Praise for *The Sawtooth Slayer*

'Gripping to the point of being un-put-downable, the core story is fascinating to anyone who enjoys crime novels, and particularly those with an interest in the use of DNA in genealogy research'
Family Tree magazine

'Highly recommended'
Who Do You Think You Are? magazine

'Once you start reading you won't want to stop – though that's what I've come to expect from this author. Highly recommended!'
LostCousins

'I was sad when I finished the book and am looking forward to the next installment'
Jonny Perl, DNA Painter

'A heck of a romp! Exceedingly well researched and well written…the best genealogy investigation writer in the world'
The Genealogy Guys

'Goodwin's best work yet'
GenealogyMagazine.com

'You really need to grab it yesterday as it does an outstanding job of teaching you the process, but almost without you realizing because it's all wrapped up in a 'What happens next?' story with interlacing plot lines and characters you'll genuinely care about'
Megan Smolenyak

'It was difficult to put it down. The reader will want to digest each word since the author describes in detail how the discovery process is accomplished'
Family Tree Archaeology

'This is not simply a crime novel with a genealogical twist; it is a masterclass in DNA'
West Middlesex Family History Society

'It's a must-read, especially if you're interested in how DNA evidence is used in investigative genetic genealogy. Nathan's writing is entertaining and informative and prompts readers to think about they can approach their own research'
Society of Australian Genealogists

'A satisfying blend of murder mystery thriller and realistic DNA-based family history research'
Waltham Forest FHS

'Goodwin keeps you glued to the book, so you don't want to put it down'
Wayne County Genealogical Society

'Nathan Dylan Goodwin has given us another heart-pounding mystery. Once you dive into this case, you won't be able to put it down'
Boulder Genealogical Society

'Another fantastically written page-turner from Nathan Dylan Goodwin'
Hertfordshire People

'It's fast-paced and I didn't want it to end'
Oakland County Genealogical Society

'You cannot go wrong spending time reading any of Nathan's books which can be read as stand-alone reads or as a series. The Sawtooth Slayer is a wonderful read on its own and continues smoothly on from the Chester Creek Murders. Now what are you waiting for?'
Wakefield & District FHS

'A recommended read'
Powys Family History Society

'This book will have you sitting on the edge of your chair as you read it'
Tuolumne County Genealogical Society

About the Author

Nathan Dylan Goodwin is a writer, genealogist and educator. He was born and raised in Hastings, East Sussex. Having attended school in the town, he then completed a Bachelor of Arts degree in Radio, Film and Television Studies, followed by a Master of Arts degree in Creative Writing at Canterbury Christ Church University. A member of the Society of Authors, he has completed several local history books about Hastings, as well as several works of fiction, including the acclaimed *Forensic Genealogist* series, the *Mrs McDougall Investigates* series and the *Venator Cold Case* series. His other interests include theatre, reading, running, skiing, travelling and, of course, genealogy. He is a qualified teacher, member of the Guild of One-Name Studies and the Society of Genealogists, as well as being a member of the Sussex Family History Group, the Norfolk Family History Society and the Kent Family History Society. He lives in Kent with his husband, son, dog and an assortment of chickens.

     NathanDylanGoodwin

       @NathanDGoodwin

By the same author

A Venator Cold Case

The Sawtooth Slayer

An Investigative Genetic Genealogy Mystery

by Nathan Dylan Goodwin

Cover design: Patrick Dengate
www.patrickdengate.com

To my first American lady friends, Heather and Michelle

Chapter One

Thursday, April 2, 2020, Twin Falls, Idaho

The highest setting on the windshield wipers was struggling to keep up with the snow. The Twin Falls County Coroner, Gene Turley, eased off the gas pedal as the screen of his black Ford coroner's van cleared to reveal four police patrol vehicles parked at angles suggesting a hasty arrival, their blue and red lights swirling in the snowy dawn skies of East Ninth Avenue.

The coroner backed up between two of the patrol cars, switched off the engine and looked out of his window. Yellow crime scene tape was strung along a row of bare linden trees that separated the sidewalk from the large red brick building of the First Baptist Church behind it. Buzzing around on the other side of the tape were a half-dozen uniformed police officers. If he had the choice, he would prefer to work with the county police who were much more laid back and allowed him to get on with his job. State police were strict and by-the-book but were reasonable to get along with. But city police, the ones who were standing in front of him right now, were his least favorite. They tended to think that they knew it all and often tried to do his job for him.

Gene took some slow breaths, then stepped out of the van with his kit bag. He was medium height, aged sixty-four years with short dark hair. He pulled on a face mask, snapped on a pair of blue latex gloves and strode over to the taped area, catching the eye of a young officer guarding the scene. He held up his identification badge and said, 'Gene Turley, County Coroner. Who's in charge, here?'

'Detective González,' the officer answered, pointing to a Latin American woman with striking green eyes, whom Gene already knew. He was pleased to see that it was her, having worked well with her on several occasions before. She was on the other side of the tape, crouching down and making notes on a pad.

He glanced in the direction of her gaze and saw the body, the pale flesh appearing beneath a crust of fresh snow. He was pleased to see

1

that a large plastic tarp had been strung up between two of the linden trees to protect the deceased from further bad weather. Judging by the lack of footprints left in the snow, the first responders had done a good job in keeping well clear of the body, respecting a wingspan perimeter around the outside of it.

The coroner took a long hard look around him, surveying the immediate area to determine the scene's safety, then he turned to address Detective González. 'Maria,' he said.

She looked up at him and smiled warmly. 'Gene,' she replied, pocketing her notebook and standing up. 'I would like to say that it's good to see you again, but it's not been long since we were last in this situation…'

'You think it's part of the series?' Gene asked her.

Detective González nodded. 'I'm afraid so, yes. But I'll wait and hear your professional opinion on it first.'

'Okay. Has anyone moved or touched the body since its discovery?' he asked.

Idaho's code stipulated that law enforcement were not permitted to move a body until the coroner's arrival, so he wasn't surprised when the detective shook her head in response. 'No, nobody's touched her.'

'Good. And who was the first responder?'

'That would be Officer James Leonard,' she said, indicating a middle-aged patrol officer, standing behind the yellow tape with his arms folded.

'And he found her just like this?' he probed.

'That's right, yes,' she confirmed.

'Do you have any witnesses?'

'None so far.'

Gene took his notepad from his bag and began to jot down details about the scene. Then he asked Officer Leonard a series of questions to ascertain if any artifacts or contamination may have been introduced to the death scene. From the officer's answers, it appeared not.

Placing his kit bag down on the snowy sidewalk, Gene took out a digital camera and proceeded to photograph the area, starting with wide shots of the street, the general crime scene and then lastly, zeroing in on the body itself.

'Detective González,' he said, ducking under the yellow tape. 'If anybody needs to approach the body, I'd like them to use the same pathway that I'm going to use right now.'

'Absolutely,' she confirmed. 'As always.'

The coroner carefully stepped closer to the body, taking photographs as he went. There were no signs of footprints or other disturbances to the inch of snow within the wingspan area around the victim, which indicated that she'd been there for several hours prior to the weather having changed for the worst.

He neared the body and then knelt beside the woman's abdomen and took his time in simply looking at her—really seeing her—and her immediate surroundings. He calmly thought on his mantra: dead bodies cannot lie; they always tell the truth. He just needed to ask her the right questions. He took more photographs, then made more notes on his pad about the positioning of the body and her general physical appearance.

The woman was naked, lying on her back, her arms by her side, palms facing upward, and her legs splayed apart. She was white with blonde hair, maybe twenty-five years old, five feet five, estimated one hundred and fifteen pounds. A black blindfold covered in snow was pulled tight over her eyes and appeared to have been tied behind her head. The soles of her feet were almost black with dirt.

Now, he needed to document her injuries. Gene took a breath and gently wiped the layer of snow from her body. He'd been doing this job for a lot of years, but the shock of witnessing such a violent end to a life never lessened. She had multiple stab wounds to the chest, ligature marks around her neck, lacerations to her feet and what appeared to be two bullet wounds to her legs. He began to make notes and photograph the injuries up close.

'Do you think this could be the missing girl?' Gene asked quietly, craning his neck around to face the detective.

She nodded. 'It does look very much like Molly Hutchison, but we'll obviously need a formal ID to confirm.

Gene touched the back of his gloved hand to the dead woman's cheek. Cool to the touch, but not as cold as the ambient exterior temperature.

He carefully pressed his thumb and forefinger on the woman's lips and tried opening her mouth, but rigor mortis had set in; he was unable to do it. He also tried lifting her right arm, but it too was rigid from that third stage of death.

Placing his head just inches above the snowy ground, Gene Turley took a closer examination of the dependent portions of the body, finding the distinct and tell-tale purple blotching of livor mortis, where the blood had settled under the mere force of gravity after the woman's heart had stopped beating.

'Death probably occurred within the past twelve hours,' the coroner told the detective, making further notes. 'I'll need to call Ada County to schedule an autopsy.'

'Of course,' Detective González said. The Ada County Forensic Pathologist performed the autopsies for the entire state of Idaho. She leaned closer, lowering her voice so that only he could hear her. 'But until that comes in—and...off the record—do you agree that this looks like this victim is the fourth in a series, killed by the same perpetrator?'

Gene thought for a couple of seconds, half-winced and nodded his head solemnly.

Chapter Two

Monday, April 6, 2020, Boise, Idaho

Detective Maria González hated the Ada County Forensic Pathologist's Office, even when she wasn't standing over the body of a recent murder victim. There was just something about the whole building that turned her stomach. Maybe it was the inherent stench of death—or perhaps the abundance of chemicals used to try to cover it up—but something reacted badly with her insides the moment that she stepped inside the front door. Today was worse. She was in the windowless room that was used for conducting autopsies, with its harsh white lighting, cream linoleum, and beige walls. In front of her, lying in a supine position on a stainless-steel gurney, was the body of Molly Hutchison whose identity had been formally confirmed two days ago. She was covered with a green sheet which Gene Turley, the Twin Falls County Coroner, gently lifted back. Standing beside Gene, holding a clipboard, was Walter Rachmal, the smart and very adept Ada County Forensic Pathologist.

Detective González was revulsed by the combined effects of the autopsy, the natural dehumanizing of a person after their death and the horrific injuries inflicted on her by the killer. Her corpse was a real mess. The usual Y-incision, which had been made from each of Molly's shoulders, around her breasts and down to her groin, had been stitched back up and the discrete incision behind the left ear that ran around the back of the head to the right ear, enabling her brain to be removed and examined, was barely visible under the fall of her long blonde hair. 'Same as the others?' she asked from beneath her face mask, hoping to expedite proceedings.

Walter Rachmal raised his eyebrows. 'Yeah. As was the case with the other three victims, Molly wasn't killed where her body was discovered. The evidence suggests that she was killed in a location as yet to be determined and that she had already been dead a few hours before being placed outside of the church.'

Detective González scribbled some details in her notebook, then looked across to the Ada County Forensic Pathologist as he drew her attention to an open flesh wound on the victim's lower left leg. 'Shot from behind. I would say, not close range but also not long distance. The bullet penetrated through her shin bone and came out the other side. Similar on the right thigh. Although, here, there's no exit wound,' he said, using his meaty hands to lift her thigh to show the bullet entry point. 'Ballistics have yet to come back to me.'

'But,' Gene Turley added, 'it does appear to be the same weapon as was used with the other victims: a .45-70.'

The pathologist continued, pointing down to her lower body. 'Bruises on both legs. Abrasions and ecchymoses on her upper right thigh. Probably from being beaten with a blunt object. No sign of sexual assault,' he said, making a point to look Detective González right in the eyes as he said it.

The pathologist stepped sideways and indicated Molly's chest as he leaned forward. 'It's difficult to see now, but there's very similar bruising here as the other three victims had in this same location.'

'He tried to resuscitate her...' she muttered, receiving a nod of confirmation. During the post-mortem of the first victim, Detective González had ventured the possibility that perhaps causing death had not been the assailant's intention and that maybe he had tried to bring her back to life. When the same evidence of resuscitation had occurred in the second and third victims, only one chilling conclusion could be reached: that the killer had in fact brought the women back to life purely in order to be able to kill them again.

'Then there's the question of the stab wounds,' the pathologist continued. 'Owing to the lack of blood loss and the yellowish-brown bruising, these all appear to have been inflicted on the body post-mortem.'

'Overkill, again,' she voiced, making more notes.

'Oh, hell yeah. It's the very *definition* of overkill,' Gene Turley confirmed, shaking his head. 'The victim was probably dead long before he even inflicted the first knife wound.'

Detective González struggled to take enough air in through her face mask. 'Jesus.'

'Cause of death—like with the previous victims—was ligature strangulation,' the pathologist continued, indicating the red and purple

6

lines cut into the skin below Molly's chin.

'Eventually, he just wasn't able to bring her back to life anymore,' Detective González concluded grimly, before adding, 'And the teeth?'

'One missing premolar, removed post-mortem,' he told her.

'Just like the other three again.'

'Yeah, exactly the same position in the mouth, too,' he confirmed, turning and picking up a clipboard. 'We're waiting on toxicology and blood work, but she had the same black capsules in her stomach as the other three victims did.'

Detective González studied the scratches on the victim's lower legs. Some were no more than superficial red marks that had barely damaged the skin, while others had cut more deeply into the flesh and had run with blood that had since congealed on the surface. She moved around to the end of the gurney, crouched down and looked squarely at the filthy soles of Molly's feet as she asked, 'Get anything from here?'

'Yes,' he answered, spinning around and picking up a small specimen jar. 'Unlike the other victims' feet, where we drew a hard blank, Molly had two different types of foliage that had penetrated the skin between her toes.'

Detective González took the jar and held it up toward the strip light, briefly examining what appeared to be two slightly different pine needles. Vegetation was not her specialty. A tree was a tree, and a bush was a bush. 'Any idea exactly which plants they might be from?'

The pathologist shook his head. 'I'll leave that to you to investigate, but suffice it to say that the evidence points to these superficial injuries'—he pointed to her lower legs—'having occurred prior to death.'

Detective González nodded. Again, it had been the same with the other three victims. Evidence suggesting that they had been trying to escape from a woods or a forest. The question was, where? Twin Falls was nestled among thousands of acres of wilderness. So far, she and her team had absolutely no clue as to what had happened to the three—now four—women between abduction and their bodies being strategically placed in various locations around the city. One thing that she did know was that the killer was a very dangerous individual who needed to be apprehended before he could strike again.

'Approximate time of death?' she asked, pen poised in readiness for the answer.

'Some point in the early hours of April second.'

'So, just like the other victims. Once Molly had died, he discarded her…' Detective González mused, wondering at the implication of that statement. With no signs of sexual assault, she wondered what purpose Molly had had for the killer. She was about to look in her notebook at one of the previous victim's details when her cell phone began to ring. Great. It was her boss, Captain Pritchard. 'Sorry. I'd better take this,' she said.

The pathologist shrugged. 'I think we're about done here, anyway. I'll be in my office if you have further questions.'

'Hopefully, I won't be seeing you again too soon,' Gene Turley said, the sides of his face mask twitching to reveal a smile.

'Let's hope not,' she agreed, turning as she answered the call.

'Detective González?' Captain Pritchard said. 'Where are you?'

'Just finishing up at Ada County,' she replied, adding, 'Molly Hutchison's autopsy.'

'Any new clues?'

'Possibly, Captain,' she said, looking back to see the pathologist peel off his latex gloves and put them into the trash. 'Two different types of pine needle were removed from in between the victim's toes, which the other women didn't have.'

'Look into it. Anything else more concrete from this latest victim?'

'Not so far.'

'Security video from the bank opposite?'

'It didn't cover the area where the body was found.'

'Witnesses?'

'None so far.'

Captain Pritchard emitted a heavy sigh. 'What about this genealogy thing? We got a good DNA sample from the first victim. Any progress there?'

'Not that I've heard, boss.'

'Well, since we've got no other leads, let's push it forward. Can you put me in on a call with them this afternoon?'

'Sure,' she agreed uncertainly.

'Talk to you later.'

The line went dead, and Detective González stared momentarily at the blank screen. Then she dialed the office of Venator, the investigative genetic genealogy company that she had retained to look into the case.

'This is Venator. Ross speaking. How may I help?'

'Hi there. This is Detective Maria González from Twin Falls Police Department. I need to speak with Madison Scott-Barnhart, please. It's urgent.'

There was a short pause at the other end of the line. 'Well, the office is currently shut down, so I'll need to pass the message along to Maddie and get her to call you back.'

'Please tell her that we urgently need to Zoom this afternoon regarding the Twin Falls case.'

'Got it,' Ross confirmed. 'I'll get in touch with her for you right now.'

'Thank you. Please tell her it's very urgent and imperative that we speak this afternoon.'

Detective González ended the call. She stared at the cell phone in her hand before her focus shifted back to the lifeless corpse of Molly Hutchison. She had to find the monster who did this. And quickly.

Chapter Three

He slowly walked the gravel path, covered in a light dusting of snow, toward the small, single-story house, knocked hard on the screen door, then took a step backward. He pulled his face mask high up over his bearded chin, grateful to have additional covering of the pockmark scars that covered both sides of his face.

Moments later, the inner door was opened and Mrs. Staniforth gazed out with a frown which almost immediately turned into a smile. 'Oh, it's you. You're back. Hi! How are you doing?'

'Good, thank you, Mrs. Staniforth. And how are you?'

She shook her head from side to side. 'A little scared, if I'm honest.' She touched her chest. 'With my breathing difficulties, I just don't know what'll happen if I get this awful virus. Then there's this madman on the loose—did you see there's another victim?'

'Well, you just stay home safe and well,' he instructed, his voice uncontrollably switching mid-sentence to a high octave, then back down again to its usual pitch. 'I don't want to see you setting foot outside, do you hear?'

She smiled. 'You're too kind, do you know that?'

'I try my best,' he said with a warm smile. 'I'm heading into town for some groceries. What do you need?'

'Oh, I do so hate having to inconvenience you like this,' she said.

'Mrs. Staniforth, do you want to see me get mad?' he asked, his voice coming out as a young girl's might.

She laughed, but he knew that it was directed at his comment, not his voice. Mrs. Staniforth was nice and—unlike everyone else in his life—would never mock the muscle tension dysphonia that involuntarily squeezed his vocal cords as he spoke. 'Now, that's something I'd pay good money to see! In the two years you've lived here, I've never heard so much as a raised word out of you.'

'Well, then, hand me a list of whatever you need, and it'll stay that way.'

'I'll be right back,' she said with a chuckle, heading inside the property and leaving the door open.

He casually turned and looked around the neighborhood. He had grown up just a few streets from here, in a house not too dissimilar to the one that he now resided in, next door to Mrs. Staniforth's. It wasn't a great part of town, and a lot of the houses around here—including his own—were in quite a bad shape. But he didn't care.

'Here we go,' Mrs. Staniforth said, reappearing and waving a piece of paper and a twenty-dollar bill through the screen.

'Just put it down and open the screen, and then I'll take it once you've moved back inside. I don't want to risk you catching anything,' he instructed.

Mrs. Staniforth nodded, placed the paper and cash down on the floor and did as he had said. 'Okay,' she called.

He moved forward past the screen, picked up the piece of paper and the money, and then took two paces backward. 'Is this it, Mrs. Staniforth? *Four* items? Come on—I'm going downtown. Anything you need at all—medicine, clothes, food, a five-star vacation to the Bahamas?'

She laughed. 'Oh, now wouldn't that just be something! No, really. You're very kind, but that's all.'

'Okay. Well, I'll see you later with your groceries,' he said, walking down the path to his black Jeep Wrangler. He climbed in, fired up the engine and drove three blocks south to Addison Avenue. He parked outside of Swensen's Markets, pulled on his blue baseball cap, raised his mask and then headed inside to get Mrs. Staniforth's groceries. He also got her some fresh white roses while he was there, picked up some beer and a bag of chips for himself, then headed out to his Wrangler.

He began the drive along Addison Avenue toward home but decided to take a short detour down Ninth Avenue. After two blocks, a mild panic set in when he saw a police patrol car blocking the road at the junction of Shoshone Street North. He slowed down behind a line of three cars, watching as a police officer spoke with the driver of the first vehicle. He glanced in his rearview mirror, wondering about turning around but a truck was already right up behind him. The officer stepped back and waved the first car through before raising his hand to stop the next.

11

There was no way now that he could turn around without arousing suspicion. He raised his facemask and inched the Wrangler forward. As he did so, the First Baptist Church came into view on the opposite street corner. He glanced across, seeing the swathes of bunched flowers on the grass under the trees. He watched as two young women comforted each other as they bent down to read the tributes.

The car in front of him pulled away and the officer beckoned him forward. He was city police—an older guy with a hard narrow face. He frowned as he motioned for the window to be lowered. 'Are you local?' he asked.

'Uh-huh,' the man answered.

'So, you'll know all about what went on over there, then,' he said, nodding his head over toward the church. 'Do you use this road regularly?'

'Not that often,' he replied, his voice coming out in a high-pitched squeak. He had to swallow down his rising anger at the sight of the officer's obvious amusement in response to the sound of his voice.

'And did you happen to use this road at any point last Thursday morning?'

The man thought for a moment before shaking his head. 'No, I was out of town,' he answered, his voice thankfully holding at a lower register this time.

The officer nodded, looking inside the Wrangler. 'They for her?'

The driver was momentarily confused. He glanced down, following the direction of the officer's gaze and seeing then the bunch of flowers that he had purchased for Mrs. Staniforth. 'Uh-huh.'

The officer's demeanor toward him visibly warmed. 'Well, it's getting a little congested over there, so I'm going to ask you if you wouldn't mind parking a little further down the road, and then walk back to lay your tributes.'

'No problem,' the man replied.

Taking two steps back, the officer waved him forward.

The man pulled across the junction and drove past the carpet of flowers that covered the area where Molly Hutchison's body had been left. A little further down the street, he pulled the Wrangler over but kept the engine running as he climbed out, carrying Mrs. Staniforth's white roses over to the edge of the sidewalk. The two women were sobbing and embracing just a few yards away. One of them looked over at him as he laid the flowers and smiled appreciatively at him.

He grinned, headed back to the truck and drove home.

Having given Mrs. Staniforth her groceries, he walked next door and entered his own house. Despite it being broad daylight outside, only thin shards of light penetrated the dim room through the tears in the drawn curtains.

He walked through to the kitchen, put the crate of beer on the table and opened a can. He drank it until the contents were all gone. Then he belched, crushed the can in his hand and tossed it to the floor.

He took another can, popped it open and carried it through to the living room, feeling happy with his life right now. He sat down on the couch with a sigh, picked up the television remote and was about to switch it on when his eyes caught one of the photos on the wall beside him.

He put the remote back down, took a swig of beer and then stood up to face the wall. Every inch of it was covered with photographs of Molly Hutchison.

It was time to take these pictures down…and start again.

Chapter Four

Madison Scott-Barnhart pocketed her cell phone with a lengthy sigh as she stared out of her bedroom window to the yard down below. She'd just finished talking with her receptionist, Ross Mole, who had informed her that the detective from Twin Falls wanted to schedule a Zoom call in two hours' time. Just terrific. Ten days ago, Detective Maria González had driven all the way down to Salt Lake City to try and convince Maddie to use investigative genetic genealogy on a live serial killer case. Her main concern—and the prime reason for her having initially declined the case—had been the potential psychological impacts on her small team. The lives of the killer's likely next victims could hang in the balance and depend upon their very work. They were used to cold cases, decades old, where time was no longer a critical factor in play. Eventually, though, Maddie had acquiesced and accepted the case, having been persuaded that law enforcement had no other viable leads. But since that day, the whole world had turned upside down with the Coronavirus pandemic, and Maddie had been forced—like most other businesses in downtown Salt Lake City—to shut down temporarily and run the office from home. She had quickly discovered that working from home was, in fact, an oxymoron and she had achieved very little since agreeing to take on the Twin Falls case.

Despite the fact that she could hear her two teenaged kids arguing downstairs, Maddie took a moment to sit down on her bed and close her eyes. She drew in a few long breaths and tried to formulate a plan. But it was no good; the racket emanating from the kids proved to be just too much. She didn't need to go ask what the problem was, though. It had been the same thing that Nikki and Trenton had argued about every day since their school had closed: sharing devices and glitchy internet to complete the work that they were being sent from their teachers through Google Classroom. She gave up trying to find that elusive moment of calm and took out her cell phone, typing a message to the team on their shared group.

Hey everyone. Hope you're all doing good. Do you remember the detective from Twin Falls, who wanted us to work on a live serial killer case? You were all into it, but I wasn't? Well, I've changed my mind and we're taking it on…the detective wants a Zoom meeting in two hours. I'd like to meet with you all first to take a look at the DNA results and see where we're starting at. I'll email the link over once I've dealt with my two fighting toddlers… I mean, teenagers.

Maddie clicked to send the message to the group, imagining how it would be received. The team had all been fired up and had encouraged her to take on the case when the detective had first proposed it. They had expressed their disappointment when they had learned that she had declined the case. But she also knew that they were enjoying the freedom that the past ten days had given them to work on some of Venator's other cases, some of which had lain dormant in the two years since Maddie had set up the company. It had been a great opportunity for them to revisit these cases to determine if any new DNA matches had come through that might help to solve them.

'Okay,' Maddie muttered to herself, walking across her bedroom to the door. Every day since lockdown had been declared, Maddie had been thankful that the house was a decent-enough size to feel as though they each had their own space. She and her husband, Michael, had bought the place back in 2006, the year after they had married. It had been their first home together, along with Maddie's eldest child, Jenna, from a previous relationship, who had been nine years old at the time. The move here had been just in time for the arrival of their first adopted child from South Korea, Nikki. Trenton's adoption from the same family had come along two years later and had made their little family complete.

Maddie followed the sound of yelling through the house to Michael's study, where she found his computer monitor smashed on the floor. Nikki and Trenton were engaged in an unintelligible game of shouting-the-blame tennis.

'What the hell's happening in here?' Maddie demanded, cutting straight through their juvenile argument.

'He's literally had the whole, entire morning on here—' Nikki tried to explain.

15

'Then I get up to use the bathroom and *she* closes all my files,' Trenton interjected.

'And then he physically pushes me off the computer and *that* happened,' Nikki continued, pointing at the smashed screen.

'Stop. Just stop. I want both of you out of here, right now,' Maddie yelled, resolutely gesturing into the hallway.

'Well, sure,' Trenton objected, 'but you can be the one to tell my teacher why my assignment isn't done.'

With the kids out of the room, Maddie closed the door and crouched down, placing her hand on the monitor as though it were an injured pet. She sighed. The computer was slow and should have been upgraded years ago, but Maddie hadn't been able to bring herself to throw it out. Like almost everything else in the room, it belonged to Michael. It wasn't hers to get rid of, despite her kids' protests.

She gazed slowly around the room. It was one of the few places in the house that she had resisted the need to update and, because it had remained largely untouched in the last five years, it had become where she felt closest to Michael. It was the one room that he would be able to walk right back into and find everything just as he had left it. Except…he probably wasn't ever coming back.

Last month the family had endured the painful milestone of the fifth anniversary since he had gone off to Green River on a fishing trip and had never come home. The intervening five years had brought no further information or clue about what had happened to Michael until last month when a detective, named Clayton Tyler, whom Maddie and the Venator team had been helping to solve a cold case, had offered to take a fresh look at Michael's file. Maddie had been surprised to find that included in the document was reference to a twenty-four-second call to his cell phone, right before it had been switched off and he had disappeared. The call had come from the office of his employers, The Larkin Investment and Finance Group. That wouldn't have aroused suspicion, except that, immediately after Michael had disappeared, the company CEO, Andrew Larkin, had issued a gag order on all of his employees, forbidding them from cooperating with law enforcement. Adding another aspect to the already complex problem for Maddie was the fact that one of her staff at Venator, Becky, was Andrew Larkin's daughter. Becky wanted to help Maddie find the truth but had so far managed to glean nothing from her father. Detective Tyler had also suggested getting Michael's truck swept again by CSI. The results that came back had startled Maddie: there had been no fingerprints found anywhere on the vehicle apart from one partial print found on the trunk catch. And the print was not Michael's. It belonged to a man named Emmanuel Gribbin, someone about whom Maddie knew very little. All the detective had been able to tell her about him was that his only criminal activity had been a DUI in Washington DC in 2014. The sum total of Maddie's own research into the man amounted to the sole fact that he had died four years after the DUI. That was it.

For the past five years, Maddie had desperately wanted answers, but she had been finding that the ones which had been forthcoming in recent weeks had not been the answers that she had hoped to get.

Maddie turned out of the study and closed the door behind her. She marched into the kitchen and found Trenton wearing headphones and playing a videogame on his tablet, and her mom sitting at the table shuffling playing cards. Nikki had evidently retreated to her room.

'You okay, Mom?' Maddie asked, taking her laptop from the counter and sitting down beside her.

Her mom faced her and smiled. 'Yes, thank you.'

Maddie fired up her laptop and headed straight for Amazon. 'Solitaire?'

'Hmm?' her mom said.

'What are you playing, there? Is it solitaire?'

'Oh, no. I thought we could all sit down together and play Go Fish.'

Maddie laughed as she began to search for new laptops online. She stopped, though, when she realized that her mom was being serious. 'Mom, it's a working day *and* it's the middle of the school day. It's not the weekend. I can't...they can't just sit and play cards. Trenton has an assignment due soon.'

'Well, he certainly doesn't look very studious to me,' her mom responded, nodding toward Trenton who was jerking his tablet left to right in some mindless car game. 'Trenton!'

Trenton did a double-take to the two pairs of eyes boring into him.

'Yeah, what?' he said, removing his headphones.

'Do you want to play Go Fish?' her mom asked.

Trenton glanced at Maddie, as though it were a trick question. 'Uh…yeah. I guess. I mean, I haven't played it since I was a kid, but…'

'Trenton has work to do, Mom,' Maddie said as calmly as she could muster. 'Trenton, I'm ordering you and Nikki a new laptop each, right now. In the meantime, I'm sure you have other schoolwork that you can be getting on with.'

Trenton marched from the room in a huff.

Her mom stopped shuffling the cards and sighed, her face hardening. 'Fine. Well, I'll just go play with your father, then.' Her mom stood up with the cards in her hand and headed over toward the door.

'Mom,' Maddie called after her. 'Dad's not going to be playing cards with you…'

Her mom paused at the doorway and turned toward her. Her face had softened into one of embarrassment. Realization had set in that her dementia had fooled her again. 'I didn't mean… forget it,' she said, hurrying away.

Maddie sighed, returning to her laptop search. As much as she loved her family, after ten days solid of being cooped up with them, she had come to realize just how much she had taken for granted all the various separate busy compartments that constituted her day-to-day life. Now, she felt incarcerated and already missing her friends, work colleagues and her two favorite sports, running and skiing. The ski slopes had closed prematurely for the season and, although she could still get outside for a run, she felt that, given the way things were at home right now, that would be as irresponsible and selfish as leaving three infants unattended. But, God, she really needed a run.

Maddie returned to the top of Amazon and switched her search to one for a treadmill. 'Wow,' she muttered at the sudden hike in prices. Still, she also figured that if she did *not* get one and was trapped in this house very much longer, she would surely go stir crazy.

A half hour later, Maddie had placed an order for an over-priced, mid-range treadmill and two over-priced, low-spec laptops, all of which would be delivered tomorrow morning. With that little job out of the way, she turned her attention back to her work, starting by emailing a Zoom link to the rest of the team. She had already received confirmation from all of them that they would be available to join the meeting.

On the kitchen counter in front of her was the piece of paper that Detective Maria González had given her with the DNA kit number for the purported Twin Falls serial killer. She felt guilty that she had done nothing with it, not even logged in to see how viable the case might be for solving. Since the arrest of the Golden State Killer back in 2018 and the raft of cases that had followed, there had been a general assumption by law enforcement and the wider public that any serious crime, where DNA evidence existed, could be solved using investigative genetic genealogy. But it wasn't really always like that. For a variety of reasons, including quantity and quality of DNA and, crucially, the number of cousin matches found in the databases, not all cases could benefit from this cutting-edge methodology.

Maddie poured herself a coffee, picked up the piece of paper and headed downstairs to the basement. At her computer, she opened the FamilyTreeDNA website and was about to enter the kit details but changed her mind, deciding instead to wait for the team meeting to view the results together.

As she looked at the kit details, a thought suddenly struck her: Ross had said in his earlier call that the meeting with Detective González was urgent. An instinctive, foreboding, sick feeling washed over Maddie. Opening a fresh tab in her web browser, she ran a Google search for *Twin Falls murder.*

'Oh, my God,' she muttered as the KMVT website opened with its main headline: *Fourth Victim of the Twin Falls Serial Killer.*

Maddie read the opening lines of the story, then closed her eyes. Another woman, Molly Hutchison, had been killed. She had died four days ago. Maddie thought back. Four days ago, she'd been fretting about the Harmons grocery delivery. There had been no flour or sugar available, and she'd spent the rest of that day trying to source some from somewhere else. It was ridiculous. While some poor twenty-five-year-old was being butchered to death, she was worrying about getting hold of two baking ingredients that she had had no immediate plans to use.

She drank some coffee and checked the time. The meeting wasn't scheduled for another forty-five minutes but she couldn't wait any longer, so she opened up the team's group chat.

Hey everyone. Are we possibly good to start the meeting now?

In the Zoom waiting room, she gazed at her own video feed and sighed at the slightly unkempt woman staring back at her with bloodshot green eyes. She ran her hands through her blonde bangs, hurriedly trying to make any sort of last-minute improvement to her appearance.

'Admiring yourself, there, Maddie?' Kenyatta asked, appearing on-screen in front of her.

Maddie laughed. 'Oh… Just seeing if I look half as bad as I feel right now. And I do. But…how are you?'

Kenyatta, a middle-aged African American grinned. 'All good, thank you. And listen, you look as amazing as always, by the way.'

'Thanks,' Maddie replied as Becky, Ross and Hudson joined the meeting.

'Hi, everyone,' Becky greeted, looking fresh-faced and full of energy, as though she had just finished a workout, which was entirely plausible for her. Her mousey hair was pulled back in a ponytail and she wore her usual thick-rimmed glasses. 'Is everyone good?'

'Yes, thank you,' Hudson replied.

'Just about holding up,' Maddie answered. 'Like everyone else in the world.' Then she thought of Molly Hutchison. 'No—all things considered—we're doing just fine here.'

'Anyone made any significant progress on the cold cases?' Kenyatta asked.

Hudson screwed up his face. 'A couple of new matches have come in for the Cleveland Cannibal case, but no major progress so far.'

'Well, I've had some luck with one of the sexual assault kits,' Becky informed them. 'Some good leads. How about you, Kenyatta?'

Kenyatta sighed. 'Yeah, slow progress here, too, with my boys. But you mark my words, I will get there.'

Maddie smiled at her doggedness. The *Boys under the Bridge* case was a pro-bono investigation for the National Center for Missing and Exploited Children that, given the current matches in the databases to which the team had access, was nigh-on impossible to solve. But Kenyatta was one determined woman.

'So, you ended up changing your mind on that hot case, then?' Hudson said.

'It was changed *for* me,' Maddie admitted. 'The detective running the case drove all the way down to the office on that last day before we closed up. Let's just say she was…very persuasive.'

'Well, I'm sure glad she did,' Kenyatta replied.

'It's going to be so exciting working on a live case,' Hudson chipped in.

Maddie raised her eyebrows. 'It's actually going to be harrowing and highly pressured.'

'Oh, for sure. That too, I know,' he concurred.

'Okay. Shall we get this meeting started and officially open the Twin Falls case?' Maddie said, taking in the faces staring back at her out of their square boxes. 'I have to say, from here it looks like I'm staring at the opening credits to the *Brady Bunch*. Anyway, let's get down to it. I just wanted us all to take an initial look at the DNA results, triage how we're going to tackle it—*if* we can do it at all, that is—prior to the detective joining us on the call.'

Maddie clicked to share her screen so that everyone could see the log-in page for the FamilyTreeDNA website. She sipped her coffee, took a quick breath, then typed in the kit number and password, before hitting *Sign In*. A dashboard of eight gray rectangular buttons appeared in front of everyone. She clicked *Matches* and waited for a few long seconds before the page was filled with a long line of people—two thousand and forty-three people, to be precise—who were unknowingly related to the Twin Falls serial killer. The key question that the whole team wanted to know was just how close the various cousin matches were coming in at.

'So, we have…eighty-seven centimorgans,' Maddie said, reading off the top match.

'Not bad,' Becky commented. 'Can you scroll down, so we can see

21

how quickly the numbers drop away to below twenty.'

Maddie slowly scrolled the page down and passed through the list for everyone to see. By the time she had reached the bottom of the first page, the amount of DNA had dropped to just twenty-three centimorgans, meaning that the ancestors that these people had in common with the killer could be as far back as seventh great-grandparents. At this stage, it was almost pointless looking through the remaining twenty-four pages of DNA matches.

'I'd say that what we've got there seems to look workable,' Kenyatta said.

'Yeah, I agree,' Maddie said, glancing up at a notification that said Detective González was waiting to join the meeting. 'The detective is here already. So, very quickly, before I let her in. Hudson, are you good to take on the Y-line and EVCs as usual? Kenyatta, if you can get those matches organized into separate clusters for us? And Becky, start working on admixture and geo-profiling. Ross, you know the drill: get me a file ready for the victim details and then start to collate data as we go. Everyone good with that?'

The team confirmed their readiness in their various allocated roles.

'Good, then I'll admit Detective González to the meeting,' Maddie said, clicking to allow her entry. Moments later, she appeared on-screen, looking more officious and sober than Maddie remembered. She was sitting at a desk and next to her was a severe-looking uniformed officer.

'Hi, Detective,' Maddie greeted.

'Hi, Maddie. I am here with Captain Pritchard who's overseeing the case,' she said, indicating the man sitting beside her.

He responded to a polite greeting from Maddie with a cursory nod of his head. Maddie introduced the Venator team, then Captain Pritchard said, 'Let's just get down to brass tacks, shall we? We've got four dead girls on our hands, up here, a killer at large and precious little to go on.' He sighed. 'My wife's done one of these Ancestor tests and she tells me they've got a database of individuals way bigger than CODIS.'

'Ancestry does have the biggest database by far, yes,' Maddie began to explain, 'but, unfortunately, we don't have access to it. We use—'

22

'What do you mean, you don't have access to it?' Captain Pritchard interjected, shuffling closer to the screen.

'The three biggest databases—Ancestry, 23andMe and MyHeritage—don't work with law enforcement, sir,' Maddie said.

'So, what are we left with, then?' Captain Pritchard asked.

'FamilyTreeDNA and GEDmatch,' Maddie answered.

'What's the size of their databases, then?'

'They have around a million users each, give or take.'

Captain Pritchard sighed and mumbled something unintelligible.

'Do you have any matches to our killer at one of these websites, Maddie?' Detective González pitched in.

'Yes, we do have matches,' Maddie confirmed. 'We've not begun exploring the results too deeply yet, but I'm pleased to tell you that it certainly does appear to be a viable case for us to agree to take on.'

Detective González blew out a breath through pursed lips and sat back in her chair. 'That is such a relief to hear, Maddie. Thank you. So, what happens now?'

Maddie replied, 'Now you need to tell us as much about the case as you can: victims, locations, autopsy reports and anything at all that you have on the serial killer himself.'

Chapter Five

Monday, April 6, 2020, Liberty Wells, Salt Lake City, Utah

Hudson Édouard was sitting at his laptop which was on a desk in the bedroom of his bungalow on Milton Avenue in the Liberty Wells district of Salt Lake City. He was a handsome twenty-five-year-old with dark hair, olive skin and a mixed heritage from Canada and French Guiana of which he was proud.

'Okay,' Maddie said, 'Detective González, you're good to take over. If you could just give us a general overview of the case first, before going into the specifics of each individual, that would be great. I'm sure my team will interject with any questions they might have along the way.'

'No problem,' she said with a smile, the first page of her presentation appearing on everyone's computer screen. It was a simple slide but one that was highly effective, consisting just of the four victims' names and photographs: *Lorena Baly. Carla Eagleton. Jasmine Jaconski. Molly Hutchison.*

Whether it was a conscious decision or not, the detective lingered on this first slide, not saying a word.

Hudson studied the photos. Although there appeared to be differences in the women's hair and eye color, there were also marked similarities. All of them were of a similar age to him, were white with a petite frame and appeared in these photos to be naturally very beautiful. In fact, now that he studied their faces more closely, none of them was wearing make-up.

Finally, Detective González spoke. 'These four young women were part of a series, all murdered by the same man. We believe that they were all drugged in their own homes, kidnapped and taken somewhere out of the city, murdered and their bodies brought back to the city before being placed outside of various churches around Twin Falls.'

'What makes you think they were taken out of the city? I mean, how do you know that?' Kenyatta asked. 'To where?'

'None of them lived particularly close to a park or woodland and, yet, they all had scratches and cuts to their lower legs and the soles of their feet were very dirty. Between the toes of the latest victim, Molly Hutchison, we got a bit more to go on. We found two types of vegetation; possibly different types of trees. We're working on that, now. We think he might have taken the women to a forest outside of Twin Falls where he let them go.'

'Sorry. Let them go?' Becky questioned.

Detective González nodded. 'Our working theory is that he released them—literally set them free—then hunted them down with a rifle favored by hunters. All of them received bullet wounds to the legs, which would have incapacitated them but not killed them. Once they were down, he strangled them to death.'

'Jesus,' Becky muttered.

'Yeah, it's real bad. But it gets worse, I'm afraid,' the detective revealed, mustering a breath. 'It appears that the killer then resuscitated the victims.'

Hudson asked, 'Why? Surely his intention was to kill them, no?'

'Yes, you're right. But...not once...rather multiple times over.'

A collective gasp was followed by a shaken, stunned silence in the assembled team.

'Once they were dead, he then stabbed them, over and over. As you'll see in a moment with the autopsy photographs—and apologies, but this is your trigger warning for what I am about to show you— there's a marked increase in the sheer ferocity of the overkill from one victim to the next.'

'It sounds like he's playing a very elaborate, sick game with these poor women,' Maddie moved on.

'They sound like anger-retaliation homicides to me,' Becky offered. 'I'm guessing little sign of sexual assault?'

Detective González's eyebrows raised, and her mouth turned down in a suggestion of being impressed by Becky's insight. 'Yes, exactly that. For the first victim, Lorena, we retrieved a small semen sample from her thigh. From the other three victims, nothing whatsoever,' Detective González revealed.

'Nothing at all? As in *no* signs of sexual assault?' Kenyatta pushed, incredulity carrying in her voice.

'That's correct. As your colleague here has just intimated, we think that the overkill—inflicting massive injuries which by far exceed the extent necessary to kill the victim—is the most important part for him. That's where he gets his gratification. Sexual release likely comes much later.'

'So, you think that the semen sample on the first victim was an *accident*?' Hudson sought to clarify.

'Most likely, yes,' the detective answered.

'Wow,' Kenyatta said.

'It's not uncommon in anger-retaliation homicides,' Becky added.

'Retaliation for what?' Hudson asked. 'You mean the victims knew him and did something to piss him off?'

'Possibly; but not necessarily,' Becky answered. 'They could be substitutes for one or several women-figures in his life, who he feels have wronged him in some way.'

'Yes, exactly that,' the detective confirmed. 'And this anger-retaliation model continues to hold in his disposal method for the victims. Once his anger is spent, he blindfolds them and takes them—'

'Wait,' Kenyatta interrupted. 'Sorry, but you say he blindfolds them *after* they're dead. Is that what you said?'

Detective González nodded. 'That's our belief, yes. He seems not to be able to bear for them to look at him and see what he's done…even though they're dead. He then leaves them out in the open, in front of apparently random churches.'

'He's ashamed of what he's done,' Becky intoned.

'Not ashamed enough to walk into a police station and confess, though,' Kenyatta commented. 'Or, worse still, to *not* do it again.'

'How were the bodies placed?' Becky asked.

'All of them were naked, arms by their side and palms facing upward, and their legs were splayed.'

'Any significance of churches—or maybe these particular churches—in this?' Hudson inquired.

'There doesn't seem to be any rhyme or reason to the selection as far as we're able to tell: the victims had no known connection to the churches; they weren't in their own neighborhoods... Friends and family can't account for it.'

'Maybe there *is* no rhyme nor reason. Sometimes there just isn't, or at least not one that we may ever know or perhaps understand,' Maddie said.

'Exactly,' the detective agreed. 'Another thing. The killer also removed a premolar from each victim post-mortem.'

'Souvenir?' Kenyatta questioned. 'Our last guy liked to take locks of hair.'

'Probably,' the detective answered.

There was a brief silence. Hudson presumed that the rest of the team was struggling to take it all in, as was he. All of the cold cases that they had investigated had been shocking to a point, but there was something more disturbing about this one. Perhaps the fact that it was

26

happening right now—rather than decades ago—gave it an even more disquieting quality.

Maddie spoke up and broke the silence, asking, 'Do you have anything at all to go on about the killer?'

Detective González shook her head. 'We simply have nothing. This guy's done his homework. The women all lived on their own. No roommates. No Ring doorbells. No security video nearby. Nobody who'll miss them in a few hours. No fingerprints or footprints. Nothing. Just his DNA from the first victim.'

'And you'll be glad to hear that that's all we need,' Maddie said with a soft smile. 'Well, that and time.'

Detective González nodded. 'I know. I appreciate that. But time is something we might not have a ton of. I gotta tell you, the longest he's gone between victims is five weeks.'

Hudson heard Maddie's mic pick up her sharp intake of breath: some cases they had cracked in a matter of days; others took significantly longer; and others were still as yet unsolved.

'And there's an escalation between cases, which will be mixed up with his sense of his getting away with it,' Becky said.

'Yes,' the detective said solemnly. 'We're *very* worried about what else might happen to any next victim.'

'Okay, does anybody have any questions about the overview before we go into the specifics for each victim?' Maddie asked the team.

When nobody came forward Detective González advanced the PowerPoint presentation to the next slide. *Lorena Baly* was typed in bold at the top of page. Below that on the right-hand side was a different photo to the previous individual portrait of Lorena. In this image, she was standing in front of a group of friends, laughing with her mouth wide open toward the camera. She was petite with long dark hair, dark eyes and was easily the most beautiful of her friends. Beside the picture was a text box containing her basic personal data.

Age: 24
Weight: 119lbs
Height: 5 feet 5 inches
Occupation: dental hygienist
Address: Poplar Ave, Twin Falls, ID

Even though the pertinent details from the presentation would be made available to them all in their shared work drive, Hudson jotted down the basic notes to help immerse himself into the finer detail of the case.

Detective González pushed on to the next slide. The named heading remained but the rest of the page morphed into repugnance, showing a close-up of Lorena's mutilated corpse. Hudson was certain that the juxtaposition between the two slides had been deliberately designed to shock. It worked. To see Lorena go from carefree smiles to the horrific image now on-screen was sickening. The text beside the image had changed from her living statistics to those centered around her death.

Kidnapped: 10 December
Murdered: 12 December
Found: 13 December

Hudson wrote the details on his notepad, then stared over his monitor out through the bedroom window to the Hawthorne Elementary School that was directly opposite his house, preferring not to focus on the image currently on-screen. The playground—usually bustling at this time of the day with kids on recess—was silent and deserted, just like every other school would be.

He returned his focus to the computer, seeing that the slide had changed, once again for the worse. This time, it was a photograph of Lorena on a stainless-steel gurney, evidently pre-autopsy. The text was equally as appalling as the image.

Two bullet wounds to right thigh
Abrasions and ecchymoses on legs, likely from a blunt object
Ligature strangulation (cause of death)
37 stab wounds to the chest (post-mortem)
Premolar removed (post-mortem)

'And these are just the grim highlights,' Detective González said quietly. She paused and then again advanced the presentation. Carla Eagleton's name, profile picture and personal information signaled the shift over to the second victim.

Hudson braced himself for another gruesome onslaught. He tilted his coffee cup—empty—and wondered if Maddie might give them a comfort break, but then figured that that seemed callous, given the immediate circumstances of what they were doing and the urgency surrounding this case.

He looked out of the window again, this time at the distant snow-covered Wasatch Mountains and the highest peak, Gobblers Knob. Unlike Maddie and Becky, Hudson was not a skier. He loved the mountains and—being a native of Madawaska in Maine, with its fair share of snow every year—he enjoyed the cold climate, but he just wasn't one for snow sports. Give him a game of basketball any day. He stared at the mountains, his thoughts drifting to the growing need to escape the clenching sense of claustrophobia brought on by the lockdown.

'Hudson?' It was Maddie's voice, pulling his gaze back to the laptop screen. 'Are you still with us?'

He smiled and nodded as his eyes settled on the brutal photo of Carla Eagleton's naked, mutilated body which somehow looked worse than that of the previous victim. Escalation, he thought, dreading what the killer had done to the other two women yet to come.

Detective González moved through the grim details for victims three and four, Jasmine Jaconski and Molly Hutchison. By the end of the presentation, Hudson was feeling vaguely nauseous and somewhat tight-chested. Thankfully, Maddie was just about wrapping up the meeting.

'Okay, Detective. I think we have everything that we need from you right now, so I'll let you leave. If the rest of you could stay on, please,' Maddie directed.

'Okay. Well, thank you all. Good luck and I hope to hear from you soon,' the detective said. Then her video feed disappeared.

'Before we all get to work,' Maddie began, 'I'd just like to remind you of the reason that I initially turned down this case: my fear that you would neglect to look after yourselves and work on it every hour God sends. Yes, this *is* more urgent than the previous cases that we've worked on, but my priority is for your well-being as well as catching this monster. You need to eat, sleep and even interact with your loved ones…no matter how challenging that can be. Seriously, I don't want you working into the early hours on this. Okay?'

'We get it. We hear you,' Kenyatta said.

'Yep,' Becky confirmed.

Hudson nodded his agreement.

'Good. And everyone knows what they're doing. I suggest we have a team briefing first thing tomorrow to bring each other up to speed. Okay, you're free to go. Hudson, could you stay on, please?'

A wave of panic struck Hudson as he watched the rest of the team say goodbye and then disappear from the meeting for what felt like minutes. His mind raced through what Maddie could possibly want with him. It couldn't be work-related, or else she would have spoken in front of everyone else. When they alone were left in the room and he saw the serious look on her face, he knew.

Maddie unmuted him. 'How are you doing, Hudson?'

'Good, thanks,' he answered. 'Cabin fever, like everyone else.'

'Right. I never thought I'd miss the office, or Harmons, or a cup of coffee from Eva's quite so much.'

Hudson offered a weak smile, waiting for her to cut to the chase.

'Listen, Hudson. Have you done anything about that private case that you were working on?' she asked.

Hudson shook his head. 'I'm paralyzed by it, Maddie. I have Abigail on my back constantly, wanting me to hand over the information, so we know the money is definitely ours; I have daily emails from Wanda Chabala, asking if I've identified the person who killed her daughter yet. And I just—'

'Okay, Hudson, let me tell you where I'm at on this. I appreciate that you're not in an easy position. But…I just can't have a member of the Venator staff taking on private jobs where the DNA has come to you illegally. This is exactly why so many people have issues with investigative genetic genealogy. They say it's like the Wild West and that we're a law unto ourselves: as long as we find the killer, or rapist, or identify the human remains, it doesn't matter how we get there. But it does matter, Hudson. It matters to me and my company. And, most of all, it matters to the very survival of this industry. We're pioneers in this field, marching ahead of official regulation and legislation, but it will catch up with us soon and we need to be showing exemplary practice when it does.'

'I know,' Hudson muttered.

'Look… I'm really sorry to have to say this to you, but you either have to end your ties with this woman and hand back any money she paid to you for this work, or…you leave Venator. If it goes public— which, being so high-profile, it will——someone will connect the dots back to the company and I just can't risk that kind of damage. This is exactly the type of ammunition critics of our work are looking out for.'

Her words were crushing, and he fought with himself not to cry.

'I'm sorry, Maddie,' he muttered. 'I didn't mean to bring you or Venator into all this… I'll resolve it.'

'Good,' Maddie said. 'You're very good at your job, Hudson. Just don't let yourself be blindsided or seduced by this poisoned chalice.' She paused, then softened. 'Go take a walk. Clear your head.'

Hudson nodded.

'I'm here to talk if you need me. Otherwise, I'll see you online in the morning.'

'Bye,' he said weakly, his quivering hand clicking to hit the leave button.

The screen went blank as did his mind.

Now what?

He put his head in his hands, trying to untangle his thoughts. A month ago, he had been accosted by a stranger who had seemed to know an awful lot about him. Over a drink in a downtown bar, she had revealed herself to be Wanda Chabala whose daughter, Francesca, had been raped and murdered, and an apparently innocent man, Brandon Blake, had been convicted of the crimes. Somehow—certainly not by legal means—Wanda Chabala had managed to obtain a DNA sample from the perpetrator, and she had offered Hudson fifty thousand dollars to conduct investigative genetic genealogy to identify the man who had raped and killed her daughter. It was a lot of money that would have funded the entire adoption of a baby that he and his wife, Abigail, had wanted to pursue. *Had* wanted to pursue. She still did, desperately so. But he just wasn't sure anymore. They had only been together for four years but, in the past twelve months or so, things hadn't been great between them. Being forced to spend every waking hour in the same house had run a highlighter over the fact that they had unwittingly been living separate married lives prior to lockdown.

Hudson picked up his cell phone and opened his banking app. All fifty thousand dollars was sitting right there, in their joint savings account, untouched and ready to go. He needed to return every cent back to Wanda Chabala and tell her that he had been unable to identify a suspect. Simple. But it was actually far from simple. He *had* identified a suspect, or at least narrowed it down to two brothers. The problem was that one of the suspects was Wanda Chabala's own husband, Warren Mercaldo. Either he had raped and killed his own stepdaughter, or his brother Jackson had. Neither one was a name that Hudson had wanted to hand over.

He looked back out through the window, feeling a profound need

31

for guidance; someone to talk to. The friends that he'd made in Utah wouldn't understand the complexities of his past life and he hadn't seen his old friends back in Madawaska for a few years. He thought of his mom and dad. He hadn't spoken to them in a long time, either. Just two or three close friends would understand. The thought of getting out and sitting in a bar with a glass of wine and chatting it all over with them was overwhelming. But he couldn't do that; he had to make the decision for himself. In a way, he supposed, Maddie had made the decision easier: it was either keep the money or keep his job. Simple. If he kept his job and returned the money, then he would almost certainly lose Abigail and, with her, perhaps his one shot at having a wife and family.

He drew in a long breath, stood up and carried his cup into the kitchen where Abigail was working on her laptop at the counter.

'How's it going?' she asked without looking up from her screen.

'Okay, I guess. The detective from Twin Falls just finished presenting the new case to us all in quite some detail.'

Abigail glanced at him with a grimace. 'Bad?'

Hudson nodded as he made himself a fresh coffee. 'How's your day going?'

'Fun, fun, fun,' she said, presumably with a heavy dose of sarcasm. She worked in the accounting department of PacifiCorp, a job she enjoyed under the normal circumstances of operating in their busy downtown office. However, she hated working from home.

'Coffee?' he asked.

'No, thanks,' she replied. 'I've already caffeinated my veins just enough to get me through the day.'

'Good luck with it,' he said, brushing past her and heading back to his bedroom office. He woke his laptop and headed directly to the FamilyTreeDNA website. It was time to forget his personal problems and get down to some work.

He entered the suspect's kit number and password and was then faced with the same dashboard as Maddie had accessed in their earlier meeting. Hudson clicked on the *Y-DNA Matches* button and was instantly disappointed to see that there were zero matches at Y-111, the highest level that the kit had been tested against. Fifteen matches were recorded at the Y-67 level, below. These were fifteen men who should theoretically share a common male ancestor whose DNA had passed from father to son down through the generations. Also theoretically, those fifteen men should share the same surname as the killer.

However, the range of surnames in front of Hudson—nine in total—were, as was most often the case, very divergent: *Rowson. Johnson. Waldman. Raič. Staley. Taylor. Scotton. Valentine. Macey.* One of those names could be the surname of the Twin Falls serial killer. Equally, they could not.

Hudson made a note of the nine surnames in a Word document and also jotted them down on the legal pad beside him.

The closest match of the fifteen men was Peter Andrew Valentine. Hudson clicked the Time Predictor tool to find out how far back he would have to go in order to find a common ancestor. It was even worse than he had feared. Even to have an 84% chance of finding the common male ancestor shared between the killer and Peter Andrew Valentine, it would be necessary to go back at least sixteen generations, a task that was utterly out of the question.

Returning to the main dashboard, Hudson looked at further details about the killer's Y-DNA. His haplogroup was listed as R1a which, Hudson read, was now most commonly found in Europe and South Asia. He pulled up phytogeographer.com and selected the option of displaying haplogroups as a heat map. A duotone map of the world loaded, and Hudson entered R1a into the search box. Splatters of vibrant pinks and yellows were clustered heavily around Eastern Europe, Russia and South Asia, denoting its highest frequency globally. Interestingly, there was no coverage over the United States.

'Hmm,' Hudson said to himself as he took a screenshot of the heat map and added it to the Word document that he would share with the team at the first briefing tomorrow morning.

Hudson's next task was to extract the killer's EVCs—externally visible characteristics—from his DNA. This stage was one that excited him, being the first real step in the team's investigations that could shed some light on the killer's physical appearance. The science of phenotyping was not perfect, but it was a good starting point when the police so far had zero leads on what this guy might look like.

Hudson clicked to download the killer's raw DNA file. Of the 677,864 pieces of DNA code contained in the plain text file, just forty held the clues toward the killer's eye-, hair- and skin-colors.

With the document open on-screen, Hudson pulled up the Hirisplex website, run by the Department of Genetic Identification of Erasmus Medical Center and began to pick his way through the file, extracting the relevant data and entering it into the Hirisplex tool.

The process didn't take him long and he held his breath as he clicked *Display Predicted Phenotype*, pulling the Twin Falls serial killer's face from the shadows.

The DNA coding pointed to a man with very pale skin, brown hair and blue eyes.

Chapter Six

'Move!' Becky Larkin said, entering the guest bedroom of her swanky Sugar House Apartment, carrying a cup of decaf coffee and flapping her free hand as though she were swatting a fly.

Ross, her best friend and roommate who was sitting at her desk, sighed dramatically. He ran his hand through his fair hair and asked, 'I thought we were hot-desking, Becks?'

Becky screwed up her face. 'No, *you* thought we were hot-desking. This is my apartment. And this is my guest bedroom that is now doubling as my home office.'

Ross stood up with a groan, scooping his laptop from the desk. 'Back to the kitchen for me, then,' he said, his face contorting with great theatrics.

Becky smiled. 'Now, there's a good boy,' she said slapping his back as he passed. He turned to give her a mock-glower before she added, 'I've made you some coffee.'

He grinned. 'It'd better not be some of your decaf crap,' he said as he left the room.

Ignoring him and setting her drink down beside her laptop, Becky reached over to the printer and took out color photographs of the four victims of the Twin Falls serial killer, then fixed them to the wall directly above her computer. She had already memorized their names. Lorena Baly. Carla Eagleton. Jasmine Jaconski. Molly Hutchison. Victim photographs were always displayed prominently in the Venator office during a case to give the team a constant reminder of the real people and why their work was of such great importance: to provide closure, to answer questions that had remained resolutely unanswered for decades and, of course, to see that justice is done. For some of the cases that the team had worked on, justice had come too late and the perpetrator had already passed. Then, the only atonement and restitution for the family and friends of the victims was a public declaration of his name. Rationales, explanations and motivations had died along with the perpetrators themselves. But not with this case. The Twin Falls serial killer was out there right now, *definitely* alive and probably about to select his next victim.

Becky sipped her coffee as she stared at the women's photographs while she cleared her head. Detective González's presentation had gotten to her. They always did. Becky couldn't stop putting herself in the victims' shoes, imagining what their last moments on earth might have been like. For Lorena, Carla, Jasmine and Molly, their final days would have started horrifically, building to an unimaginably brutal and terrifying end.

It was time to find this monster.

Becky drank more coffee and woke her computer. On-screen in front of her were some of the cases that she had been working on over the past few days. Since the office had shut down ten days ago, the Venator team had been working on cases independently. Her focus had been on applying investigative genetic genealogy to some of the backlog of rape kits that the team had taken on. Since there was no federal law mandating the tracking and testing of rape kits, an unbelievable 400,000 such kits were found in 2014 languishing untested in police and crime lab storage facilities around the country. SAKI— Sexual Assault Kit Initiative—was now providing federal grants to help end that hideous backlog. Having identified the suspects in two such cases in the past ten days, the latest one that Becky was working on was a serial rapist from Houston, Texas, who had been active in the 1980s. She was certain that, with just a little more time, she would be able to provide his name to law enforcement. With some reluctance, she closed this file, vowing to return to it as soon as possible.

She took a sip of coffee and then pulled up the FamilyTreeDNA website, entering the Twin Falls killer's kit number. From the main dashboard, she selected *myOrigins* which took her to a page that displayed an estimate of the killer's admixture, or ethnicity as it was sometimes described. Personally, she preferred the term geo-ancestry. The science was advancing, but it wasn't yet at a point of reliable accuracy. Like with much in the world of investigative genetic genealogy, estimates, approximations, hunches and guesswork had to be combined with dogged, systematic and meticulous, traditional genealogical research until a final conclusion could be reached.

'Interesting,' Becky commented, looking at the geo-ancestry estimate for the Twin Falls serial killer.

Eastern Europe 47%
West and Central Europe 29%
North and Central America 19%
Iberia <5%

It appeared from the data that the killer had strong links to Europe, notably the Eastern parts. She needed to drill down further into his heritage and so, opened GEDmatch.com in a new web browser tab. Directly after the Zoom meeting had ended this morning, Maddie had uploaded the killer's DNA to this site, which would hopefully give the team more options to help track him down. Although the cousin-matching aspect wouldn't be available for another twenty-four hours, their tools for admixture analysis were available immediately.

Given the overwhelming European nature of the killer's heritage, Becky selected the Eurogenes tool to analyze the admixture further. She entered the kit number and then hit continue.

Volga_Ural 30.23%
Italian 21.33%
Eastern_Euro 16.06%
East_Central_Euro 12.04%
Central_Euro 11.35%
French 4.34%
North_Caucasian 1.23%

'Well, that needs Googling,' she muttered to herself, having never seen Volga Ural listed in admixture results before and having no clue as to where it referred. She read that, according to Wikipedia, Volga Ural *is a historical region in Eastern Europe, in what is today Russia.*

They were an interesting set of results, Becky thought as she entered the details into her working document. Clearly the killer had a strong Russian and Italian heritage.

She scanned down the remaining columns, noting that there was no African or Asian DNA present in the results.

With the geo-ancestry analysis completed, Becky turned her attention to her favorite aspect of the job. It was something that she had studied as part of her degree and master's in criminology at Simon Fraser University in Canada and involved a micro-analysis of the crimes, with the aim of trying to work out what type of an individual they were dealing with. As part of her work, she also geo-profiled the locations in which all aspects of the crimes had taken place to ascertain if patterns could be formed that might give an indication of where the killer lived, worked or hung out.

Becky accessed the Venator cloud drive and opened up a new

subfolder within the *ACTIVE CASES* folder that had been created for the Twin Falls case. This shared area would inevitably grow in content as the case progressed, but for now it contained just the detective's PowerPoint presentation, the DNA kit log-in details and a more-in-depth file on the murder victims, as provided by the Twin Falls police department, which was what Becky now clicked to open.

According to the file, Lorena Baly had been abducted from her home on Robbins Avenue on December 10, 2019. With no signs of forced entry, it was believed that Lorena had opened the door to the killer and possibly allowed him inside. A series of photographs of her living room showed it to have been the locus of the attack: a small side table had been knocked over, a glass vase smashed, and the contents of a coffee cup spilled on the cream carpet. Two cushions from the sofa were also on the floor, but, tellingly, there was no sign of blood in any of the pictures which covered every angle of the room. Becky read the accompanying text which confirmed that no blood had been found in the room, nor had it been anywhere else in the house, and nor was there evidence of a sexual assault having taken place. The police theory, backed up by the autopsy findings, was that Lorena had been attacked and overpowered almost as soon as she had opened her front door. Having given Lorena barbiturates to make her drowsy, the killer was able to get her into his vehicle with little struggle. Had there been any witnesses they would likely just have assumed that Lorena had been intoxicated and was being helped into a vehicle by a friend.

Becky skipped through to the details for the second victim, Carla Eagleton, who had been abducted from her home on Harmon Park Avenue, Twin Falls at some point on January 30, 2020. Again, there had been no signs of forced entry and, judging by the accompanying text and images, the killer seemed to have overpowered Carla as soon as he had stepped through the door. Here also, no blood at the scene and no signs of sexual assault.

Just nineteen days later, Jasmine Jaconski had been abducted from her home on Alturas Drive. Becky studied the crime scene photographs of her house. An initial attack appeared to have taken place in the entrance hall, which had continued through to the kitchen where several plates had been smashed on the stone floor. Becky swallowed hard when she saw a toppled knife rack, its contents spilled on the countertop. Jasmine had apparently fought to save herself but had failed. The forensic team had found no evidence of blood, nor of a clean-up operation. He had overpowered her, drugged her and then removed her from the house, just like the previous women in the case.

The final victim—the final so far, Becky had to remind herself—Molly Hutchison, had been taken from her home on Wendell Street exactly one week ago. No signs of forced entry and no signs of a struggle. Either Molly had been more easily overpowered or the killer had taken the time to tidy up the place a little before bundling her out of the house, which, given how he'd acted with the other women, seemed unlikely.

The killer clearly ticked the FBI Behavioral Science Unit descriptors for what an organized killer looked like. The murders were clearly planned, restraints used in the attacks appeared to belong to the killer, a display of control over each victim had taken place and a vehicle had been used during the commission of the murder.

But what of his motivation? The majority of serial murder cases involved offenders who kill for sexual reasons. Becky agreed with Detective González's assessment that the killer fell overwhelmingly in the anger-retaliation category, but she wanted a deeper analysis of the killer's primary motives in committing the murders. She pulled up a PDF version of an FBI monograph, created by the National Center for the Analysis of Violent Crime. The document was her go-to guide in cases involving serial murder.

The file stated that primary motivations fell into five categories: *sexual, anger, mental illness, profit* or *other*. Becky carefully read the descriptions for each model. Only one matched perfectly: anger.

Anger was defined as a motivation in which an offender killed victims based on personal pent-up hostility which was projected towards a person or group represented by the victim. The victim could have been a symbol of this hostility, or may have just been an available, vulnerable target to the offender.

His motivation had been, as she suspected, anger. The level of post-mortem injuries seen in each victim had been nothing short of frenzied overkill.

Becky moved on to the next section of the document, which defined the relationship between the offender and victim as one of either *stranger, targeted stranger, acquaintance, relative / familial* or *customer / client*. At this point, it was difficult to settle firmly on what the relationships might have been, but since the police had so far found no link between the women, it pointed to one of the first two options. She read each of the descriptors carefully.

Stranger was defined as no known relationship between the offender and the victim. Targeted stranger was defined as a situation where the offender knew who the victim was, but the victim had no knowledge or familiarity with the offender.

Becky's gut instinct was directing her toward the *targeted stranger* relationship. Given how much planning had gone into the murders, the killer had probably come to know the victims—all single women, living alone—very well but without their knowing it and probably without ever contacting them prior to his attacks.

The next part of Becky's role was to analyze the locations in which the bodies had been left to try to figure out why he had chosen those particular places. The fact that he had placed the bodies in full public view indicated that he had no concerns about their being discovered. Was this arrogance? Becky wondered. Was he so confident in his own meticulous planning that he knew that he wouldn't get caught? She wasn't convinced. There was something about the victims' being blindfolded and left outside of churches that made her question this theory.

Returning to the case file document, she took her time to study each of the four photographs of the victims as taken by the coroner in the location where they had been found. The killer had certainly not been in a hurry. Each of the women had been positioned on their backs, their arms by their sides with their palms facing upward and their legs splayed apart. It was a confusing image to attempt to understand. The blindfold suggested that the killer perhaps felt remorseful, as he couldn't bear for them to look at him despite their being dead. The churches suggested a possible desire for repentance or forgiveness, but the degrading positioning of their open legs strongly indicated a desire for further humiliation in a final expression of his anger-retaliation.

Becky flicked between the images several times, straining to understand what might have been going on in the killer's head at the time, but she failed to draw any firm conclusions; the diorama the killer had created made no sense to her.

Having made some notes of her findings so far in preparation for the briefing tomorrow morning, Becky switched to geo-profiling the known locations connected to the case by applying the circle hypothesis—merging several studies' outcomes, based on the work of leading forensic psychologist, David Canter—that found that in upward of eighty-five percent of serial murder cases, the killer lived within a circle defined by a diameter drawn between the killer's two furthest offences. Opening up Google Maps, Becky began to plot the locations where the bodies had been disposed.

A while later, Ross entered the guest bedroom. He leaned on the doorframe and asked, 'How you getting on, Becks?'

Becky rotated her chair to face him. She rubbed her eyes, realizing then that she had not moved for a long while. 'Good, I think,' she replied. 'And you?'

Ross nodded. 'I've added all names, dates and places so far associated with the Twin Falls case to a file and then, more crucially perhaps, I started cooking us dinner.'

'God. Wait. Is it really that time already?' Becky said, craning her neck to see the laptop clock. 'Jeez.'

'I've poured us a glass of white. Why don't you wrap it up for the day? Remember what Maddie said about not burning out...'

Becky nodded and yawned. A glass of wine was exactly what she needed right now. She stood up and followed Ross out to the open-plan living area. From the kitchen, something that smelled amazing was cooking in the oven. 'What are we having?' Becky asked, as Ross handed her a wine and chinked his glass lightly against hers.

'Baked chicken thighs,' he revealed, quickly adding, 'Don't worry, it's one of my healthier meals.'

Becky smiled. 'Sounds just about perfect—thank you.' She sipped the wine and wandered over to the balcony that offered spectacular views of the Wasatch Mountain Range. She emitted a long and protracted sigh.

'What was *that* about? Jerome? Or your dad? Or missing getting out for exercise, maybe?' Ross asked.

She smiled and glanced over her shoulder at him. He knew her too well. She thought for a moment. 'All of the above...I guess.' She had managed to go on just two dates with Jerome, a guy whom she'd met climbing right before lockdown. After a string of hopeless relationships, Jerome had seemed like a good guy, but the current absence of spontaneity was a big problem and the things that they most had in common—outdoor and extreme sports—were all closed or currently prohibited. She couldn't even meet the guy for a damned walk outside. The combination of not knowing each other very well and how little they had going on in their lives had meant that their

41

recent conversations on FaceTime had quickly dried up and uncomfortable silences had started to creep in.

'Where are you at with your dad?' Ross queried. 'You know I don't really like to pry.'

Becky laughed. 'Oh my God! Said the queen of prying herself.'

Ross smiled. 'I'm being a good friend and roommate, and letting you talk to me when you're good and ready.'

Becky shrugged. Three weeks ago, she'd had it out with her father, telling him that she knew that he had placed a gag order on all of his employees, preventing them from speaking to the police who were investigating Michael Barnhart's disappearance. His defense at the time had been blunt and concise: he had had to make dozens of business decisions every day and wouldn't be discussing the matter any further with her. If she had pushed him, it would have been the end of their relationship. Despite the potential implications, she had revealed everything to Maddie in a tearful conversation. Although it was selfish to admit it, Becky had been relieved when Maddie had told her not to probe her father on the subject any further. But in the subsequent days, when she had heard nothing at all from her parents, her resolve to help Maddie had been reignited.

'Is sitting down and talking with him face to face out of the question?' Ross asked gently, placing his hand on her shoulder.

'My dad was very clear about *not* talking about it.'

'Do you have any ideas about who phoned Michael right before he disappeared? Or why your dad would stop his employees from cooperating with the police?'

'None whatsoever,' Becky replied, sipping her wine. 'But I'm sure as hell determined to find out.'

Chapter Seven

Monday, April 6, 2020, Salt Lake City, Utah

Kenyatta Nelson clicked to leave the Zoom meeting. 'Well, now, that was intense,' she mumbled to herself, setting her laptop off to one side and standing up to stretch. She was glad that Maddie had changed her mind about the Twin Falls case, but she knew that the next few days were going to be tough on the Venator team. Everyone had been assigned roles that would keep them occupied for the rest of the day but, after the briefing tomorrow morning, they would all be dedicated to a single focus area: the complex process of building the killer's family tree from the people with whom he matched on FamilyTreeDNA and GEDmatch. Kenyatta's job, today, would be to get those cousin matches into related clusters, ready to be assigned at the morning briefing. But, first, after all that gruesome information and all the gory photographs, she knew that she needed to take a short break.

She slowly ambled across the living room to the kitchenette in her tiny house on East Seventh Street. She pulled open the refrigerator and took out a cold can of Coke which she popped open. After taking a mouthful, she exhaled. Since the pandemic had taken hold, her feeble attempts at dieting had gone out of the window. She vowed things would change once life returned to normal, not that there was any sign of that on the horizon right now.

This darned pandemic, she thought, not for the first time today, as she stared at the refrigerator door with a photograph stuck on it of her with her three sons on a day out at the Natural History Museum of Utah. It was a selfie, taken two summers ago in the Past Worlds exhibition with the four of them pretending to be terrified of the dinosaur skeleton looming directly behind them. She smiled at the returning memories; it had been one great day in what had been a fantastic summer break. Things had been okay back then. She'd just gotten the job at Venator, her seventeen-year marriage to Otis had been happy and secure, they had enjoyed a comfortable home together and their three boys had been thriving in it all. But everything had changed just a few months later. Four days before Christmas, her beloved mom had been out shopping and had dropped dead of heart failure, right in the middle of the City Creek Shopping Center. Kenyatta could still feel the crushing devastation from that day as though it had been only hours ago that the call had come in from her distraught father. Hindsight had magnified the anguish and heartache of her mom's death to become the eventual earthquake that had caused the tsunami of what had followed. Three days after her mom's passing, on Christmas Eve, her father had suffered a massive stroke while planning his wife's funeral. He had died the following day and Kenyatta had had to spend the holiday period organizing a joint funeral for both her parents. Kenyatta's slide into a mire of deep depression had been swift and destructive and had been the reason that Otis had given her for his wanting a divorce and sole custody of their kids. Therapy and medication had offered her a lifeline toward trying to establish a new path for herself in her mid-fifties.

Through watery eyes, Kenyatta tried to smile at the photo of the four of them. Despite her court-mandated visitation rights, Otis had refused to let her see the boys since the pandemic had begun because of the work that she did, volunteering with the city's homeless population. 'God only knows what diseases you'll pick up,' he'd scorned on the phone, despite her protestations about various safety protocols and wearing protection. A scheduled court appearance in eleven days would hopefully determine a more permanent shared-custody arrangement for the kids, now that she was better.

Kenyatta drank more of her Coke, then walked back into the living room area and sat with her laptop on her thighs, ready to start work on catching this Twin Falls demon. 'Your days as a free man are numbered,' she muttered, entering the FamilyTreeDNA website. Under the heading of *Autosomal DNA Results & Tools*, Kenyatta clicked *Matches* which loaded the page that Maddie had accessed during the team meeting earlier today. It showed the names of the two thousand and forty-three men and women who were all somehow related to the Twin Falls serial killer. At the top of the list, with eighty-seven centimorgans of shared DNA, was a man named Samuel Green. Kenyatta ticked the checkbox beside his name and then hit the *In*

Common With filter button which produced a new list of sixty-four people who matched both Samuel Green and the Twin Falls killer. Somewhere, at some point back in time, all these people shared at least one common ancestor. Having removed all the matches that fell below the unworkable ten-centimorgans threshold, Kenyatta was left with just eight names which she downloaded into a CSV file and put into a folder on the shared drive, labeled *Cluster One*. Then, she returned to the FamilyTreeDNA website and did the same thing for the second closest match, a lady by the name of Heather Newton, who shared seventy-nine centimorgans of DNA with the killer. Kenyatta repeated the process of finding everyone who was in common with both Heather and the killer, this time producing a CSV file containing five names. She labeled the file *Cluster Two* and saved it to the shared drive. She worked through the first page of results, ensuring that every person had been included in at least one genetic network cluster. After more than an hour's work, she had saved seven clusters to the Venator shared drive, which, for some reason, wasn't as many as the exercise would usually produce. In theory, each cluster should represent seven distinct common ancestors or couples in the killer's direct ancestral line. As of tomorrow, it would fall to the team to share out the clusters to work on identifying who those common ancestors were and then to figure out how they all related to one another.

Kenyatta sighed. There was nothing in the refrigerator. At least, nothing that she really wanted to eat. What little food she had in there was either way too healthy or way too unhealthy for her current requirements. What she fancied more than anything right now was sitting down with her kids in the Pig and a Jelly Jar restaurant five blocks away and eating their amazing sausage gravy and biscuits. But, of course, like pretty much everywhere else in the world, they had been shut down.

She looked at the time. She had just under an hour until she would need to leave to go help out at the SLC Homeless Kitchen. No time to cook anything decent now, anyway. She decided to eat over there with the homeless.

The journey from Kenyatta's house to downtown Salt Lake City was bizarre. It was as though she had strolled onto a post-apocalyptic movie set. The streets were almost deserted and when she boarded the Green Line Trax, she sat alone in an eerily empty car. Just one woman—a nurse, judging by her uniform—boarded further up the tram. There were cars on the streets, sure, but they were few and far between, and every person that she saw in and out of vehicles was hidden behind a face mask. A pack of zombies wouldn't look at all out of place under these circumstances, she thought with a smile as she alighted from the Trax and took the short walk to Pioneer Park in the city center. Thankfully, there had been no snow for a couple of days now and the sidewalk was clear.

'Kenyatta!' a voice extolled as she approached. It was her colleague, Jim, with his usual booming voice. He was standing just off the sidewalk behind a long folding table that held everything needed to run the outdoor SLC Homeless Kitchen.

'Hi, Jim. How are you?' she asked cheerily, not standing as close to him as she might have done ordinarily. He was a good-looking, six-foot-tall man with broad shoulders and a bushy, salt-and-pepper beard that was protruding out from under his facemask. On his head, he wore a deerstalker hat that flapped down over his ears.

'All the better for seeing you,' he said, then frowned. 'Are you early?'

She smiled, not that he would have seen it easily owing to her mask. 'I'm early. Thought I'd eat here…with you guys. I couldn't face eating alone again, not to mention that I have nothing appetizing in the house.'

'I'm the same. I get it,' he agreed. 'It's one thing to *choose* to eat alone but totally another to have no choice in the matter.'

She had not known Jim all that long and didn't like to pry. He lived alone, didn't wear a wedding band, and had never mentioned partners or kids. He was a former banker—or some similar such line of work—and was now giving something back to the community in his retirement.

'What's the soup?' Kenyatta asked him.

'Tomato,' he replied.

'Perfect,' she said, glancing down the street as their first visitor of the evening was coming into view and heading toward them. 'You might want to crank that heat up; David's coming.'

'It's almost there,' Jim replied, slightly increasing the heat of the two pots.

'Hi, David,' Kenyatta greeted as he approached them. 'How are you doing?'

The elderly African American man with curly gray hair ambled closer, carrying three large trash bags. 'Yeah, not so bad, not so bad,' he answered. 'Soup ready yet? I could smell it way back as I was coming along.'

Jim removed the lid from the first urn and peered inside. 'Just a couple more minutes,' he answered.

'Hot drink for you…while you're waiting?' Kenyatta asked.

David nodded. 'Coffee. Black with two, please.'

Kenyatta moved toward the pot of hot water. 'Say, David. Have you seen my friend, Lonnie, up at the shelter at all?'

David's mouth turned downward. 'Lonnie? Let's see. I haven't seen Lonnie in days—not since the world went all to hell. No. I ain't seen him once up at the men's resource center.' David shrugged.

'I worry about him,' Kenyatta said, as much to herself as to anyone else.

'Hey. Lonnie's been out there a long time; he's a true survivor.'

'Well, I sure hope you're right on that,' Kenyatta said, handing David his drink.

'Thanks.'

'You're welcome.'

'Why don't you go see him if you want,' Jim suggested to Kenyatta. 'Take him some soup and bread…'

Lonnie's usual hang-out wasn't far, just one block away on West Second Street. 'Well, are you sure?'

Jim opened his arms out. 'I think I can cope, so long as you come back. You've got at least fifteen minutes, I'd say, before the usual crowd arrives.'

'Thanks, Jim,' she said, opening up the bag of bread and taking out two slices, while he ladled hot soup into a cup. 'See you in fifteen, then.' She carried the food one block over to a derelict building that

47

was in serious need of demolition. A pile of trash bags, newspapers and blankets in the covered entrance was where Lonnie liked to call home.

'Lonnie?' Kenyatta called. 'Anyone in there? Is anybody home? It's me, Kenyatta. I got you some soup.'

A familiar, reassuring rustling came from somewhere inside the filthy camp. 'What flavor?' he called out.

Kenyatta sat on the steps to the entrance and smiled. She always found it amusing that somebody reduced to begging on the streets could be so downright fussy with their food. 'Tomato.'

Lonnie made a snorting noise, then began shuffling out from the rubbish. He stood up, showing that he was tall and painfully thin. Behind his facemask, a toothless mouth was set in a scraggly, gray beard. He was dressed in the only set of clothes that he owned: pants, shirt, tie and jacket; all dirty. Lonnie sat down on the same step as Kenyatta but kept his distance. It had been Lonnie who had first warned her about the seriousness of the virus as it had approached, asking her to get him the mask and gloves that he now wore.

'Nice day, huh?' he commented with a glance to the sky.

'This the first time you've been out, today?'

He shrugged, extending his hand out to take the soup and bread. 'Thanks, Kenny.'

She hated his shortening of her name, but she didn't ever correct him or let on that it bothered her. 'How have you been?'

'You know,' he replied, pulling down his mask and loudly slurping the soup.

'You've not been up to the shelter?'

Lonnie shook his head, then met her gaze. 'Don't you see? That's what they want. Put us all in one giant room together, introduce the virus and, shazam, it spreads like wildfire and you suddenly don't have such a problem with homeless folk anymore.'

'That's so cynical, Lonnie.'

'I'm a very cynical person, you see, Kenny,' he answered. 'By the way—tell whoever made this soup that it ain't all that bad. Slightly too much salt, mind, but it's okay.'

Kenyatta laughed. 'I'll be sure to pass that on.'

'So, are you out of a job, now everything's shut down?'

'No, we're working remotely from home.'

For some reason that she couldn't fathom, Lonnie burst into laughter. 'Catching the bad guys from a computer at home, huh? What you working on?'

'It's a live case; not a cold one. Serial killer on the loose,' she said, keeping the details deliberately vague.

Lonnie raised his eyebrows. 'That so?' His brain processed this, then he shot her a sideways glance. 'Not in this city, though, right?'

'No, you don't need to worry; it's not Utah.'

A short moment of silence was broken by Lonnie muttering, 'Working remotely...'

'What was your line of work, Lonnie?' she asked, knowing almost nothing about his background or past.

'Oh, you know, this and that. Tried my hand at various things over the years.' He drank more soup. 'Jack of all trades, you might say.'

'Where did you do your Jack-of-all-trading?' she pressed.

Lonnie took a breath, and then stuffed a whole slice of bread into his mouth. 'Here and there. I passed through most states at one time or another. Except Hawaii. I might just retire there, though.'

Kenyatta laughed. 'I think you'd have a real nice retirement in Hawaii, but I won't be delivering soup and bread to you there anytime soon.'

'That's too bad,' Lonnie said, handing her the empty cup. 'Thanks.' He pulled his face mask back up and wordlessly shuffled back inside his make-shift home.

'Goodbye then, Lonnie,' Kenyatta called. She waited a moment for a reply that never came, then headed back over to Pioneer Park.

'Looks like I got here just in time,' Kenyatta observed, placing a hand in the small of Jim's back as she passed behind him to face the line of six homeless men and women.

'Was he home?' Jim asked, filling a bowl with soup.

'Yeah, he was home,' Kenyatta replied. 'He's Lonnie, the same as ever,' she said. 'He complimented you on the soup, wouldn't you know? But said—now, how did he put it—it was maybe a little too salty.'

'Ha. I'll be sure to remember that next time,' Jim chuckled.

Kenyatta sat down on her sofa with a contented sigh. The lights in her living room were subdued and Ella Fitzgerald was crooning softly in the background. It had been an enjoyable evening at the SLC Homeless Kitchen, and she had come away buoyed by the experience; the type which was quite hard to come by at the moment.

She opened her work laptop and paused. She could make a start on one of the clusters for the Twin Falls suspect case, or she could carry on with the *Boys Under the Bridge* investigation. She couldn't help herself and opted for the latter, opening the forty-three-page document that she had created for her work on the case. It was pro-bono work for the National Center for Missing and Exploited Children and involved trying to identify two boys whose bodies had been found murdered and dumped under a bridge in 1994 in Penrose, Colorado.

The boys had been brothers—aged around four and six—with a strong Asian heritage. Their closest cousin match was a man named Elborn Nodecker who shared just fifteen paltry centimorgans of DNA with them. All other matches fell below the ten-centimorgans mark, where false positives became more likely, making Kenyatta wonder if the boys had come from someplace where DNA, for regular genealogy purposes, simply wasn't common. The case, as it stood, was pretty well unsolvable and she knew that the rest of the Venator team thought that she was a little crazy even to entertain trying, but she felt that she owed it to the two brothers; nobody else in the world was working to identify them, much less solve their murders.

Kenyatta was about to pick up where she had left off with trying to track down more of Elborn Nodecker's ancestors, but she paused, having not checked for fresh cousin matches in several days. She knew both the boys' kit numbers by heart and logged in at FamilyTreeDNA to run a check. As expected, no new matches.

She logged in to GEDmatch for the elder brother and ran a *One To Many* search which compared his DNA to the rest of the database. The page loaded and Kenyatta couldn't quite believe what she was seeing: a new match.

Her phone pinged with an incoming text message that seemed to chime in perfectly with the revelation on-screen in front of her. 'Oh my gosh,' she exclaimed, her hands quivering as she excitedly studied the new information. It was a lady by the name of Angela Spooner who matched the boy with 37.3 centimorgans of DNA. According to GEDmatch's approximation, Angela was just 4.29 generations back to a shared common ancestor.

Kenyatta could not hold back her tears. This match was still very low and there were no guarantees that it would end up being any better than Elborn Nodecker, but for the first time on this case, she felt something that she hadn't truly felt before: hope.

She wiped her eyes with the back of her hand, logged out of the elder brother's kit and logged in with that of the younger brother.

'Wow. Just wow,' she said, seeing that he matched Angela Spooner with a slightly higher 40.1 centimorgans. She looked across the data given and saw that Angela had transferred her DNA to GEDmatch from MyHeritage two days ago. If Angela were willing to provide information from her cousin-matches and admixture reports from that site, it could help Kenyatta significantly.

Kenyatta carefully copied Angela Spooner's email address and pasted it into a new message. She thought for a long time about how best to compose the email. It was very rare for the team to make contact with the public regarding their trees, but she felt, in this instance, that it was justified. This could be her one and only shot. On the odd occasion that the team had sent emails such as this, they were usually vague about the specific nature of the case that they were working on. This time, however, Kenyatta believed that full disclosure and honesty could be her best option.

Dear Angela

I'm emailing you with tears in my eyes. I work for an organization called Venator in Salt Lake City – the short version of what we do is that we use genetic genealogy to discover the identities of people who have committed a serious crime as well as indentifying unknown human remains.

For several months now, I have been trying to identify two young brothers who were murdered in Colorado. The closest cousin match for a very long time was with a very low 15 centimorgans of DNA. You match the brothers with a significantly better 37.3 and 40.1 centimorgans.

Trying to identify these two poor boys has become something of a labor of love for me; I won't stop trying until the day I can replace the grave marker (currently dedicated to 'Two Unknown Brothers') with one that gives their full names, and someone is arrested for their murder. There is more information about the young brothers on the NamUs website (National Missing and Unidentified Persons System) if you'd like to take a look.

Their ethnicity results point to an Asian heritage—do any of your direct ancestors that you know of have links to this broad geographical area?

I appreciate that you probably didn't take a DNA test in order to help provide a name to unidentified human remains, but I can't begin to stress how much help you could be to these poor boys.

I look forward to hearing from you.

Kind regards

Kenyatta Nelson

Kenyatta exhaled then re-read through the message twice. She had laid it on a little thick and it probably went way over her usual professional line, but she couldn't afford to waste this one opportunity. 'Oh, good heavens above!' she said nervously, and clicked to send the email.

It was gone.

She stared at her screen, anticipating a bounce-back or a rejected-email-address notification. But nothing came. Kenyatta dearly hoped that that meant Angela Spooner would soon read and reply to the message.

She continued to stare at her inbox, every now and then clicking to refresh it, despite the fact that new emails came in automatically.

Then she remembered that a text message had arrived earlier. She picked up her phone to read it. It was from one of her twin sons, Gabe. Her instinctive smile at his contacting her faded when she read the message.

Mom, Dougie's dead. It's horrible.

Kenyatta gasped. Dougie was the family retriever, so named because her twin boys—who had been two years old at the time when they bought him as a puppy—refused to call him anything other than Doggie. Kenyatta and Otis had just about managed to persuade them that Dougie would be an acceptable close alternative. She loved that dog.

That's so sad, she wrote back. *How are your brothers taking it?*

Jon's upset, Gabe replied immediately. *Troy's in shock, I think. He found him and isn't really saying anything at all.*

I can imagine, she typed back. *So sad. He was 12 years old and that's okay for a retriever.*

Gabe's response shocked her deeply. *Someone killed him, Mom. He was stoned to death. Troy found him in the street outside our house.*

'Oh my God,' she cried out. Who would do such a thing to that beautiful, harmless creature? Then she thought about all that she had been told this morning about the Twin Falls serial killer and cast her mind back over all the other horrific cases that she'd worked on. There were *plenty* of disturbed sickos out there who would indeed do such a cruel thing.

Kenyatta wept. She cried for Dougie. She cried for the four victims of the Twin Falls killer. She cried for the *Boys under the Bridge.* And she cried for herself.

She desperately needed someone to talk to.

She picked up her cell phone and scrolled through her contacts, settling on a name and clicking to call.

Almost immediately, it was picked up. 'Jim,' she said softly. 'I'm sorry to call out of the blue like this but I'm all alone here, and really need someone to talk to right now.'

'Of course, Kenyatta. Of course,' he answered. 'You sound upset. What is it? What's wrong?'

Chapter Eight

'Mom..? Mom..?' Trenton called impatiently from the front door. 'There's a guy here…from Amazon. Says he wants to deliver laptops and a treadmill. Is this for real?'

Maddie hurried into the hallway from the kitchen. 'Get right back inside,' she directed Trenton, wafting her hands at him.

'It's okay, he's masked and half-way down the drive,' Trenton retorted. 'Did you really order a *treadmill*?'

Maddie nodded, although she was now wondering if she hadn't made a giant mistake. After all, there was literally nothing stopping her from going outside for a run.

'Awesome!' Trenton exclaimed. He turned and shouted, 'Hey, Nikki! You'll never guess what Mom just bought us!'

'Bought her*self*…*my*self,' Maddie corrected. 'I bought it for *me*.'

'What, and you're not going to let us use it?' Trenton countered.

'We'll talk about it later,' she replied quietly as the delivery driver placed the two boxed laptops down a few feet from the door, then hastily took a giant step backward.

Maddie moved forward warily and picked them up, handing them directly to Trenton. 'Can you set these up? Both of them?'

Trenton rolled his eyes. 'Like, yeah. Obviously. Blindfolded,' he said, hurrying off with the devices toward the kitchen. He stopped short, turned back and kissed Maddie on the cheek. Then, with a voice that she rarely heard but recognized as belonging to his younger, more polite self, he said, 'Thanks so much, Mom.'

'You're welcome,' she replied, slightly taken aback.

The delivery driver wheeled a monstrously large box up the drive on a handcart. 'Can I leave this here?' he asked, stopping three feet from the front door.

'Would you mind terribly bringing it inside?' she responded.

'I'm really not supposed to…but okay,' he acquiesced.

Maddie moved back and watched as he manhandled the box to inside the hallway. 'Thank you so much.'

'Oh…Trenton wasn't joking, then?' Nikki asked, appearing from the living room and gazing at the huge box. 'Where's it going, exactly?'

Maddie took a breath before answering. 'Your dad's study.'

'Oh…okay. I thought that was being kept…like…in case?'

'I'm just going to move everything downstairs to the basement for the time being,' Maddie explained.

'And we get a home gym? Cool,' she said, but Maddie couldn't tell if she was being genuine or judgmental.

'It's just a treadmill, Nikki,' Maddie felt obliged to say.

'Uh-huh,' Nikki said, returning to the living room. 'Thanks for the laptop, Mom,' she called back.

'You're welcome,' she answered as she stared at the huge box now dominating the entrance hall and not feeling remotely like setting the damned thing up.

Maddie entered the kitchen and smiled at one of those sights that she rarely saw: Nikki leaning over Trenton with her hand on his shoulder as he set up one of the new computers for her. Despite their regular protestations to the contrary, they did love each other and that made Maddie happy. All the other stuff really didn't matter, she thought as she made herself some coffee. 'Do you guys need anything before I head down to the basement to work?'

'Better internet,' Trenton said, without looking up.

Nikki shrugged and looked at Maddie. 'He's right; there's just not enough bandwidth for the three of us sometimes.'

Maddie drew in a long breath. 'Right. I *will* look into this later on. Can you cope for the next few days?'

Another shrug from Nikki. 'I guess it really depends on if we're all streaming video-calls at the same time.'

Trenton glanced up at her. 'Maybe you could keep your video turned off for your work meetings?'

'Oh sure. That'll make the briefings interesting,' Maddie commented. 'How about…maybe *you* could not play video games until we get it fixed…'

'Don't even joke about that,' Trenton replied.

Maddie picked up her coffee and headed down to the basement. The three spacious rooms down there had been used for a variety of purposes over the years, their most recent incarnation being as a hang-out area for the kids to watch movies or have parties and sleepovers with their friends. Maddie had cleared the smallest of the rooms, intending that to become Michael's new study. The largest room, which had walk-out patio doors to the yard, was her temporary home office. She had already moved a desk, a bookcase and two large whiteboards from the Venator office down there.

She sat at her desk and logged in on the laptop. While she waited for it to boot up, she sipped some coffee and considered what best to do first. It was going to be a busy day. Later this morning, she had an interview scheduled with Scott Fisher, the host of *Extreme Genes*, one of the top genealogy radio shows and podcasts in the world. She had been asked to record a segment for a special episode dedicated to the capture of the Chester Creek murderer. She also needed to sort out the lack of internet, but she had just under a half hour until the first scheduled team briefing and she had things that she needed to do to set up for that.

The day so far had run away with itself, and Maddie had achieved very little by the time she logged in on Zoom. Hudson was already in the waiting room. She worried about him and questioned whether she might have been too hard on him yesterday. No, she reasoned, she had not. He needed to make a decision and she hoped that it would be the right one. She simply could not have a member of her staff going rogue like that; it was exactly the kind of misapplication of the tool that detractors and criminal defense lawyers seized upon to attack the fledgling industry. He was an excellent genetic genealogist and understood the science behind their work better than any of them. If he did decide to leave Venator, then she sincerely hoped that his termination date would be after the Twin Falls case had been concluded.

Maddie was wondering whether to admit Hudson into the meeting already and ask if he'd decided what he was going to do, but then Kenyatta dropped into the waiting room too, followed immediately by Becky.

'Hi guys,' she said, starting the meeting with a smile. 'And how are you all enjoying prison life?'

Kenyatta's mouth was moving, her face very animated, but no sound was coming forth.

'Kenyatta, you're on mute,' Maddie grinned.

Kenyatta squinted at the screen, then quickly unmuted herself. 'Gets me every time,' she laughed.

'I think you were in the process of telling us how you were? Or at least that's what it looked like from here,' Maddie said.

Kenyatta opened her hands as though she were squeezing an invisible box. 'I'm emotionally all over the place... Sort of conflicted,' she began with a wan smile. 'Our dear little retriever, Dougie, died yesterday, and it was quite horrible. Apparently, he was *stoned* to death.'

'Oh, God. What on earth...? I'm so sorry,' Maddie said. 'That's awful. Did they find the person who did it?'

Kenyatta shook her head. 'Not that I know of. But you know I'm not exactly on Otis's speed-dial these days.'

'Sorry to hear that. It's bad enough that we get to see the worst of human depravity at work, let alone have it spilling into our personal lives,' Becky commented.

'Uh-huh,' Kenyatta agreed. 'It's so sad. I loved that little dog... But, the reason I'm feeling so conflicted... I—we—have a new match to the *Boys under the Bridge* on GEDmatch with a whopping forty centimorgans of DNA!'

'Wow,' Maddie said, as she admitted Ross into the meeting. 'For *that* particular case, that's high.'

'It sure is. I'm just waiting on a reply from the test-taker.'

'That's so awesome. I'm so pleased that you've had a little good news after what happened to your poor dog. I can't get over that,' Becky said.

'If there's anything we can do, Kenyatta,' Maddie said.

'Thank you. I'll be sure to say if I need you,' Kenyatta assured her.

'And what about you, Hudson?' Maddie asked, noticing that he was sitting back in his chair and not really engaging. 'How are you?'

Hudson shot forward with a smile and answered cheerily, 'Yeah, great thanks. Can't wait to get into this case.'

Maddie didn't buy his cheeriness, but she used his comment to segue into getting the briefing started. 'Okay, so let's get going with the Twin Falls serial killer case. I must confess that I've done literally nothing, so I'm hoping you guys have something to bring to the table. Anyone desperate to start the ball rolling?'

'I'm happy to start,' Hudson said, again a little too keenly.

'Over to you, then,' Maddie said.

Hudson cleared his throat. 'Okay, starting with phenotyping,' he said, glancing down at a notepad in front of him. 'The evidence points toward the killer having very pale skin, brown hair and blue eyes.'

'Great start,' Maddie chipped in, noting the details on the whiteboard behind her. She used a blue marker pen, meaning that the results were only indicative, not conclusive.

'Haplogroup is R1a,' Hudson continued, 'which was identified in the remains of 'Mal'ta boy' who belonged to a tribe of mammoth hunters that roamed Siberia twenty-four thousand years ago.'

Maddie grinned. 'That's *real* helpful, Hudson. I'll keep an eye out in the matches for a Siberian mammoth-hunter,' she joked as she wrote the haplogroup on the board in red marker, denoting that it was a confirmed fact.

'But what is really interesting about this haplogroup is its distribution. Take a look,' Hudson said, sharing his screen with the team.

Maddie leaned in closer, taking in the heat map of the world, with bright colors concentrated heavily over Russia, Eastern Europe and Asia.

'Not commonly found in the U.S.,' Becky observed.

'Yeah, that's right,' Hudson confirmed.

'That ties with what I found out about his geo-ancestry,' Becky concurred.

'Interesting,' Maddie said, noting down the very broad locations on the white board. 'So, we could be looking at fairly recent immigration into America from one of those locations… Good work. Anything else?'

'Y-Line,' Hudson began. 'Unfortunately, no matches at Y-111. At sixty-seven, we pick up fifteen men with nine different surnames that I'll put on the screen now.'

Hudson brought up a document containing the nine surnames which appeared in the killer's male line, one of which *might* be his. Glancing between the screen and the whiteboard, Maddie scribed the names. *Rowson. Johnson. Waldman. Raič. Staley. Taylor. Scotton. Valentine. Macey.*

'Raič?' Kenyatta asked. 'Is that name originally from one of those haplogroup locations?'

'Yes,' Hudson confirmed. 'Bosnia and Herzegovina, Croatia, Serbia and Slovenia have the highest frequency.'

'And how closely related are these fifteen individuals to our killer?' Maddie probed.

Hudson screwed up his face. 'Not close. We'd have to go back about sixteen generations to hit an eighty-four-percent match with the closest person on the Y-line.'

'That's a shame,' Maddie said. 'But good work, Hudson. Any other discoveries from your side of things?'

'That's all from me. Over and out.'

'Thank you. Becky, do you want to feed back next?'

'Sure,' she said, sliding her thick-rimmed glasses up onto the bridge of her nose and straightening herself in her chair. 'So, starting with the geo-ancestry from FTDNA,' she said, pulling up a screenshot showing the percentage breakdown of the killer's geographic heritage. 'As you can see, just under fifty-percent of the killer's geo-ancestry is currently attributed to Eastern Europe and, if we drill down into that aspect of his DNA, we get this.' The screen changed to an image showing a colorful pie chart centered between a reference key and a text breakdown of the killer's European heritage.

'*Volga Ural?*' Kenyatta read. 'Where the heck's that?'

'Yeah, I had to Google it,' Becky said. 'It's in Russia now, but historically in Eastern Europe.'

'Okay,' Maddie said. 'So, what we've got so far strongly indicates that we're looking at a white male with immigration history from Eastern Europe.'

'But look at the next result,' Becky said, drawing a circle with her mouse. 'He's almost a quarter Italian.'

Maddie wrote the detail onto the whiteboard. The information could become very useful when the team began to construct the killer's family tree.

'Moving on,' Becky said, 'we're definitely looking at anger-motivated killings where he's taking some kind of revenge out on a targeted stranger. He probably knew the victims, but they likely did not know him. They're probably women that he's chosen specifically because they represent a person or people that he despises. He'll spend time making sure they fit his profile so that he can feel justified in his actions. Despite how utterly barbaric this guy is, he'd probably have trouble just killing some random nobody and would even possibly think that certain types of murder are wrong.'

'Wow,' Kenyatta muttered. 'That's messed up.'

'So, now looking at the circle hypothesis,' she said, pulling up a map of Twin Falls. A semi-transparent purple circle was laid over the city center, with two red pins forming its diameter. Becky ran her mouse around the left-most pin and explained, 'This is Wendell Street where Molly Hutchison, the fourth victim, was abducted. And this'— she indicated the right-most pin—'is Harmon Park Avenue from where the second victim, Carla Eagleton, was taken. There's a high chance that the killer lives somewhere in or close to this circle.'

'Could you possibly zoom in a little,' Hudson asked.

'Sure,' Becky answered, pushing into the map.

Hudson winced. 'That's most of Twin Falls.'

'Yes, it is,' she agreed.

'But it gives us something to work with,' Maddie replied. 'Anything else?'

'That's it from me.'

'Thank you,' Maddie said. 'Kenyatta, before you assign the genetic network clusters to everyone, I'm going to take a look at what's come up on GEDmatch.'

Maddie took control of the screen and entered the Twin Falls serial killer's kit detail into the GEDmatch website. Unlike the limited dashboard yesterday, all options were now available. Maddie selected the *One-To-Many* tool and a list of 12,269 names appeared, all people who were genetically connected to the killer.

'Ninety-one centimorgans for the first match is good,' Becky observed.

'Uh-huh,' Maddie agreed. 'But look after that—the second match is only forty-two.' She scrolled a short way down and was quickly into matches below ten centimorgans. 'Kenyatta, can you work out where this first strong match fits in among the clusters, or create a new one, if necessary, please?'

'With pleasure,' she replied.

'Great. Before you do that, do you want to assign us our clusters?'

'Okay,' Kenyatta began. 'I've only identified seven workable genetic networks; there are possibly more now we have GEDmatch to consider. Becky, since you were the first to break a cluster on the last case, you've been given genetic networks one and two. Hudson, you've....'

Maddie was distracted from the meeting by Trenton stepping into the basement and flapping his arms.

'Mom, he's on YouTube right now!' Trenton exclaimed.

Maddie quickly hit mute and turned to face him, wondering to whom he could be referring. Her heart jumped as her thoughts ran down a line of thinking that maybe he was talking about Michael. But why would he be on YouTube?

'Your guy, Wayne Wolsey. He's in court live on YouTube, right now.'

'I thought that wasn't until this afternoon?'

Trenton shrugged. 'It's now.'

'Thanks,' she said, unmuting herself and interrupting Kenyatta. 'So sorry, guys. Trenton has just informed me that Wayne Wolsey's live on YouTube. Let me try and get it up and we can watch it together.'

As Maddie brought up the website, she heard the rest of the team murmuring with anticipation. This was a big deal. Together, the Venator team had identified Wayne Wolsey as the suspected Chester Creek serial killer. This was his first court appearance.

Everyone fell silent as Maddie shared her screen.

The view of the courtroom was over the judge's right shoulder. The left of the frame was filled with viewers; press and family, Maddie supposed. And in the center, standing inside a cage—which looked like something straight out of *Silence of the Lambs*—was Wayne Wolsey himself.

This was the first time that Maddie had seen him in any other form than the couple of photos that had been used widely across the media in the past couple of weeks since his arrest. He was standing aloof, his chest puffed and his chin in the air, wearing a bright-orange jumpsuit. His lank, gray hair was pulled back over a balding scalp, giving him a cadaverous appearance.

The judge was part-way through reading the allegations against Wolsey. '…Count two, alleges that on or about January 1, 1983, in the county of Delaware, you did intentionally cause the death of another human being by the willful, deliberate and premeditated killing of Terri Locke, in violation of 18 Pa.C.S.A. § 2502(a). Count three, alleges that on or about October 28, 1983, in the county of Delaware, you did intentionally cause the death of another human being by the willful, deliberate and premeditated killing of Sadie Mayer, in violation of 18 Pa.C.S.A. § 2502(a)…'

The judge paused to allow a cacophony of camera shutters to fall silent, then continued his oration, looking directly at Wolsey. Maddie wondered what would happen next. Her team had been asked to solve the murder of three women, but, in the course of their investigation, had found one other possible victim, plus discovered that Wolsey's own wife, Fiona, had mysteriously disappeared. When detectives had searched Wayne's trailer, they had found souvenirs—or maybe trophies—in the form of locks of hair from eleven different women.

'Yes!' Kenyatta cheered and clapped the air at the news that Wolsey was also being charged with the murders of Tandy Howard and Fiona Gregory.

Wolsey appeared indifferent to the charges, staring only at the bars above him.

The judge asked, 'Do you have a lawyer, Mr. Wolsey? Can you afford one? Or are you asking the court to appoint you a lawyer?'

Wayne Wolsey looked right at the judge, but to Maddie, it appeared as though he were staring through the camera lens directly at her. She shuddered as he grinned, and she needed to avert her eyes an instant. 'I have a lawyer.'

'Is that the public defender?' the judge asked.

Wolsey nodded, still grinning.

'Let me appoint the public defender,' he replied, switching his attention to the smartly dressed woman standing close to the cage. 'Miss Hargreaves, do you accept representation on behalf of your office?'

'Thank you. Yes, Judge. I accept the appointment to represent Mr. Wolsey. I acknowledge receipt of the complaint. Judge, I would also like to reserve the right to make any later objections to any potential penalty or punishment with reference to this complaint. Mr. Jackson, the attorney for the Commonwealth, and I have agreed on a preliminary hearing date of April 28 at 8:30 in this department.'

As the judge confirmed the date and delivered his closing comments, Maddie's gaze roamed over the assembled crowd. The members of the press were indifferent, the public—presumably a mixture of the murdered girls' friends and family—were jubilant and emotional. Then she spotted Detective Clayton Tyler sitting on the second row, wearing a suit. She felt an unexpected surge of pleasure at seeing him again. During their brief interactions on the Chester Creek case, they had gotten along well. Becky was adamant that he liked her, and Maddie had eventually admitted to herself that, had things in her life been different and he not lived more than two thousand miles away, maybe she'd have gotten to know him somewhat better. As she looked at him, she was surprised—and a little saddened, if she were honest—that he hadn't called or emailed to let her know that Wolsey was appearing in court today.

Maddie's attention was jarred by the continuous clicking of camera shutters. She looked across the screen to see Wayne Wolsey being led out from the back of the cage. The judge stood, exited off-camera and the live feed went dead.

Maddie took a quick breath. 'That was short but sweet.'

'I'm so glad he was charged with those other two murders,' Becky said. 'But that's still not *all* of them.'

'Whatever happens,' Maddie said, 'Wayne Wolsey is *never* getting out of jail.'

'Unless it's to the mortuary after a lethal injection,' Hudson replied.

Maddie felt inclined to agree with the sentiment. 'So, back to work on nailing another monster. Sorry, Kenyatta. I think I interrupted you assigning the clusters. What did I miss?'

Kenyatta repeated what she'd told the rest of the team while Maddie had been distracted by Trenton.

'Great. So, are there any questions, or are you all good to make a start on the case?' Maddie asked, taking down that she was responsible for trying to identify clusters seven and eight.

'I'm good to go,' Kenyatta answered.

'Can't wait to get started on it,' Becky confirmed.

'I'm ready,' Hudson added.

'Okay, let's have an end-of-day briefing tomorrow afternoon,' Maddie suggested. She thanked the team and then ended the meeting.

Maddie exhaled loudly. It had been quite an intense morning already. She needed more coffee, so she headed back up to the kitchen, taking a look at her cell phone as she went, and finding that she *had* received a message from Clayton Tyler prior to the court broadcast; only, she had somehow missed it.

Hey Maddie. How are things with you? Holding up against the challenges of the pandemic? Any news yet from the team looking into Michael's disappearance? Just to let you know, Wayne Wolsey will be in court in about an hour. Here's the YouTube link if you want to watch. Take care, Clayton

Maddie found herself smiling as she entered the kitchen, grateful for his getting in touch. She poured some coffee and then replied.

Hi Clayton. Really good to hear from you. Yeah, we're coping with life, I think. Thank you for asking. The team has just started on a new case, working remotely of course. I somehow missed your message but caught Wolsey being charged with the murders. It was great to see the result of our joint hard work. I haven't heard back from the detective looking into what happened to Michael. I'll chase him down later. How are things with you?

She hit the white arrow and the message was sent. Then, she picked up her coffee and returned to the basement. Her first job had got to be adding more bandwidth, she reasoned. A task which ended up taking her over an hour to sort out. She settled for a far faster package—also more expensive—which, she was reliably assured, would suffice with all that was taking place in her house right now.

She was just checking on the kids and her mother when her cell phone rang.

'Hello?' she said, not recognizing the number.

'Hey, Maddie. It's Scott Fisher here from *Extreme Genes.*'

'Oh, hi there,' she replied, looking at her watch and wondering where on earth her day was disappearing. She'd not yet even opened her clusters to begin work.

'It's great to talk to you. I'm a big fan of Venator's work. You've done an amazing job getting those bad guys off the streets, let me tell you.'

'Thank you,' she said, heading down to the basement. 'I'm a fan of yours, too. I listen to the podcast when I go running.'

'Well, that's great to hear. So, how are you and your team dealing with working through the pandemic? I hope it hasn't stopped you cracking these cold cases?'

'No, not at all. Actually, we're working on a live case right now... Although I probably shouldn't be telling you that... I'll come back on the show once he's caught.'

Scott Fisher laughed. 'I'll hold you to that and good luck with it. So, we're looking to record about a thirteen-minute segment that I can edit down into the final show about the Chester Creek murderer. Obviously, there'll be some things you can't talk about, and I'll probably do another dedicated episode once the trial is over and everybody's free to talk about it. Are you ready for me to hit the record button?'

Maddie wasn't really, but she cleared her throat anyway. 'Ready as I'll ever be.'

'Great,' Scott replied. There was a moment of silence, then he said, 'Welcome to America's family history show, *Extreme Genes* and ExtremeGenes.com. It's Fisher here, your radio roots sleuth on the program where we shake your family tree and watch the nuts fall out. Today we have a very special episode dedicated to the Chester Creek murders which you are all probably very familiar with. After almost forty years languishing as a cold case, it's finally been solved using this cutting-edge investigative genetic genealogy technique that's being used up and down the country to put these bad guys behind bars. I'm going to be talking to the boss of Venator, the company based in Salt Lake City that identified Wayne Wolsey as the prime suspect in these horrific murders. Madison Scott-Barnhart, it's great to have you on the show. Can I call you Maddie?'

'Thank you for having me. And yes, please do call me Maddie.'

'Why don't you start by telling us a bit about your company, Venator. Where does the name come from, exactly?' Scott asked.

'So, *venator* means hunter in Latin, which I thought was an apt title when I set up the business back in 2018.'

'Ah, I see—interesting. Very good. And how does it feel to have hunted down the Chester Creek murderer? It must have felt good, seeing Wayne Wolsey standing behind bars in his first court appearance?'

'You know what? I felt a lot of things, seeing him in that cage. But the overriding emotion was one of pure relief. I'm just so glad that this monster is no longer living his everyday life without a care in the world, while the family and friends of his victims have had to suffer almost forty years of daily torture.'

'Absolutely,' he agreed. 'You and your company are to be congratulated for providing that closure. Good job.'

'Thank you,' she said.

'Could you tell us about the early stages of the investigation and how you initially approached the task?'

'Sure,' Maddie answered. Then, at some length, she explained how her team undertook their work. Scott led the interview through the various steps of investigative genetic genealogy to the moment of Wayne Wolsey's discovery as the Chester Creek murderer and subsequent arrest.

A half hour later, the interview was over. She considered that it had gone well and had enjoyed the process, which wasn't often the case with such media interviews. Usually, they were exercises in educating the public about investigative genetic genealogy and correcting misunderstandings about the procedures and practices. This time it was good just to talk about the company's most recent success.

But now, Maddie needed to focus on the team's current live case. She clicked to open the file labeled *Cluster Seven* in the TWIN FALLS KILLER folder on the Venator shared drive. A simple spreadsheet opened in front of her, giving her the seven individuals who had uploaded their DNA to either the FamilyTreeDNA or GEDmatch websites and who were related to each other…and to the killer.

The first thing that Maddie did was to check the surnames of those seven people against the Y-DNA matches that Hudson had found, but there was no overlap. There were also no names within the cluster that were obviously Eastern European or Italian.

As was usual practice, Kenyatta had ascribed the lead name of the cluster to the person with the highest amount of shared DNA in the hope that they might be the easiest to research, although it very often didn't work out that way. In this case, Joey Seymour had been designated as the cluster lead with eighty-four centimorgans of shared DNA, an amount that FamilyTreeDNA estimated to put him and the killer somewhere in the second-to-fourth-cousin range. That seemed pretty close but actually could be much more remote in reality.

She signed in at FTDNA using the killer's kit log-in details, finding Joey Seymour on the first page of the cousin matches. She was heartened to see the family tree icon beside his name; although once she clicked to see how detailed it was, she found that it just contained Joey's name—with no accompanying useful biographical data—and some basic information about his deceased mother.

Gina Westlake born 1953, London, England, UK - died 2018, Edmonton, AB, Canada

'Well, it's a start,' Maddie said, exhaling as she logged in at Ancestry and created a new speculative family tree with Joey Seymour as the home person. She added his mother's details to the tree and then clicked *Search on Ancestry.* A variety of suggested records populated the screen. Some would be relevant and correct, others not. Maddie scrolled down until she found the first record pertaining to Gina

Westlake's death. Where possible, she liked to start at the end of a person's life since these records were often bountiful in their genealogical information. An obituary from the *Red Deer Advocate* on Newspapers.com, dated October 20, 2018, was suggested as potentially relating to Gina. The date and location appeared possible, so she clicked to read it.

Seymour, Gina of Edmonton, Alberta went to be with her Lord Oct. 11, 2018, surrounded by her loving family at the age of 65 years. Gina was born on February 19, 1953, in London, England. She emigrated to Alberta, Canada in 1974, where she met her future husband, Marcel. She had a great devotion and compassion for her family and friends, which was shown by her strong love and support. Gina is survived by her loving husband, Marcel of Edmonton, two children, Adam Seymour also of Edmonton and Joey Seymour of Williamstown, Ontario; also her parents, Lawrence and Evelyn Westlake of London, England...

'Perfect,' Maddie muttered to herself as she copied the names of Gina's family across to the speculative tree that she was beginning to build. She was delighted with this initial trove of information as it would have been provided by the family itself and, therefore, was much more likely to be accurate. She still needed to verify the information using documented sources, but this was a great start. Maddie now had the names of both of Joey's parents and one set of his grandparents.

Given the information that she already had, Maddie decided to pursue Joey's maternal grandparents, Lawrence and Evelyn Westlake. On Ancestry, she clicked to go to the *England & Wales, Civil Registration Marriage Index, 1916-2005* and ran a search. She entered Lawrence Westlake's name into the search boxes and Evelyn—with no surname—as his spouse. There were two hundred and twenty-one results, although only the first five showed the correct spelling for the groom and only one—the top result—had a bride with the correct first name.

Name: Lawrence G. Westlake
Registration Date: 1950
Registration Quarter: Jan-Feb-Mar

Registration District: Islington
Inferred County: London
Spouse: Evelyn Simons

It appeared to be the right one. But, before Maddie added the information to the speculative family tree, she ran a search for Gina's birth in the *England & Wales, Civil Registration Birth Index, 1916-2007*. Just one result confirmed the information contained in the obituary, that Gina Westlake had been born in the March quarter of 1953 in the district of Islington to a woman with the maiden name of Simons.

Maddie added the information to Joey Seymour's family tree and then ran a search in the *1939 Register* for England and Wales. As she expected, neither produced a result due to the fact that they were still alive and thus covered by data protection.

Maddie thought for a moment. They were both still alive in October 2018, but that didn't necessarily mean that they were still alive now. She wasn't an expert in records for the U.K. and so, needed to spend some time locating information as to how up-to-date death indexes were. Picking up her cell phone, Maddie typed out a message to the rest of the team.

Ideas for finding a death in England in the past few months??

While she waited, Maddie accessed the Ancestry hints that had been generated for the couple, clicking on what was usually her last resort: *Ancestry member trees*. Sometimes they could be the key to unlocking a whole family mystery or were a helpful short-cut, but so very often the trees uploaded and repeatedly shared by the public were wildly inaccurate. One person did have Lawrence Westlake in their tree, but Maddie could immediately see that it pertained to the wrong person and Evelyn didn't show up in any searches either, which pointed very strongly to the fact that they were still alive and would only show up in public trees as *Private*.

Maddie returned to the English birth index, entering Lawrence's name with a possible birthdate window of 1914-1934. There were thirty-seven results. Just as Maddie began to scrutinize the list, her cell phone beeped the announcement of a new text message from Kenyatta.

Try these:
funeral-notices.co.uk
gov.uk/search-will-probate
deceasedonline.com

Maddie thanked her and then clicked the first link. It sent her to a website that she had not heard of before; a database of over 4 million notices of death that had appeared in U.K. newspapers. She typed in Lawrence's name but had no hits. Then she tried Evelyn's and also had no luck. She went back into the text message and hit the second link which took her to a page on the U.K. government website, where searches for wills in England and Wales could be made. She entered Lawrence's name and then Evelyn's but again was faced with the same conclusion: *No results.*

Just as Maddie was about to click the link to *deceasedonline*, Hudson added to the message thread.

I presume you've checked the government's own General Register Office website? Deaths run to the end of 2019: gro.gov.uk

Maddie thanked Hudson, admitting that she hadn't checked the official government website but was now about to do so. She typed in Lawrence Westlake's name and received one index result.

Name: Westlake, Lawrence Gilbert
Death: Q1/2019, Kent
Year of Birth: 1928

The entry was too brief to know if it related to the correct man and to get more detailed information would require purchasing a physical copy of the death certificate, which would take time that Maddie just didn't have. Keeping that web page open, Maddie visited the final link suggested by Kenyatta, taking her to deceasedonline. One match for Lawrence.

Name: Westlake, Lawrence Gilbert
Cremated on: 2 February 2019
Recorded at: Kent & Sussex Crematorium (Kent)
Date of death: 19 January 2019

This entry undoubtedly related to the person that she'd just found on the government GRO website, but there was still nothing that confirmed that this man was definitely Joey Seymour's grandfather. Maddie decided to pay the £2 fee for an immediate download of the cremation register, which appeared as a typed transcript on her screen.

Authority: Kent & Sussex Crematorium
Cremation date: 2 February 2019
Last name: Westlake
First names: Lawrence Gilbert
Date of death: 19 January 2019
Age: 91
Marital status: married
Denomination: Methodist
Occupation: retired teacher
Residence: 16, Bramley Road, East Peckham

Maddie smiled, feeling sure that the entry held sufficient clues to prove or disprove that this man was indeed Joey Seymour's grandfather. Returning to her previous searches for Lawrence's birth in the indexes, she found that the top entry confirmed that she had found the correct person.

Name: Lawrence G Westlake
Registration Date: 1928
Registration Quarter: Jan-Feb-Mar
Registration District: Islington
Inferred County: Greater London

There were no other Lawrence Westlake's born within a ten-year window of 1928. His age and middle initial were also correct. It was sufficient proof for Maddie to add the details to the growing speculative tree that she was building for the family. Lawrence's birth index reference had also provided a clue to her next search: his mother's maiden name, Murton.

Two hours later, Maddie began to feel hungry. She yawned and stretched as she stared at Joey Seymour's family tree, pleased with her work. She was viewing it as a pedigree, showing each of Joey's direct ancestors whom she had so far identified. She had managed to work the Westlake, Murton and Simons sides of his tree back to the great-great-great-grandparent level.

It was time for lunch, but first she wanted to call the detective who had been working on Michael's disappearance. She dialed the Emery County Sheriff's Department, a number that she knew from memory. In the first weeks after Michael had failed to come home, she had called the office daily, demanding answers that they had been unable to give.

When the call was picked up, she asked to be put through to the detective working Michael's case.

'Detective Scullion,' his familiar voice answered after a short wait.

'It's Maddie,' she said, knowing that he would recognize which Maddie immediately.

'Oh, hi, Maddie,' he said brightly. 'How are things with you?'

'Fine,' she replied crisply, having grown to hate his disingenuousness. 'Did you get my email with the new information from the CSI sweep of Michael's truck?'

'Yeah, yeah,' he said, the telephone sounding as though it were being shoved onto his shoulder while he brought up case notes that he probably otherwise had no intention of accessing anytime soon.

'So, now you have the name of the guy—Emmanuel Gribbin—who must have done something to Michael,' Maddie said.

'Yeah,' Detective Scullion said, tapping keys in the background. 'I looked him up and found a DUI in Washington DC in 2014. It looks like the guy died in 2018 and that's about all I got.'

'Great work,' she couldn't help but say. '*I* told you all that information.'

'Yeah, but the guy's dead… What do you want me to do? Dig him up?'

'And that's your only possible line of investigation?' Maddie asked incredulously.

'Listen, Maddie. It's just not enough to go on, okay? I've got like six homicide cases piled up on my desk, not to mention a whole bunch of cold cases—with bodies and *actual* evidence, you know—that need my attention. If something else more concrete comes to light, I'll be sure to look into it, okay?'

'What about the phone call he received from The Larkin Investment and Finance Group? And the gag order that Andrew Larkin placed on his employees?'

Detective Scullion laughed. 'I can't go after Larkin Investments, as well you know.'

'But why would he silence his employees like that, if he had nothing to hide?' she asked with increasing desperation.

'It could be for a hundred reasons. And *not* the one you're thinking. No big business wants the cops snooping around and interviewing their employees.'

A sudden wave of emotion hit Maddie as she realized that, once again, nothing at all was going to be done to find out what had happened to her husband. A lump caught in her throat, and she couldn't speak anymore. Without saying another word, she ended the call and burst into tears.

She waited until the upset and frustration had abated, then she went upstairs to fix some lunch. She groaned at the site of the huge, boxed treadmill still blocking the hallway.

She found her mother reading in the living room and Nikki working on her new laptop with her headphones on.

'Everyone okay in here?' Maddie asked.

'Uh-huh,' Nikki answered.

Her mother lowered her book and said, 'I think I'll make dinner tonight.'

'You don't need to do that, Mom,' Maddie said, a little too hastily.

Her mom rolled her eyes. 'What? You think maybe I'll forget to take the food out of the carton and put it in the oven and burn the whole house down? Or I'll forget how to cut vegetables and chop my hands off?'

Maddie couldn't help but smile. 'No, Mom. It isn't that. I just don't want you to be stressed by unnecessary tasks, that's all.'

'It isn't unnecessary,' her mom responded. '*Someone* has to do it and it might as well be me, since you three are all so absorbed in your work. Do I look stressed? Frankly, I'm bored of all this sitting around.'

Maddie looked at her mother, not knowing how to respond. The day would come soon enough when she would be entirely unable to cook a dinner. Today wasn't that day. 'Okay, you can make dinner, but the second it becomes a problem, you ask one of us to help out.'

'Thank you,' her mother said sincerely.

Maddie took a grilled cheese sandwich back down to the basement, picking up with her research into another set of Joey Seymour's maternal great-great-grandparents.

'Mom!' came Trenton's shout.

Maddie stood up and hurried to the bottom of the stairs, fearing that something bad must have happened owing to the ferocity of his yell. 'What? What's wrong?'

'Nothing,' he answered. 'Dinner's ready and I've been calling you for like hours.'

'Sorry… I've been a little consumed with the case. I'm coming right now,' she said, calming herself before heading up into the kitchen to find her mother and Nikki seated at the table, waiting patiently with their dinner in front of them. Nikki pulled a strange face at Maddie, her eyes dancing to the plate of food in front of her.

'I made your favorite,' her mom said proudly.

Maddie sat at the table and scanned her plate. 'Oh good. Mashed potatoes, canned corn and hamburger gravy. Yummy.'

Her mom beamed. 'See, I told you I've still got it.'

'Your favorite?' Trenton asked, jabbing his fork into the mashed potatoes and pushing them around his plate.

'Uh-huh,' Maddie confirmed.

'Since when?' he demanded.

'Since she was a very young girl,' her mom answered.

Maddie nodded, then, when her mom was distracted, mouthed to Trenton, '*Shut up!*'

'Okay,' Trenton said, dragging out the word uncertainly, then eating some of the food and grimacing. 'I'm not *really* that hungry, Grandma.'

'Eat!' Maddie uttered quietly but sharply.

Trenton sighed and half-heartedly ate some potatoes. He faced Maddie as he struggled to eat his current mouthful. 'Have you heard anything back from Defective Scorpion yet?'

'*Detective Scullion,*' Maddie corrected. 'Yes, as a matter of fact, I have. I called him earlier. It's not great news, though, I'm afraid: he's not going to do anything about the new information.'

'What? You've got to be...' Trenton stammered.

'But why not?' Nikki asked.

Maddie shrugged. 'I pushed him—I really did—but he said that with Emmanuel Gribbin being dead already, and with nothing much in the system about him, there was really nothing more that he could do right now.'

Trenton dropped his cutlery down onto his plate and stormed from the kitchen.

'Are we ever going to find out what happened to Dad?' Nikki asked quietly.

'I don't know, honey. But you know...I will never stop trying.'

Chapter Nine

Tuesday, April 7, 2020, Twin Falls, Idaho

He was sitting in near darkness in his dirty living room with no idea of the time. He stared fixedly at his tablet screen, his tired eyes coming in and out of focus on her Facebook profile photo, anger and hatred pumping out of his heart. She was exactly like all the girls at school, who'd scorned him. Exactly like all those women his father had brought back to the house when he was a little kid. All of them mocking him.

He was exhausted, his eyes involuntarily closing. Only the whirr and chatter of the printer was keeping him awake. He had spent the entire night wading through hundreds of Twin Falls girls' Facebook profiles. Using their publicly viewable Friends list, he would jump from one girl to another until he found the right one who needed to be punished. Just a short time ago, he'd found her. She had posted hundreds of selfies, pouting absurdly at the camera with her icy blue eyes goading him from every image. She was the type who could—and did—date any guy that she wanted. He knew immediately he saw her that she needed punishing for all the men she'd scorned, deceived, snubbed and ridiculed from the moment she'd grown breasts.

The printer stopped and the house fell silent.

The man put his tablet down on the couch beside him, stood up and walked over to the printer, taking the stack of color photos from the tray.

He stared at the blank wall, pockmarked with the sticky-tape remnants of the previous girls' pictures. He wanted to put the new pictures up right now, but he needed sleep more.

Putting the photographs down on the couch, he picked up his tablet and took one last look at her profile picture. He still had a lot more research to do, but he went to bed bitterly rolling the name Debra Towers around his mouth.

By 8 a.m. the next morning, one entire wall of his living room was covered with photographs of the girl. Every picture he could find of her was up there. He had easily found her address on a background-check website and, from her regular postings and updates on social media, was getting a pretty good idea of her life routines.

He stood back and smirked.

He'd found the girl and now he needed to select her final place of repentance. He would administer the punishment on behalf of all men everywhere and then she would ultimately have to answer to God to justify her behavior.

The man strode purposefully from the room, pulled on his baseball cap, raised his facemask and headed out of the house to his Wrangler.

He drove around with no particular route or plan in his mind, pulling up outside various churches around the quiet city. Several he ruled out because of their neighboring buildings or security cameras, but one he found was perfect: the First Christian Church. It was just three blocks down from the First Baptist Church on Shoshone Street North.

He stared up at the grand old building with tall windows, columns out front and a wide staircase leading up from the sidewalk to its entrance.

He smiled at the idea of Debra Towers laid out on the steps in her final act of atonement.

Chapter Ten

Wednesday, April 8, 2020, Twin Falls, Idaho

Detective Maria González was waiting in line outside of Jim Bob and Son Bakery on Second Avenue. She was next, but the customer in front was taking a ridiculous amount of time; time that Maria just did not have, right now. She needed to get back to the office and move this case forward. She had worked numerous homicide investigations in the past and this one had some of the hallmarks of the kind that tended to fall quickly off the radar and into cold-case territory. Just before she had left the office, a report had come back on the two different types of foliage found between Molly Hutchison's toes. According to a professor from the Department of Plant Sciences at the University of Idaho, one of the specimens was from an Engelmann spruce and the other was from a Douglas fir. Any hopes that she had had that perhaps the two species would only overlap in a localized, specific area of Idaho were completely dashed; both tree species were widely distributed in this part of the country.

The customer stalling at the bakery window—a masked old lady to whom Maria gave an acknowledging nod of the head—finally moved off. Maria gazed through the open window, eyeing the shelves of different donuts.

'Ah, Detective,' the young male server greeted. 'Good to see you. How are you?'

'As well as can be expected,' she replied, her answer covering all bases in her life at the current moment in time.

'The usual?'

'Actually, we've got quite the growing team on the investigation now. So, I'll get two assorted dozen boxes, please. Oh, and a coffee.'

'The case with that serial killer?' he asked. 'Any luck with that?'

'We're working on it,' she replied, watching him box up the donuts. He placed them on the counter, then poured some coffee.

'That's thirty-three fifty-eight, please,' he said, holding out a credit card machine at arm's length.

Maria tapped her card and took the donuts and coffee.

'Good luck catching him,' the server called after her.

'Thanks,' she responded without turning back, then muttered, 'I think I'm going to need all the luck I can get with this one.'

The roads were so empty that Maria was able to cross three lanes, walking diagonally north over to the police department, without a single vehicle even coming into sight or earshot. Despite being in a hurry to get back, Maria slowed her pace and turned her face toward the sun. It was still cold out—fifty-five according to the weather on her drive in, this morning—but the snow had almost completely melted, and she hoped that it would stay that way. The drawbacks of having snow on the ground at a crime scene—mainly water damage—far outweighed any potential benefits of finding clues like tire tracks or footprints.

Maria stepped up onto the sidewalk beside the building, her eye passing over the large V-shaped sign that announced TWIN FALLS PUBLIC SAFETY to both directions of passing traffic, and entered the single-story administration part of the station. She headed down a hallway through to the open-plan Criminal Investigation Division office that she shared with the department's other eight detectives.

'I got donuts,' Maria called, eyeing the assembled group. 'Although…maybe not enough.' On an ordinary day, there would be five or six people in the office at any one time. Today, there were at least twenty-five working specifically on this case. Some were at computer terminals, some on phones and some gathered round talking together.

'Now, that's what I like to hear,' one of her colleagues responded, rising from his desk and heading over to pick out a donut. 'I got the blueberry!' he declared, taking a giant bite. 'Thanks, Maria.'

She nodded and sat at her desk, taking a sip of coffee.

'Detective González,' Janet Tibbs, one of the Community Service Officers, called over to her. 'The autopsies for Lorena Baly and Carla Eagleton are in. I've just emailed them over to you.'

'Thanks,' Maria replied, tapping and sliding the mouse to wake her computer. She opened the two attachments from Walter Rachmal, the Ada County Forensic Pathologist, drinking her coffee as she read through the documents. The only three new pieces of information in each file were the ballistics report, toxicology and the pathologist's conclusion. As suspected, the killer had shot the victims with .45-70 ammunition at medium-range, probably while they were fleeing through woods or forest. Since it was the belief that the killer was a hunter, considerable department resources had been aimed at talking to local hunting groups, conservation officers, park rangers, and gun and ammo shops within a wide area. So far, the only thing of value to come back was information about the post-mortem tooth extraction. According to several keen hunters, a requirement of a successful bear hunt on state land was a mandatory harvest report, whereby a premolar is removed from the presented skull to the Fish and Game Regional Office.

This affirmed the police department consensus that the killer was very likely a hunter. Consequently, details of every man issued a license to hunt in the state in the past two years were currently being collated.

Maria moved on to toxicology. Only two drugs were found in Lorena and Carla's bloodstream:

<1.5mg/l amobarbital and <1.5mg/l secobarbital in bloodstream

She took in a long breath. She was fairly certain what the combination of the two drugs would do to a person, but she picked up her desk phone and called Walter Rachmal's office just to be certain.

'Maria, hi,' he greeted once she had been put through. 'I sincerely hope you're not calling to tell me you've got another body…'

'No, no. And I hope it stays that way,' she answered. 'Just a quick question about the tox report. Could you describe for me the impact on the person of amobarbital and secobarbital, please?'

'Sure. The combination of these drugs taken together makes a central nervous system depressant. The effects they could potentially have on an individual at a mild dose could be confusion, dizziness, headache, slurred speech, and drowsiness. At a life-threatening dose, they could potentially lead to slowed respiration, cardiac arrest, unconsciousness, coma, or death. In these cases, the toxicology report estimates that the quantity found in the two victims' bloodstreams would have been enough to make them very weak, but *not* unconscious.'

'Easily overpowered and probably quite disoriented, in other words,' Maria muttered.

'Exactly.'

'Okay, thank you.' Maria ended the call. She called over to her colleague, Janet Tibbs, who was helping assimilate reports. 'Hey, Janet. Have the families been informed of the autopsies yet?'

Janet looked up from a computer terminal and shook her head. 'Not yet.'

'Okay, get on that, but I want the autopsies sealed. I do not want the public getting their hands on this information.'

Janet nodded.

Maria read the concluding statement from the Ada County Forensic Pathologist, which confirmed what she already knew: despite many horrific injuries, some of which had occurred post-mortem, the two women had died from ligature strangulation.

Maria sent the two documents to the printer, then carried the paper over to the large bulletin boards that were being used to display the key facts and findings of the current case. She pinned the autopsies to the board, stood back and slowly looked over everything that they knew so far...which amounted to very little. She stared at the four victims' photos, trying to work out what might link them to a bear hunter. The women's names had been cross-checked with all known hunting clubs and the Fish and Game Regional Office hunting license databases, but no link could be established, and family members confirmed that the women themselves had no known interest in hunting, nor had they had any friends who were hunters.

'Hoping for divine inspiration by any chance, Detective González?'

Maria turned to see Captain Pritchard observing her. 'Just reflecting.'

Captain Pritchard raised an eyebrow. 'Where are we at with this investigation?'

Maria brought him up to speed with the autopsy highlights, then she told him about the hunting leads that they were pursuing. She ended with the report from the Department of Plant Sciences at the University of Idaho.

'What about this genealogy thing? They got anything yet?'

'It's still early days with that line of inquiry,' she answered.

'Let's videocall them, see if they've got anything for us to go on yet,' he instructed.

'Uh...okay,' Maria said, heading back to her desk and opening Zoom on her computer. She clicked to invite Maddie and waited.

A few seconds later, Maddie appeared. 'Hi, there. Sorry, did we have a meeting scheduled?'

'No,' Maria answered. 'I'm here with Captain Pritchard, and we were wondering if you had anything to update the investigation with?'

'Uh, well, we don't usually provide updates along the way—'

'Listen,' Captain Pritchard interjected, 'I don't want to press too hard, here, but this isn't a cold case from forty years back. I've got a serial killer on the loose, right now in my city.'

'Anything you can give us would be a big help,' Maria added.

'Okay,' Maddie started. 'What we have currently is… We have *suggestive* clues from the DNA that point toward the suspect's being a white male; in fact, someone with very pale skin, brown hair and blue eyes.'

'Great—our first inkling of what he looks like,' Maria said, noting down the details.

'Although, that only narrows it down to about seventy-seven percent of the population of Twin Falls,' Captain Pritchard pointed out in a barbed voice. 'Anything else?'

'We believe that he comes from Italian and Eastern European heritage,' Maddie answered, rising irritation now evident in her voice.

'Will this guy be speaking like an Eastern European or an Italian?' he quizzed. 'English not his first language, that it?'

'I can't say for certain. He could be a first-, second- or third-generation immigrant; we simply don't know yet. But we should…'

Maria observed Captain Pritchard in the camera view on-screen, concerned that he was about to boil over, something she'd witnessed plenty of times in the past. He closed his eyes and rubbed a hand over his mouth, clearly exasperated. 'Anything else? Anything.'

'He probably lives in Twin Falls, somewhere between'—Maddie paused and glanced to one side, referring to something off-screen—'Wendell Street and Harmon Park Avenue.'

'The DNA gave you his address, huh? That's clever,' Captain Pritchard scoffed. 'Of course he lives in that area; those are two of the victims' home addresses you've just given me, right there. I wasn't exactly expecting him to live in New York City. What else?'

'With all due respect, sir,' Maddie said, 'Investigative genetic genealogy doesn't work in bite-sized chunks; we don't get definitive answers until the end. If we can be left to just get on with our jobs…'

'Okay,' he conceded, nodding.

Maria breathed out slowly, relieved to see that her boss was backing down.

'Tell us the moment you have anything to go on.'

'We will. Goodbye,' Maddie said, leaving the meeting.

Captain Pritchard stood up, grabbed a jelly donut, and marched out of the office.

Maria stood up and decided to call the room to silence. 'Just a little update from the investigative genetic genealogy team: the guy we're looking for is very likely to be white with brown hair and blue eyes. He also has Italian and Eastern European ancestry, but we don't yet know how far back that might be. Michelle and Reuben,' she said to the two analysts whom she had been given for this investigating team, 'can you go back over the hunting license database and cross-reference it with this new information? The rest of you, hold these new facts in mind as you continue your work. Thank you.'

The room returned to its previous busyness. Maria pinned the information from Maddie to one of the bulletin boards. Despite Captain Pritchard's mocking of the vagueness of the information, it would be very helpful when it came to narrowing the suspects list. Not that they had any suspects so far. As she stood in front of the bulletin board, she had a troubled feeling that it would remain that way before another woman would be abducted.

Chapter Eleven

Wednesday, April 8, 2020, South Jordan, Utah

Maddie headed up to the kitchen in urgent need of some coffee. She paused at the top of the stairs, finding the house was suspiciously peaceful. Nikki and Trenton were in their rooms, studying; or were supposed to be studying, at least. The issues over computers and internet service seemed to have been resolved for the moment.

Maddie entered the kitchen, finding her mom lacing up her shoes. 'Going out into the yard for some air?' she asked.

Her mom stood up and, with an air of indignation, said, 'No, Maddie. I'm going *outside* for a walk. I won't go near people and I'll even cross the road if someone comes toward me. *And* I'll double-mask.'

They both knew that the pandemic wasn't the biggest worry that Maddie had about her mom going out into the big wide world: it was more that she'd end up coming home in the back of a police car as she had done two weeks ago after trying to force her way into her previous home.

'Why don't I come with you?' Maddie said. 'Just give me two or three minutes to get myself organized.'

'No,' her mom rebutted. 'You're busy with work and I would like to go for a walk alone. Don't worry, I've got the address written down, right here…just in case'—she pulled a piece of paper from her pocket and waved it in front of Maddie—'*and* your phone number. I just want to go around the block, Maddie. That's all.'

Maddie was conflicted but she smiled and found herself conceding. 'Okay. You have a good time.'

'Thank you,' her mom said, heading out into the hallway. 'When is this monstrosity being moved out of the way? It's like an obstacle course.'

Maddie rolled her eyes. That damned treadmill. It definitely had been a stupid impulse purchase. 'Soon,' she promised.

The door slammed shut and Maddie felt an instant tightening knot of worry. She rushed to the curtains and peered through, spying on her mom walking down the drive. The contentedness on her face was enough to tell Maddie that she had made the right decision in allowing her mother to leave alone. Not that she was certain that she could have prevented her mother from going out, even if she'd wanted to.

While she was making the coffee, Maddie ran a Google search for GPS devices for dementia patients, promptly feeling bad that she was now actively considering discreetly planting something on her mother's person, knowing that she likely wouldn't readily give her consent to such an intrusive step. She scrolled past several advertisements for key fobs, wrist bands and watches until one website—*projectlifesaver.org*—caught her attention and she clicked on it to read more.

Project Lifesaver is the premier search and rescue program operated internationally by public safety agencies and is strategically designed for "at risk" individuals who are prone to the life-threatening behavior of wandering.

Maddie couldn't say that her mom was *prone* to wandering exactly, but she did like to walk, and she did get disoriented. And things were only going to get worse as time went on. She read more about the project and became increasingly convinced that it was a sensible route to take for her mom's safety and her own peace of mind. She would need to enroll her mom in the project by finding a member agency which, once Maddie had inputted her zip code, she found to be the North Salt Lake City Police Department, some 19.37 miles away. Her thumb hovered momentarily over the agency phone number, but she decided to do it later. Right now, it was time to get back to work.

Back down at her computer in the basement, Maddie brought up the speculative tree that she had been creating for Joey Seymour. The next task in Maddie's research was to identify the parents of one of Joey's great-great-grandmothers, May Vera Buxton, who had married a man named Leslie George Farthing in the village of Lyng in Norfolk, England in 1859. A copy of the original marriage certificate in the *Norfolk, England, Church of England Marriages and Banns, 1754-1940* record set on Ancestry had provided May's father's name: John Buxton.

Searching the 1851 England Census, Maddie found May Vera

Buxton living in the village of Lyng, Norfolk as a sixteen-year-old girl. The household was headed by her father, John, a journeyman blacksmith and below him was listed May Vera's mother, Elizabeth, and five children.

Maddie saved the document to Joey Seymour's speculative tree, then set about trying to identify Elizabeth Buxton's maiden name. She clicked the newly created profile for Elizabeth and viewed the hints that Ancestry suggested might relate to her. A marriage, taking place in Norwich, Norfolk two years prior to the birth of their first child was a strong possibility.

John Buxton of the Parish of Lyng, single man, blacksmith and Elizabeth Adams of this Parish, single woman were married in this church by Banns this sixteenth Day of September in the Year One thousand eight hundred and twenty-eight…

Their names and John's occupation were a match to Maddie's previous findings. Then she remembered something from the 1851 Census that she had just saved to the tree: John and Elizabeth's youngest son had been named William Adams Buxton, his middle name being an obvious reference to Elizabeth's maiden name. Maddie was contented enough that the record was correct to save it to the speculative tree. That was another ancestral couple identified.

She returned to May Vera Buxton's husband, Leslie George Farthing. In the same way that their marriage certificate had provided May Vera's father's name, so too did it provide Leslie George's father's name: *Matthew Farthing - A labourer.*

'Madison, I'm back,' her mother called down the stairs. 'I got brought home in the back of a trooper car.'

Maddie rolled her eyes and gave a wan smile. 'That's real funny, Mom.'

'I know. I thought so, too. Do you want anything to eat or drink, down there?'

'No. I'm good, thank you. Could you just go and check on the kids, please?'

'Sure,' her mom replied.

'Thank you,' Maddie called, clicking to view Leslie George Farthing on the 1851 England Census, where he was residing in the delightful-sounding place of Primrose Green. His father, Matthew, was stated to be an agricultural laborer and his mother, Mary, a dressmaker. In a new web browser tab, Maddie ran a quick Google search for Primrose Green, finding that it was a very short distance from the village of Lyng in Norfolk. Next, she ran a marriage search for Matthew Farthing with a spouse named Mary.

'This is just too easy,' she said to herself as the first result offered appeared to be correct. Matthew Farthing had married a Mary Loveday in Lyng in 1830, one year prior to the birth of their first child. Maddie smiled as she added the entry to the speculative tree. *Mary Loveday of Primrose Green*', she read aloud; it sounded to her so very quaint and so very English.

Another ancestral couple located and named.

With the Farthing and Buxton sides successfully tracked down, Maddie switched to researching the Simons side of Joey Seymour's maternal family. She had just pulled up the profile page for Noah Simons, when she heard someone walking slowly down to the basement. At that pace, it could only be her mom. Maddie looked over at the doorway, waiting patiently. Sure enough, her mom did eventually appear, carrying a plate.

'I know you said you didn't want anything, but it's lunch time and you can't just spend the day down here in this dungeon without any sustenance,' she said, placing the plate down in front of Maddie's keyboard.

'Thanks, Mom,' Maddie said, glancing down at what looked like a cheese and tomato sandwich. 'Are the kids okay? They're being remarkably quiet.'

Her mom nodded reassuringly. 'They're fine. Let sleeping dogs lie. Isn't that the saying? Quiet is good.'

'Hmm, not always,' Maddie countered and took a bite of the sandwich. 'Lovely. Thank you for this.'

'You're welcome,' her mom said, shuffling slowly back up the stairs.

The sandwich was good. Her mom seemed happy. The kids were quietly working. Her cluster research was moving forward nicely.

Maybe lockdown wouldn't be as painful as she had first feared.

Maddie spent the afternoon in a work cocoon, suddenly noticing the time by chance at 4:16 p.m.: fourteen minutes before the end-of-day briefing. 'Oh, my God!' she exclaimed, once again unsure where all the time had vanished to. She had not moved from the very spot since before her mom had delivered her lunch several hours ago.

She quickly set up a link to the Zoom meeting, emailed it out to the rest of the Venator team and used the bathroom, before sitting back down at her computer to gather her thoughts.

Becky and Ross were the first to arrive. 'Hi, you two. How are you? Ready to kill each other yet?'

'I would if I thought I'd get away with it,' Ross quipped.

'Ignore him. We're good, thank you. You?' Becky asked.

'Life is surprisingly calm in this house; and long may that continue to be the case,' Maddie answered. 'Here's Kenyatta and Hudson. Hi, guys. Are you both okay?'

'Oh, hanging in there,' Kenyatta said with a chuckle. 'Waiting impatiently for the end of the plague.'

'Well, if the Spanish Flu is anything to go by, that won't be for quite a while yet,' Hudson commented.

'Why, thank you for that little uplifting reminder, Hudson,' Kenyatta replied. 'Any other good tidings you'd like to share with us? Maybe pestilence, locusts or the death of firstborns?'

Hudson grinned. 'Sorry. It's just that the... I'll stop talking now.'

Maddie smiled, then said, 'Probably best. Okay, let's get on with the second briefing for the Twin Falls case. Everybody good to go?'

The team confirmed their readiness and Maddie opened the meeting by sharing her screen which was displaying Joey Seymour's pedigree. 'I might as well go first. As you can see, I haven't done too badly, having concluded my work on the maternal side for the lead person in my cluster. Out of sixteen possible great-great-great-grandparents, I've identified twelve ancestral couples. The other four are nearly impossible to locate. What you can't see there is that all twelve of those people were born in east England, predominantly in the counties of Norfolk, Suffolk and Essex. So, keep an eye out for any of those names or locations cropping up in your research. I don't know… My gut tells me that, given what we know about the killer's heritage, the link between him, Joey Seymour and the rest of the cluster isn't going to be found around this half of the tree,' she said, drawing the cursor in big circles around Joey Seymour's maternal half for the team's benefit. 'We'll see as I make more progress on the paternal side. Kenyatta, would you like to go next?'

'I sure would,' she answered, sharing her screen. 'So, this is the pedigree view for Jeffrey John Dockerty who matches the killer with seventy-nine centimorgans. As you can see, I've really struggled with his maternal side. I just can't seem to get anywhere with his grandmother. But,' she said, emphasizing the word, 'I do have a *potentially* interesting lead on his paternal grandmother's line, which I literally just found a half hour before this briefing.' She clicked to view the profile of a woman named Carmelina Lombardo. 'This lady here was born in Sicily, Italy. According to the 1930 U.S. Census, she immigrated here in 1908 and both her parents were listed as having been born in Italy.'

'That sounds promising,' Maddie said. 'Well done. Keep going. Hudson? What joys do you bring us?'

'Okay. My cluster lead is Valerie Kerouac,' he said, sharing his screen. 'And her name kind of got me excited, wondering if it might be of Eastern European origin. Turns out, it's French and, after some research, it transpired to be her husband's surname, so completely irrelevant. Her birth surname was Paige.' Hudson clicked to display Valerie's pedigree for the team. 'I've managed to identify eight of Valerie's great-great-great-grandparents, mainly concentrated in New Jersey, New York and Connecticut. That's about it, so far.'

'Great start,' Maddie commented. 'Becky?'

Becky blew out some air. 'Well, I had to switch out Samuel Green, my cluster lead. He was our top match at eighty-seven centimorgans, but I could literally find *nothing* out about him at all. I don't know what's going on there. Adoption or a pseudonym or…I don't know. Anyway, I picked the next person down in the cluster,' she said, bringing up the profile page of Latasha McNaughton, 'and I've had more success. Even though she—'

'Mom,' Nikki announced, suddenly appearing at the foot of the stairs.

'One second, guys,' Maddie interrupted, hitting mute and then facing her daughter. 'Nikki, this can't keep happening. I'm on a work call. Is this urgent?'

'Yeah, it is. It's Trenton. He's gone.'

'What? What do you mean, *gone*?'

Nikki handed Maddie a handwritten note.

Mom, I know you'll be mad and try to find me, but please don't. I need answers about Dad. I'll be back in a couple of days and won't do anything stupid. I promise. Don't worry. Love, Trenton

'When did you find this? Where was it?' Maddie demanded.

'I just found it in his room.'

'Well, he can't have gone far—'

'He took Dad's truck,' Nikki announced.

'What?' Maddie stammered. 'Jesus. Right, I need to leave this meeting and get out there in my car. He can't have gone far.'

'Shall I call his friends?' Nikki asked.

'Great idea. Yes, thank you,' Maddie said, before unmuting herself. 'Guys, family emergency: Trenton's absconded in Michael's truck, so I'm going to have to leave. You carry on without me and we'll have another briefing tomorrow at the same time.'

There was an unintelligible babble as the team spoke over one another to wish her well as she darted from the room and up the stairs. Nikki was in the kitchen on the phone already. Her mom was wringing her hands, watching on helplessly.

'Do you think I should call the police?' Maddie said to nobody in particular.

Her mother looked vacantly at her, but Nikki nodded her head.

Maddie pulled out her cell phone and dialed 911. Her initial uncertainty around whether reporting his absence immediately was too premature was quickly allayed by the operator who insisted that there was no waiting period to report a child missing. Maddie felt instantly sick when she was told that Trenton's disappearance would also be reported to the National Center for Missing or Exploited Children as was procedure. This was an organization that she dealt with in a professional capacity on a regular basis, very often with unhappy outcomes.

As Maddie was led through a series of questions, her anxiety and sense of dread increased. The hours of anguish following Michael's disappearance resurfaced, now with a fresh layer of terror. She couldn't go through this again, not with Trenton. Despite the present evidence to the contrary, he was a sensible kid, she tried to tell herself.

Having gone through the basics of Trenton's date of birth, address, physical description, school and doctor's details, she was asked a question to which she did not know the answer. She lowered the phone and said to her mom, 'They want to know when he was last seen here? When was that? Lunchtime, just after you brought the sandwich down to me? Do you remember what the time was?'

Her mom's startled, mortified face gave rise to a new realization for Maddie. 'You didn't check on them, did you?' she asked quietly.

'I'm so sorry,' her mom replied. 'At first, I presumed they were just quiet and working. Then, I clean forgot.'

'For God's sake, Mom. One simple request: check on the kids for me. Now look what's happened,' she ranted. 'Nikki, when did you last see your brother?'

Nikki thought for a moment. 'Maybe around ten this morning. I'd just finished Math and heard him coming out of the bathroom. Nothing since then.'

Maddie hadn't seen him since breakfast, a fact that made her feel like a terrible parent. How had she failed to check in on him? What if he had fallen over and knocked himself out? Or had felt unwell and choked on his own vomit? How on earth had he managed to leave the house without anyone noticing?

Maddie solemnly relayed the news to the operator that her fourteen-year-old son had not been seen for almost seven hours.

Had they checked with friends and family? Yes.

Was there anywhere else, where he might have gone? Seven hours in a truck could get him hundreds of miles away. But she was suddenly sure she knew where he would have gone: Green River.

Chapter Twelve

Thursday, April 9, 2020, Liberty Wells, Salt Lake City, Utah

Hudson re-read the email from Wanda Chabala that had just come in.

Hudson,
Warren and I will be in the city on Saturday and need to meet with you. I suggest Pioneer Park at 1pm.
Regards, Wanda

The worry and foreboding returned to him, tenfold. The email was the most terse and direct so far. *Need* to meet with you. Had something happened? Had they made discoveries of their own? Did she want her money back because he was taking too long in giving her answers? In a strange kind of way, that might be the best-case scenario here; that she demands her money back. But were that to happen, he wouldn't ever be forgiven by Abigail, Brandon Blake would still be in jail for a crime that he didn't commit, and Warren or Jackson Mercaldo would be walking free, having raped and murdered Francesca Chabala; it was hardly such a *best-case* scenario.

Hudson found himself doing the same thing that he'd spent a lot of time doing in the past few days: gazing absent-mindedly at the Wasatch Mountains, while his mind raked over the myriad of problems in his life, sifting through for some overlooked nugget of hope or other solution.

He stood from his desk, walked over to his bedroom door and quietly closed it. Then, he took out his cell phone, opened up his contacts and scrolled down to *Mom*. He stared hard at her home phone number for some time, took an unsteady breath, and then tapped it.

She answered almost immediately, which didn't afford him the time to think about what he might say.

'Oui?' she said, in her familiar clipped way. Like over eighty percent of the residents of Madawaska, Maine, she predominantly spoke French at home.

'Mom, it's me,' he said, his throat tight.

He heard her take a breath. 'Sarah?'

'No, it's Hudson,' he clarified. 'How are you doing? Are you coping okay with lockdown?' he asked.

The line went dead, just as he had predicted it might.

He pocketed his cell phone.

He had to get out of the house, but he also had to work. He couldn't turn up to this afternoon's briefing having done nothing but fret and mull over personal matters that could not be resolved. But work was a problem in and of itself. Right before the email from Wanda Chabala had arrived in his inbox, Hudson had been working on Valerie Kerouac's genetic network, in particular her paternal grandmother, Carmela Costello, who had hailed from New York. But he had hit a New-York-style genealogical black hole. The city was currently being sued by the activist not-for-profit organization, Reclaim the Records, for withholding or charging extortionate fees for access to their vital records. Some New York documents had already been digitized by FamilySearch, including the one to which he currently needed access: *Brooklyn birth certificates, 1866-1909*. The problem was that this file, like several others that he would likely need, was only available to view in person on the network at the Family History Library downtown...which was shut for the foreseeable future.

Hudson would have no choice but to arrive at this afternoon's briefing and admit that half of his cluster's paternal family were currently untraceable. He considered switching out his cluster lead for someone else but couldn't justify the loss of all the work that he'd done to that point. He had to hope that the link between Valerie Kerouac, the rest of the cluster and the serial killer was to be found on Valerie's maternal side for which he had yet to do any research. Hopefully this side of the family would not involve New York City.

Pulling up Valerie Kerouac's profile in the speculative tree that he had created for her, he suddenly had an idea. What if the internal Wi-Fi at the Family History Library was still working? He knew from past experience that the signal extended a good few yards outside of the building itself. There was a small chance that, if the Wi-Fi was still working, he would be able to access the documents that he needed without having to be inside.

Hudson smiled for what felt like the first time in a long while. Getting out of the house and taking a walk, possibly making some headway with identifying Valerie Kerouac's grandmother, overrode his deep-rooted fears of being outside during a pandemic. Science was his thing, and the science was telling him to get his groceries delivered, wash his mail and not leave the house under any circumstances, especially not for trivial reasons such as tracking down a Brooklyn birth record. But he had to get out.

He shut the lid of his laptop, stuffed it into his shoulder bag and hurried out of his bedroom. In the hall, he pulled on his coat and shoes, then called out, 'I'm just heading down to the library.'

'Okay, see you later. Wait, what?' came Abigail's obviously surprised reply. She darted out of the kitchen where she had been working. 'What do you mean? It's closed, isn't it? And besides, we're in lockdown.'

'Uh-huh,' Hudson answered, quickly explaining his plan.

Abigail screwed up her face. 'But what about staying safe and not going outside until it's all over? This isn't like you, Huds. What's going on?'

Hudson forced a smile. 'I'm not going to go near anyone, just sit close to the library and use their Wi-Fi for a few minutes. Honestly, I also just need to take a walk.'

'I'll come with you. Hold up,' she said. 'Just give me ten minutes to wrap up this presentation and I'll—'

'I'd like to go alone, if that's okay? I need to clear my head.'

'Oh…okay, sure,' Abigail replied. 'Go ahead.' She turned around and went back into the kitchen.

'I won't be too long,' he said, attempting to sound much lighter of mind than he felt. He waited for a moment for a reply, but when one wasn't forthcoming, he opened the front door and stepped outside.

As he headed away from the house, Hudson felt close to tears. The sense of relief at being outside was profound and much more far-reaching into his soul than he could have predicted. Just getting air and feeling the sun on his face was instantly restorative.

The walk to the Family History Library would usually have taken over an hour at Hudson's fast pace but, today, he walked leisurely, appreciating his ever-changing surroundings that he had taken for granted. It was weird being out and seeing the roads so deserted. He passed a few walkers and joggers, pulling up his mask and taking exaggerated measures to get out of their way.

In the end, the walk took almost an hour and a half. He reached the library and smiled fondly, not realizing quite how much he had missed the place. Although he and the rest of the Venator team were predominantly based in their office in the Kearns Building on Main Street in downtown Salt Lake City, trips to the Family History Library were very regular for genealogical resources that weren't available online.

Hudson marched purposefully toward the main entrance. He peered inside on the off chance that someone might be in there, but the lights were off and the automatic doors did not open for him. He looked at the pair of low, symmetrical concrete walls containing flowerbeds that ran outward from the entrance in a circular backward sweep. He chose a spot in the sunshine, sat down on the wall and took out his laptop. Opening a new tab in a web browser, he watched the Wi-Fi symbol in the top-right corner, waiting and hoping. Seconds later, it suddenly turned blue with full signal strength and confirmed that he was indeed connected to their internal network.

Smiling to himself again, Hudson clicked to view the scanned image of Carmela Costello's birth certificate that he'd been unable to see from home. It loaded on-screen, instantly providing him with exactly the information he needed.

Name: Carmela Costello
Sex: Female
Birth Date: 15 Mar 1900
Birthplace: Brooklyn, Kings, New York, United States
Race: White
Father's Name: Anthony Costello
Father's Age: 20
Father's Birthplace: Italy
Mother's Name: Selina Mary Dickson
Mother's Age: 19

Mother's Birthplace: Brooklyn, New York

Hudson was excited to see that Valerie Kerouac's paternal great-grandfather had been born in Italy. He wondered if this family line held the unfortunate distinction of containing the direct ancestors of the killer currently murdering young women around Twin Falls. The thought of catching him spurred Hudson on, banishing the other life problems that repeatedly crept forward into his thinking.

It appeared from Carmela Costello's birth record that her parents had met after Anthony Costello's immigration. Hudson opened the 1900 U.S. Federal Census, hoping that it would provide the answers. If his memory served him correctly, the census had been taken on June 1, so he *should* be able to find the young family living together. He inputted all the information that he knew about Anthony, his wife Selina and their three-month-old daughter, Carmela into the search boxes. The top result was correct.

Name: Anthony Costello
Age: 20
Birth Date: February 1880
Birthplace: Italy
Home in 1900: 188 Greenpoint Ave, Brooklyn Ward, Kings, New York
Immigration Year: 1896
Marital Status: Married
Father's Birthplace: Italy
Mother's Birthplace: Italy
Naturalization: Alien
Occupation: Baker
Spouse's Name: Selina Costello
Marriage Year: 1899
Number of living children: 1

The information was exactly what Hudson wanted. It also provided similar detail for Selina's New-York-born parents whom he would pursue once he had taken the Italian branches back as far as was required.

First, he needed to try and find Anthony Costello's marriage to Selina Dickson. He returned to the FamilySearch catalog and clicked on *New York, Brooklyn, marriage certificates, 1866-1937*. These records were also only available in the library. He entered the known details and was pleased when he saw a copy of the couple's marriage certificate, rich in genealogical detail.

Name: Anthony Costello
Age: 19
Father's Name: Angelo Castiglia
Mother's Name: Marie Randazzo
Spouse's Name: Selina Mary Dickson
Spouse's Age: 18
Spouse's Father's Name: Joseph Dickson
Spouse's Mother's Name: Mary McQuillan
Marriage Date: 23 Jul 1899
Marriage Place: Kings, New York

Hudson now knew the names of four of Valerie Kerouac's great-great-grandparents. He was intrigued to see that Anthony's father's surname was given as Castiglia, not Costello. To get beyond the names of Anthony's parents, Hudson needed a much more specific birth location than *Italy*. His hunch was that Anthony had arrived in the U.S. via New York—possibly through Ellis Island—so he accessed the *New York, U.S., Arriving Passenger and Crew Lists, 1820-1957* records on Ancestry, entering Anthony's name, birth year and arrival year of 1896.

The first page of the results list was filled with a variety of suggestions for various Anthony Costellos, but their arrival dates in the U.S. were way out. Hudson spent some time checking the list but didn't find a person whom he considered to be correct. He switched the search to *Anthony Castiglia* and was presented with a new set of results.

The fifth entry looked possible.

Name: Anthony Castiglia
Age: 16

Departure Port: Palermo
Arrival Date: 25 March 1896
Arrival Port: New York, New York, USA
Ship Name: Ems

It *could* be the correct Anthony, but there was insufficient evidence for Hudson to be certain. A departure place of Palermo pointed to a possible location of Sicily, but it was just too tenuous to be sure. He needed something much more concrete.

Hudson brought up the hints suggested against Anthony Costello's name in the speculative tree. The 1920, 1930 and 1940 censuses simplified his place of birth, all reporting just the country of Italy. The final hint suggested a record in the *U.S., World War II Draft Registration Cards, 1942*—or the Old Man's Registration as it was sometimes known. Hudson clicked to view a color copy of the original document.

Name: Anthony Costello
Gender: Male
Registration Age: 62
Birth Date: 3 Feb 1880
Birthplace: Calatabiano, Catania, Sicily, Italy

The document also gave Anthony's 1942 address, next of kin—his wife, Selina—and a physical description, but the information that Hudson wanted was the exact date and location of birth, which this document provided. He remembered that Kenyatta had mentioned a connection to Sicily in the briefing yesterday but, with all the usual flurry of names, dates and locations, couldn't now recall the specifics. Opening the Word document that Ross maintained for the Twin Falls case, Hudson searched for potential links to Sicily. *Carmelina Lombardo, born 1888, Sicily, Italy.* That was all the file contained so far. Hudson made a mental note of the surname and copied Anthony Costello's place of birth into Google maps, immediately grateful to find that the draft registration document had narrowed it down from the whole of Italy to a small commune on the island of Sicily.

Italian records were not his specialty, so he turned to the

FamilySearch website, navigating through to the Research Wiki page on the genealogical records for the Catania Province. He read down the page, finding that the civil registration of births, marriages and deaths began in 1809 and that *After this date, virtually all individuals who lived in Italy were recorded.* It was a promising start to finding Anthony Costello's birth and hopefully next, his parents' marriage and their births. However, as he read on, he learned that all civil records were kept at the local registrar's office, only some of which had been digitized. Following several links within the FamilySearch site, Hudson found his way to the *Registri dello stato civile di Calatabiano (Catania), 1820-1929* record set. Once again, the documents were only available on either microfilm within the library or online via their Wi-Fi.

Having read that the term, *nati*, meant births, he clicked to view *Nati 1866-1888.* Fortunately for Hudson, he had an exact date of birth, as the 3,320 scanned images had not yet been indexed. He soon reached February 1880 and found an entry with what he thought was the surname of Castiglia.

'O-h, y-e-s,' he said, zooming in to the image and trying to decipher what was written there. Apart from the surname, the handwriting for the rest was hard to read. '…*è nato un bambino di sesso…*' he attempted to read aloud. Something about a baby.

'Sounds like fun,' a man's voice suddenly said from close by.

Hudson was startled to see someone sitting a couple of feet along the wall from him, grinning. He was African American, around Hudson's age, with short dyed-blonde hair, wearing an orange puffer jacket, and sitting with a laptop on his legs, exactly as Hudson was. 'Uh, yeah. I guess you could say that,' Hudson answered.

'You're borrowing the Wi-Fi to access their records, too?' the man asked, still grinning.

Hudson nodded. 'New York,' he explained.

'Ah, I get it, man,' he replied.

'Actually,' Hudson clarified, 'I've emigrated from New York back to Sicily, but I can't speak Italian—or read it, for that matter as you might have noticed—so I'm a little stuck.'

'Sorry. Can't help you there, man.'

'It's okay. I've got a contact who's an Italian genealogy specialist,'

Hudson said, downloading an image of the entry and then emailing it to his friend, Stephen Caraccia, hoping that he might come back right away so that he could move backward in time through the *matrimoni* documents for Calatabiano.

'Is this your own family tree you're researching?' the man asked.

Hudson shook his head. 'No. This is part of a case I'm working on for an investigative genetic genealogy company.'

'Oh, wow. That sounds cool, man.'

'Yeah, I guess it is. What about you?' Hudson inquired. 'What brings you here?'

'I'm a professional genealogist, so doing some case work, plus I work with Megan Smolenyak at Unclaimed Persons, finding family for bodies with no known next of kin.'

'That must be interesting, too,' Hudson commented.

'Yeah, it can be a lot of things, but I guess interesting is an accurate all-round description of what I do. It's a quiet but disturbing epidemic. There are so many bodies going to the grave without the knowledge of their family; it's awful,' he said.

'Do you have much success?'

'Yes, actually. We've been able to find next of kin for more than four hundred people so far,' he replied.

'That must be very rewarding,' Hudson replied.

'Yeah, it is. I guess it's the same for you, though? Do you do suspect cases or unidentified human remains?'

'Both,' Hudson answered. 'At the moment, we're on the trail of a serial killer.'

'Wow,' the man said. 'That's awesome. I'd like to get into that work, one day.'

'It can get a little intense,' he warned.

'I can imagine,' the man said. 'I mean, I already find it really hard to switch off at the end of the day with the work *I* do, so I guess it's even tougher for you.'

'It sure can get that way,' Hudson agreed.

'Well,' he said, pushing down his laptop lid, 'that's me done draining the library's Wi-Fi.' He stowed his laptop into his backpack and stood up. 'It was nice to meet you. I'm Reggie, by the way.' He mimed shaking Hudson's hand at a distance.

'Hudson. Good to meet you, too,' he said, copying the air handshake.

'Good luck with your bambino,' Reggie said, giving a wave as he walked away.

Hudson watched him leave, then, as he was at an impasse with Anthony Costello, switched his attention to Anthony Castiglia's wife, Selina Mary Dickson. He opened her profile page, noting that she had been born in Brooklyn, New York in 1881.

Hudson found her birth certificate easily in the *New York, New York City Births, 1846-1909* record set at FamilySearch.

Name: Selina Mary Dickson
Sex: Female
Birth Date: 26 Sep 1881
Birthplace: Brooklyn, Kings, New York
Race: White
Father's Name: Joseph Dickson
Father's Birthplace: New York
Mother's Name: Mary McQuillan
Mother's Birthplace: New York

He saved the document to her profile, confirming that which had been stated on her marriage certificate to Anthony. The next obvious step would be to take a look at the family on the 1890 U.S. Federal Census, but it had largely been destroyed by fire in 1921. He knew that by the time of the next census in 1900, Selina had been married and living with her husband and young daughter, Carmela, so Hudson ran a search for her parents, Joseph and Mary, in New York at that time.

As he scrolled through the search results, Hudson saw an email come in from Stephen Caraccia.

Hi Hudson
Please find attached the translations and data.
Thanks
Stephen

That was quick, Hudson thought as he opened the attachment, headed *BIRTH RECORD TRANSLATION & DATA EXTRACTION.*

City, County, State, Country: Calatabiano, Catania, Sicily, Italy
Subject's Name: Anthony Castiglia
Date of Birth: 3-Feb-1880, 2:30 a.m.
Father's Name: Angelo Castiglia
Father's Age: 30
Father's occupation: Farmhand
Deceased?: No
Mother's Maiden Name: Marie Randazzo
Address: Via Teatro Communal

Hudson smiled. The record confirmed the details from Anthony and Selina's marriage certificate. Next would be to try and track down the marriage of Angelo Castiglia and Marie Randazzo.

The day quickly slipped away, and Hudson was surprised by the time when Kenyatta sent out the Zoom link to the afternoon's briefing in just under thirty minutes. There was now no time to walk home. He took out his cell phone, seeing that he had an unread message from Abigail.

Where are you???

He replied that he was still at the library but would be home after the briefing. He put his phone away and carried on researching until the meeting started.

'Hudson, hi,' Kenyatta said, admitting him. 'Wait a minute, where are you? That looks like the library…'

'It is. Here's a life hack for you: if you need to look at the digitized records only available *inside*, sit on the wall *outside* and use their Wi-Fi.'

Kenyatta laughed. 'How long have you been there?'

'Almost all day,' Hudson admitted.

'Jeez, you must be freezing.'

102

'Well, my butt is numb and frozen solid, but otherwise I'm okay. I've really enjoyed just being out of the house. Anything from Maddie today?'

'No, nothing. I texted her this morning, but she hasn't replied. I don't want to pester her, but I'm worried for the poor boy.'

'Yeah, me too. I messaged her last night, but I haven't heard anything back, either.' He shrugged. Despite the ultimatum that she had given him, he felt deeply sorry for her and would like to have been able to help in some way. 'I wish there was something we could do.'

'Me too. I feel so helpless. I can't imagine what she's going through right now,' Kenyatta commented, as Ross and Becky joined the meeting. 'Hi, guys.'

'Hi,' they both greeted in unison.

After an exchange of pleasantries, questions about Maddie's absence and Hudson's location, Kenyatta started the briefing. 'Okay. Well, since I'm chattering on, I may as well start the proceedings. I am still at a dead-end with my cluster lead's maternal side. I don't know what the problem is, but I just can't find corroborative records. I *have* made some progress, though'—she paused to bring up the pedigree for Jeffrey John Dockerty—'on his paternal side.'

Hudson studied the screen intently, seeing names from the isle of Sicily: *Napoli. Lombardo. Patané.* Nothing that crossed over with his own discoveries, though.

'I think there's good documentation on FamilySearch, but my knowledge of Italian only extends to varieties of pizza and pasta, so I've referred some records over to Stephen Caraccia.'

Hudson laughed. 'Me, too. I hit Sicily today.'

Kenyatta's eyes widened. 'Oh, wow. Do any of these names show up in your research? Or any of the places?'

Hudson shook his head. 'Not so far, but I need to look on Google Maps to see how far your locations are from mine. I think this is really promising, though, as a place where our clusters might converge.'

'Well, that's great, since I'm getting next to nowhere on Jeffrey Dockerty's maternal side,' Kenyatta said keenly. 'So, do you want to go next, Hudson, while we're in Sicily?'

'Sure,' he said, sharing the pedigree page for Valerie Kerouac. 'I'm still focused on her paternal side at the moment. Her great-grandfather, Anthony Castiglia, emigrated from Sicily to New York, having his name changed to Costello at Ellis Island.' Hudson grinned.

Kenyatta and Becky laughed loudly.

'What's so funny about that?' Ross asked.

'It's just a stupid myth that gets perpetuated that immigrants were forced to change their names when they arrived here,' Kenyatta explained. 'But it's nonsense.'

'Not helped by *The Godfather* movie,' Becky added.

'But he *did* change his name, didn't he?' Ross questioned, clearly not understanding.

'Sure, but that would have been *his* choice,' Hudson replied. 'Nobody was forced to change their names when they arrived here.'

'I see,' Ross said.

'Anyway,' Hudson continued, 'I think, given what Kenyatta has found, that I need to keep going with these lines, then see if I can triangulate the rest of my cluster, as opposed to working on Valerie's maternal side.'

'Good plan; I'll do the same,' Kenyatta agreed. 'Becky, how have you gotten on today?'

'Well, I don't think I'm going to win the twenty bucks for the first orange slip on this case,' she said, holding her hands up in defeat. She was referring to a light-hearted incentive for the Venator team, rewarding the first person who identified the ancestor or ancestral couple common to their particular genetic network. 'I told you yesterday that I'd switched out my cluster lead for Latasha McNaughton, but she's not proving much easier,' she said with a laugh. The pedigree on-screen showed Latasha's parents' names, her two maternal grandparents and all four maternal great-grandparents, but that was it. 'As you can see, I've got several states around the U.S., including Ohio, Kansas and Michigan. There's also this guy'—she clicked on one of Latasha McNaughton's maternal great-grandfathers, Adam Kowalski—'who was born in Poland, so potentially getting closer to the areas found in the killer's geo-ancestry. That's it.' Becky sat back in her chair.

'Great work, everyone,' Kenyatta said, overly enthusiastically.

Hudson guessed that she was trying to compensate for Maddie's absence. 'Unless I hear otherwise, carry on with your investigations and we'll have another briefing at four-thirty tomorrow afternoon. Any questions?'

'No, ma'am,' Hudson replied.

'Only one,' Becky said, 'Remind me why was I given cluster number one?'

Kenyatta laughed. 'Punishment for winning the twenty bucks on the last case, missy.'

Becky sighed. 'Well, I won't be winning it this time around. Okay, same time tomorrow.'

'Goodbye, honeys,' Kenyatta said, ending the meeting.

During the briefing, the sun had moved behind the Family History Library and Hudson now began to feel deeply cold. He should pack up and head home. He checked his cell phone. Nothing back from Abigail, which could only mean one thing: that she was pissed at him. The coldness that he was feeling now was nothing compared with that which he'd feel when he got home. He packed his laptop away and began the walk home. This time, however, instead of staying on South Temple until East Fifth Street, he turned down Main Street, unable to reconcile the deserted buildings with a normal five o'clock on a Thursday afternoon. The Trax stops were empty, the City Creek Center shut, all the stores, coffee shops, restaurants and banks that he was passing were closed up. He paused outside the Beerhive Pub and stared into the dark, lifeless interior, desperately wishing that he could go inside, get a large wine and forget his troubles. But actually, that was exactly where the Wanda Chabala trouble had all started. She had accosted him right here, out on the street, and they had gone in to talk over the situation. A big part of him wished that he had never accepted her invitation, but it wasn't just about him; many other people's lives were intimately entwined. He realized that his indecision was compounding the heavy burden of this impossible situation. He needed to do *something*. He had to hand back the money and withhold from Wanda the identities of the two suspects. Opening his cell phone, he typed a response to Wanda Chabala's email.

105

Wanda,
Yes, I think it's time we met to discuss the situation. I'll see you at 1p.m. in Pioneer Park on Saturday.
Hudson

He clicked send, even though he had no idea which way the meeting was going to go.

Hudson exhaled, needing to move away from the painful reminder of the pub. Just a few yards on was the Kearns Building. He stopped outside and tried the door. Locked. He looked up to the fifth floor, where the Venator office was, wishing that life would hurry up and get back to some kind of normal.

As he continued his walk home, his phone pinged with the arrival of a text message. It was from Abigail.

Hudson, I don't know what's going on with you right now, but I'm not going to allow anything to get in the way of our plans. I've told the adoption agency that we're good to proceed and to take the money from my account. We'll chat about it later.

Hudson opened his banking app and checked the balance of their joint savings account. Zero. Abigail had preempted his decision and moved all fifty thousand that he had been going to give back to Wanda Chabala into her own personal account.

Chapter Thirteen

Friday, April 10, 2020, Salt Lake City, Utah

Becky Larkin sighed, stretched and yawned. It was almost lunchtime and she needed to take a break. She stood up, stretched again, and walked out into the open-plan living area. Ross was sitting at the kitchen counter, typing something into his laptop. 'Hey,' he greeted. 'How's your work going?'

'Slower than I'd like,' Becky admitted, getting a glass of water. 'But I've made good progress with my cluster. And yours?'

'Still compiling all the lists of names, dates and places that you all generated yesterday.'

'Could I just take a quick peek at that, please?' she asked, peering over his shoulder.

'Sure,' he said, leaning out of her way.

Becky rolled the mouse down the list of names, but nothing jumped out from the rest of the team's research that crossed over with hers. She moved into the kitchen and picked up the blender. 'Smoothie?'

'I'd rather a wine, but I guess it's a little early,' he answered. 'So…sure, thanks. Oh, by the way… I took a call on the Venator divert line about the SAKI kit you're working on; they wondered if you had any updates?'

Becky grimaced. 'I'm close to identifying the guy, but I just need a *little* more time. Give them a call back and tell them I'll update them on Monday. I'm going to have to give it some time this weekend.'

'Sure?' he pressed.

'Yeah,' she answered. 'I mean, it's not like I can go out and do anything else with my time, now, is it? I'm just stuck here…with you.'

Ross blew her a big kiss. 'Love you, too.'

Becky smiled as she began loading the blender with fruit from the bowl. 'Has Maddie checked in with you, at all?' she asked him.

Ross shook his head. 'Nope.'

'That's really worrying. I thought Trenton had his head screwed on,' she said.

'Who knows what's going on in his head. It can't be easy not knowing what happened to his dad: one day he's there; the next he's gone. No explanation.'

'I know…' Becky said, blitzing the smoothie. 'I just hope she finds him quickly. Can you imagine how she must be feeling, having her husband *and* son go missing?'

'Have you thought any more about your dad and trying to find out what he knows?' Ross asked.

'Constantly,' she replied, handing Ross his drink, 'But I don't ever come to any firm resolution on it. Ideas welcome on that one.'

'Thanks,' he said. 'I'll think on it.'

'Right. Back to it,' Becky said, taking her smoothie off into the guest room, settling back down at her computer.

'Briefing warning!' Ross called out, making some weird siren noise.

'What?' Becky cried, being dragged out of her research rabbit hole and back into the real world. She looked at the clock. Somehow, it was 4:28 p.m. 'God…' she mumbled. She had not moved from the computer since she had sat down with her smoothie at lunchtime. She went off to use the bathroom, then hurried back to her computer to click the Zoom link that Kenyatta had sent. 'Hi,' she said, hoping that she didn't appear as absent as she felt.

'How are you all doing?' Kenyatta asked.

'Okay, I guess,' Becky answered.

'Fine,' came Hudson's clipped reply. He didn't look very happy, Becky thought as she selected his video feed for a moment. She picked up her cell phone and sent him a text.

Hudson, are you okay?

Becky saw Hudson look down at his cell phone for a few seconds. Then a message came back.

Yeah, fine. Tired.

Becky gave him a smile, not buying that he was okay. It could be a symptom of lockdown, or maybe he *was* just tired; it seemed to be a universal thing that people just weren't sleeping great at the moment. However, even before the pandemic, she somehow got the impression that Hudson's homelife wasn't anywhere near as wonderful as he would make it out to be.

'Anything from Maddie?' Ross asked.

Kenyatta nodded her head solemnly. 'Just one brief message that said she was down at Green River, where they think Trenton might be but that search and rescue hadn't yet found him, yet.'

'Green River? Where Michael disappeared?' Becky stammered.

'I'm guessing so,' Kenyatta replied.

'Oh my God,' Hudson commented.

'I keep looking at my cell,' Kenyatta admitted, 'hoping for some good news, but nothing so far.'

'Poor Maddie,' Hudson said.

'Yeah, exactly,' Kenyatta agreed. After a reflective silence, she added, 'I think the best thing for us to do right now is to carry on with this investigation. Okay?'

'It's hard, but yeah,' Becky said.

'Uh-huh,' Hudson said.

'So,' Kenyatta began, 'Hudson, you're starting today, *per favore*, because I'm hoping that the good Lord is on our side and you're going to show me how our Sicilian lines match up.'

'Well, with a lot of translation help from Stephen Caraccia, I've managed to get the names of all four of my cluster lead's great-great-great-grandparents who hailed from Sicily. Recognize any of them, Kenyatta?'

'*Castiglia. Randazzo. Puglisi. Caruso…* Well, I've got *Russo*, but not *Ca*ruso,' she read. 'Nope. None of those match so far, but I'm not done yet in that area. Okay. Good work, Hudson. Any triangulation within your cluster?'

'Not yet.'

'Well, here's my progress so far,' Kenyatta said, replacing Hudson's screen with her own. 'I've been concentrating on the Sicilian side and have identified—also with a ton of help from Stephen Caraccia, I might add—six out of eight Sicilian great-great-great-grandparents.

They're mainly concentrated around the city of Syracuse, on the east coast.'

Becky focused on the surnames and locations, seeing nothing at all that even came close to her own research.

'The link has to be there,' Hudson said. 'Syracuse is like sixty miles up the coast from Calatabiano where my cluster are from.'

'Well, it looks as though you two are storming ahead, unlike me,' Becky commented, folding her arms in mock-annoyance.

'Ah, don't get upset now, honey,' Kenyatta said with a smile. 'Why don't you tell us what you *have* found?'

Becky shared her screen, showing the pedigree of her cluster lead, Latasha McNaughton.

'That's good going,' Kenyatta praised.

'I guess so,' she half-heartedly agreed. Becky had successfully confirmed the identity of all eight of Latasha's great-grandparents, six out of sixteen great-great-grandparents and eight great-great-great-grandparents. 'But I'm getting nowhere fast with finding this woman's birth or locating her parents,' she said, clicking on the profile of Virginia Torres who, according to her son's birth record, had been born in Mexico around 1878. It was always a tough call when somebody they wanted to track down proved elusive. Did they keep persevering? Or move on to someone else and risk a whole line going unsolved?

'What we're not seeing,' Hudson commented, 'are Russian or Eastern European names or places. Isn't that a little weird, given how high this guy's ethnicity pointed toward these areas?'

'Yes, but,' Kenyatta replied, 'we've only been working on four out of seven of the genetic networks; there's plenty of time yet.'

'Plus, very few DNA kits get sent out to Russia and its neighboring countries,' Becky added. 'So, there will naturally be fewer people in the database from those areas.'

'Let's keep going,' Kenyatta said. 'But, at this point, I do feel obligated to take on Maddie's role and voice, here, and tell you all *not* to work over the weekend.'

'And are *you* going to be taking that advice of yours?' Becky asked, raising her eyebrows and leaning in closer to the camera.

'Why, of course,' Kenyatta said, laughing. 'I'll be putting my feet up and doing nothing, both days. Anyone have anything else to ask or add or…?'

When nobody spoke up, Kenyatta wished everyone a good weekend and ended the briefing.

Becky sat back in her chair. She still had so much work to do on this case, but she had also promised an update on the Sexual Assault Kit Initiative by Monday.

She turned at the sound of footsteps approaching the guest-room door and, as if by magic, Ross was standing there holding two very full glasses of white wine. 'Party time,' he said.

Becky smiled, closed her laptop and wandered over to him. She took the glass, chinked it against his and took a swig. 'That's better. So, what are your plans for tonight? It is Friday, after all.'

'I thought we would start off at the Sugar House Pub, before going on to the Tap Room for a couple of drinks and before heading into town. Maybe Gracie's or Beerhive? End the night tomorrow morning at Durango? What do you think?'

Becky screwed up her face. 'Or—brace yourself—we could put on our PJs, stay home, eat snacks and watch Netflix?'

'Just like every other night,' he said, tapping his glass to hers again. 'Cheers to another fun night in at casa de zero options.'

'Cheers.'

They both moved into the living room area and sat down.

'Did you get all your work done?' Becky asked him.

'Pretty well, yeah. I keep wondering… Are you feeling confident that we'll all catch this guy before he strikes again?'

Becky took in a long breath. 'I'm really not sure. Up until this afternoon's briefing, I was very confident. I mean, Venator's running at a, what, eighty-five-percent success rate? There aren't many cases that we've taken on that are still unsolved, but I don't like the lack of matches for this Eastern European side.'

'Is he identifiable without that part of his family being found?' Ross asked.

'Good question. Technically, yes. But it would depend on how long his family has lived in the U.S. If we've got three generations, we could do it. If he's a first-generation immigrant, it will be *very* difficult.'

'But what about—'

Becky's cell phone began to ring. She took it out of her pocket. 'Jerome,' she announced, staring at the screen.

'Aren't you going to take it?'

'I don't know if I've got the energy… We just don't have enough history to be able to talk about stuff at the moment…' She continued to look at the phone screen until he stopped calling.

'Are you dumping him?' Ross asked. 'Can I have him?'

Becky smiled. 'No… I don't think so, anyway. It's lockdown. All the things we have in common we can't do, and nothing significant happens each day that warrants talking about. Plus, I *can't* talk about my work for obvious reasons, and we've banned all conversation about the pandemic; so, it doesn't leave much to say… I'll call him back later. And, no, you can't have him. Find your own.'

'I'm not even bothering to *try* and meet a guy right now. I mean, really, what's the point? Virtual dating? No, thank you. I'll wait it out,' he said.

'According to Hudson's prognosis, we might have a long wait,' Becky warned.

'Yeah, well… That's Hudson for you.'

'Did he seem normal to you today?' she asked.

Ross rolled his eyes. 'He's *never* normal with me; I genuinely think he doesn't like me, you know?'

'Hudson likes everyone,' Becky countered. 'He just seemed a little off at the briefing. Something's up, I'm sure of it.'

'Detective Larkin on the case again,' Ross quipped. 'Speaking of which… Any ideas to move the Michael Barnhart situation forward?'

Becky shook her head. 'My dad is barely talking to me about anything, right now. There's zero chance of him telling me who called Michael just before he disappeared, or why he placed a gag order on his employees. I can't go rummaging in his offices at work or home. His staff are barred from speaking with anyone, plus he'd be certain to get wind of me snooping. Short of doing nothing at all, I figure there's only one thing that I can do.'

'And that is…?'

'Talk to Lois Strange again. If she could just tell me the names of some of Michael's co-workers, maybe they would talk to me about what projects he was working on at the time when he disappeared.'

'Just playing Devil's advocate, here… But, isn't there still a risk it could get back to your dad that you're interviewing his employees?'

Becky shrugged. 'Got any better ideas?'

'No,' he replied.

'Do you know what?' Becky said, polishing off the rest of her wine and picking up her cell phone. 'To hell with it. As they say… If he's got nothing to hide, then he's got nothing to worry about.' She opened her phone.

'What are you doing?'

'Calling Lois Strange,' she replied, pulling her name up from the contact list. 'I'm going to need more wine for this.'

Ross mumbled something, then went over to the refrigerator for the opened bottle as Becky tapped on Lois's cell phone number to connect.

She answered almost immediately. 'Becky, hi. How are you doing?' Lois asked.

'More fortunate than a lot of people,' she answered. 'You?'

'Just a *little* concerned about our wedding in the fall. We're still making plans, still being reassured by everyone involved that everything will be just fine. But, still, it's a big worry.'

'I'm sure it'll all be over by then,' Becky said, hoping that her tone sounded more optimistic than she felt.

'I'm assuming this isn't a social call?' Lois correctly intuited. Having been best friends for several years, their relationship had faltered when Lois had been working as Becky's father's personal assistant and had accused him of sexual harassment. Becky's clumsy attempt at impartiality—not least because she hadn't known whom to believe—had effectively put an end to her friendship with Lois.

'I do want to pick up with our friendship again,' Becky said, her cheeks flushing with embarrassment. 'After this is over, we need to go for a social catch-up drink. But you're right, I'm calling about that problem that I spoke with you about when we met downtown a couple of weeks ago.'

'Michael Barnhart?' Lois said. 'I told you everything I knew, which I realize wasn't much. I've not held anything back, Becky. As I'm sure you can imagine, I've absolutely no allegiance to your dad or his company.'

'No, I know. And I appreciate your help. I'm just really struggling to understand why my father would try to cover up whatever happened to Michael.'

Lois made a low, scoffing grunt.

'Could you tell me anyone's name who was working closely with Michael right before he disappeared?'

Lois took in a long breath and didn't answer for some time.

Ross walked over and handed Becky her glass, now refilled with white wine. She silently mouthed her thanks to him over her phone and took a sip, still waiting for Lois to answer.

'First of all, anything I say did *not* come from me... Agreed?'

'Absolutely,' Becky confirmed.

'Second of all, you've got to remember that I was your father's PA, so I didn't really know the ins and outs of what each employee was working on.'

'I know, but any names you can suggest would be a huge help to me.'

'In the few months before Michael disappeared, I'm sure he was working on a finance package for a big infrastructure company in Haiti. Two of the other guys on the project were Artemon Bruce and Jay Craig.'

'Excellent,' Becky said, jotting down the information. 'Are they still at the company, do you know?'

'I've no idea anymore. Sorry.'

'Do you know anything more about this project in Haiti?' Becky pressed.

'Literally nothing. The Larkin Investment and Finance Group dealt with *hundreds* of projects around the world. As far as I know—or could tell, at least—there was nothing unusual about this particular one.'

'Thank you. Anything else you can recall?'

'I don't think so, Becky. But if I remember any more...'

'Thank you so much. I really do want to meet up as soon as we can.

Would that be okay?'

'Yeah… But I think we need to have a face-to-face conversation about what your father did to me, and I need to hear it from you that you believe me. Because that really hurt, you know?'

The comments hit Becky hard, and she felt a heavy guilt over the way that she had dealt with the situation between Lois and her father. She could have asked more questions at the time rather than trying to steer a diplomatic course between the two of them. 'Okay. We will,' she finally answered.

'Take care of yourself. Goodbye,' Lois said.

'You, too. Bye,' Becky said, ending the call.

Ross eyed her eagerly. 'Well?'

'Two names of people who worked with Michael Barnhart on a project. Some infrastructure finance thing in Haiti.'

'Sounds…dull,' Ross commented.

Becky looked at the names on the piece of paper, then looked up at Ross. 'Instead of Netflix, would you be willing to help me track down Artemon Bruce and Jay Craig?'

'Anything to assist the indomitable Detective Larkin,' he replied, raising his glass.

Chapter Fourteen

Friday, April 10, 2020, Twin Falls, Idaho

He was wearing his baseball cap and face mask as he turned onto Adams Street. The road was much quieter than usual what with everyone being imprisoned in their own homes, too scared to go outside. That suited him. He drove on a short distance, then pulled up beside a wire fence. On the other side was some kind of a detached garage with a large empty lot around it. He watched the building for some time, making certain that there was nobody around, and then looked over at the property directly opposite. An evergreen tree concealed most of the front of the house and all he could see of the single-story building was the screened front door that led out onto a deck. The house had a gray tiled roof and was dressed in a wide pinkish siding. The garden, edged by a variety of mature shrubs, was nice and private, he observed with a satisfied smile.

He spent some time checking through the windshield, looking in his mirrors, double-checking the garage to his left and making sure that nobody was in the immediate vicinity. Then, he bent over and gathered up a lanyard and a navy-blue jacket from under his seat. He put the jacket on and pulled the lanyard over his head, and lastly picked up the clipboard from the passenger seat.

With one last check around him, he stepped out of the Wrangler and crossed the street to the little bungalow that he'd just been watching. He walked up the drive, onto the deck and knocked on the door.

After a few seconds, the internal door opened and she appeared, squinting through the screen at him. Despite being in her pajamas with messy bed-hair and no makeup, she was still very beautiful.

'Hi there,' he said. He glanced down at his clipboard. 'Debra…Towers?'

She nodded, her eyes falling to his lanyard.

'My name's Steven Bright and I work for Falls Fiber Utility. Basically, the guys who lay and fix all the internet cables under the roads around here.'

'Okay,' she said uncertainly, tying her auburn hair back behind her head.

'We're just doing a kind of spot-check on bandwidth, now that everyone's trying to work from home, and working out where we need to prioritize upgrading the old copper cables over to the fiber network.'

'Right... So, do you need to come in or...?' she asked, looking again at his lanyard.

He laughed—a little too strongly—and his voice flipped up an octave before falling back down again, 'No, no need for that; especially not with the pandemic and all. Just a couple of questions here on the doorstep, if that's okay?'

Debra tried to conceal her reaction to his voice. She overcompensated by giving him a wide smile of acceptance. 'Sure.'

'Great,' he said. 'First off, how have you found the speed of your internet since the lockdown started?'

Debra glanced upward in thought for a second, then answered, 'Yeah, fine. I can't say that I've noticed much of a difference.'

'That's great to hear,' he said. 'And, actually, your neighbors have said pretty much the same thing all the way along. Okay. So, no slowdown. Are you working from home or placing any extra demands on the internet than you would have done, say, two months ago?'

She nodded. 'Yeah, sure. I'm working remotely now but I was at the office a couple of weeks ago.'

'So, like most people, home twenty-four seven?'

She nodded and sighed. 'Unfortunately, yes.'

'And what about the other occupants of the household?' he looked at his clipboard and laughed. 'I'm supposed to ask about kids and streaming video games, but you're clearly way too young to have kids.'

Debra smiled. 'No, it's just me and my cat, here.'

'Great,' he muttered. He took another look at his clipboard, feigning close scrutiny. 'I think that's it... Yup, we're all done. Um, you probably won't see me again. That is, unless we intend to upgrade the network in the area, as I said. Thank you for your time, today. Have a good one and stay well.'

'You're welcome. You, too. Goodbye,' Debra said, closing the internal door.

117

He set off back to the car, whistling. He climbed into the Wrangler, fired up the engine and removed his jacket, tossing it onto the passenger seat. Just as he went to pull away, he noticed a spray of blood spatter across the back of it.

Chapter Fifteen

Friday, April 10, 2020, Green River, Utah

Maddie was standing on the spillway that terminated at the Green River, staring at Michael's truck, the only non-emergency vehicle in the parking lot beside the track that led down to the water. In a cruel echo of the past, it was now parked in the exact spot where it had been back when Michael had seemingly abandoned it in 2015. Clutching a plastic coffee cup to stop herself from shivering, she was simultaneously numb and raw with emotion. She hadn't slept for two nights. She was still wearing the same clothes that she'd been wearing when Nikki had interrupted the Zoom call with her team.

All around her was a hive of activity. Ground search and rescue teams—working under the jurisdiction of the local Sheriff's office—were applying all their resources to find Trenton. Unlike with the investigation into her husband Michael's disappearance, progress was being made, most likely because of Trenton's age. For any missing person under the age of twenty-one, it was mandatory for law enforcement to enter the details into the FBI's National Crime Information Center. Consequently, in a crushing twist of irony, her son now appeared with her husband in the *Utah's Missing Persons* database online.

Maddie stood like an island on the spillway, staring at the truck while police and search and rescue teams worked around her. The past two days had been a hazy, tangled mess of time that could just as easily have been a few hours or several weeks. She couldn't recall what her last meal had been, just that every now and then a kind person assisting with the search would offer her a sandwich or a can of soda. She couldn't fault the investigation so far. Maddie had directed police to Green River as being the most likely place to find Trenton. Michael's truck had been immediately found but there had been no sign of Trenton. The Incident Commander—an employee of the Forest Service—had coordinated law enforcement and search and rescue teams, identifying the high-hazard and high-probability areas to prioritize searches. The Incident Commander, a short, stocky man with a thin gray moustache and a bald head, had solemnly informed Maddie that, given all that she had told him, the high-hazard and high-probability areas to be searched first intersected at one obvious location: the Green River itself.

This worrying conclusion became a reality when tracking experts had confirmed that they had traced Trenton's foot impressions down to the riverbank; but from there the trail had gone cold. It wasn't until two hours ago that searchers on horseback—used because they could cover terrain inaccessible by other means—had tracked his movements to the John Wesley Powell float-in campsite, seven miles downstream. An hour ago, a group of hikers had reported seeing someone of Trenton's description packing up his tent before continuing downriver in a rubber raft. Maddie's initial elation that they had been on the verge of finding him was now quickly trampled on by the Incident Commander who informed her that Trenton was probably around three and a half miles upriver from the Red Creek Rapids.

'Should we be worried about that?' Maddie asked him pointedly.

'How is he at negotiating rapids?' came his reply.

'He's certainly *been* on rapids before, but I don't think he's ever had to navigate any by himself...'

'Hopefully, he'll be fine, then,' the Incident Commander responded. 'I've got an experienced team of ground search and rescue making their way on horseback to the spot where the Red Creek converges with the Green River.'

'Will they get there before he does?'

'Hopefully,' he said, using that same word again. 'But there's no direct route.'

As he walked off, Maddie ran a Google search for the rapids.

Red Creek Rapid is the largest and most dangerous rapid in the first 30 miles of the Green River below Flaming Gorge Dam...

She read on with tears in her eyes, not really absorbing what she was reading.

At low flows (1,200 cfs and below) a majority of Green River guides drop off their passengers prior to running either side of the rapid… River left is a semi-dangerous class II rapid… You will likely hit rocks…the river right side is a class III rapid. The strong river currents push boats hard towards the cliff wall…

'Oh, God,' she sighed, not really understanding all that she had just read, but fully appreciating the seriousness of the situation. Closing the webpage, the browser returned her to the last-viewed website: *Utah's Missing Persons*. Trenton's photo and basic description were now at the top of the page. She hoped to God that he wouldn't still be on there come the end of the day.

At the top of the website, Maddie clicked on a link that she had checked in on at least once a month for the past five years: *Utah's Unidentified Persons*. Fifteen unidentified human remains were on the list, dating between 1982 and 2016. Only two—occurring in 2016—could have been Michael, but their biographies and physical descriptions thankfully did not match his.

Maddie was about to pocket her cell phone when she was struck by a sudden surge of anger toward Detective Scullion. She wouldn't have been standing here right now in this nightmare of a situation, had he taken Michael's disappearance at all seriously in the first place and put in even a fraction of the resources that she had witnessed here in the past two days. She took a photo of Michael's truck with the melee of search and rescue personnel around it and texted it with a message, stating *Trenton's missing* to Clayton Tyler.

She pushed her cell phone into her pocket just as it started to ring. It was Clayton. 'Hi,' she answered.

'What's going on, Maddie?' he asked.

Maddie took a deep breath and gave him a short summary.

'Jesus,' he replied. 'Is there anything I can do for you?'

His question suddenly made her wonder why on earth she had sent him the picture. What *did* she want from him? She'd told hardly any of her friends, family or colleagues what was going on and yet, she'd just informed someone whom she barely knew. Was it a cry for his professional help?

'Maddie?' he pressed. 'You still there?'

'Yeah, still here. No. I… I don't need anything, thank you,' she said, answering his question. 'I just thought I'd let you know where I'm at and what's happening.'

'Do you want me to come down there? To help out in the search? Or just to be with you? I don't think there are any flights, but I could totally drive down there and be with you.'

Maddie felt her eyes moistening again and bit her lip, as she now realized how inappropriate it had been for her to have contacted him like this, and also how kind his offer was, given that he lived in Pennsylvania. In the two days that it would take him to get here, it would all hopefully have been resolved. 'No, it's fine. Thank you, though. I'd better go.'

'Let me know how things progress, okay? And if you change your mind—'

'Sure. Thanks,' she said, ending the call with a knot of guilt adding to the tangle of emotions that she was currently feeling.

Maddie looked over at the Incident Commander who was holding a radio away from his mouth while he spoke to two members of the search and rescue team in front of him. She watched as they hurried off and he then went back to speaking on the radio. He glanced upward, then at his watch. He put the phone away and unfurled a large map, laying it out on the hood of one of the several emergency vehicles parked on the slipway. Maddie walked quickly over toward him, sensing that there had been some kind of a development.

'Have you got him?' she asked.

He shook his head. 'Listen. I'm sorry. We're not going to get there in time.'

'What do you mean?' she demanded.

'Trenton will hit the rapids before I can get search and rescue down there,' he said bluntly, scratching the top of his head.

The way he had said 'hit' made Maddie feel like she might vomit on the spot. 'So, what are you going to do about that?'

'I've got another team getting as close to the rapids as they can by road and they're about to put a drone up.'

'Well, that's sure going to save his life, isn't it?' Maddie stammered angrily.

'It's the best I can do,' the Incident Commander replied. 'I've got teams hiking toward the rapids—including trained emergency personnel—a boat not far behind him and teams down at Indian Crossing Campground, ready to intercept right away when he gets there. If we can at least monitor his progress, then we can make better decisions about how best to help him.'

Maddie looked helplessly at the map before them as the Incident Commander's radio crackled and a female voice said that the drone had just come into sight-range of Trenton's raft approaching the rapids.

'Maybe it's best if you go and wait in your car, and I'll get someone—' the Incident Commander began.

'No chance,' Maddie interjected, moving in even closer so that she could hear the voice better on the other end of the radio.

'Target is just approaching the rapids, now,' the voice informed them.

Maddie shot a glance at the Incident Commander whose face betrayed nothing.

'Target on river-right of the rapids.'

River-right, Maddie recalled, was *a class III rapid. The strong river currents push boats hard towards the cliff wall.*

'Raft overturned. Raft overturned. Repeat. Raft overturned. Target is in the water.'

Chapter Sixteen

Saturday, April 11, 2020, Salt Lake City, Utah

'Yahoo!' Kenyatta cheered, doing a dance in her seat. She was sitting in her living room, wearing an incongruous combination of pajama bottoms and a smart work blouse. She had styled her hair and applied a little make-up. Completing the contradictory ensemble were comfortable socks and her pink fluffy slippers. She was all ready for her therapy session in twenty minutes. But for now, she was totally focused on the two emails sitting at the top of a very long line of messages, all of which required some level of attention today. The two emails in question made her clasp her hands together with outright elation.

The first was from Stephen Caraccia, the Italian genealogist, who had sent through a translation of a marriage record that she was desperate to see. She already knew the paternal side, so she skimmed down to the bride's information.

Date of wedding as reported: Promise 2-Feb-1838, Wed 4-Feb-1838
City, County, State, Country: San Giovanni, Catania, Sicily, Italy
Bride's Name: Paola Pernicano
Bride's Age: 22
Bride's Residence: Calatabiano, Catania, Sicily
Bride's Birthplace: Calatabiano, Catania, Sicily
Bride's Occupation: -
Bride's Father's Name: Vincenza Pernicano, age 52
Bride's Mother's Name: Rosa Messina, age 52

The document provided Kenyatta with a further generation that she could add to the speculative tree that she was creating for her cluster lead, Jeffrey John Dockerty. But, before she did that, she just *had* to take a look at the second email calling to her from her inbox. It was from Angela Spooner.

Dear Kenyatta

Thank you for your email regarding my DNA link to those poor boys. Sorry to have taken a few days to get back to you, I've been unwell.

When I checked the box to allow law enforcement access to my DNA, I never reckoned on it actually helping to solve a crime. I'd already made up my mind to do whatever I could to assist you, but then once I'd looked at the boys' profiles on NamUs I was totally convinced. Just heartbreaking. How can so many kids' bodies go unidentified like that? Does nobody miss them?!

I'm willing to help in any way I can, just let me know what you'd like me to do.

Your email mentioned that the boys' ethnicity pointed to Asia. One branch of my family comes from Thailand—could this be where the boys came from??

Best wishes, Angela

Tears welled in Kenyatta's eyes as she re-read the email. She replied, thanking Angela profusely, and politely asked if she would mind taking some screenshots of her ethnicity reports and also any cousin matches that Angela could connect with certainty to the Thai side of her family.

Kenyatta was suddenly feeling very optimistic about life.

She went to the kitchen and poured herself a glass of water, ignoring the craving that she was having for a Coke. She returned to the living room and pulled up the details for the rest of cluster six. She hoped that finding another person to triangulate against would be a simpler process now that she was in possession of the names of the likely common ancestral couple and their geographical location. Just one out of the five names in the cluster had a family tree which she opened to view on the FamilyTreeDNA website.

'My goodness. Look at the time!' she suddenly shrieked, noticing that her therapy session should have started two minutes ago. She quickly returned to her emails, scrolled down to the Zoom link she had been sent yesterday and joined the meeting.

'Hey, Kenyatta,' her therapist, Tabitha, greeted warmly.

'Hi, so sorry I'm late,' she apologized.

'That's no problem. How have you been since our last session?'

Kenyatta thought for a moment. 'You know, it's been a strange week. Workwise, everything is going really well. In fact, I'm deputizing for my boss for a few days, and that's...uh...'—she struggled to find the right way to describe how work made her feel—'giving life a busy and time-consuming flipside.'

'Okay,' Tabitha said. 'And on the other side?'

'Well, obviously Otis. He won't let me see the kids because of my work with the homeless. My lawyer has advised to not do anything at the moment that might jeopardize the court hearing that's in less than two weeks. In fact, him keeping them away from me could play in my favor...or so I'm told.'

'Right. And have you had any contact with your children at all? Any phone calls? Text messages?'

'Luckily, they've all got their own cell phones, so I hear from them fairly regularly. Gabe messaged me on Monday to say that the family dog of twelve years was killed by some lunatic, which was horrible to hear.'

'Sorry to hear that. I imagine that's made your week much harder?' Tabitha asked.

'It all got too much for me and I ended up crying on the phone to a friend...which was a little embarrassing.'

'Is this one of your close friends that you've talked about before with me?'

Kenyatta shook her head. 'No. This is a guy from the SLC Homeless Kitchen.'

'Okay. So why did you choose him to unburden to?'

The question flummoxed Kenyatta.

Hudson Édouard was sitting once again outside the Family History Library with his laptop resting on his thighs. This time, he'd brought a cushion from home and had a coffee in his hand, which he'd managed to buy from a grocery store en route, to help keep out the cold. He'd been here for two hours so far, borrowing the Wi-Fi from inside the building to access the library records. Truth be told, he didn't need to be here at all; the documents that he was currently working on were all available online from home, but that was the one place where he couldn't face being right now. His relationship with Abigail was at an all-time low and they were currently scarcely speaking. When he had arrived home on Thursday, they'd had a big fight and Abigail had refused point-blank to transfer the fifty thousand dollars back into their joint account, ready for him to return to Wanda Chabala. Hudson had then dropped the bombshell that he wasn't feeling certain that he wanted to proceed with an adoption after all. As he had expected, Abigail had been devastated by the news, but she still refused to hand over the money and they were now at an anguished stalemate.

Hudson checked the time again. He had just under an hour until he needed to walk over to Pioneer Park and meet with Wanda Chabala and her husband, Warren Mercaldo. He felt sick about the meeting but tried to switch it off and concentrate on the other task in hand: trying to find at least one other person from within cluster three who triangulated with Valerie Kerouac and the killer. His gut told him to look at Valerie's Sicilian ancestors for that link.

With the names of the other seven men and women from the cluster jotted down on a notepad beside him, Hudson logged in at the FamilyTreeDNA website, where he accessed the killer's cousin matches. From that list, he selected Valerie Kerouac's name, then checked the *In Common With* box beside it. The seven cousin matches appeared at the top of a long list, all of them likely descended from the same person or couple. Hudson scanned down the list, looking for shortcuts. None had an attached tree and none had an Italian-sounding name, so he selected the one with the next highest amount of shared DNA, a person by the name of Alexandra Cripps. Her profile contained only the minimum amount of required information: her email address.

Hudson opened the BeenVerified website and under the *Email Search* tab, he pasted in Alexandra Cripps's Gmail address. A few seconds later, the background-check company produced a list of associated data. The website was usually accurate, but not always, and the amount of information it contained varied considerably from search to search. The results suggested that Alexandra Cripps had been born in November 1975. Various addresses and phone numbers were listed, all pointing to her life being based in New York City.

Before Hudson moved on, he created a new speculative tree with Alexandra Cripps as the home person. Even though the information was as of yet unverified, he added the suggested birth date of

November 1975. Then, he returned to BeenVerified, moving down the page and clicking on *Social Media*. The only associated account listed was an Instagram profile which he clicked to view. He was pleased to see that Alexandra was a particularly prolific poster of photographs on the site, varying from what appeared to be nights out with friends, social events, pictures of young children and some old photos that Hudson hoped might yield some useful genealogical information.

The most recent image, posted two days ago, was a picture of Alexandra centered between two women of a similar age. They were dressed smartly and appeared to be standing outside of a bar or restaurant. The caption beside the photo read, *Best night out with my girls!* Various people had liked and commented on the photo, but it contained no genealogical data that Hudson could harvest. He clicked the arrow to the right of the photo to see the next image; this was of a young boy looking up at a police officer with the Statue of Liberty in the immediate background. The picture had a haziness to it and, when combined with the outdated fashion of the boy and the police officer, it suggested to Hudson that the photo had been taken some twenty or thirty years ago. The caption read, *Happy birthday, benny boy! This is where it all started!* Someone named Ben Cripps was tagged, and Hudson clicked through to view his profile. Benny Boy was now a serving officer in the New York police. Other people had posted with various comments, one of which said, *Next year, the Big 4-0!*

Hudson noted down Ben's name and a possible birth date of 1981. His working assumption was that Alexandra and Ben could be siblings.

The next photo was of a park or garden, just the sky and some flowers. It had lots of likes and a few positive comments but, again, nothing that helped Hudson.

He clicked on and then smiled. It was a photo of a funeral program. In the center was a picture of an old lady, surrounded by superimposed pink roses. Some text below the image showed it to be titled, *In Loving Memory of Barbara Cripps*. Alexandra's accompanying caption for the image read: *A year ago today our hearts were broken the only consolation is that you're with grandpa again after 30 years apart we love you grandma.*

Hudson went to the GenealogyBank website and ran an obituary search for Barbara Cripps, filtering the search down to 2019. There was just one result, and that was found in *The Buffalo News*, dated April 16, 2019. From the date and location, Hudson was almost certain that it was the correct person. He clicked to read the full obit.

CRIPPS-Barbara of Greece, NY, April 11, 2019. Barbara was predeceased by her husband, William A. Cripps; parents, Edith and Paul Burke Sr.; brother Paul Burke Jr. and sister, Lorraine Dalton. She is survived by her son, Richard Cripps and his children, Alexandra, James and Benjamin; her daughter, Michelle and her daughter, Carol Ann; great-grandchildren, Antony and William; extended family of cousins, nieces and nephews. Barbara was born in Buffalo, NY and resided in Rochester for over 30 years...

The obit went on to detail Barbara's life story, but for the moment, Hudson had a whole trove of genealogical information that he could now add to Alexandra Cripps's speculative tree. For now, though, there was still no sign of any familiar surnames which might connect Alexandra to Valerie Kerouac.

Hudson spent some time adding the new names to the tree, researching them and checking out the hints that Ancestry suggested. When he had the names of all four of Alexandra Cripps's grandparents and several great-grandparents, he ran some searches in the family trees that the public had uploaded to Ancestry, MyHeritage, FindmyPast and WikiTree. At the latter website, Hudson found what he had hoped to find: a tree for Alexandra's grandfather, William Cripps. The tree, complete with detailed source information, listed his father as David Cripps, born in New York and his mother as Giosepa Romano, born in Sicily.

Hudson couldn't help but grin widely when he saw the names of her parents: Augustu Romano and Valentina Randazzo from Calatabiano, Catania in Sicily. Valerie Kerouac's great-great-great-grandfather had been called Silvestra Randazzo from Calatabiano. Although WikiTree didn't go beyond Valentina Randazzo, Hudson was certain that, judging by the date of her birth, she would prove to be a daughter of Silvestra. He just needed to get her birth record from FamilySearch and have it translated to confirm.

'Do you think they'd mind that this has become our office?' a voice that Hudson recognized asked, seemingly out of nowhere.

He looked across to see that Reggie had arrived and was now sitting a few feet away on the wall, opening up his laptop with a broad smile and pointing toward the library behind them. 'They're very forgiving people,' Hudson answered. 'I'm sure they'll be okay with it.'

'Did you get anywhere with your bambino?' Reggie asked.

It took Hudson a moment to realize what he was talking about. 'Oh, yeah. I got a translation, and it looks like I'm working along the right lines.'

'Well, that's good to hear, man.'

Hudson pulled up the FamilySearch website, returning to the now-familiar Research Wiki page for Catania in Sicily, when he noticed the time. 'Oh, God. I'm going to be late. What is it with time, these days?' he said, more for Reggie's benefit than his own, as he hurriedly stowed his laptop and notepad in his bag. 'Nothing personal. I gotta run. See you back here at the office at some point, I'm sure.'

'Hey. Black coffee with one sugar, next time,' Reggie called after him.

Hudson turned, smiled at him and put on his face mask. As he walked away, the enormity of what was about to happen washed over him and he suddenly felt nauseous. Every time he had tried to prepare himself mentally, or rehearse what he might say, a crippling haze had entered his brain. He was sure that, when he came face-to-face with Wanda and Warren, he'd end up saying very little that was intelligible.

It took twenty minutes for Hudson to get to the closest entrance of Pioneer Park. No specific meeting point had been discussed, so he paused to look around. The park was one block square, each side lined with skeletal trees. On the far side were tennis courts and a kids' playground, not exactly where he might expect to find Wanda and Warren waiting for him.

He decided to take the path which crossed diagonally near to the center of the park, where he would get a better view of the whole place.

As he strode on, Hudson felt quite breathless and his heart began to race. He pulled his face mask down, took some deeper, deliberate breaths and slowed his pace. Taking an extra minute to locate them was hardly going to change anything.

Then he saw them. They were sitting unmasked on a bench not far away, facing in his direction. Wanda raised a hand to him but did not offer a smile. Warren just stared, watching him draw closer.

Hudson pulled up his face mask again, but then realized that they wouldn't be able to see him smiling, so, instead, he greeted them with an over-the-top, 'Hi!'

'Hudson, this is my husband, Warren Mercaldo,' Wanda introduced him perfunctorily.

Warren nodded his head once but said nothing, continuing his steady stare at Hudson. He was a tall, beefy, no-nonsense kind of guy, and any vague notions that Hudson might have entertained about moving to accuse either him or his brother of being the ones who had killed Francesca Chabala evaporated instantly. It suddenly dawned on Hudson that he was standing just a few feet away from someone who could well have been a rapist and murderer. He fought the strong temptation to take a few precautionary steps back.

'How are you?' he asked Wanda in a feeble voice.

'Honestly?' she said. 'I'm getting kind of desperate now.' She was as well-dressed as she had been the last time that he had seen her, wearing an expensive-looking coat, gold earrings with her curly, black hair styled neatly to her shoulders. She stared at him…waiting.

'I can understand that,' Hudson said.

'Oh, *your* daughter was raped and murdered, huh?' Warren barked brusquely without warning. 'Well, poor you.'

Hudson looked at him. 'No… I just meant that I understood—'

'My wife doesn't want your understanding. She wants the answers that she paid you to get,' he said icily.

'Have you found him?' Wanda demanded.

Hudson shook his head. He was about to give the standard spiel that Maddie would give out to the detectives whom she was unable to help at a given moment because the DNA matches simply hadn't been strong enough…but changed his mind. 'I can't find him. I'll return all the money.'

'How kind of you,' Warren said, revealing a slight snarl. 'Told you it was a waste of time.'

'Why can't you find him?' Wanda asked, ignoring her husband. 'What's the problem? Is it the quality of the DNA? I can get a hold of more if that's the issue.'

'No, it's not the DNA. It's inconclusive,' he said, taking a quick glance at Warren. 'I can't give you one person's name and that's the bottom line, here.'

Hudson watched as Wanda visibly changed. Her previous upright posture sagged as she exhaled at length. He could only imagine what was going through her mind and he had every sympathy. He glanced again at Warren, not seeing any obvious change in his disposition.

'What do I need to do?' she said, emotion rising in her voice. 'Just tell me.'

'We have several cold cases in our office that are waiting on the shelves, currently unsolved, but we're certain that one day we'll crack them. It will just take the right person to come along and take a consumer DNA test, upload it to one of the websites we use, and then we'll be able to solve it.'

'So, you're telling me to be patient, is that it?' Wanda said. 'To sit back and do nothing.'

Warren sighed, looked down toward the ground and then cracked his knuckles.

'I'm saying that I can't help you,' Hudson answered.

Wanda turned to her husband, placed her manicured hand onto his black jeans, and said, 'Go and get the car.'

For a brief moment, Hudson panicked and wondered if he was about to be bundled into the back of it and taken God knows where for a beating.

Warren stood up and glared at Hudson, before following her instruction and striding away apace.

Wanda watched him leave.

'I'd better be going,' Hudson said, realizing that his life wasn't in any danger after all. 'I'm so sorry.'

Wanda stood up and grabbed his arm tightly. 'You think it's him, don't you?' she asked, nodding her head toward her husband's disappearing figure.

'What?' Hudson said, shocked at how she could possibly have reached that conclusion based on what he had just said.

'You think my husband raped and killed his own stepdaughter?'

He couldn't tell from her flat tone what she was feeling. 'What makes you say that?' he countered tentatively.

'You're not the first genetic genealogist I've employed to look into this. The last one told me that the DNA was good, plenty of matches on FamilyTreeDNA, the closest being four hundred and twenty-two centimorgans. Then suddenly—' she stopped and went quiet '—exactly as you've done…she handed me back all the money and said she couldn't solve it. Of course, I took her at her word and moved on to you. Now, you look me in the eyes, and you tell me you were not able to identify a single suspect.'

Hudson felt sympathetic and met her gaze. 'I identified two suspects…'

'Go on.'

'Warren and Jackson Mercaldo,' he blurted out.

Wanda took in a sharp, shocked intake of breath, clearly taken aback. 'Warren…*and* Jackson…?'

Hudson nodded. 'DNA can't distinguish between full siblings.'

Wanda raised her hands to her mouth as she looked over in the general direction that Warren had walked. Thankfully, there was now no sign of him. 'How am I to find out which of them was responsible?'

'Either or both of the men need DNA-testing and you've got to get law enforcement to get their samples into CODIS; that will reveal the true identity of your daughter's murderer.'

'And how do I go about doing that?' she asked.

'Listen, I'm way out of my depth on this one,' he replied. 'I never should have taken the case on. You need to speak with your lawyers or contact Crime Stoppers or… I'm just not sure.'

Wanda held his hand in hers and looked him in the eyes. 'You're one hundred percent certain that it was Warren or Jackson—*my* Warren and Jackson—not some weird coincidence that their names are just the same?'

'I'm certain,' Hudson answered. 'But a final CODIS check would confirm it for you.'

A car horn blared loudly from the side of the park and Wanda let go of Hudson's hand as they both looked over to see a white SUV waiting for her beside the road.

'Thank you, Hudson,' she said softly. 'I appreciate how hard this must have been for you.'

'I'll return the money,' he said with false confidence, not knowing how he could really get it back from Abigail or, even possibly by now, the adoption agency.

'No. Keep it,' she insisted. 'You did exactly what I asked you to do.'

'But...' he began, watching as she walked over toward the very man who may well have raped and murdered her daughter.

It wasn't yet a good outcome for Brandon Blake or Francesca Chabala, but things had been taken out of his hands now, and his earlier decision had been rendered immaterial, all of which made for a better outcome for him at least.

Hudson removed his mask and breathed out, feeling the weight of the world sliding from his shoulders.

Becky Larkin was sitting at the breakfast bar, nibbling at a piece of buttered toast, feeling nervous. Late last night, she and Ross had tracked down phone numbers for Artemon Bruce and Jay Craig, the two guys who had been working with Michael Barnhart immediately prior to his death. Becky hadn't phoned them yet because—as she had insisted to Ross—by the time they had found the correct people, it had been too late to call. She now realized that fear had been the driving force of her procrastination. Her investigations into her father's business were about to cross a very serious line. If he should get wind of it, she knew that she would never see him or her mother again, and she would likely be turned out of her apartment which was not hers, but was owned by her parents. But she could not stop her inquiries; she owed that to Maddie, if nothing else. Besides, after what Lois Strange had accused her father of, Becky had a heartfelt need to find some tangible evidence that he wasn't the villain in this story. She was still clinging to the hope that a perfectly rational explanation existed for the decision to gag his employees and that Michael's disappearance had nothing to do with him or his business.

Ross appeared in the doorway with a white bath towel wrapped around his waist. 'What did they say?' he asked, entering the kitchen.

'Not much…because I didn't actually call them yet,' she answered. 'I will do it after my breakfast.'

Ross raised his eyebrows. 'You've been eating one piece of toast for like an hour. Just call them and get it over with already.'

'I will. I will. Just stop hassling me,' she snapped, standing up and carrying her plate over to the sink. She slunk past him out of the kitchen and entered the guest bedroom, closing the door behind her.

Becky picked up the yellow legal pad upon which she had written all the details of the two men who'd been working on the Haiti-based finance project with Michael Barnhart. She closed her eyes for a few seconds, trying to clear her mind. Then she tapped the first of the two numbers into her cell phone and hit the green circle to connect a call to Artemon Bruce's home phone.

'Hello?' a female voice answered.

'Hi there. Could I speak with Artemon Bruce, please?' Becky asked.

'May I ask, who's calling?' she asked.

'My name's Becky Larkin,' she responded, uncertain of how much truth she should divulge at this stage. She had no intention of misleading or lying but also didn't want to give too much away too soon.

'Okay… And what do you want with Artemon?' The woman sounded terse, a little defensive maybe.

Becky felt that she had no option now but to give the full truth upfront. 'My father is Andrew Larkin, the owner of the company your husband works for. I need some information about someone who worked on a finance project with Artemon, a man called Michael Barnhart.'

The line went dead.

'Hello? Hello?' Becky said, looking at the screen to verify that the call had indeed been disconnected. She clicked *Recents* and dialed the number back. The call went straight to voicemail. 'Hi, this is Becky Larkin. I'm not sure what just happened, there. Reception, maybe. But, if you could get Artemon to give me a call back, I'd really appreciate it.

Thank you.'

Becky dialed the number for the other man. Once again, a female voice answered. 'Hi there. Could I speak with Jay Craig, please?'

There was a short pause. 'Um, I'm sorry. He passed away a few years ago. Can I ask who's calling?'

'Oh, I'm so sorry,' Becky said. 'My name is Becky Larkin. My father is the owner and CEO of The Larkin Investment and Finance Group.'

'Okay… Then, surely you knew that my husband had died?'

'No, I'm so sorry. I did not. I'm trying to get some information. I believe your late husband worked with Michael Barnhart on a project, right before Michael disappeared in 2015?'

Another pause. 'Right…'

'I was just wondering if you knew anything about what he was working on with Michael at that time?'

'And are you phoning on behalf of your father?' she countered.

'No, not at all,' Becky replied. 'In fact, he doesn't know that I'm reaching out, and if he did… Well, let's just say, it wouldn't go down too well. I work with Michael's wife, Maddie, and we're trying to find answers as to what happened to Michael.' Becky waited for the woman to speak, but when she didn't, Becky continued anyway. 'Apparently my father placed a gag order on employees, preventing them from talking to the police who were trying to find out what happened to Michael, and I just want to understand why he did that. Anything you can help with will be treated with complete confidentiality; I can assure you.'

'How do I know that?'

The question surprised Becky. 'Why wouldn't it be?'

The answer of silence spoke volumes.

'Have you been threatened by my father or one of his employees?' Becky asked.

'I'm sorry, but I can't help you. Jay preferred to keep his work life and our family life as two entirely separate worlds: I didn't ask what he was up to; and he didn't tell me. Now he's gone, and I can't offer you anything. Sorry.'

The call ended and Becky was left feeling completely perplexed.

She left the guest room, finding Ross watching TV in the living room.

'Sorry for snapping before,' she apologized.

Ross paused the TV and smiled. 'I forgive you, darling wife.'

'Thanks,' she said, slumping down beside him. He placed his arm around her as she began to relay what had just happened. 'So… I just tried calling Artemon Bruce and Jay Craig, right?'

'Oh, God. I feel there's a story coming, here,' Ross commented.

'Yeah. A woman answered Artemon's phone, asking who I was, and when I explained, she hung up on me. Another woman also answered Jay Craig's phone, and when I explained to her who I was, she said she couldn't help me, as he was dead, and she then hung up as well.'

Ross drew back in surprise. 'That's a little weird, don't you think?'

'Yeah… It did feel weird. Both women were *really* defensive and *really* didn't want to talk to me…'

'But why?' Ross asked.

Becky shrugged and leaned forward on the sofa. 'I'm going to do some more digging. Try and find another way to contact Artemon Bruce, since he seems to be the only one left alive, who worked on this Haiti project.'

'Need help with that?

'Always,' she answered with a wry smile. 'I'm going back to basics on him: I'll take background checks; you take social media.'

'You've got it,' he said, heading over to the breakfast bar where he proceeded to open his laptop.

Becky returned to the guest room and picked up her laptop. She paused in front of the photographs of the four murdered victims of the Twin Falls killer. 'I won't be long,' she whispered to them and left, carrying the laptop to the kitchen where she then hopped up onto the stool beside Ross.

'Facebook and Twitter were easy enough,' Ross commented. 'Not one Artemon Bruce. Trying Instagram and TikTok, next…'

Becky ran background searches through Spokeo, TruthFinder, MyLife and BeenVerified. First, she accessed Artemon Bruce's work history, finding a lengthy career in various financial institutions, culminating in The Larkin Investment and Finance Group from 2011 to the present day.

'Nope. Nothing on Insta or TikTok,' Ross muttered. 'Snapchat next.'

Someone born in 1969 with a solid background in finance didn't seem a likely candidate to have a Snapchat profile, Becky thought, but anything to track him down was worth a try.

Under the *Relatives* option at BeenVerified, only one person was listed: Jackie Bruce. Becky wondered if that had been the person with whom she had spoken; that being most likely his wife.

'No Snapchat profile,' Ross confirmed. 'LinkedIn next.'

Becky continued looking into Artemon's work history.

Seconds later, Ross exclaimed, 'Got him!'

Becky craned her neck to see his laptop. A LinkedIn profile for Artemon Bruce was on-screen. His profile photo was clearly a professional headshot. He was sitting at a quarter-turn, looking at the camera with a fixed smile. His short dark hair, with flecks of gray, was well-trimmed and his suit looked smart. Below his name was a short job description: *Overseas Finance Director at The Larkin Investment and Finance Group.*

'Typically vague,' Becky commented.

'This is weird,' Ross said, using that word again to describe the situation. He scrolled down the page. 'His last post on here was back in 2015, and prior to that he was fairly prolific, posting every other day, by the looks of it. You don't think…'

'I'm on it,' Becky said, intuiting his thoughts. She opened up Newspapers.com and ran a search for Artemon Bruce. Various articles came up, mainly to do with sponsorship deals, but the most recent was the one that Becky clicked to view. 'Jesus.'

Finance Director death investigation
The investigation into the June 22, 2015 death of Artemon Bruce has ruled that the deceased died by his own hand. Artemon Bruce, 47 of Summit Creek, disappeared from home on June 16 and his body was found 4 days later in a bedroom in the Hampton Inn across the state border in Rock Springs, Wyoming. A hotel maid found Bruce's lifeless body on the afternoon of June 22 when he failed to check out of his room. He was discovered in the bathtub, where Bruce had

apparently cut his wrists. The Sweetwater County Medical Examiner and Coroner ruled Mr. Bruce's death suicide.

'So, he's dead, too?' Ross mumbled. 'How did Jay Craig die, exactly?'

'One way to find out,' Becky said, opening a new tab and running a search in the same database. She clicked the top result, and together they read the short article in silence.

Dec.21, 2015, Reno, Nevada
Jay Craig, a finance assistant for a company based in Salt Lake City, was found dead in the trunk of his rental car in a parking lot at Reno-Tahoe International Airport. Police are asking for witnesses to come forward.

'Wow...' Becky said, looking aghast at Ross.

'That's an amazing coincidence, don't you think?' he said. 'The three people who all worked together on this mysterious project in Haiti all died or disappeared within, what, a few months of each other?'

'Small wonder those two women didn't want to talk with me...'

'Are you going to share this with Maddie?' Ross asked.

Becky sighed. Whatever Maddie was currently going through, the last thing that she needed to hear right now was that two of Michael's close colleagues had wound up dead around the same time that he had disappeared. No. Becky needed more information about the Haiti project, but she had no real idea of how she was going to get a hold of it.

Maddie was sitting outside her son's room in a private waiting area of the Gunnison Valley Hospital to which Trenton had been rushed, following his rafting accident yesterday. Under the surveillance cameras of an overhead drone, his boat had hit the Red Creek Rapids and flipped over. For several long seconds, there had been no sight of him, only his empty raft continuing downriver, all the while being buffeted around. The wait for any news or information from the Incident Commander had been absolutely agonizing, made much worse by the fact that none of the search and rescue teams had been anywhere near

139

him; only the useless drone, passively watching everything unfolding thirty feet below. He'd only been under the water for a matter of seconds but to Maddie it had felt like several minutes.

'Target is up,' a voice on the radio had finally said. 'Target is gripping a rock, hanging on against the flow.'

It had been a long while since Maddie had prayed, but at that moment, she had closed her eyes and asked for Trenton to be given the strength to hold on until help arrived.

The news over the radio had been desperately slow to arrive and Maddie had several times begged the Incident Commander to request a further update.

'They'll tell me when there's something to say,' he had repeatedly told her. 'If there's nothing to say, then it means Trenton is still okay. The situation won't have changed. One major thing in his favor is that he's wearing a life vest.'

Maddie had considered taking issue with his use of the word *okay* but then had thought better of it.

Moments later, the search and rescue team on horseback had caught up to him and successfully hauled him out of the water.

Although he had suffered no obvious injuries, and he hadn't been under the water for very long, he had been suffering from hypothermia and been taken to the Gunnison Valley Hospital for treatment and observation.

Maddie now checked the time on her cell phone: 4:26 p.m. There was still a possibility that Trenton would be discharged today. She had not slept and not showered in days, despite the doctors informing her that Trenton was in no danger and that she could go check herself in at a nearby hotel. But she wanted to be here, just in case.

She unlocked her phone and stared at all the little red notifications beside the text, Messenger and email apps. She hadn't been able to face any of them before. The only people whom she'd really kept up to date with how things were going, down here, were her two daughters, Jenna, her eldest, and Nikki who was managing to hold everything together back home. Jenna had been poised to get herself somehow from Florida to Utah, until Maddie's firm insistence and the apparent lack of flights had convinced her to stay put.

She looked at the Venator message thread, feeling so far outside of the loop with regard to the latest investigation, but knowing that the team would be working hard in her absence; harder probably. She typed out a short message.

Hi all. I'm so sorry for the radio silence. I'll fill you in with all the details later, but Trenton has been found alive and well. Catch up with you all on Monday. Maddie

She sent the message, then began replying to other concerned friends and family. After twenty minutes, she was up to date with her texts and messages, but, according to the goading red and white notifications, she still had 162 unopened emails to deal with. Now was not the time, she thought, pocketing her cell.

Maddie exhaled loudly, stood up and paced over to the small window as she had done many times in the past twenty-four hours. The waiting room looked out over a tiny parking lot behind the hospital canteen, where nothing changed from one moment to the next. Just a bunch of cars. She turned back into the bland room and exhaled again. There was nothing here but a water cooler, a fake plant and two lumpy chairs.

Underneath one of the chairs was Trenton's backpack that had also been pulled from the river by the search and rescue team. She took the bag out from under the chair and crouched down over it. She recognized it as being one of Michael's old ones from the garage. She unfastened the straps and slid back the waterproof zipper. Tentatively placing her hand inside, Maddie could feel that the contents—so far, just Trenton's clothes—were bone dry. She felt a flashlight, distress flare, several empty chip bags, a container of some kind, box of matches and a book. At least he had gone prepared.

Maddie went to stand up from her crouching position but immediately became light-headed and started to tumble backward. She reached out for the rucksack, but that wasn't enough to hold her as she rolled onto her back, flat out on the floor.

Maddie lay there for a moment, then began to laugh at what on earth she must have looked like. The emotions of the past few days overwhelmed her, and she found her laughter morphing into sobbing.

She was crying for what had almost happened to Trenton and from sheer relief at what had not.

A quick knock on the door was followed by a nurse entering the room. She was instantly shocked to see Maddie lying on the ground, crying now hysterically. 'Oh, my gosh. Are you hurt, ma'am?' She glanced over to locate the emergency button that the room had on the wall.

Maddie grinned, appearing to be some deranged lunatic. 'I'm fine, thank you. Really, I am. I just tried to stand too quickly and fell right over.'

'Okay,' the nurse said, offering Maddie a hand to help her up. 'If you're sure… I came to inform you that Trenton has just been discharged; you're free to take him home.'

'Thank you so much,' Maddie said, crying again. 'And sorry about that.' She pointed at the floor and noticed that the top half of Trenton's rucksack contents had spilled out onto the floor. 'Lovely. My son's dirty underwear,' she said, stuffing the clothing back inside the bag.

'No need to apologize,' the nurse said. 'I'll leave you and go tell Trenton that you're coming shortly.'

'Thank you.' Maddie pushed a pair of sweaty socks into the bag and then noticed that the book that had fallen out wasn't a book at all. It was a journal of some kind. She knew it wasn't her right to pry but, given what Trenton had put her through these past days, she gave herself permission to open it, nonetheless.

She began flicking through. The contents immediately surprised her: beginning from the moment when he had arrived in Green River, it was a meticulous analysis of the possible scenarios that could have befallen Michael. He'd documented all the walking routes out of the slipway and drawn maps of where each led. He'd noted the conditions of the paths and the kinds of plants and trees that might impede movement. He'd made careful notes about the water temperature and depth as he'd moved downriver. He'd listed the major roads nearby and the close proximity of Dutch John Airport. He'd listed all the campgrounds within a ten-mile radius and their opening hours and various facilities.

Right at the back of the book was a page, titled *Theories*. Below it, Trenton had scribbled notes on several potential scenarios, offering evidence for each and scoring them a likelihood rating out of ten.

Banged his head / amnesia / no memory of former life. Does this ever happen except in the movies? 0/10 (mom's rating 10/10)
Got lost walking in the wilderness. Dad was smart and always prepared. He had provisions, water and a cell phone. 0/10
Eaten by a bear / attacked by wildlife. As above: Dad was smart and always went prepared! He carried a knife, knew to keep food and toothpaste, etc. away from where he slept. Where are his remains? 1/10
Got caught in the rapids and drowned. Dad knew that river well and knew how to navigate rapids. He was an excellent swimmer and always wore a life vest. Where's the body? 2/10

Maddie found that her hands were quivering as she read the final entry.

Foul play: someone attacked and overpowered him. Several possible scenarios. Since a fingerprint was found on the trunk catch, most likely is that he was bundled into the back of his own truck and driven off somewhere close by, then the truck was returned to the slipway. Where did they take him? Dead or alive? 9/10

Chapter Seventeen

Sunday, April 12, 2020, Salt Lake City, Utah

Although Kenyatta was missing her friends at the City Presbyterian Church, today she was kind of glad that she couldn't attend even if she'd wanted to. The church pastors had organized for something they had aptly named *Virchurchal Praise* which was currently playing in a background tab on her laptop. She was only half-listening to it as she sat in bed, sipping coffee. Angela Spooner had replied to Kenyatta's email, but instead of supplying the requested screenshots, she had handed over her MyHeritage username and password to Kenyatta, telling her that she could log in to do whatever she needed to do. It was far from usual practice to be given access like this, but Kenyatta deemed it her only viable option right now. She intended to go in, just the once, and take screenshots and details of everything that she needed.

Having logged in, Kenyatta navigated to Angela Spooner's family tree, easily locating her great-great-grandparents, Arthit and Preeda Tang, who had both been born in Khao Wang, Thailand. Kenyatta spent some time creating a new family tree for the couple within the Venator account. Although she didn't yet have any firm evidence to support her hypothesis, Kenyatta was certain that the *Boys under the Bridge* would somehow be related to this branch of Angela Spooner's family. Only once she had copied across all the details that she felt she might need did Kenyatta switch to analyzing Angela's DNA. She clicked on *DNA Matches*, finding that Angela had 6,728 people genetically related to her. But what Kenyatta needed to find was at least one of those people who also descended from Arthit and Preeda Tang.

Kenyatta started by filtering the DNA matches by ethnicity. She scrolled down the list and chose *Thai and Cambodian*. The top cousin match from the filtered list of 257 names was a woman named Kanda Phasuk. According to the website, they shared 89.3 centimorgans of DNA.

Kenyatta was filled with hope when she spotted the words below Kanda Phasuk's name. *Appears in a family tree with 2034 people that she manages.* Clicking on *View tree,* Kenyatta was taken to a pedigree view of Kanda's ancestors. She grinned when she saw that Arthit and Preeda Tang were listed as Kanda Phasuk's great-great-grandparents.

Returning to the previous page, Kenyatta scrolled down to the bottom, where the 22 chromosomes were set out as horizontal gray lines, getting shorter as they descended. Highlighted on three of the chromosomes were the purple rectangles that showed where Angela Spooner and Kanda Phasuk shared their DNA. Kenyatta needed a way to triangulate this data with the boys but, right now, she couldn't, as Kanda hadn't transferred her kit to GEDmatch, and Kenyatta was prohibited from uploading the boys' DNA to MyHeritage. Running a search within *Shared Matches* was pointless if Kenyatta didn't know for certain that Kanda Phasuk definitely was related to the boys.

She typed out an email to Angela.

Dear Angela
Thank you so much for allowing me to access your account. It has been really useful. I think we're on to something with the Thai side of your family. To be more certain, it would really help to have someone else descended from Arthit and Preeda Tang have their DNA in GEDmatch. You have a third cousin on the website called Kanda Phasuk who also shares Arthit and Preeda Tang as their great-great-grandparents. May I have your permission to contact her and explain the case?
Kind regards,
Kenyatta

She sent the email, then thought about her options. She could spend the entire day, or week, or month working on Angela Spooner's tree, as she had done with Elborn Nodecker, aimlessly adding names to a giant tree in the hope that a miracle might occur along the way; or she could take the sensible option and wait for Angela to reply. Having a third person to triangulate with would cut her research work down immensely and give her a definite set of common ancestors from which to work. As much as it pained her, it was time to switch off from the boys.

She picked up her cell phone and sent a morning greeting text to each of her three sons. She was missing them terribly and told them so.

She hadn't liked to upset them further by asking how they were all dealing with Dougie's death, but the most recent text that she'd had from Jon said that he was really missing him. Despite Kenyatta directly asking him, Troy had said nothing at all about Dougie's death, which made her wonder if he was internalizing his grief for the poor animal. Maybe she should suggest that he talk to someone about it, she considered, thinking about her own therapy session yesterday. She'd worked hard unpacking a lot with Tabitha but found herself being defensive over questions about the nature of her relationship with Jim.

'Is he someone you would consider dating?' Tabitha had asked her during their Zoom therapy session yesterday.

Kenyatta had laughed. 'Dating Jim?'

'Yes.'

'No,' she'd replied, a little too curtly.

'Why not?'

'Because…' Kenyatta had tried to explain but had been unable to form the end of the sentence. In the end, she'd managed to say, 'Because I hardly know anything about the man.'

Tabitha had shrugged. 'That's what dating's for; that's the point.'

'But I don't want to date,' Kenyatta had said flatly.

'Listen, I don't *need* you to go on a date with him, or anyone else, I'm just curious why you're holding him at arm's length from this therapy session…and yet, he was the one person in your life that you picked up the phone and called when you were in distress.'

'Can't he just be a friend?' Kenyatta had defended. 'Would you have asked me to date him if he'd been a woman?'

'As I said, I'm not asking you to date him, Kenyatta; I'm trying to gauge where he sits in your life. If you see more possibility with him than mere friendship, then that could have implications—positive and negative—for your own wellbeing and mental health.'

'Can we move on to something else, please?' Kenyatta had asked.

'Of course.'

The therapy had left Kenyatta feeling rattled. It had also been the first time that a session hadn't ended with her feeling lighter and more able to deal with her problems.

Setting her laptop to one side, Kenyatta climbed out of bed and looked out of her bedroom window into her small yard. Why *had* she been so defensive about Jim? Was it about him in particular? Or was it just the idea of dating anyone again? The very idea of sitting down in a restaurant or someplace, getting to know someone new, was outright terrifying. Plus, there was no space in her life right now for anyone else. She had deliberately and consciously filled the gap that Otis and the kids had left in her life with her work commitments.

She looked at the time. In a little over two hours' time, she was supposed to be taking a shift with the SLC Homeless Kitchen downtown. Jim would very likely be there. She picked up her cell phone and texted the organizer to say that she wasn't feeling well and wouldn't be coming in, today.

Kenyatta went to the kitchen, poured herself an orange juice, then headed back to bed where she began to work on triangulating within her cluster on the Twin Falls case. If she couldn't work on the *Boys under the Bridge* case and didn't want to volunteer at the soup kitchens today, then she was determined that she was going to find the common ancestors that linked her genetic network together.

Abigail was sitting in the living room bawling her eyes out. Hudson placed his arm over her shoulder, but she shrugged it off. 'Don't,' she warned him.

'You can keep the money,' he repeated.

She glowered at him. 'And what, tell the adoption agency that I'm going ahead *by myself?*'

Hudson shrugged. 'I don't know…'

'What do you mean, *you don't know?*' she stammered. 'My husband is living here with me, but only *I* am adopting the baby… How would that sound? What do you want, Hudson? A divorce? You want out, is that it?'

'No,' he answered, hearing in his cadence that he didn't fully believe his own reply. 'I'm just not sure, right now, about adopting. It's a separate issue from our marriage.'

'Not for me, it isn't. This is what I wanted—we've both wanted—and talked about since the day we met. I don't understand what's changed…'

'I can't explain it,' he began. 'It just doesn't feel right at this moment in time. Maybe it's just with what's going on in the world. I mean, Jesus, Abigail, we can't even go to a restaurant or see our friends.'

'That's just an excuse, Hudson, and you know it is. Besides, you don't get a baby sent out by return mail once you've sent in the application; it can take up to a year, as you well know.'

'Abigail, I don't want to upset you, but I—'

'Too late, Hudson. You've ripped out my heart.'

Her words devastated him.

She glanced up and said, 'You can be the one to tell the adoption agency that you've changed your mind. I'm not doing it.'

'Abigail, I just—'

'Leave me alone,' she blurted.

Hudson knew better than to push. He stood up and left the room, returning to his bedroom. He closed the door and exhaled, wishing that he could express his feelings better. But how could he when he didn't understand them fully himself? All he knew was that, deep down, he did not want to adopt a child right now. *Was* it the pandemic? Was he just getting cold feet now that the moment to apply had arrived? Was it Abigail? Or did he just not want kids after all? He didn't know and the constant self-analysis was draining him.

He sat at his computer and checked his emails. Close to the top was an automated message from the adoption agency saying that they had received their application. He stared at it, then hit delete. He should contact them and tell them to pause their application process, but right now he just couldn't face taking that giant step forward. Later.

The next email was the translation of Valentina Randazzo's birth record that he had been waiting for from Stephen Caraccia. He clicked to open it.

City, County, State, Country: Calatabiano, Catania, Sicily, Italy
Subject's Name: Valentina Randazzo
Date of Birth: 19-Sep-1850
Father's Name: Silvestra Randazzo
Father's Age: 28

Father's occupation: Laborer
Deceased?: No
Mother's Maiden Name: Marie Longo
Address: Via Teatro Communal

If he'd been in a better mood, he might have been more jubilant about this development. As it was, Hudson barely smiled at the fact that the birth record confirmed that two people from cluster three, Valerie Kerouac and Alexandra Cripps, both shared Silvestra Randazzo and Marie Longo as their shared common ancestors, which meant that the Twin Falls serial killer also descended from this Sicilian couple.

With this genetic network now completed, Hudson opened up *Cluster Four* from the shared drive. Kenyatta had assigned a guy, named Jacob Sauer, as the cluster lead with eighty-one centimorgans of DNA shared with the killer. There were six other men and women in this genetic network, although none of them had a surname that he recognized as being connected to the case so far.

Hudson was pleased to find that Jacob Sauer had included a tree on the FamilyTreeDNA website. However, when he came to view it, he found that it consisted of just Jacob himself and was without any accompanying dates or locations. Undeterred, he copied across Jacob's Comcast email address to the Spokeo website and ran a background search from it. The results confirmed his name, gave his age as 71 and his current address in Minneapolis. Two people were listed under *Family Members.*

Mark Sauer, age 36. Jacob and Mark have resided together in a single-family house in Bay City, MI.
Belinda Sauer, age 70. Jacob lives with Belinda in a single-family house in Minneapolis, MN.

Wife and son? Hudson wondered, looking at their ages. He noted the data on his pad and then continued scrolling down to *Personal.*

Jacob Sauer is 71 years old and may be married. He was most likely born in Jan 1949.

149

Hudson used this information to create a speculative family tree for Jacob as the designated home person. Next, he ran a marriage search for Jacob and Belinda. He tried all the major genealogy databases without success, so switched to searching his social media for clues instead. He started with Facebook, generally the preferred company for someone of Jacob's age, but Hudson found that there were literally dozens and dozens of profiles matching his name. When he filtered the search parameters down to the city of Minneapolis, he was left with just three men. The profile photo of the first possibility looked like a much younger man than someone born in 1949, the second had been left blank and the third was of a red dragon flying out of a fire. Hudson clicked on the second profile, finding it almost desolate. This man had just three friends listed but, crucially, one of them was called Mark Sauer. He clicked Mark's name, thankfully finding a much fuller, more active profile. Most importantly, though, the privacy settings were public, and so, Hudson began to trawl slowly through everything that Mark had ever shared.

Various job and education achievements were peppered around social posts. *Studied at University of Minnesota School of Social Work. Studied Psychology at Wesleyan University. Former Youth Advocate volunteer at Tubman.*

The posts that Hudson really wanted to see, however, were the personal ones. Posts that mentioned family, anniversaries, deaths and birthdays were the ones filled with the real genealogical treasure.

It didn't take too long to hit on a grainy photo of a man and woman standing side by side, looking at the camera. The man, with receding hair and a thick black moustache, had his hand on the woman's shoulder. She wore large glasses and had her gray hair cut into a bob. It was definitely an older photograph but posted on December 5, 2019, without any accompanying description at all. Hudson clicked the image and read the seven comments that had been made by Mark Sauer's friends and family.

Gerry Black: Handsome couple!
Mark Sauer: My grandparents. We lost my grandpa 6 years ago today.
Jenny Hook: I remember Frank and Sue very well from my time in Bay City.

Lovely couple, they were. Sending love to you and your dad.
Mark Sauer: Thank you.
Mary Metcalf: I miss them both terribly. She was the nicest sister I could have wished for.
Gerry Black: Don't worry there not lost they are in The Network looking at your every move…they love you dearly.

Hudson wasn't sure if *The Network* was a reference to heaven or perhaps the *Matrix*, or another obscure universe that he hadn't heard of, but generally the comments had given him some clues upon which he could work. First, he clicked on Mary Metcalf's profile, finding in a suffix her maiden name, Miller. Pulling the various threads together so far, it appeared as though the couple in the photograph could be Sue Miller with Frank Sauer who had possibly died in December 2013.

Switching over to the GenealogyBank website, Hudson ran a search for an obituary for Frank. The top result, from the *Star Tribune* newspaper, was correct.

Frank M. Sauer, 86, of Apple Valley, died December 1, 2013, at Essential Health-Virginia. Frank was born Oct 27, 1927, in Weld County, Colorado, the son of Caspar and Mabel (Balakin) Sauer, who both preceded him in death. Frank was a dedicated Bible study teacher and enjoyed helping others to reach their potential. Survived by wife, Sue; son, Jacob (Belinda); grandchildren, Mark and Liza; brother Benjamin (Janet); and other relatives.

Hudson's interest was piqued at Frank Sauer's mother's name: Mabel Balakin. Could this have its origins in Eastern Europe? he wondered, running a quick Google search to answer the question.

Balakin. This unique Russian name refers to someone who is 'very talkative' or can chatter constantly.

Hudson grinned. As always, he would need further corroboration, but he couldn't help but wonder if he might possibly have just stumbled upon the first branch of the Twin Falls killer's Russian family.

Becky Larkin was thrown off course. She was sitting at her computer in the guest room, working on her SAKI case, when a cryptic text message from an unknown number had arrived on her cell phone. She read it with bated breath for the fourth time.

How do I know I can trust you? WC

Ordinarily, she would have deleted the message and blocked the caller, but in light of her recent inquiries into Michael Barnhart, something was telling her not to.

WC...

Becky rolled her chair over to the guest bed where she had an assortment of untidy papers. She rummaged around, pulling out the notepad that she had used yesterday to record what she had found out about Artemon Bruce and Jay Craig. She ran her finger down the page until she came upon her notes from the background check on Jay Craig. A family member of the same age and living in his house was listed as Willamina Craig. *WC?*

Hi. I don't know how I can prove to you that I'm trustworthy. I get your reticence. You could contact Michael Barnhart's wife, Maddie. She'll vouch for me and tell you that I'm trying to help her to find out what happened to her husband. I haven't spoken to my father since I confronted him about why he placed a gag order on his employees and refused to help the police. I'm sorry to say it, but I think he knows what happened to Michael. I think the project that Michael was working on before he disappeared might have something to do with it. If you know what that was, I'd be so grateful to hear it. Michael's wife and children would really appreciate some answers.

Becky sent the message.

'Becks,' Ross said, appearing at the door, staring at his cell phone. 'Apparently I'm E-M35.'

Becky swiveled around to face him. She pushed her glasses back onto the bridge of her nose. 'I'm sorry, what?'

He looked across at her. 'My Y-DNA results have just come back

152

and I'm looking at them now. My haplogroup is E-M35.'

'Great,' Becky said flatly.

Ross opened his hands in a gesture of incredulity. 'What do I do now?'

Becky laughed. 'What do you mean? Dance? Have a celebratory drink?'

'I *mean*, what does it mean?'

Becky's cell phone began to ring from the desk beside her. It was WC calling, she was sure of it. 'I have to get this, Ross. The best person to speak to about Y-DNA is Hudson.'

'—Who hates me,' Ross replied.

'Well, this will give you something to bond over,' she said, picking up the phone. 'And he does not hate you.'

Ross exhaled, muttered, 'He does,' then turned from the room, closing the door for her behind him.

'Hello?' Becky answered warily but also trying to sound as pleasant and reassuring as she could muster.

For a few seconds there was silence on the other end, then WC spoke. 'I'm not going to talk for long and I don't have much to tell you at all. All I know is that the three men were working on a finance package for Haiti. It was some big-time construction deal worth millions… You know, following the 2010 earthquake?'

'Okay,' Becky said, scribbling notes as she listened, while also trying to confirm if this was the same person with whom she'd spoken when she'd called before to speak to Jay Craig. She thought it was. 'Do you know what the project involved or what the three men were doing?'

'Just doing their normal jobs as far as I'm aware,' she answered.

Becky was starting to imagine that the finance package could not have been altogether above-board. The trio had somehow found themselves in hot water over a deal gone bad. She voiced her theory.

'I don't think so, no,' came WC's reply. 'I've got some of the paperwork here and it all seems legal and aboveboard…'

Becky decided to tackle the elephant in the room head-on. 'Why, then, do you suppose all three men committed suicide, were murdered or disappeared within a year of one another?'

'I don't know,' she eventually answered.

153

'You said the project was in response to the 2010 earthquake. When exactly were they working on it? Right up until…until they each died or disappeared?'

WC took in a long, considered breath. 'I don't honestly know when it all started or ended. Jay didn't talk an awful lot about his work. Frankly, he knew that it wasn't often exactly scintillating conversation. He was stoked about going out to Haiti with Artemon and Michael, but when he got back, things were different.'

'How so?'

'He became very quiet and spent much more time alone. I asked him outright what he'd seen out there, but he wouldn't talk about it.'

'When was this trip to Haiti, exactly?' Becky asked.

'I can probably find the exact dates for you, but it was around January 2015.'

'Michael Barnhart disappeared in March 2015, Artemon Bruce allegedly committed suicide in June 2015 and Jay was murdered in December 2015.'

Becky's shocking statement was met with a silence that suggested WC had drawn the same conclusions a long time ago.

'Is there anything else that you can think of that might help me? Did Jay ever talk specifically about Michael vanishing?' Becky pushed.

WC gave a sardonic laugh. 'When he disappeared, Jay really spiraled. I mean, he was so down that he didn't even go to work for a while. Yet, he didn't once talk to me about Michael. God knows what was going on in his head…'

'Can you send me over the exact dates of the Haiti trip and also any copies of the paperwork you have for the project?'

'I guess so… But it can never be traced back to me, do you understand? I'm serious.'

'Totally,' Becky said. 'Thank you.'

The call ended.

Becky looked at her notes, more confused than ever but also more certain that her father or his company were behind what had happened to determine the fates of those three men.

She stood up for a moment before heading into the living room where Ross was looking at his cell phone.

'Well, that was totally unhelpful,' he said to her.

'What was?'

'Hudson,' he replied. 'I called him up, told him my haplogroup and asked what it all meant, but he barely gave me anything more than I've since found on Google. I asked what his haplogroup was and he said he'd never taken a Y-DNA test, so he had no idea. Then he said he was busy and hung up. I told you he hated me.'

'Something's going on at home. Don't take it personally,' Becky commented. 'So... Wanna know what I've just found out about Michael, Artemon and Jay?'

Ross pocketed his phone, patted the sofa beside him and said, 'Rebecca, dear, tell me *everything*...from the beginning.'

And so, she did.

Maddie couldn't recall a time when she'd been as pleased to open her own front door as she was now. The welcoming committee was waiting as she and Trenton entered the house.

'Welcome back, you idiot,' Nikki said, pulling her brother into a hug.

'Thanks,' he muttered sheepishly.

Maddie had worried that he might be angry or defiant to have his little expedition cut short by her and dozens of search and rescue personnel; but from the moment when he was pulled out of the water, he was suitably remorseful and grateful. He'd even admitted that he didn't know how much longer he could have held out, had the boat not picked him up when it did. She secretly hoped that this new, humbler version of her son might stick around for a while.

'You've put your mother and all of us through absolute hell,' Maddie's mom scolded, standing with her arms folded and very much not about to pull him into any sort of forgiving embrace.

Maddie couldn't help but smile. 'It's okay, Mom. He won't do it again.'

Her mom rolled her eyes and wandered off, saying, 'He might not come back next time...just like his father before him.'

'I am sorry, Mom,' Trenton said to her, for the hundredth time since his rescue. 'I just wanted answers, and after Defective Scorpion said he wasn't going to do anything, I just took it upon myself.'

'So, come on then. What *did* you find out?' Nikki asked.

'I won't know until I cross-refer my findings with the police report,' he answered vaguely.

'Nothing, then,' Nikki retorted.

'Hey! At least I made an effort.'

'—And nearly drowned,' Nikki muttered, before addressing Maddie. 'Notice anything different?'

Maddie stared hard at her daughter. She was exhausted and struggled to see any change in her. Her hair? Looked the same as it always did. Clothes? No, they were her usual. She leaned in closer, praying that she hadn't had a piercing of some kind put somewhere. 'Open your mouth.'

Nikki looked rather confused but did as she was asked. No piercing.

'I give up,' Maddie said.

'Look around you,' Nikki said, gesturing to the hallway.

'She's talking about the treadmill,' Trenton clarified, unimpressed.

'Oh,' Maddie said, looking down at the floor where it had been deposited and remained. 'Where did you put it?'

Nikki nodded and pointed to the door of Michael's office.

'You built it yourself?' Trenton asked, pushing open the door and looking inside. 'Does it actually work?'

'Of course, it works. I used it this morning,' Nikki replied. 'In fact, even Grandma has been on it for nearly an hour.'

Maddie's eyes widened. 'Please, God, tell me only a gentle walk?'

Nikki laughed. 'No. Thirty minutes of uphill sprinting. Of course a gentle walk, Mom. She made some sarcastic remark about being able to exercise without the worry of getting lost, but I think she really liked it.'

'Well done,' Maddie said. She glanced around the place, and added, 'Somehow, I feel like I've been away for weeks.'

'No offence, Mom, but you look super wrecked,' Trenton observed. 'I'm going to my room to lie down.'

'Yeah, and whose fault is that?' Nikki called after him. She turned back to Maddie. 'Go and sit down and I'll bring you some coffee.'

'I'm not going to argue with that,' Maddie said, wandering into the living room and slumping down on a sofa. After the uncomfortable hospital chairs and the lumpy bed of the cheap motel where they'd had to stay last night, Maddie felt as though she was collapsing into a vat of cotton candy. 'Oh, my gosh,' she breathed.

'Maybe you should go to bed, too, Mom?' Nikki suggested from the kitchen as she made their drinks.

'Can't. I've got too much to catch up on,' Maddie answered. 'And I need to let Jenna know we're home.' She took out her cell phone and sent a short message to her eldest daughter to let her know that they were home, safe and well. Before Maddie could put her phone away, Jenna started to ring, wanting to FaceTime.

Before Maddie answered the call, she saw herself in the front-facing camera. 'Jesus, seriously.' She sat up and raised the phone above her eye level to try and smooth out some of the sags and dark circles under her eyes. 'Hi,' she finally greeted, trying to sound more awake and look sprightlier than she felt by far. 'How are you?'

'I'm good. How are you two doing?' Jenna asked.

'I'm exhausted to my core and Trenton is embarrassed to his core.'

'He's an idiot to the core, is what he is,' Nikki intoned, as she placed a coffee down in front of Maddie.

'Thank you,' she mouthed.

'Is he physically okay?' Jenna asked. 'No broken bones or hypothermia?'

Maddie shook her head and yawned. 'No lasting damage, thank God.'

'Well, that's something that he's okay. Did he find anything out after all that?'

'Yeah,' Nikki responded, 'that he's a total idiot who can't negotiate rapids and rocks.'

Jenna laughed.

'I don't think so,' Maddie answered. 'Not really. But hopefully it knocked the sense of helplessness out of him that drove him to do it in the first place.' Maddie took a breath, drank some coffee and then asked, 'So, anyway. Let's get back to some normality. What's going on with you?'

'Well, I have some news that I was waiting to tell you.'

Oh God, she's pregnant, Maddie immediately guessed. And at twenty-three years of age, still too young. Maddie offered a weak smile and was poised to absorb the news.

Jenna held up her left hand, revealing a gold band with what looked to be an inset diamond. 'Rick proposed!'

'Oh, my God!' Maddie yelled. 'Jenna, that's amazing news.'

'Congratulations,' Nikki called, eagerly rushing over and squeezing herself into shot beside Maddie.

'Tell us everything!' Maddie said.

'Well, you know what Rick's like...' Jenna began. But Maddie didn't really know what Rick was like since she'd only ever met him on the one occasion. 'He'd spent the afternoon converting our guest room; champagne, French music, candles, and the Eiffel Tower projected onto the wall.'

'The Eiffel Tower?' Nikki questioned.

'Uh-huh. He'd booked us a surprise trip to Paris, but which had to be canceled,' Jenna answered. 'So, at that very moment we should have been in a champagne bar at the top of the Eiffel Tower. Then he got down on one knee and asked me to marry him.'

'Oh, that's very romantic!' Nikki said.

'And obviously I said yes!'

'That's really such wonderful news, Jenna. I am so pleased for you,' Maddie said, as tears began to well in her eyes. 'I wish I could hop on a plane down to Florida and congratulate the pair of you in person. He's such a romantic.'

'Yeah, about that,' Jenna said, grimacing.

'There's more?' Maddie asked.

'Well, he's got some old-fashioned ideas about how this whole process should have played out and, even though we are where we are, he's asking about my father...'

'Oh,' Maddie said, very much taken aback.

'He thinks it only right that he should ask him or, at least, *tell* him that we're planning on getting married...'

Nikki screwed up her face. 'You've never even met your dad, Jen.'

Jenna shook her head. 'I know, it's weird and I told him so, but he just thinks that the man has a right to know.'

'And do you think that, too?' Maddie asked.

'No... Yeah... Maybe. From what you've said about him, he wouldn't give a damn, anyhow,' Jenna commented. 'I realize it was a long time ago when you were back in college and when you told him you were pregnant, he bailed, but do you know where he might be, these days?'

Maddie's heart was suddenly racing and adrenalin thundering around her body. Until today, Jenna had always accepted that her father had not wanted anything to do with her, and had never before asked probing or uncomfortable questions about him, which had suited Maddie. She turned to Nikki and said, 'Honey, could I talk to Jenna alone for a moment, please?'

'Sure,' Nikki said, pushing her face closer to the camera. 'Talk to you soon. Congrats!'

'Bye, Nikki.'

Nikki left the room and closed the door behind her.

'I know you're embarrassed, Mom,' Jenna began, 'but you don't need to be.'

'Do you really want to ask his *permission* to marry, Jenna?' Maddie stammered.

'Of course not, not in *that* way. I don't know, I guess Rick's questions have just made me wonder about him more, lately. He might have changed. Being told you're going to be a dad at age nineteen is probably a lot to take in. I mean...'

Maddie was shaking as she confessed, 'I never told him that I was pregnant.'

Chapter Eighteen

Sunday, April 12, 2020, Twin Falls, Idaho

It was one in the morning and Debra Towers was still awake. He was sitting in the back seat of his Wrangler, wearing black pants and a black shirt, looking directly out the window at her house. Except for her living room, the house and surrounding neighborhood were pitch dark and quiet.

From the backpack beside him, he took out a can of beer, popped it open and took a long glug. That felt better. He had been sitting out here for over two hours, waiting for her to go to bed. He was getting impatient, but if he had to wait all night, then so be it. He was ready.

He finished the beer, crushed the can in his hand and took another from the bag.

At last, there was movement inside the property: Debra was crossing the front room. Then, the light went out and the house blended almost seamlessly into the darkness that surrounded it. The nearest streetlight was at the end of the road; nowhere near close enough to provide any illumination over Debra's house or yard, which was just how he wanted it.

He drank more beer. A nervous energy, which he had recognized from this moment with the other four girls, tingled in his bloodstream. He finished the beer, his hands lightly quivering as he crushed the can and tossed it down into the passenger floorboard where other empties lay. He took another beer, chugged it in one go and squeezed the can until the sharp folds of aluminum cut into his hand.

His heart was racing as he felt inside the backpack and pulled out his night-vision monocular headgear which he carefully fastened to his head, positioning the single lens down over his right eye. He closed his left eye, switched on the device and gazed out of the rear passenger window. Out of the blackness, Debra's house suddenly appeared in a high-contrast, monochromatic green.

He smiled as he slowly surveyed the neighborhood.

No signs of life anywhere.

He picked up his backpack, opened the car door, stepped down onto the street and quietly pushed the door shut.

He gradually turned three-sixty, paying close attention to Debra's house, her neighbors' and the empty garage behind him. When he was sure that nobody was around, he crossed the street to approach her property.

Keeping to the hedge line on the right, he walked up the drive, the night-vision aid guiding him toward her house. He paused when he reached the first window but couldn't see inside because of a thick curtain. The same was true of the next window.

Creeping to the backyard, he grinned; an inch of light—all he needed—spilled out from a gap between her bedroom curtains. He switched off the night-vision device and moved toward the window, almost pressing his face against the glass.

He nearly swore out loud. The bitch had a guy in her bed. Of course she did. That was exactly her type. The Chad was sitting up, bare-chested, grinning like he couldn't quite believe his luck, and watching as she rubbed cream into her face.

He continued to watch as she got into the bed beside him. The damned guy laid back and switched off the lamp on her nightstand, plunging the room into darkness.

He fumbled with the switch on the night-vision aid but quickly thought better of it and roughly tugged it from around his head. He had no desire whatsoever to see what that disgusting pair got up to in the dark.

His previous excitement turned to rage as he rushed back down the drive to the Wrangler. Panting agitatedly, he got in, fired up the engine and took off.

'God damn her,' he said in a high-octave pitch, as he slammed his fist into the steering wheel.

Chapter Nineteen

Monday, April 13, 2020, South Jordan, Utah

Maddie was feeling overwhelmed. The one thing that she needed last night, above all else, was a good, long sleep, but it had never happened. Her mind had refused to switch off for very long and, when it did, her dreams taunted her with vivid depictions of Trenton drowning in the Green River rapids. She saw him release his last breath out underwater and panicked screaming on his face as he was forced to inhale water. She had awakened in a hot sweat and, after that, every time she had closed her eyes, she saw Trenton's terrified face as he drowned. She gave up trying to sleep at just past four o'clock in the morning and went downstairs to the basement.

She stared at the computer screen, her eyes refusing to focus. She was trying to work through her backlog of unopened emails that had risen to two hundred and eighty-six. She'd already deleted the easy ones, read a few important ones and was now left with fifty-nine which required more careful attention.

Maddie clicked on another email. It was a long one. She skimmed it. The gist was that someone wanted Venator to pick up a case of three murdered schoolboys in Arkansas. The person had set the case out in detail, including various links to news outlets and social media pages. Maddie sighed as she responded with her carefully worded standard reply that it wasn't ever up to her to seek out new cases, but rather that law enforcement had to initiate the contact. The number of similar such inquiries had risen dramatically since Wayne Wolsey's arrest.

She angled her coffee cup, which revealed that it was drained. She promised herself that after ten more emails, she would go and make another.

The next message was from the company which had supplied the treadmill, asking how her running was coming along. 'Non-existent,' she mumbled, hitting delete.

The following three emails were another type of which she got several each day: people asking her how they could get into investigative genetic genealogy. Her replies were always the same: get *a lot* of experience helping adoptees to find their birth parents and gain experience working on complex cases like families with endogamous populations, South American or African American heritage. She also liked to provide a reality check in the form of a link to a webpage that summarized some of the more brutal and harrowing cases that she had been involved in in order to remove some of the misperceived glamorized notions about the profession.

She clicked to read the next message in the list. It was from someone, named Eva Hyatt, and simply read, *FYI*. A zipped file was attached, helpfully labelled, *file*. She was about to move it to her junk folder but something about the name seemed familiar. Did she know someone by the name of Eva Hyatt? Not that she could recall. Perhaps it was connected to a past case?

Maddie looked at the email for several seconds, then decided to unzip the attachment, hoping that her computer's antivirus software would intervene, should it be harmful.

The folder opened, revealing more than twenty files comprising a mix of photos, videos and Word documents. Some of the file names gave a clue as to what the combined folder might contain: *ROI. DUI Questionnaire. Arrest video. Pre-arrest video. Car1. Miranda. Sample results. DMV record. Prints.*

Maddie hoped to God that this was what she thought that it might be.

She clicked to open the document labeled *ROI*.

Report of Investigation
Date: Oct 3, 2014
Offence: DUI
Name: Emmanuel Gribbin
Address: 4814 Tuckerman Street, Riverdale Park, Maryland

Maddie could not believe what she had in front of her. Before she read the rest of the report, she returned to the main folder and clicked on *Arrest_video.mov*. A video player opened with a white play button in the center of the screen. She hit the button and watched in

163

astonishment. It was a dusky evening and a camera—presumably being worn as a bodycam by law enforcement—moved toward a light-blue Ford Club Wagon pulled over in a quiet suburban side street. Maddie noticed that the camera lingered on the Maryland license plate, before proceeding to the open, driver's side window. And then she saw Emmanuel Gribbin for the first time. The man whose fingerprint was the only one found after a CSI sweep of Michael's truck. In all likelihood, the man she was now looking at was the last person to have seen Michael alive.

Maddie hit pause and stared at him. He was middle-aged, slightly overweight with black and gray hair swept back untidily over his head. He had a gray moustache and several days' worth of stubble on his face. She could tell from his glassy eyes that he was way over the limit.

She stopped the video and returned to the folder and opened other files at random. There were images of his car, his fingerprints, mug shots, an evidence voucher for the towing of his vehicle, a detailed DUI questionnaire about the day that had led up to the arrest, a summons copy, voucher for property seized and breath test results.

It was beyond amazing for her, but, in her shattered state, the information was overwhelming. The contents of this folder required her full, uncompromised attention which she could not currently give.

She yawned and then looked at the time: 5:14 a.m. She could try going back to bed, but she knew that sleep wouldn't come. She wanted more coffee. She yawned, stretched, then stood up and carried her empty cup upstairs. The house was still in silent slumber. Maddie entered the kitchen and placed her cup down on the counter.

She dithered, wondering if she should get more coffee or force herself to use the treadmill. Exercise had always helped clear her head, and if ever she needed her head cleared, it was right now. She moved across the hallway into Michael's office and switched on the light. Maddie smiled at the pride-of-place positioning of the machine, right in the center of the room. She stood on the treadmill and gradually inched up the speed from a slow walk to a gentle jog.

Her heart rate began to increase, and her breathing got faster as she notched up the speed even more. She gritted her teeth and ran at full pelt, trying to push aside invidious thoughts as they crept into her mind. But she couldn't keep them out, try as she might.

She kept coming back to the DUI. If she could just focus on it long enough, it might prove to contain information that could help her to work out how Emmanuel Gribbin was connected to Michael. She wondered who Eva Hyatt was and why she had sent her the files. Either way, she was very grateful. Then it struck her. It was so obvious that she was certain, in her normal state of mind, she would otherwise have figured it out straight away. The report had been sent by Detective Clayton Tyler who had wanted to remain anonymous and so, had—rather clumsily, in her opinion—chosen the name of the bakery opposite the Venator office, Eva's, and the hotel in which he had stayed when visiting Salt Lake City, the Hyatt. Eva Hyatt. Not exactly a genius name, but it was random enough that only she would understand the email's provenance…eventually. She would thank him—somehow—later on.

Sweat was flying off her face and the pace of the machine was starting to beat her, but she was determined to carry on pushing.

'Mom? What are you doing?' Trenton suddenly asked from the door, scaring her so that she nearly lost her footing.

She was barely able to draw enough oxygen to run anymore; to talk at the same time was simply impossible. She knocked the pace down to a gentle jog and managed to answer, 'Baking a cake.'

'Very funny,' he replied. 'Why are you running in your pajamas?'

Maddie glanced down, having not realized what she was wearing. 'Fashion,' she muttered breathlessly.

Trenton rolled his eyes and left the room.

At least things were feeling more settled between the two of them, she considered; unlike her relationship with her eldest child. After Maddie had dropped the bombshell yesterday that she'd never actually informed Jenna's father that she had become pregnant by him, Jenna had hung up and, so far, had not responded to Maddie's pleas to talk about it some more.

She dropped the treadmill speed down to a walking pace and tried to normalize her breathing. The guilt that Maddie had carried with her for all these years had not lifted from her as she had expected it might. The lie had seemed the best option—and the easiest—at the time when, aged six years old, Jenna had first asked about her father. Soon after that, Maddie had met Michael and any residual questions that Jenna had had about having a father in her life vanished when he had willingly taken her on as his own daughter.

She'd try and call Jenna again in a couple of hours when it was a more reasonable time of the day. For now, though, she just wanted to shower.

Maddie was back at her desk in the basement. Although she had pushed herself on the treadmill, she felt much more energized for it. She had cleared all her remaining unread emails and gone through the contents of Emmanuel Gribbin's DUI folder several times over, making relevant notes as she went. Later this evening—perhaps over dinner—she planned to share her findings with her mom and the kids. But for now, she needed to get back to pulling her weight on the Twin Falls case. She was surprised that none of the team had yet closed down their genetic network clusters. Or, perhaps they had, but hadn't liked to say so with all that was going on in Maddie's personal life.

She had tried calling Jenna several times but was sent straight to voicemail. Knowing how Jenna handled such things, she would need a little time to get her head around the situation, then she'd be willing to talk.

Opening the speculative tree that she'd created for Joey Seymour, it took Maddie a few minutes of working back through his pedigree to remind herself of where she'd gotten up to last Wednesday before Trenton had run away.

She had taken Joey Seymour's maternal lines back to the great-great-great-grandparent level, positively identifying twelve out of sixteen individuals. Four she had deemed too difficult, given the time and resources at her disposal. If she failed to find the person or couple who linked cluster five, then she would have to come back to trying to find these four people.

Maddie returned to Joey Seymour's profile, then clicked on his father, Marcel. All that she knew about him thus far had been taken from his wife's obituary.

She emigrated to Alberta, Canada in 1974, where she met her future husband, Marcel… Gina is survived by her devoted husband, Marcel of Edmonton.

Maddie started working on the theory that Marcel had been born in Alberta sometime around 1953 when his wife had also been born. He had still been alive and well in Edmonton, Canada upon her passing in 2018.

Turning to the Research Wiki page on FamilySearch, Maddie looked up what vital records existed for Alberta.

Births:
1870-1898

Marriages:
1870-1946
1898-1942

Deaths:
1870-1968
1870-1971
1914-1946

'Not helpful,' she commented, before opening Newspapers.com and running a search for Marcel Seymour between the years 1930 and 2020.

104,580 Matches for Marcel Seymour

Slightly too many, Maddie thought, as she selected Canada from the drop-down filter menu of locations. On the right-hand portion of the screen, a map of Canada appeared with the number of search results for each province. Below that was a chronological breakdown in decade chunks for corresponding search results. Knowing that Gina Westlake had arrived in Alberta in 1974, Maddie clicked on the map for that particular province, then on the 1970s.

From *Result Type* on the menu bar, she selected *Marriages* and the number of matching articles dropped to just twelve. She clicked the first link, taken from the *Edmonton Journal*, dated March 14, 1978.

Seymour-Westlake
Mr. and Mrs. Walter John Seymour of Edmonton take pleasure in announcing the forthcoming marriage of their son, Marcel Seymour to Gina Westlake, daughter of Mr. and Mrs. Lawrence Westlake of London, England. The wedding will take place May 18, at 2:30 p.m. in Strathcona Presbyterian Church.

Maddie took a screenshot of the article and added it, with source information, to Joey Seymour's speculative tree. Her research into Gina Westlake confirmed that this pertained to the correct Marcel Seymour. She was now in possession of his father's full name. The following article was for the marriage proper. Maddie read through the details of the ceremony, searching for further genealogical information. The only additional piece of potentially helpful detail was that the best man had been Marcel's brother, Harold.

Maddie added the article to Marcel's profile, then added his father, Walter John Seymour, and brother, Harold. Since the Ancestry hints had not yet appeared, Maddie clicked *Search on Ancestry*. A long list of documents was suggested that might relate to Walter John Seymour in some way. She didn't have the time to check each and every one for its relevance; at this stage she just wanted to build a quick but accurate tree, so she filtered the search to *Birth, marriage & death*. Skimming quickly down the page, Maddie's eyes settled on what she was searching for: *Canada, Find A Grave Index, 1600s-Current*. She clicked on the result. It was a profile for Walter John Seymour. So far, however, there was insufficient evidence to know that it was the correct person.

Walter John Seymour
Birth 1922, Saskatchewan, Canada
Death 2009
Burial Westlawn Memorial Gardens

She scanned down the page for further information, pleased—in a morbid research kind of way—that there were other family profiles listed.

Parents
John Seymour 1891-1972
Frances Seymour 1893-1964

Spouse
Anna Wacker 1925-2013

Child
Harold Seymour 1950-1982

The addition of Harold Seymour, who had been the best man at Marcel's wedding in 1978, made Maddie believe that she was working along the right lines. She clicked Harold's name to bring up his FindAGrave profile. Although it displayed a picture of his memorial and gave full birth dates, death dates, and locations, there was no biography.

Maddie turned back to Newspapers.com and searched for Harold's death. There was just one result in the *Edmonton Journal* of November 18, 1982.

One Dead in Two-Vehicle Pileup
A 32-year-old Edmonton resident was killed on Thursday in a two-car pileup. The car in which Harold Seymour was a passenger was traveling northbound on 66ᵗʰ Street when the driver, Mr. Seymour's brother, Marcel, began making a left turn, police said. The passenger side of the car was hit by a delivery truck heading south. Firefighters had to cut the roof out before the driver and passenger could be taken out of the wreckage to hospital. The driver of the car and truck were treated for minor injuries. Harold Seymour, son of local businessman Mr. Walter Seymour was pronounced dead at the scene. Police are appealing for witnesses to come forward.

The article and the FindAGrave profiles, when taken together, were sufficient evidence for Maddie that she was working on the correct family. She saved the information to Joey's speculative tree and then began to research Walter John Seymour's parents, John and Frances.

With fifteen minutes to go until the briefing, Maddie paused her research, contented with what she had managed to achieve today, and went upstairs to check on her mom and the kids.

'Everything okay up here?' she asked her mom, who was sitting in the living room doing a crossword.

She looked up with a smile. 'Perfectly okay, thank you.'

'Good,' Maddie replied. She wanted to ask when the last time was that her mom had seen the kids but didn't want her to feel the emotional burden of having to be their gatekeeper. Maddie wandered upstairs, finding Trenton's and Nikki's bedroom doors both closed. She tapped on Trenton's first and couldn't help feeling relieved when he answered from within.

'Go away if you're Nikki,' he called.

Maddie rolled her eyes and pushed open the door but didn't enter the room. For some reason, his blinds were drawn, the room was in darkness, and he was working at his desk under a lamp. 'Are you okay?'

'I'm still here, if that's what you mean.'

'That wasn't what I meant,' Maddie lied. 'I was asking if you were okay.'

'Sure.'

'Good,' she replied. 'I'm just about to do the briefing, then I'll get the dinner.'

Trenton suddenly became animated. 'Can we get a take-out from Door Dash? Like Red Robin?'

'Yeah, I guess so,' Maddie agreed.

Trenton pulled down a tightened fist. 'Yeah!'

Maddie closed his door and then checked on Nikki.

'Do you want me to cook?' she asked in response to Maddie telling her that she was about to do a team briefing.

'That's very sweet, but Trenton has just talked me into getting a

Red Robin, once I'm done with the meeting.'

'Cool,' Nikki replied. 'Southern Charm burger for me, then, please.'

'I can't hold that in my brain at the moment. I'll be back in a while to take orders.'

Maddie returned to the basement with just a couple of minutes to spare before the meeting began. She prepped her files and then opened Zoom. Everyone was already in the waiting room, which Maddie took to mean that they all would have plenty to say.

There was a chorus of greetings back and forth, then Kenyatta said, 'Good to have you back, boss.'

Maddie grinned. 'It's great to be back, but I must admit I feel so detached from this case; like I've been away for several weeks.'

'You'll get back into it soon enough,' Kenyatta encouraged.

'How are you doing? How's Trenton?' Becky asked.

'We're both fine,' Maddie said, giving a rundown of the events that had taken place with Trenton. She didn't mention not sleeping, the DUI folder or Jenna's engagement, not wanting to get too sidetracked with her own domestic issues. 'Despite all that, I've worked really hard today,' she said, sharing her screen and segueing into the briefing proper. 'This is Joey Seymour's pedigree and, as you can see, I've managed to close down eight of his paternal great-great-great-grandparents' lines, taking me to a grand total of twenty out of thirty-two.'

'Good job,' Kenyatta commended.

'Thanks. The locations have mainly been England, Canada and Kansas up till now. Any of these names or places appearing in your research?' When the team replied in the negative, Maddie asked, 'Okay, so who wants to go next?'

'I will, although I don't have any grand revelations,' Becky said, forestalling any expectations, before sharing a pedigree for Latasha McNaughton. 'I'm almost done with this one's direct ancestors, now. There are four great-great-great-grandparents that I can't find, so tomorrow I'll be switching focus to linking someone else in the cluster to Latasha's tree.' Becky screwed up her face and leaned in closer to the camera. 'I have to say that none of these names or places are particularly jumping out at me. I've got a concentration around the

California-Arizona area and one branch from Missouri…but that's it so far. I'm *definitely* not getting the orange slip this time round; that much is certain.'

'No, but I will!' Hudson chipped in with an exuberant smile.

'Me too! Me too!' Kenyatta called with a laugh.

'Have you both closed your clusters?' Becky demanded.

'Yep,' he confirmed.

'Sure have,' Kenyatta said.

'Way to go,' Maddie said. 'Shared first prize goes to Kenyatta and Hudson, it seems, people. You each get an extra ten bucks in your next pay packet. Don't squander it, now. So, Hudson, do you want to go first and tell me what I'm writing on the first orange slip?'

Hudson pulled up the profile page for Silvestra Randazzo in his speculative tree and shared it with the team. 'This guy, along with his wife, Marie Longo,' he began, circling around her name with his mouse and cursor, 'are the common ancestors for Valerie Kerouac and Alexandra Cripps. Silvestra and Marie came from Calatabiano, Catania in Sicily. Cluster three is officially closed.'

'Well done, Hudson. Great job,' Maddie praised.

'*And*, I've made some promising progress on cluster four,' he said, displaying Jacob Sauer's pedigree for everyone to see. 'I was really excited to find that Jacob's paternal grandmother was named Mabel Balakin, which—according to our good friend, Google—is a distinctly Russian name.'

'Wow,' Becky said. 'At last, some links to Eastern Europe.'

'*And*…' Hudson started, receiving a groan of dismay from Becky, 'Look here.' He clicked on the profile for Caspar Sauer. 'Mabel *and* Caspar were born in Rohleder, Saratov, Russia.'

'You are on fire, Hudson,' Maddie said, giving a little clap.

'And where is Rohleder? I hear you ask,' Hudson continued as he brought up a map for them to see. 'In the Volga region of Russia.'

'Just where his geo-ancestry predicted,' Becky chimed in.

'And that's where I'm at,' Hudson said. 'I really wanted to make sure that I was on the right track with this couple—really pinning down the records after their arrival in the U.S.—before embarking on what records I might be able to find for Russia.'

'Excellent work, Hudson,' Maddie praised. 'Kenyatta, didn't you have links to Sicily in your cluster, too?'

'Indeed, I did. And that's exactly where I found the common ancestral couple for cluster six. Here,' she said, sharing her screen.

Maddie looked carefully at the two names: Vincenza Pernicano and Rosa Messina, also from Calatabiano, Catania in Sicily. 'I feel like you guys must be on the verge of a *purple* slip, don't you?' Maddie stated, referring to the next stage in the investigative genetic genealogy process, where two genetic networks would become linked together, taking them a generation closer toward the killer.

Kenyatta laughed. 'Given the size of Calatabiano, I don't think it will be too long until we find a Randazzo marrying a Pernicano.'

'This is great work, everyone,' Maddie said. 'You've all done fantastically, and I know I *really* need to catch up. Does anyone else have anything to add, before I head off to place a Red Robin order?'

'I think that's about it from us,' Kenyatta said. 'Enjoy your takeout. I've got an exciting chicken salad to look forward to.' She sat back in her chair with a sigh.

'Enjoy. Have a good evening, everyone,' Maddie said. Once everyone had said goodbye, she ended the meeting, then put her computer to sleep, wanting to switch off psychologically for the evening. Before she headed upstairs to gather the orders for their takeout, Maddie tried to call Jenna again. This time, she picked up.

'Hi,' Jenna said, without expression.

'Hey. Look, I'm sorry, Jenna.'

'What for? Lying to me my entire life? Not telling a man that he had a child? For keeping me away from him?'

'Yes, all of that, but mainly for not telling you everything.'

'What was wrong with him, exactly?'

'Nothing,' Maddie admitted. 'I was young and scared and didn't know what to do when I found out that I was pregnant. He was a nice guy, but I wasn't ready to settle down for the rest of my life with him.'

'But you were ready to saddle yourself with a *child*...alone?' Jenna asked.

'That was different,' Maddie tried to defend, although she knew she had no real defense. 'I knew from the moment I found out that I was pregnant that I had to keep you, but just you and not him, too; not in the circumstances that I was in twenty-three years ago. As you grew up, it just became ever easier to hold to the lie. Michael came along and we became a complete family unit that I knew I could never have provided for you with your biological father. I am sorry, Jenna. Really, I am.'

Her apology was met with silence.

'Do you want to know his name?' Maddie asked, voicing a question that she never thought that she would have to ask.

Jenna fell silent. 'I don't know yet,' she finally said. 'How am I supposed to make up for twenty-three lost years with this guy? He's a complete stranger to me; and I am to him. Weren't you studying in England around that time? Do you even know where he is?'

'Uh-huh.'

'Does he have his own family?' she asked. Maddie could hear that she was crying.

'I do believe he's married with kids, yes,' she replied.

'You know, Mom,' Jenna said through her sobbing, 'you spend every waking moment looking for truth, helping people and insisting that everyone around you meets this high moral standard that you've set, and yet…I just didn't think you were this kind of a person.'

Jenna ended the call and Maddie was utterly crushed.

Chapter Twenty

Detective Maria González was sitting at her desk in the Criminal Investigation Division office, exhausted. She had existed on less than four hours' sleep every single night since the first murder had turned into a series and now it was clearly starting to tell tales on her ability to concentrate. She finished her fourth coffee as she looked over all the bulletin boards for the second time so far this morning.

House-to-house inquiries were continuing within the circle identified by the investigative genetic genealogy team, but as of yet had yielded no results. Names were being taken and cross-referenced against hunting license databases and known associates of the four victims. Searches among the same databases for Italian or Eastern European names had also so far drawn a complete blank.

Maria headed over to one of the analyst's desks, Reuben Wright, a young nerdy guy who was excellent at his job. 'How's it going?' she asked, having tasked him on Friday with working out how the killer might be getting hold of amobarbital and secobarbital, given that they weren't over-the-counter drugs.

Reuben sat up straight and ran his hand through his floppy side-parted hair. 'Well, as you know, amobarbital and secobarbital are schedule-two drugs, meaning that they have a high potential for abuse and are considered dangerous.'

'Uh-huh,' Maria said, wanting to speed things up.

'Since doctors can no longer prescribe them, we have three possible scenarios: one, this guy is stealing them from a hospital setting where they can still be used for controlled sedation, but I think this would be the most difficult way to obtain them; two, he buys them from the black market from another country that doesn't consider these drugs to be illegal. Possible, but not likely. I think he buys them illegally off the street just like he would heroin or cocaine. Red Devils, Pink Ladies, Lilly, Reds and Blues, Double Trouble—take your pick— they're all out there on the street if you only know where to look for them. Locally, I've identified several dealers where he could be getting hold of the drugs.'

'I was hoping you wouldn't say that,' Maria commented.

'Sorry,' Reuben replied with a casual shrug.

'Okay, give me the names of the local dealers and we'll have them questioned,' Maria directed, heading back to her desk where she found a new email from Professor Steiner from the Department of Plant Sciences at the University of Idaho. He had been the person to identify the two samples of foliage found at Molly Hutchison's autopsy. Maria had asked him something that she knew was way out of left field when she had asked him if he would mind checking the trees for the two closest parks to where the killer was suspected to live.

Dear Detective González

Happy to comply with your request. In fact, I went further; my wife and I did a tour of the city's parks over the weekend. Neither species of tree was found at the First Federal Bank Park nor the Frontier Park. However, I did identify several examples of Douglas fir at the Rock Creek Park. Having said this, I could find no examples of the Engelmann spruce, which is to be expected since it is mainly a high-altitude tree. As per my previous correspondence, it is my belief that you are looking for a mountainous forest area outside of the city itself.

Please don't hesitate to contact me if I can be of further assistance, although I'm not sure that I can convince my wife to accompany me on a tour of all Idaho's mountain ranges!

With my best wishes.

Simon Steiner

Maria wasn't at all surprised by the email, but she had wanted confirmation from an expert. And now she had it. The killer might well live some place in Twin Falls, but he was taking his victims out of town to hunt them down and eventually murder them.

She glanced over at the large map of Twin Falls that adorned one of the walls of the Criminal Investigation Division office. The problem was that the city was surrounded by hundreds of square miles of mountainous, forested areas. She realized that right now it was a waste of time to focus any more resources on foliage.

On her computer, she pulled up the list that the analysts had compiled of every man who had taken out a hunting license in the past two years. There were seven hundred and twenty-two names. Maria read through them all, her gut telling her that the killer's name was on there somewhere. When she had voiced as much to the team, it was pointed out that the licenses were only for hunting on state land; if the killer had his own land, then he wouldn't need a license. But something about the molar removal made Maria believe that, at least at some point in the past, he had held a state hunting license.

'Michelle,' she called over to one of the analysts who had compiled the list. 'Can you extend your search through the hunting licenses back ten years, please?'

'Ten?' she asked, reacting with trepidation at the scale of the task.

'Uh-huh. Ten,' Maria confirmed.

Chapter Twenty-One

Tuesday, April 14, 2020, Liberty Wells, Salt Lake City, Utah

Hudson clicked send on the email to the adoption agency. It disappeared from his screen, leaving him feeling hollow inside and yet, paradoxically, mightily relieved. He had copied Abigail in on the message, telling the agency that they would need to pause their application until the pandemic was over so that they could have a more settled and certain financial situation prior to proceeding. Hopefully, that delay would buy him enough time to figure out what on earth was going on in his mind. Abigail was still barely speaking to him and, for the past few days, had made her own meals and eaten alone in her bedroom, despite his offering to cook for them both.

He gazed out of his bedroom window to the thick clouds currently shrouding the Wasatch Mountains. The house felt more oppressive than ever before; the only temporary respite that he'd experienced since lockdown had started had been his trips to the Family History Library. Although he knew that he shouldn't be going out and was much safer staying home, he was saddened that he no longer had the real need to be able to justify his going there.

Before he settled down to work, he had an important email to send.

Dear Maddie

I'm just writing to let you know that I have had a meeting with Wanda Chabala about the private case that I was working on. Having told her that I could not give her a name and offered to hand back the money, she worked out that her husband was a suspect. As things stand, she's said that we can keep the money.

Therefore, because I was not able to fully back away from the case and return the money, I am offering my resignation. If you find it appropriate, I will stay on for the duration of this current case and then leave.

Yours sincerely,

Hudson

He clicked send and the message was gone. Another weight off his shoulders, which was instantly replaced by an equally heavy one of needing to find a new job at a time when almost nobody in the world was recruiting. He should tell Abigail about the email that he'd just sent to Maddie, but he couldn't face the arguing that would undoubtedly follow, so instead he forwarded the sent message to her.

He tried to switch his focus back to the Twin Falls case by pulling up the speculative tree for Jacob Sauer. Hudson had completed a lot of work on Jacob's paternal grandparents, finding that both had been born in Rohleder, Saratov, in the Volga region of Russia.

Hudson's bedroom door suddenly flew open. 'What the hell's going on, Hudson?' Abigail stormed.

She'd evidently read the email to Maddie, then.

'You're not just content with wrecking our chances to adopt a child; you're now threatening our home and entire livelihoods?'

'Don't overreact. I'll find something else,' he tried earnestly to reassure her. 'Besides, you earn enough to cover the mortgage and basic bills, at least. We're not in any danger of losing our home or livelihoods.'

'I seriously cannot believe you're being so blasé about this. You are literally in self-destruct mode and are a completely different person than you were even just a month ago. Is there someone else in your life? Is that it?' she demanded.

Hudson couldn't help but laugh off her assumption, given their current confined circumstances. 'No, there's nobody else.'

'I'm glad to see that causing me such deep distress and breaking my heart is quite so amusing to you…'

'Abigail, I didn't—'

'I don't want to hear it,' she yelled, and promptly left, slamming his bedroom door shut behind her.

Hudson sighed and gazed out of the window into the clouds which were still doggedly clinging on, finding it an appropriate metaphor for his feelings right now.

He needed to focus on work.

He looked at his computer screen, having utterly forgotten whatever he'd been working on just two minutes previously. It was no good. He decided that he was just not going to be able to concentrate here.

Closing his laptop, Hudson stowed it in his rucksack, along with his notepad and pencil, pulled on a coat and, without saying anything to Abigail, headed out the front door. He felt an instant, enveloping blend of gratitude and guilt for being outside and free. He walked purposefully, trying to empty his head of all the personal stuff going on at home before he reached the FHL.

As he was walking away from home, he remembered that that guy, Reggie, had asked him to bring coffees next time that he would be working outside the library, and this thought took Hudson on a minor detour through Liberty Park over to Salt Lake Coffee Break, hoping that it was open for take-outs at least, despite almost everything else still being closed.

He was in luck. The place was indeed open with a limited menu for take-outs, all served through a side window, and Hudson ordered two coffees before continuing on to the library.

When he arrived and sat at his usual spot, he found himself unexpectedly crestfallen to discover that Reggie wasn't there. Then he felt a little dumb to have considered that he would have been. He set down the coffees and took out his laptop.

Apart from being a little colder—in temperature, at least—there was no difference between working here or working at home, but somehow it felt so much less repressive and much more conducive to making some progress. Here, he was much better able to compartmentalize and lock away constant thoughts of Abigail, the adoption agency and their marital problems.

He drank some coffee and reminded himself of where he was up to with investigating Jacob Sauer's grandfather, Caspar Sauer. Several U.S. censuses had cited his place of birth as Rohleder, Saratov, Russia. But Russian genealogy was notoriously difficult. There was nothing in the way of vital records offered on the FamilySearch Research Wiki, but one thing at the bottom of the *Russia Genealogy* page caught his attention. Under *Research Tutorials*, he spotted a link to a video, titled *The Volga German Settlements in Russia*. The video was 48 minutes long— perfect to listen to on his walk back home. For now, though, he was intrigued just to read the brief description beneath the video player: *Catherine the Great invited Germans to settle the area along the Volga River around 1764-1767. Some 27,000 Germans came and settled here.*

Hudson ran a Google search for genealogy records for Rohleder, Saratov, Russia, where he knew Caspar Sauer had been born. The fifth result, volgaparishes.com, looked as though it might prove useful to his research.

The website was headed with a map of the villages surrounding the Volga River and was titled *Volga Parish Records*. Hudson scrolled down the page, finding that the parishes were divided into two sections: *Bergseite—mountain side—*and *Wiesenseite—meadow side.*

Rohleder Parish was close to the bottom of the latter section which Hudson clicked to view.

Births 1801 to 1857
Marriages 1801 to 1869
Deaths 1801 to 1857

According to various U.S. censuses, Caspar Sauer and his wife, Mabel Balakin, had both been born around 1890, way outside of the transcriptions within this database.

Hudson sipped his coffee and thought for a moment.

Accessing MyHeritage, he pulled up their *Collection Catalog* and filtered the search down to records from Russia. Nine record sets came up. He clicked *Russia Births and Baptisms 1755-1917* and searched for Caspar Sauer's and Mabel Balakin's birth.

No Results were found for your search

'Great,' he muttered, returning to the previous page and clicking on *Russians Immigrating to the United States.*

No Results were found for your search

Hudson opened the genealogy resource site, CyndisList.com, to see what other resources there might be for Germans who lived in Russia and then immigrated to the U.S.A. Under *Germans from Russia*, he found a link to an obituary database from the American Historical

Society of Germans from Russia, covering the period 1899-2012.

Hudson searched for Caspar Sauer among the 539,878 obituaries within the digital archive. The third result appeared to be correct.

'Hi,' a voice said from beside him.

Reggie was standing beside him with a grin on his face. Hudson picked up the spare cup from the wall. 'Black coffee. One sugar,' he said, offering it to him. 'Should still be warm enough to drink.'

Reggie laughed. 'Ha, thanks, man. I was just kidding, you know, when I said to bring me coffee. I didn't think anywhere was even open.' He took a sip of the drink. 'Perfect. Thank you.'

'You're welcome,' Hudson replied, watching as Reggie sat down and took out his laptop. 'What are you working on today?'

'An Unclaimed Persons case. A young guy who was hit by a car in Kansas City last summer. No next of kin came forward after his death, so I'm trying to track down any family members. What about you?'

'Oh, trying to trace back a German family who lived in Russia and immigrated to the U.S.'

'Sounds simple enough,' Reggie said with a laugh.

'I'm hoping this obit I just found is going to help me,' Hudson said, gesturing to his laptop screen. He looked at Reggie, wondering if he too came here as a place of escape, rather than out of necessity for work. He didn't feel that he knew him well enough to ask.

'Fingers crossed,' Reggie said, drinking his coffee before tapping at his keyboard.

Hudson returned to the obituary that he hoped might pertain to the correct Caspar Sauer.

Der Kirchenbote Vol.84 No.2. 13 Nov 1965
SAUER, Caspar
Caspar Sauer, son of George and Maris (nee Zeiler) Sauer was born February 7, 1890, in Rohleder, Saratov, Russia where he was baptized by Pastor Samuel Dietrich and after thorough instructions in religion was confirmed by Pastor Roos. With his parents, the Sauer family came to America in 1892, settling in Weld County, Colorado where the deceased was engaged in cabinet making. He married Mabel Balakin on March 13, 1912, and they had 9 children. After a short illness, he died October 20, 1965, at the age of 75 years. His survivors include his widow,

Mabel and children George, Caspar, Lydia, Paul, Sara, Frank and Gertrude. "I am the Way and the Truth and the Life."

Hudson was delighted that it not only confirmed his findings thus far, but also provided the names of Caspar's parents. He took a screenshot, attached it to Caspar's profile and then added George Sauer and Maris Zeiler to the tree.

Even though it was highly unlikely that George and Maris had wed before the terminus of the transcriptions in 1869, Hudson opened the marriage records at volgaparishes.com. He slowly worked his way backward in time until 1850, when he ended his search without having found any of the relevant surnames.

'Thanks for the coffee, man,' Reggie said, shaking the empty cup. 'If you're back here tomorrow, I'll gladly repay the kindness.'

'If it means escaping from my wife's wrath, then yes,' Hudson answered, instantly regretting what he had just blurted out.

Reggie took it as a joke and laughed. 'Yeah, same. Except I live with my parents still. This cold spot right here'—he slapped the hard concrete under him—'is *so* much better than being stuck at home.'

Hudson nodded his empathic agreement as they both returned to their respective projects. For his, he returned to Google for some suggestions of where to look next for records. At volgagermans.org, he found a twenty-eight-page PDF, entitled *Volga German Genealogy Research: Documenting Your Ancestors Lives in America and Canada*, which he set about digesting.

Hudson was hungry, thirsty and, what was more pressing, needed to use the bathroom. It was just past two o'clock in the afternoon. If he left now, he'd have plenty of time to walk home and get himself ready before the briefing. He packed up his things, chatted a little more, and then said goodbye to Reggie.

'I'll be back in the office around ten, give or take,' Reggie said with a smile.

'Okay, I'll see you then,' Hudson replied, giving a wave and wandering slowly in the direction of home.

As he walked, he allowed his thoughts to roam back to the Wanda

Chabala case. He wondered what she would do next. He had checked the Minneapolis local news several times since Saturday and run Google searches for any updates on the Francesca Chabala case, but nothing new had been reported. Was Wanda biding her time? Doing more investigating to determine which of the brothers was responsible? Getting a surreptitious DNA test? Hudson couldn't imagine that he would be able to continue acting normally at home, if he harbored such similar suspicions about his spouse.

Maddie hadn't yet replied to his resignation email, and he guessed that perhaps she'd talk to him after today's briefing. He didn't have any more to say on the subject, however; it was up to her as to when she would let him go from Venator. Although he did not want to leave at all, he was at peace with the decision that he'd made. What he didn't know yet, though, was what was going to happen to all that money which Abigail had siphoned off for the adoption process.

He arrived home more than an hour after leaving the library. 'Hey,' he called out when he entered the hall. Abigail's bedroom door was closed, and she didn't reply. So, it was going to be like that, then.

In the kitchen, Hudson made himself a sandwich and a drink, then went to his bedroom, closed the door and carried on working, right up until the briefing started.

'Hi, guys,' Maddie said, welcoming the team.

'How's everything with you?' Kenyatta asked. 'Has Trenton settled back down?'

'Knock on wood… Everything's great. Back to doing schoolwork and annoying his sister. Nothing could feel more normal around here. As far as I'm aware, he hasn't hatched any further escape plans; so that's something to be thankful for, I suppose.'

'Well, that *is* something,' Kenyatta said with a laugh.

'Are you all okay?' Maddie asked.

Even though he'd dropped a hand grenade into his marriage and the job he loved, Hudson somehow managed a reply in tune with the rest of the team. 'Yeah, good, thank you.'

'Okay, then,' Maddie said, sharing her screen with Joey Seymour's pedigree on it. 'Let's get on with the briefing, shall we? It's been a good day for me, research-wise. Having found twenty-eight of thirty-two of

184

Joey Seymour's great-great-great-grandparents, I then started working on triangulation within the cluster, and guess what? The mother's maiden name of the next person whom I picked from the cluster matched with one of Joey's great-great-grandmothers. Obviously, I homed in on this branch of the tree and, about an hour ago, found the ancestral couple who link together cluster five. Say hello to John Murton and his wife, Minnie Davis, from England.'

'Hi, y'all,' Kenyatta said, waving comically into her camera.

'Well done,' Becky enthused. 'Another cluster closed.'

'Thanks. I'm glad to have it closed. Hudson? What have you been working on today?'

'So, I've been continuing with genetic network number four for Jacob Sauer,' he said, pulling up his pedigree, 'mainly focusing on the Russian side of his family who, it turns out, are actually *German* émigrés.'

'Oh, okay…' Maddie said, leaning in.

'A lot of the parishes along the Volga River were settled from the 1760s by German families. I have to say that it hasn't been easy to research them, and I think it's highly unlikely that I'll get back too much further than great-grandparent level. Although there were censuses taken in 1850, 1857 and 1897, they're not comprehensive, not all translated and most of the 1897 Census was destroyed in a fire.'

'Now, isn't that always the way…?' Kenyatta muttered. 'I tell you, fire is the biggest enemy of the genealogist.'

'Hear, hear,' Becky chipped in.

'I don't know exactly why,' Hudson began, 'but several of these German-descended families left the Volga region at the same time in 1892; the Sauers and the Balakins were among them. Obviously, this is prior to the 1897 Census that was destroyed and a *long* way off the previous census of 1857.'

'Do you think there's more to pursue, here, Hudson?' Maddie asked. 'Or are you better off switching to triangulation within the cluster and hoping for the best?'

'I think I'd prefer to work up Jacob Sauer's maternal side, as I've done nothing at all there. You never know if this whole Volga area is just a red herring; or there could be a Russian influence on both sides of his tree.'

'Yeah, I agree,' Maddie concurred. 'Good work. Actually, now I've closed down my genetic network, I could work on triangulation within your cluster. Stay on after the meeting and we'll talk about it.'

Hudson nodded along, presuming that Maddie was using this as a ruse to discuss the terms of his resignation. He suddenly felt nervous and began to think ahead to what she might say. Was she even going to let him see this case through? Or could this be his last briefing? Was this Maddie stepping across to take over his workload? As his thoughts began to spiral, he realized that he was no longer paying attention to what was now being said in the briefing. Kenyatta's screen was mirrored on his and she was in full swing, explaining where she was up to.

'...and they seem to come from the Illinois area. At least back to the early 1900s. Anyone spot any familiar names?'

Hudson quickly scanned the tree, not seeing any overlaps with his own clusters.

'Well, let's see. I've definitely got a Smith in my genetic network,' Becky commented with a wry smile.

'And it's a John Smith, too,' Maddie observed. 'Just what you need. Okay, anything else from you, Kenyatta?'

'Oh, I think you've heard enough from me today,' she replied.

'I don't think we could ever hear enough from you,' Maddie countered. 'But I will hand over to Becky if you insist.'

'That I do,' Kenyatta said, sitting back in her seat with a grin.

'Okay. Well, I still haven't closed down my genetic network yet,' Becky complained with a roll of her eyes as she shared her screen. 'But...I am making headway with Summer Eckhart's paternal line. So far, they're from Maine and Vermont. The names of Summer's four paternal great-grandparents were Eckhart, Bruno, Skinner and Ferrari. I've obviously still got work to do getting each of these lines back another couple of generations, but I've got this feeling the link is going to be Summer Eckhart's maternal side. We'll see. That's all from me. Hopefully, by tomorrow's briefing, I might have finally closed this genetic network.'

'As always, great work today, folks,' Maddie said. 'Keep going with it and we'll meet again this time tomorrow.'

Becky, Ross and Kenyatta all said goodbye and left the meeting.

Hudson suddenly felt very alone and vulnerable.

'So,' Maddie opened, 'how are you doing, Hudson?'

He nodded. 'Okay, I guess.'

'I'm not sure you can be, if I'm honest,' Maddie replied softly.

Tears welled in Hudson's eyes. 'No. I'm not sure, either, to tell you the truth of the matter.'

'Do you want to talk about it?'

He shook his head, emotions suddenly preventing him from being able to speak at all.

Maddie gave him a little time, then said, 'Listen. This pandemic is holding a magnifying glass over us all. Tiny problems are suddenly big problems, big problems are suddenly apocalyptic problems.' She sighed. 'I got your email and I realize that I was pushing you to take action… Do you know what Wanda Chabala is going to do with the information she's now in possession of?'

'No,' he said weakly.

'Hey. I want you on my team, Hudson. You're an excellent genetic genealogist and scientist, and I'd hate to lose you. But I also cannot afford for Venator to be dragged into the Chabala case in any way. So, let's park your resignation for the time being and see how this thing plays out. Okay?'

He nodded.

'Now, is there anything I can do? I don't know… Do you want to take some time off, perhaps?' she asked.

Hudson internally shuddered at the idea of being cooped up at home with nothing to occupy his time or mind. Although there was a great deal of uncertainty in his life, he knew that taking time off would be a bad idea. 'I really don't want to do that, no. That would be an unwise move. I need the distraction.'

'I get it. But if you want even a day or just a half-day, take it.'

'Thank you.'

'Think it through. If there's anything else I can do…' Maddie said.

'No. Thanks, though.'

'Well…if you need to talk, you know where I am. Any time.'

'Thank you,' he repeated.

'Take the evening off,' Maddie instructed. 'That's an order. We'll liaise in the morning about my taking on the triangulation of your cluster.'

'Okay. Talk to you tomorrow, then. Bye,' he said, leaving the meeting.

Hudson stood up, exhaled, and wiped his eyes. It was time to speak candidly with Abigail, to try and clear the air in some way. Maybe they could sit down and have dinner and a glass of wine together this evening, he thought, heading out of his bedroom.

He moved across the hall and knocked lightly on Abigail's door. No answer. He hovered, then tapped more loudly. Still nothing. 'Abigail, please can we talk?' No answer. 'This toxic environment isn't good for either of us. Please, can we just talk?' When she didn't answer that time, he sighed in resignation and walked to the kitchen to get himself a large wine.

As he went to take the bottle out of the refrigerator, he noticed a note on the counter.

I think we need some time apart.

Chapter Twenty-Two

Wednesday, April 15, 2020, Salt Lake City, Utah

'God, why do I let you talk me into these things?' Ross complained, grimacing as he stretched his arms above his head, following a YouTube workout.

'Fit in body, fit in mind, Rossy,' Becky chanted, switching off the TV and going over to the kitchen. 'And now for a protein shake for breakfast.' She opened the refrigerator and took out two bottles, handing one to Ross.

'Thanks,' he said, taking a long swig. 'What are you working on, today?'

Becky exhaled. 'I'm this close'—she squashed an inch between thumb and forefinger—'to wrapping up my SAKI case and identifying the Houston serial rapist... But, with Hudson and Kenyatta closing down their first genetic networks, I feel totally behind and need to get on with mine. I can see today being a *really* long day.'

'Can't you push the SAKI case back to the weekend and prioritize with this live case?' Ross suggested.

'I guess...' Although it made some sense in terms of priorities, it wasn't as simple as that for Becky. She felt the burden of the unsolved rape cases from the 1980s acutely, thinking about those six women who were out there, trying to get on with their lives, all the while knowing that their rapist was probably still going about his normal life, possibly even continuing to commit more serious crimes. But she also felt the weight of this live case, where some poor, unsuspecting woman's life could be in immediate danger. 'Could you email them for me and let them know my update will take a little longer?'

'Sure,' he said. 'Anything back from the restroom yet?' Ross asked.

'No, nothing from WC,' Becky answered, ignoring his attempt at humor. 'Do you think I should send a message to the number that called me? Or might that scare her off?'

'Hang fire just a little longer, then do it,' Ross advised. 'What about your parents? Heard anything from them?'

'Nothing whatsoever. I should text my mom, I guess,' Becky said,

189

drinking more of her protein shake. 'But not now. Now, I'm going to jump in the shower.'

Within forty-five minutes, Becky was sitting in front of her computer and feeling ready to work. On her screen was the profile page for one of her cluster lead's paternal great-grandmothers, Alice Bruno. In what Becky took to be a double-whammy affront to genealogy, Alice had been born on June 3, 1890, just one day after the federal census had been taken; the same census that would later be destroyed by fire.

According to the 1940 census, Alice had been born in Montpelier, Washington County, Vermont. Her marriage certificate had given her parents' names as Henry and Maud Bruno. Becky used this combination of information to search for the family on the 1910 census.

Four results

She clicked to view a copy of the original images. Ancestry had helpfully highlighted the relevant family in yellow and green on each page. The third result appeared to be the right family and corroborated the data that she had already harvested.

Bruno, Henry L E, head, male, black, 48 years old, married 24 years, occupation hotel cashier, father's birthplace Vermont, mother's birthplace Vermont
Bruno, Maud, wife, female, black, 46 years old, five children, all alive, no occupation, father's birthplace Vermont, mother's birthplace Canada
Bruno, Annie E, daughter, black, 23 years old, single, occupation nurse
Bruno, Alice, daughter, black, 20 years old, single, no occupation

Becky saved the census report to each member of the family, then began to focus on Alice's father, Henry L. E. Bruno. His age in 1910 pointed to an approximate birthdate of 1862, so she ran a search in the 1870 Census for him.

She took a look down the results list. Only the top five of seventy-two suggestions were for someone named Henry Bruno, the rest were spelling variants. She checked each of the top five entries, all of which could possibly be correct, but which could equally be incorrect. Needing further verification, she switched her focus to finding Henry and Maud's marriage instead, hoping that their parents' names might have been included on the record. According to the 1910 Census, their marriage had occurred around 1886.

Using the Research Wiki at FamilySearch to navigate records for Vermont, Becky was presented with a colorful map of the state, with each separate county clickable for their genealogy records. Becky didn't know where Henry and Maud had married, but, given that they were recorded as living in Washington County on the census, she opted to start her search there. She clicked the county on the map and a page of information loaded, at the bottom of which were links to vital records.

Becky selected *Marriages 1791-1974* which were held by FamilySearch themselves and entered Henry Bruno's details with a five-year window around the possible marriage date. A page of possibilities loaded, but the name of Maud Bailey in the *Relationships* column revealed that the third result down was correct. She clicked to view a copy of the original document.

MARRIAGE - GROOM
Name of Groom: Bruno, Henry L. E.
Residence of Groom: Washington, Vermont
Date of Marriage: December 5, 1886
Age in Years: 24
Occupation: Merchant
Place of Birth: Burlington, Vermont
Father's Name: Wellington P. Bruno
Birthplace: -
Mother's Name: Myrtle (Wilson)
Birthplace: -

Becky downloaded the entry and then added it along with the information it contained to Summer Eckhart's quick and dirty tree. She returned to the vital records page, clicking on Maud Bailey's name and seeing her half of the marriage entry.

MARRIAGE - BRIDE

Name of Bride: Bailey, Maud
Residence of Bride: Washington, Vermont
Age in Years: 22
Occupation: -
Place of Birth: Washington, Vermont
Father's Name: Silas Bailey
Birthplace: -
Mother's Name: Arvilla Burdick
Birthplace: -

Once Becky had saved the information to the tree, she double-checked that the four surnames of Bruno, Wilson, Bailey and Burdick hadn't appeared anywhere on Latasha McNaughton's tree. They hadn't, which meant that she had still yet to find the point of triangulation between the killer, Latasha McNaughton and Summer Eckhart.

Becky sighed. Even though she knew that this process could be protracted, she felt anxious to close down her cluster and get started on her second as soon as possible.

She got up and went to the kitchen, taking her cell phone with her. 'Want anything to drink?' she asked Ross who was watching back yesterday's briefing and adding to the master file for the case surnames that had been mentioned.

'Wonderful idea. Coffee, please.'

'Coming right up,' she said, switching on the machine. As she waited for the drink to be made, she typed out a quick message to her mom, hoping that having that out of the way and off her mind might allow her to focus more on her work.

Hi Mom. How are you both doing? Are you managing to get enough food and provisions? How's Dad's business doing?

She re-read the message, thinking that it sounded somehow so disingenuous. Of course they would have enough food and provisions, they were very wealthy and generally got whatever they wanted in life. She was in no doubt whatsoever that the kitchen would be sufficiently stocked to feed a small village for several months. She thought her

192

question about her dad's business could be misconstrued or, given her own illicit investigations, might arouse his suspicions. So, she deleted that part and hit send.

She finished making Ross's coffee and placed it down on the counter next to him.

'Thanks,' he muttered, looking from the screen over to her. 'Do you think we're going to solve this one? In time, I mean.'

'What makes you ask that?'

'Just looking over the case notes... So much seemed to be made of the killer having this Russian ethnicity, but only Hudson has found any links to this area, and he warned that what he'd found was quite limited.'

'Well, we've still got four out of seven clusters to close down. Any of those could have Russian or Eastern European links in them.'

Ross seemed satisfied by her answer, nodding and returning to his work. But, in truth, she shared his unease, too. Yes, there were still four clusters to close, but they were all now being actively worked and, so far, no links had been established to the locations indicated in the killer's geo-ancestry.

She made herself a coffee and asked Ross, 'I was thinking earlier... How are you getting on with your Y-DNA results?'

'Oh, I've given up on Hudson and have signed up for a Legacy lecture by Mags Gaulden on the weekend. I'm hoping she'll have all the answers for me.'

'Oh, cool. She's good. You'll be an expert by the end of that session, for sure,' Becky called over her shoulder, carrying her coffee back to the guest bedroom. Clasping the mug between her hands, she gazed at the photos of Lorena Baly, Carla Eagleton, Jasmine Jaconski and Molly Hutchison. She hoped that the niggling worry that she and Ross seemed to have about not tracking down this killer—or maybe not in time to save another victim, at least—would pass as the investigation progressed.

She drank some coffee, then carried on with her work. She pulled up Summer Eckhart's other paternal great-grandfather, Lewis Skinner. All she knew about him so far was his name which had been stated on his daughter, Louisa Skinner's marriage record.

To know more about Lewis Skinner, Becky needed to find Louisa on the 1940 Census, a year after her marriage to Abel Eckhart. The newlywed couple were easy to find, living in Andover Town, Oxford County, Maine, the same place given as Louisa's birth.

Now Becky knew that Louisa had been born in Maine, she set about locating her on the previous census. She entered her details into the 1930 U.S. Census search engine, adding the names of her parents. There was just one result, in Andover Town.

Skinner, Lewis, Head, male, 32, married, age at first marriage 20, born Maine, farmer, father's birthplace Maine, mother's birthplace Massachusetts
Skinner, Laura, Wife, female, 32, married, age at first marriage 20, born Maine, father's birthplace Maine, mother's birthplace Canada
Skinner, Louisa, Daughter, female, 11, born Maine
Skinner, Elgin, Son, male, 10, born Maine

Becky saved the census return to Louisa Skinner's profile and added the new information that she now knew about her parents. Assuming that Lewis and Laura's marriage to each other had been their first, Becky ran a search in the Ancestry *Maine, U.S., Marriage Records, 1713-1922* record set. She quickly located a copy of their union in South Paris, Oxford County. The record contained further information, including their birth locations, but crucially it did not contain details of the couple's parents.

Taking Lewis Skinner's birth first, she conducted a search in the *All Maine, U.S. Birth Records, 1715-1922* collection. There were two results, the first looking as though it might be accurate.

RECORD OF BIRTH
Child's Name: Lewis Skinner
Date of Birth: April 13, 1898
Place of Birth: So. Paris, Me
Sex: m
Living or Stillborn: l
Father's Name: Llewellyn Skinner
Father's Birthplace: So. Paris, Me

Father's Occupation: Machinist
Mother's Maiden Name: Carrie Welch
Mother's Birthplace: Boston, Massachusetts
Mother's occupation: Housewife

It took Becky a few seconds to do a double take back to Lewis Skinner's mother's name. Carrie Welch. With a twinge of excitement, she opened the quick and dirty tree for Latasha McNaughton, displaying her family as a pedigree. Just as Becky remembered, Latasha's paternal grandmother had been named Judy Ann Welch from Morgantown, West Virginia. Was there a link between her and Carrie Welch from Boston, Massachusetts? She sincerely hoped so.

Becky clicked on Judy Ann Welch's profile, following the trail through all the research that she had conducted into her paternal line until she reached Latasha McNaughton's great-great-great grandparents, Clifton Welch and Julia Manefield of Manchester, New Hampshire. They were potentially the common ancestral couple that Becky was looking for.

There was one way to find out; by tracing Carrie Welch's birth record.

Returning to FamilySearch, Becky checked the location of vital records for Boston, Massachusetts, finding that they were on Ancestry. She followed the link through and entered Carrie Welch's details into the *Massachusetts Town Vital Collections, 1620-1988* record set. Becky held her breath as she clicked the top result and was taken through to a scan, titled BIRTHS REGISTERED IN THE CITY OF BOSTON. She scrolled down the page and, close to the bottom, released her breath.

Date: December 7, 1874
Name of Child: Carrie Welch
Sex and Condition: female
Place of Birth: 1 George Street, Boston
Names of Parents: Clifton and Julia Welch
Residence of Parents: Boston
Occupation of Father: Marble Cutter
Place of Birth of Father: Manchester, New Hampshire

Place of Birth of Mother: Ireland

She had done it: Clifton Welch and Julia Manefield were the common ancestral couple for Latasha McNaughton, Summer Eckhart and the Twin Falls serial killer.

Becky slumped back in her chair, overwhelmed with relief that she'd closed the cluster and would be able to have something concrete to say at their team briefing later today.

Before she moved on to deal with her other cluster, she added the birth record and then merged the two quick and dirty trees into one.

Despite being delighted with her findings so far, there was no time to waste and, with that in mind, Becky opened the file labeled *Cluster Two* from the shared Venator drive. Kenyatta had assigned a woman, named Heather Newton, who matched the killer with seventy-nine centimorgans of DNA, as the cluster lead. Although Heather had not uploaded any kind of a family tree, she had added four ancestral surnames: Duke, Gagne, Warren and Eadie. Becky copied Heather's Gmail address over to Spokeo and kicked off her research with a background check.

Heather Newton, Age 63
Aka: Heather Warren
Who was born in April 1957, Houston, TX
Current Address: Rosemary Dr, Baytown, TX

Becky scrolled down to *Family*.

We found 2 relatives for Heather

Raymond A. Newton, 76
Raymond, 76, has previously lived with Heather in League City, TX
Born July 1944. Married. 3 Phone numbers. 2 Emails.

Erica J. Newton
Erica has previously lived with Heather in League City, TX
Single. 2 Phone numbers. 1 Address.

Becky's initial interest was drawn to the *Aka* reference under her name. Working on the assumption that Warren had been Heather's maiden name, Becky began to run searches for a marriage between her and Raymond Newton.

'Are you still alive, Becks?' Ross called out.

Becky closed her eyes for a moment and yawned. 'I don't think so,' she replied.

'Wine?'

'What? It's like lunch ti—' She caught the actual time: 4:08 p.m. Yet again, the day had somehow run away with itself. She realized that she hadn't left her office chair in more than five hours. 'I'll have one after the briefing.'

Becky was pleased with what she had achieved today. She planned to have a quick comfort break, do the briefing, have dinner, and then continue working.

She checked her emails to see if anything had come in from WC, but it hadn't. Then she checked the messages on her phone. Three unread. The most recent was from Jerome.

Hi Becks. How's your day been? Fancy a virtual date on Saturday? I'll organize the food and movie.

Becky frowned at her cell. How could he organize food and a movie on a virtual date? It made no sense. She would reply after the briefing, she thought, returning to the other two messages. Lois Strange was next.

Hey Becky. I've been thinking about you and wondered if you'd made any progress on what we talked about?

Becky couldn't help but notice that Lois shared the same reluctance to communicate frankly and openly as Artemon Bruce's and Jay Craig's widows, and she could only put that down to genuine, enduring fear of a person or people working within her father's company. She was still

197

clinging to the thin and dying hope that perhaps her father's involvement in whatever was going on was minimal.

The last message was from her mom.

We're doing okay, thank you. Getting a little cabin fever now but we realize we're in a more fortunate position than most. How are you doing? If you need anything, please ask. Are you able to work from home?

It had none of her mom's usual pleasantries and there was no mention of her father at all, but at least she had answered.

'Miss Larkin, this is your ten-minute warning,' Ross yelled in a weird attempt at some sort of British accent.

She would have to reply to the three messages after the briefing, she thought, hurrying off to get a water and use the bathroom.

Becky arrived back at her computer and clicked the Zoom link to the afternoon's briefing. Amazingly, she was the first to arrive.

'Hi, there,' Maddie said. 'How are you?'

'I feel like I've just been dragged backward out of a rabbit hole, and one that I hadn't finished exploring by far, truth be told,' Becky admitted.

Maddie laughed. 'Yeah, right. That's how I feel every day. Are you finding that, without other people around you in the office and the other elements of our normal daily routines, the time just vanishes; like at triple speed?'

'Totally,' Becky agreed, telling Maddie that Ross had just offered her wine and she had gone to protest that it was lunchtime until she'd noticed the real time. 'I declined the wine, by the way.'

'Tempting, though,' Maddie commented, admitting Ross, Hudson and Kenyatta to the meeting.

'Oh, hi, Becky,' Ross said. 'You made it on time, then?'

Becky grinned. 'Of course,' she said, pretending to look at her watch. 'You're cutting it a little close, though.'

'Ha ha,' he replied.

'How are you, Kenyatta?' Maddie asked.

Becky zoned out of the exchange when she noticed her cell phone light up with a message from WC. She subtly clicked to open it out of shot. There was no message, just a 45-page document attached that was entitled *haiti_finances.pdf*. She sent the document to the printer, silenced her cell phone and returned her full attention to the briefing underway.

Maddie had just shared her screen with the team. 'As I was only assigned one genetic network—now closed—I've been working with Hudson on cluster four. No triangulation achieved yet and I'm back to all eight great-grandparents of Andre Hook. I've got Scotland, Ireland and various states in the U.S., but nothing is standing out up to this point. Hudson, do you want to give an update on the cluster lead?'

'Sure,' he said, displaying his screen for the rest of the team. Becky thought that he looked a little brighter and more upbeat than he had, yesterday. 'I've identified all four of Jacob Sauer's maternal great-grandparents and four great-great-grandparents. They seem mainly to be located around Arizona and New Mexico. But my gut is telling me that the link is not on this side, but rather on the paternal side: the Germans living in Russia. So, we'll have to see…'

'Thank you,' Maddie said. 'Kenyatta?'

Kenyatta rubbed her hands together. 'I bring good tidings…potentially. Yesterday, I said I was working on the paternal side of my cluster lead, Ray Marshall. Well, although I've got a few lines that have hit a brick wall, it's kind of done. So, a couple of hours ago, I switched over to Ray's maternal line. Take a look at this,' she said, clicking on his profile and running a mouse-cursor circle around his mother's name.

'Barbara Getman,' Maddie read.

Becky wasn't sure what they were supposed to be getting from this name. She couldn't recall its having come up before now.

'Now take a look at this,' Kenyatta said, switching tabs to the website forebears.io which showed a distribution map for the Getman surname.

'Oh, wow,' Hudson said.

'That's interesting,' Becky added, looking at the world map on her screen. All countries of the world were delineated with a color scheme ranging from gray—no incidence of the surname—through to deep red—the highest incidence of the surname—and various shades in between. Russia was the only country painted deep red.

199

'And if I scroll down,' Kenyatta said, moving to a frequency chart below, 'you can see Russia is at the top, followed by the U.S., then Belarus, Kazakhstan and other Eastern European countries.'

'This is really promising,' Maddie said with a wide smile. 'Well done. And where is Barbara Getman from, exactly?'

Kenyatta switched back to Ray Marshall's speculative tree. She clicked on Barbara, which revealed her place of birth to have been Denver, Colorado. 'I've done a little research,' Kenyatta began, 'and there's a substantial Russian-speaking community in Denver.'

'Okay, great,' Maddie said. 'And what about her parents?'

Kenyatta ran her mouse around the *Family* section of the speculative tree. The two boxes for Barbara Getman's parents were empty. 'That's tomorrow's job.'

'I've just quickly Googled how far it is from Denver to Weld County, Colorado where my Sauers and Balakins settled and it's just over fifty miles,' Hudson revealed.

'That could well be a point of connection. We'll see,' Maddie said. 'Excellent. Anything else, Kenyatta?'

'What more do you want, blood?'

Maddie laughed. 'Over to you, then, Becky.'

'Saving the best for last,' Becky said, picking up an orange piece of paper that she had printed off, holding it up and flaunting it in front of her camera.

'An orange slip!' Maddie said, moving closer to her computer screen to read the information on it. '*Clifton Welch and Julia Manefield of Manchester, New Hampshire*. Great job!'

'So, now we've got eight of the Twin Falls killer's great-great-great-grandparents,' Kenyatta said with a broad smile. 'We're so on to him, team.'

'Let's hope so,' Maddie said. 'Anything else, Becky?'

'Well,' she replied, 'Heather Newton—maiden name Warren—is the lead for cluster two. The families are almost all Texas-based on both sides, but I've only gotten back to the grandparent generation.'

'Great, thank you,' Maddie said. 'Do we have any questions to take, anyone?'

Becky asked, 'Have you heard any more from Detective González?'

'Nothing,' Maddie said. 'I'm taking it that no news is good news.'

'Let's hope so,' Kenyatta said.

After a short silence, in which Becky assumed that everyone's thoughts had been caused to recall the dark and pressing reality of this case, Maddie said, 'Okay. Well, if that's everything, then I'll go ahead and end the meeting and let you all get on with a well-earned, restful evening. Thanks for your efforts, everybody. See you tomorrow.'

'Bye,' Becky said, leaving the meeting.

A second later, Ross was at the guest room door. 'Did you see Hudson's screen?'

'What? The tree he's working on?'

'No. One of the web browser tabs he had open was for Utah Adoption Specialists.'

Becky's eyes widened with intrigue. 'Oh... Maybe that explains his weird moods. Maybe he and Abigail are having trouble conceiving and...' She shrugged. 'They're going through the adoption process, which isn't easy from what Maddie's said before.'

'Why doesn't he just tell us so that we understand?' Ross asked, leaning on the doorframe.

'It's private stuff. It might not go through and then they'll have everybody constantly asking how it's going. I kind of get it.'

'Do you want that wine now?'

'Absolutely. Oh, and WC sent through the documents,' she said, wheeling her chair over to the printer where she picked up the stack of paper before following Ross out into their living room.

Becky sat down and waited for Ross to arrive with the drinks.

'Here you go,' he said, handing her a full glass and sliding in next to her.

'Thanks,' she said, taking a sip, then setting the drink down on the coffee table and turning to the first page of the Haiti finance document.

'Well, that's an hour of my life that I won't get back,' Ross quipped when they had finished reading the final page of the dry report.

Becky sighed as she switched the pile of papers for her second glass of wine. They had read the monotonous document, page by page, but had not understood it at all. It was largely made up of figures, data and terms of business for building contractors. Neither one of them had gleaned anything nefarious or slightly dubious from the file; or even anything remotely interesting for that matter. But then, they weren't finance experts.

Ross reached for the TV remote. '*Schitts Creek*?'

'We've seen the whole thing twice,' Becky replied in disbelief.

Ross shrugged. 'And…?'

'You go ahead. I'm going to think about what to do with this document,' she said, picking up the papers and heading back to the guest room. Jerome. Why hadn't she thought of him sooner? He was studying for a business degree and it could provide them with something to talk about. She clicked to reply to his previous message about a virtual movie and dinner date on Saturday.

Hi. That sounds great - how's it going to work though?? Could I ask you a favor? I have a highly confidential finance / contract file that I need someone to look over for me. Would you mind?

She sent the message. His reply came back immediately.

Sure, send it over!

So, Becky did just that, asking him not to mention it to anyone at all.

Chapter Twenty-Three

Thursday, April 16, 2020, Salt Lake City, Utah

Kenyatta's alarm went off at 6 a.m. She groaned slightly, not ready to wake. But still she swung her legs out of the bed and made her way into the kitchenette, switched on the light and, once her eyes had adjusted to the harsh strip lighting, took a can of Coke from the refrigerator and sat down on the sofa in the living room. Before she started work, she took her cell phone off the charger, seeing that she had a message from Troy; the first one since Dougie had died, despite Kenyatta sending repeated texts asking if he was okay.

Hi Mom. We all miss you and keep asking Dad when we're going to see you next. He says we can see you when you stop working with the homeless. Can you stop please?

The message speared into her heart and paralyzed her capacity to think for a moment. She desperately wanted to see her kids and would do anything, including stopping her work at the SLC Homeless Kitchen, in order to spend time with them. But Otis was just channeling his general spite toward her and using his power over her simply because he could; not at all in order to protect their children from the virus. Her lawyer thought that Otis's withholding access to the kids, despite her altruistic work, would work in her favor as an example of his ongoing unreasonable behavior. She didn't know what to do except take time to think on it. She typed out a message back to Troy.

I miss the three of you SO very much. I'm not sure your father will permit access even if I did stop working with the homeless. I'll talk to my lawyer and work out what we're going to do so that I can see you all as much and as soon as possible. How are you doing?

She put her cell phone down and took a moment to compose herself. She couldn't dwell on the situation with her kids, or else she would end up like she'd been after her parents had died, something that she was certain Otis was trying to effect by stealth. She had to put on a brave face and continue until the all-important court hearing.

She opened her laptop and clicked the web browser that was ready and waiting: GEDmatch. After Angela Spooner had sent a message to her third cousin, Kanda Phasuk, introducing Kenyatta and explaining the case, Kanda had uploaded her DNA to the website yesterday morning. Her kit should have finished being analyzed and uploaded and should now be fully searchable.

Kenyatta logged in to the kit belonging to the eldest of the *Boys Under the Bridge* and clicked *One-To-Many*.

'Oh my!' she gasped, glancing upward and mouthing, 'Thank you!'

The closest match to the boy was no longer Angela Spooner, but Kanda Phasuk. They matched with seventy-seven centimorgans of DNA, double that of Angela. According to GEDmatch, Kanda was just 3.77 generations away from the boy.

Kenyatta wept tears of joy.

At last, she had a pair of direct ancestors for the brothers.

She dabbed her eyes on the sleeve of her pajamas and took in a deep breath. Then, she copied Kanda Phasuk's kit number and ran a *One-to-One* search against the elder brother. A small table loaded showing the chromosome numbers, overlap positions and number of centimorgans per matching chromosome. Kenyatta copied the contents of the table across to DNAPainter.com and logged in using the boy's kit details. She clicked PAINT A NEW MATCH and pasted the data across from GEDmatch. Not knowing definitively whether the boys matched with Angela Spooner on their maternal or paternal side, Kenyatta could not ascribe the four downloaded segments to either base pairs, but rather to an additional layer named SHARED OR BOTH.

She was pleased to see that there was overlap with four chromosomes between the boy, Angela Spooner, and Kanda Phasuk, which suggested that these portions of their DNA had come from their shared ancestors, Arthit and Preeda Tang of Khao Wang in Thailand.

She sipped her Coke and then logged in at MyHeritage using Angela Spooner's details. On the DNA menu, she selected *DNA Matches* and scrolled down to Kanda Phasuk. The vital information that all of these people were not just related to Kanda and Angela but also to the two brothers swelled Kenyatta's heart. She began to take screenshots and make notes on the sixty-seven people who were all linked via DNA to Arthit and Preeda Tang, intending to go on to investigate every single last one of them.

The first person who matched both women was someone by the name of Anong Bunmak. He shared 60.6 centimorgans of DNA with Angela and 50.9 centimorgans of DNA with Kanda, putting him in the third-to-fifth-cousin bracket.

Kenyatta clicked his name, then scrolled down to *Shared Ethnicities and Genetic Groups*, seeing that he was 70.6% *Thai and Cambodian.*

She was pleased to see that Anong had included a basic family tree back to all four grandparents. His maternal grandmother was listed as Ying Tang. Was Tang a common surname in Thailand or could this be how he related to Arthit and Preeda Tang?

Taking still more screenshots and notes, Kenyatta worked her way down the list of shared matches between Angela Spooner and Kanda Phasuk, wanting to harvest as much information as she could, just in case her access to Angela's account were to be revoked.

At 8:30 a.m. Kenyatta's cell phone alarm went off again. She ignored it for a moment, finishing taking details of the cousin match that she was currently working on while her cell phone buzzed on noisily beside her. Setting an alarm was the only way that she could force herself to stop working on the boys' case.

She made a note of where she had got up to, silenced the alarm and then set her laptop to one side. After taking a quick shower and eating some granola for breakfast, Kenyatta returned to the very same spot on the sofa. Turning to her Venator work, she picked up her laptop and began working on her cluster, specifically on identifying the parents of Barbara Getman. The 1940 Census had listed her birth as having taken place in 1907 in Denver, Colorado—not the best place to research if birth records were needed. The state of Colorado had a 100-year closure rule, so, technically, Barbara Getman's birth record should be available. However, Kenyatta had found in her past research that the records had only been added up until the early 1900s, the precise date of which she couldn't recall but was about to find out.

The vital records were held by Colorado State Archives. On their website, Kenyatta checked to see what was held for Denver and was relieved to see that the birth index ran from 1875 to 1909. So, provided the information on the 1940 Census was correct, she *should* find the record of Barbara Getman's birth. Kenyatta entered her name, selected the county of Denver, then hit the search button. *1 record was returned.* Kenyatta was in luck.

Name: Getman, Barbara
Record Type: Birth / R46
County: Denver
Date: 1907

She clicked Barbara Getman's name, highlighted in blue, which revealed further vital details.

Date of birth: August 15, 1907
Parents: Getman, Henry & Anna Kaufmann

Kenyatta added the new details to Ray Marshall's speculative tree, then turned to the 1910 Census to search for the family. Now that she knew the names of Barbara Getman's parents, Kenyatta discovered the family easily, living in Denver, Colorado. As she scanned across the page, she smiled happily. 'Yes!'

Getman, Henry, Head, male, white, 26, married 5 years, Birthplace Russia, Father's Birthplace Russia, Mother's Birthplace Russia, Immigrated 1906, farmer
Getman, Anna, Wife, female, white, 24, married 5 years, 1 child living, Birthplace Russia, Father's Birthplace, Russia, Mother's Birthplace Russia
Getman, Barbara, Daughter, female, 3, single, Birthplace Colorado

Although Kenyatta was delighted to find a link to Russia, she knew that she had her work cut out finding any more specific details of Henry and Anna's place of origin. Before attempting to find which part of Russia they had come from, Kenyatta concentrated on their time in the U.S., hoping that later records might reveal more about their early lives.

When Kenyatta clicked the link to join the afternoon briefing, she was feeling pleased with herself. Despite the constant pull of her desire to get back to work on the *Boys Under the Bridge* case or to text her sons, she'd managed to maintain her focus on cluster seven, specifically working on the Russian side of Ray Marshall's family.

'Hey, guys,' Maddie welcomed as soon as everyone was present. 'How are we all doing?'

'Not bad,' Kenyatta answered. 'Want an amazing piece of news?'

'Definitely time for some good news, I think,' Maddie answered.

'I have finally tracked down a *definite* pair of ancestors for the *Boys Under the Bridge*.'

'Awesome. Oh, that is fantastic,' Maddie congratulated.

'Oh, wow, that's amazing,' Becky said.

'Good work,' Hudson chimed in.

'Thank you,' Kenyatta said. 'Boy, does it feel good to have something concrete to go on.'

'So, come on. Spill. Who are they and where are they from?' Maddie asked.

'Arthit and Preeda Tang of Khao Wang in Thailand,' Kenyatta announced, hoping that, with just a little more information on the family, Maddie might accede to elevate the status of the case to one that the whole team could work on and finally crack. Even with giving the brothers names, however, Kenyatta knew that the case would be far from closed; she would immediately be advocating and actively campaigning to have the criminal case into their murders re-examined. She would not rest until their graves had a name and their killer was behind bars.

'Do you have more leads to work on?' Maddie asked.

'Oh, yeah, plenty,' Kenyatta said enthusiastically and with slight exaggeration.

'Keep us posted,' Maddie said. 'Okay. Let's make a start on this afternoon's briefing.' The speculative pedigree for Jacob Sauer appeared on everyone's screens. 'I've been working with Hudson on cluster four and, even though there have been two of us on it'—she laughed—'progress hasn't exactly been *exceptional*.'

'No, you can say that again,' Hudson concurred with a smile.

Maddie continued, 'I've managed to get Andre Hook's paternal side back to all except two at the great-great-great-grandparent level. Take a look at the names and locations. The maternal side is nearly done, although I do have four great-great-grandparents missing, which of course means eight of the generation above are also absent. This *could* present a problem, but we think we can see where Andre Hook's family might intersect with Jacob Sauer's. Hudson—do you want to take over?'

'Absolutely,' he said, overriding Maddie's screen with his own and clicking on the profile of Elisabeth Hohnstein, one of Andre Hook's great-great-grandmothers. 'Elisabeth was born around 1843, somewhere in Russia. Maddie and I haven't yet been able to ascertain exactly when or where, though.' Clicking on another web browser tab, Hudson brought up the speculative tree for Jacob Sauer, selecting his grandmother, Mabel Balakin. 'Mabel's mother was called Elisabeth Hohnstein.'

'Wow. Same person?' Kenyatta asked.

'I don't think so,' Hudson answered. 'Mabel was born in 1890, so highly unlikely. But, given all the work that Maddie and I have done on these two trees, this is either a massive coincidence or the likely area of triangulation. Basically, I'm hoping that tomorrow we might have a breakthrough.'

'Fingers crossed,' Maddie added. 'Becky, do you want to go next?'

'Sure,' she said, and displayed the pedigree for Heather Newton. 'As I said yesterday, both sides of Heather's family came from Texas but, pushing back into the next generation at the great-grandparent level, I've now picked up some emigration from England, Ireland, and Portugal, plus a couple more U.S. states. The only thing jumping out at me so far is that one great-grandmother, a Marjorie Govier, lived in Salmon, Idaho.'

'That could be interesting,' Hudson commented.

'Yeah, that maybe could be what brings all these families to the state of Idaho,' Maddie added. 'Keep going and perhaps prioritize your searches there? Kenyatta?'

'I've got a link to Russia!' Kenyatta cheered, doing a mini dance in her seat.

'Well done,' Maddie said, giving her a clap. 'Do tell.'

'But it's not *all* good news,' she warned, pulling up the profile for Ray Marshall, then navigating through to his mother, Barbara Getman. 'Both of this lady's parents are identified and both were born in Russia in the 1880s. They immigrated to Denver in 1906, a year after their marriage. I've managed to track down one document that refers to their place of birth and it's right here,' she said, running her cursor around the name Voronezh, 'which is to the west in Russia, not far from the border with Ukraine.'

'How far is that from Rohleder where my Germans lived?' Hudson asked.

'I somehow knew you'd ask me that,' Kenyatta replied with a smile. 'Depending on which route you take, anywhere from 360 miles to 430 miles.'

'Oh,' Hudson said. 'So not close by, then…'

'Not terribly, no.'

'What are records like for this area?' Maddie asked.

Kenyatta screwed up her face and shook her head. 'Let's just say that I'm not overly confident about getting back past Henry Getman and Anna Kaufmann. I've reached out to my Russian expert, Marina Brizhatova, to see if she can suggest anything.'

Maddie exhaled. 'We might have a problem if we can't link up the Russian sides of the killer's tree. I take it you've checked other people's family trees at all the usual sites?'

Kenyatta nodded. 'Sure. Nothing.'

'Well, all we can do at the moment is keep on going,' Maddie said. 'You're all doing so great. If there's nothing else, we'll bring the briefing to a close. Have a good evening and we'll talk some more tomorrow.'

The team said goodbye to one another and left the meeting.

Kenyatta stood up, her body aching from having sat in the same spot all day long. She was supposed to be helping out at the SLC Homeless Kitchen tonight, but she felt conflicted. First of all, Jim would be there. The questions that Tabitha had raised at their therapy session on Saturday had resurfaced several times, most often in the early hours of the night when she had been unable either to answer them or shake them off. She wasn't sure what seeing him would do now that these questions had been asked and left so open. Then there were the kids, specifically Troy who had directly asked her to stop her work with the homeless. He of all her three boys needed her the most. He always had. She guessed that Dougie's death was hitting him the hardest and, knowing what he was like with internalizing everything, he was probably not dealing with it well. Otis wouldn't notice. He'd just think that, because Troy wasn't expressing his grief, he mustn't be feeling anything. Kenyatta had felt every possible emotion toward Otis over the past couple of years but, right now, she deeply despised him. Faith and therapy were doing nothing to lessen that hatred.

'To hell with him,' Kenyatta said, marching into her bedroom to get changed.

Ten minutes later, she was walking downtown toward Pioneer Park.

'Hey,' Jim greeted as Kenyatta strolled over toward him. 'What's going on with you? You look different.'

Beneath her face mask, Kenyatta smiled and glanced down at herself. 'Well, this is from this season's don't-give-a-hoot pandemic collection.'

Jim laughed. 'Well… It suits you.'

'Yeah, so Gucci has told me,' Kenyatta said, doing a twirl.

'If you've got it…' Jim said.

'Oh, I've got *plenty* of it,' Kenyatta said with a laugh. 'How are you?'

'Not bad, thanks. Trying not to look at the news constantly and caught between wanting to know what's going on in the world and dreading knowing what's going on in the world.'

'I think that's the same for everyone,' she agreed. 'I get told off for doom-scrolling on Facebook.'

'Is that what they're calling it?' Jim asked.

Kenyatta shrugged and chuckled. 'So my son tells me, yes.'

'Doom-scrolling,' Jim repeated. 'I like that.'

'Is everything good here?' Kenyatta placed a hand on each of the soup pots, feeling that they were up to temperature.

'Yeah, I think so. And here comes our first guest,' he said, nodding across the park to one of their regular visitors, Betty, who hobbled along pushing a stroller full of filthy dolls.

'Have you enough for the kids today?' Betty asked when she reached them.

'No. Sorry, Betty,' Kenyatta answered. 'Just enough for you.'

Betty raised her eyebrows and mumbled something incoherent. On first meeting Betty, Kenyatta had said that there was plenty of soup for the dolls and watched as Betty had seated them all around and attempted to feed them, pouring it everywhere.

'Here you go,' Jim said, handing Betty a bowl and spoon. 'Just enough for you.'

'What about them?' Betty asked, indicating the dolls.

'Maybe they could get some tomorrow…if there's enough,' Kenyatta answered.

'Hmm, maybe,' Betty said, wandering off and dragging the stroller behind her. Coming in the opposite direction, and passing her, was Lonnie. 'Only enough soup for me today, they said. Can you believe it?' she complained to him.

'They're just dolls, Betty,' he told her. '*Plastic* dolls. I keep telling you. They can't eat any more than my damned boots can eat.'

Betty appeared impervious to the comment and kept walking toward a bench nearby.

'What is it today, Kenny?' Lonnie asked her.

'Well, hello to you, too. It's pea and ham for your information.'

'Now, why in God's name would you go and put *peas* into a soup?' Lonnie demanded.

'Give you some fresh greens,' she answered. 'Keep your strength up. Do you want any, or not, my friend?'

Lonnie looked around the park, unabashedly weighing his options to see if there might have been a better offer someplace else. He sighed. 'Okay, I'll take a bowl.' He sniffed and flicked his gaze between Jim and Kenyatta. 'You two sure look like you're getting along.'

'Of course we get along,' Kenyatta jumped in quickly.

211

'No, I mean *get along*. You know, get along, get along,' he clarified.

Jim laughed. 'I'll have you know, this lady here is a Gucci model. The last person she'd want to *get along* with is this hairy old banker.'

Lonnie found this hilarious. 'I like what you did there. Nice.'

Kenyatta hurriedly passed Lonnie a bowl of soup, wanting to change the subject. 'Bread roll?'

Lonnie nodded, took the food and walked over to the bench where Betty was sitting with her stroller of dolls. He sat at the opposite end of the bench to her, lowered his face mask and began to slurp the soup.

Kenyatta took a casual glance at Jim. She decided to tackle the elephant in the room, head on. 'What you said just then…about me not wanting to get with someone like you. That happens not to be correct.' She was deeply embarrassed and totally out of her depth, but she tried to maintain a cool air, as though she had just said something perfectly ordinary that meant nothing to anyone.

He seemed genuinely stupefied. 'Oh…well. I—'

'You're not interested in me in that way,' Kenyatta finished. 'I know. And that's fine. Let's just move on. Here comes David.'

Jim touched her arm. 'Wait. I didn't say that. I would totally, uh…date? Is that the word I'm looking for?' he laughed. 'I don't really know what I'm doing. I've been a widower for almost ten years now, and was married for nineteen years before that, so I haven't *dated* anyone in a very long time.'

Kenyatta beamed at this unanticipated response. 'Neither have I. I guess that means we're both sitting in the same boat, then.'

'I guess so. Do you want to go on a…date?' Jim asked.

'Yes!' she answered. 'But there's the tiny, hindering issue of the global pandemic to bear in mind.'

'Could *this* be our first date?' Jim suggested with a chuckle.

'Do you know, I guess it could be,' she answered.

'Well, we've got food, fresh air and great conversation,' he said.

Kenyatta watched Lonnie handing his soup to Betty and said to Jim, 'And live entertainment on tap.'

They both stood watching as Betty proceeded to pour Lonnie's gifted soup all over the dolls' faces.

Kenyatta looked at Jim and smiled, feeling something honest and warm inside which she had not felt in such a very long time.

Chapter Twenty-Four

Friday, April 17, 2020, Twin Falls, Idaho

He was sitting at his computer in the kitchen at the back of his house. Fragments of light pierced through the tears in the old curtains that hung over the window and door. Although he wasn't oblivious to the worn-through linoleum beneath his feet, the stack of unwashed dishes and the half dozen flies drawn to the light of his computer screen, he had more important things to deal with for the moment.

In front of him was the Reddit post that he'd put up on Sunday night.

The Bitch has turned to type. I went over to see her and she had a Chad in her bed. Her time is coming…

Several comments had been left.

ElliotT: "Her time is coming". Why wait? One less woman on the planet.
Death2Girls: I don't know why your surprised, dude. Make her suffer
UglySelf96: Bye bye biatch
AntiChad: First attractive guy that came along she's in bed with. A better one comes along tomorrow she'll switch. On repeat. That's women.
WLM: Give her covid

He read the final comment, considering its merit. Novel idea but not nearly enough suffering for Debra Towers.

He slammed his fist down hard onto the kitchen table as he glowered at her pouting face smiling out at him from her Facebook profile. He glared at her, his anger boiling inside of him. He hadn't felt this level of internal frenzy with the other girls; his rage had been quelled once he'd meted out their punishment. Debra Towers was really going to get it as soon as Chad was out of the picture.

She'd posted several times this week, most recently last night. A disgusting photo of the two of them grinning with their arms around each other with the caption, *Homemade pizza!* Where had this Chad even come from? He'd been so careful to select Debra because she lived alone and was single. Typical woman, that's exactly what she was. Just like AntiChad had commented, it would be a different, better-looking guy by this time next week.

The more he stared at her profile photo, the angrier and more disgusted he became. She literally had no shame.

His hands quivered and his eyes teared up. He clenched his fists and then slammed them both down on the table.

'Stop staring at me!' he yelled out at Debra, his voice became high-pitched and neared screeching at a point.

He closed Facebook, before he punched a hole in her head through the screen.

He needed something to calm himself down. He took a can of beer from the fridge, then accessed an invite-only online game, which Death2Girls had created, called *Utopia100*. A black page loaded, containing nothing other than a *username* and *password* box. He completed the details which took him to his profile page. *Welcome Rodger. Which weapon today?* Below that question was a range of options: *Guns. Knives. Crossbows. Chemicals.* He clicked on the first option which brought down a sub-menu of over twenty different gun types. He chose the gun that he had personally asked the creator to add to the site's inventory: a 6.5-in barreled Marlin 1895 Trapper.

His breathing was fast and short as he clicked *Go!* and entered a virtual near-lifelike street scene. The game was first-person shooter with the barrel of his prized Trapper jutting out from the lower center of the screen.

The virtual street was supposed to be Laredo, Texas, busy with realistic vehicle and pedestrian traffic. Some folks were walking, some talking and some entering and leaving the shops. It was just like an everyday Main Street, U.S.A. except that all the men in the game were white. The object of the game was to work through the top 100 cities ordered by population in the U.S., removing every single woman until you'd conquered them all. New York City was the big prize. Laredo, where he was at, was number 87.

He slowly panned the camera around in the game and saw a beautiful, young, blonde woman in a skimpy t-shirt and shorts, strolling toward him, looking all provocative.

With his hands shaking, he raised the Trapper, waited for her to be in point-blank range, then fired a shot into her forehead. Where most shooter video games failed, Death2Girls had done an awesome job in making the death depiction realistic. Blood and brain matter went everywhere, and the girl slumped backward onto the sidewalk, her body jerking for several seconds. The other pedestrians didn't care, didn't so much as look at her, even; they were on his side. He angled the camera to watch her dying, then waited until the counter in the top-right corner changed. *Roasties 11,404 / 128,076.*

He smiled and some of his earlier rage subsided.

Across the street, he spotted two women walking in the opposite direction. He ran across the street behind them. He wanted to call out, to make them turn around and show him the fear in their eyes, but the creator, Death2Girls, hadn't managed to achieve that level of detail yet. But he was working on it.

Instead, he fired a shot into the back of one of the women, reloaded and repeated the method for her friend.

Just as he was about to lean over and savor watching them die, there came a sharp knock at his door.

'Damn it,' he said, hating it when he was yanked out of that world where he had supreme power. He listened but didn't move to open the door. He lowered the volume on his computer, just as a bell sounded twice and the counter changed on his screen to read, *Roasties 11,406 / 128,076.*

Whoever was outside his house tried knocking again.

'Go away, already,' he whispered, scratching his chin with irritation.

The knocking stopped and he returned to the game.

He didn't know how much time had passed when someone tried knocking again. The counter at the top-right of his computer read, *Roasties 13,111 / 128,076.*

He sighed.

'Are you in there? It's me, Mrs. Staniforth,' she called.

He hit the *Exit* command and received the message: *Thank you for your service, Rodger.*

'Coming, Mrs. Staniforth,' he replied, moving through the hallway along to the front door.

She was standing well back, wearing a face mask. 'Oh, I'm so sorry to trouble you but I was wondering if you could pick up my medicine from Target later on? Like before... There's no real hurry at all, but I just...'

'Of course, absolutely,' he said.

'Thank you so much,' she cooed. 'You're such a nice young man.'

'You're very welcome.'

'Say, what did you think of the police knocking earlier?' she asked.

'Police? Oh, was that who it was? I was in the bath when they came by. What did they want?' he asked, his voice oscillating between various pitches as he spoke.

'They were conducting house-to-house inquiries about this awful serial killer who's on the loose,' she explained.

'Oh, God. Really?' he stammered. 'What did they ask?'

'Now let's see. Who lived in my house, my name and if anyone living with me *hunted*, of all things.' She laughed at the last statement, while he shuddered inside.

'Hunted?'

'Uh-huh,' she confirmed with a shrug.

'But why are they calling on *us*?'

Mrs. Staniforth shrugged again. 'Maybe they think he lives around here in our neighborhood. Can you imagine?'

He shook his head, not liking what he was hearing one bit. The rage was boiling up inside him again. Mrs. Staniforth knew that he liked to hunt. 'What did you tell them?' he asked, his anger affecting his voice and making his last word come out as nearer a mouse squeak.

'I told them my name, that I lived alone and that I'm almost housebound, never mind going off hunting.' She laughed, with which he felt obliged to feign joining in. 'Anyway, I'll let you get back to what you were doing. I take up enough of your time as it is. And thank you so much for looking out for me; not many people your age would be so kind.'

'You're welcome, Mrs. Staniforth.'

'Bye for now,' she said, walking off down his path.

He closed the door, gritted his teeth and rushed into his bedroom where he threw his backpack onto the bed. He took out his Trapper and held it fervently in his hands.

It was time to do some real hunting.

Chapter Twenty-Five

Friday, April 17, 2020, South Jordan, Utah

Maddie was at her desk in the basement, holding open her mom's crossword book. She had always been fast at crosswords, so it had come as quite a shock when Maddie had found the book tucked down the back of the sofa earlier this afternoon. Assuming that it had ended up there by mistake, Maddie had tossed it onto the coffee table. The page it had fallen open on had forced Maddie to pick it back up and take a better, closer look. Over half of the words on the page had been crossed out multiple times with thick black pen lines. Maddie looked at one answer that had been very heavily erased. *Orange language of the East (8)* ~~Japanese. Chinese.~~ *Mandolin.*

Maddie found evidence of the same errors, frustration and anguish on every page where her mom had attempted the crossword.

She exhaled. It was time to stop procrastinating. She dialed the number for the North Salt Lake City Police Department. 'Mandarin,' she said to herself as she closed the crossword book.

'Pardon me?' the operator spoke unexpectedly in Maddie's ear.

'Sorry, I——. I was just talking to myself. Uh, I'd like to enroll my mom in Project Lifesaver, please.'

'I'm really sorry, ma'am, but we're not currently processing any new applications for Project Lifesaver. Due to covid, we can't conduct home visits.'

Maddie understood and thought that all the while she would be working from home, the chances of her mom absconding were much lower. The front door stayed locked twenty-four seven at the moment. 'Will you give me a call as soon as she can be enrolled, please?'

'Absolutely. I'll take your details, and someone should get back to you.'

Maddie gave her details, thanked the woman and ended the call.

She carried the crossword book upstairs, replacing it at the back of the sofa where she had found it, an apt metaphor for how she felt that she was dealing with her mom's dementia right now. She went up and checked on the kids, finding that both were on Google Classroom, miraculously doing what they were supposed to be doing.

She left Trenton's room feeling grateful that the house had returned to something like normality. The calmness that had come with their return from Green River on Sunday had remained and it was for this reason that Maddie hadn't yet brought up the DUI folder with the kids. The last thing that she wanted was to trigger Trenton into gadding off on another madcap escapade with the new information. Maybe she would tell them tonight. Or maybe she'd leave it until the weekend.

Maddie took a glass of water down to the basement and got her paperwork and speculative trees organized for the briefing which was due to start in five minutes.

She opened Zoom and she could see Hudson in the waiting room. She'd been working with him again today on his cluster. He wasn't himself and she was worried about him. There was definitely more going on in his life than solely the anxiety over this Wanda Chabala case and its implications with him and Abigail adopting. Maddie's confrontation with Jenna on Monday had softened her response to his resignation email. Had it been the day before, she would likely have accepted it, despite his being such an asset to the team. But Jenna's words—effectively saying that Maddie was riding along on some moral high horse—had struck home. She did her best in life, but she had made mistakes in her past; still made mistakes now.

Kenyatta, Ross and Becky joined the waiting room.

Maddie drank some water, then opened the briefing. 'Hi there, folks,' she greeted. 'Are we all good?'

'Great, thank you,' Kenyatta answered. 'And your good self?'

'All is well in the Scott-Barnhart household today,' Maddie replied with a smile and a sigh.

'We're good,' Becky confirmed.

'Ross, would you agree with the 'royal we' there?' Maddie asked.

Ross grinned. 'Well, you can imagine what it's like living with her...'

Becky screwed up her face. 'Oh, shut up.'

'See what I mean,' Ross said.

'How are you, Hudson?' Becky asked.

'Good thanks,' he said, giving a weak smile that didn't fool anyone.

Maddie stepped in. 'Then let's make a start. Hudson, you made the breakthrough today, so please take the virtual floor.'

Hudson arranged his desktop so that two speculative trees were open, side by side. 'As you know, Maddie and I were trying to find the common ancestors for these two guys, Jacob Sauer and Andre Hook. Both had an Elisabeth Hohnstein in their ancestry but who were at least one generation apart. Well, today, with a bit of luck and a lot of deep digging, we made a breakthrough. Andre Hook and Jacob Sauer share Vladislav and Kristina Hohnstein as a common ancestral couple,' he explained, clicking to show the two men's ancestry as pedigrees, culminating in the same ancestors.

'Way to go!' Kenyatta praised. 'That's…ten genetic network clusters closed down, now.'

'Getting closer,' Becky added.

'They came from Tolyatti in Russia,' Hudson continued, showing a screenshot from Google Maps that he had annotated. The snaking blue line that ran north-east to south-west across the map was labelled as the *Volga River*. Around half the way down the river, a red circle had been drawn over Saratov and, directly to the west, another drawn around the city of Voronezh. Tolyatti was north-east of Saratov.

'It all looks so close,' Kenyatta commented. 'But it's not, really, is it?'

'No, it isn't. We're talking a few hundred miles apart. Still, somewhere in this triangle is part of the genealogical heritage of the Twin Falls killer.'

'We'll find it,' Maddie said. 'Becky, do you want to go next?'

'Sure,' she replied, sharing the tree that she'd created for the cluster two lead, Heather Newton. 'If you recall yesterday, I said that Heather's great-grandmother, Marjorie Govier, was perhaps an area to focus on because of her living in Idaho. Well, today, I did just that, taking her lines back two further generations. Three out of four lived in Idaho, so I think I'm onto something. These are the four surnames that I think could—*perhaps*—be more recent in the killer's ancestry.'

Maddie looked closely at the four surnames: *Govier. Lonsdale. Hesp. Williams.* None of them looked familiar. 'Since this is our only link so far to Idaho, I think you're probably right, Becky,' Maddie agreed.

'Keep your eyes peeled for those names when we start doing the reverse-genealogy. Good work. Kenyatta, it's your turn.'

Kenyatta slumped forward in her chair and rested her head on her desk.

'Oh dear. That bad, huh?' Maddie questioned with a laugh.

Kenyatta sat back up and complained, 'Yeah, it's that bad. Worse, actually. I've spent literally the *whole* day working on the Getmans and Kaufmanns, but…nothing. My Russian genealogist friend, Marina Brizhatova, came back to me and said that Voronezh has a very poor collection of historic documents because it was bombed heavily during the Second World War. Three buildings containing seven hundred thousand storage units were destroyed.'

'You're kidding?' Maddie said.

'No. So, this afternoon I switched focus to triangulating within cluster seven and I've gotten nowhere fast there, too.'

'Okay,' Maddie said. 'Do you think you might find the link with more time, or has it reached the point to call it?'

Kenyatta paused for thought. 'I don't think there's any merit in trying to push back on the Getman and Kaufmann lines; I really don't. If the point of triangulation is anywhere above Henry Getman or Anna Kaufmann, then I'll never find it.'

'Okay, so give it just a few more hours, then we'll call it. We're doing really great, here, folks. If we can close down clusters two and seven, then we're onto the reverse-genealogy phase. And, since we've heard nothing more from the Twin Falls law enforcement, hopefully we're one step ahead of the killer. I know you're going to work this weekend, but take plenty of breaks.'

'We sure will,' Kenyatta said with a laugh.

'Oh, yeah,' Hudson concurred.

'I've got a whole weekend of fun-filled activities and excursions planned,' Becky chipped in.

Maddie smiled. 'Yeah, yeah, yeah. Talk to you later.'

Once everybody had said goodbye, Maddie ended the meeting, feeling a great sense of pride in her team. She didn't want them to burn out, but she suspected that this case—as awful as it was—was offering them a much-needed distraction from all that was depressing and going on in the world right now.

Maddie stood from her desk and headed upstairs to the kitchen, finding Nikki, Trenton and her mom all playing cards at the kitchen table.

'Do you have any nines?' Trenton asked.

'No. Go fish!' her mom said with great enthusiasm.

Maddie smiled at the joy in her mom's face. Actually, on the kids' faces, too. 'Looks like you're having fun,' she said, half-wishing she hadn't disturbed them.

'I'd forgotten just how much I used to enjoy this game,' Nikki said. 'Why did we ever stop playing it?'

'I don't know,' she lied, knowing full well that they'd stopped playing anything together as a family when Michael had gone missing. After that, they had each settled into their own personal ways of enjoying life around one another; Trenton with his video games, Nikki with her reading and art, and Maddie with her work. Maybe lockdown was the perfect time to try to reclaim some of what had been lost.

'What's for dinner?' Trenton asked her.

'Good question,' she replied, pulling open the refrigerator.

'Can we get takeout?' he asked.

'No. Frankly, it's getting to be too much of a habit. I'll make us something,' Maddie replied, her eyes scanning over the little food on the shelves in front of her. 'Does leftover chicken something or other work for you?'

'I love leftover chicken something,' Nikki said.

'Can we have it with fries something?' her mom asked.

'Sure,' Maddie answered. 'Chicken something with fries something and maybe a healthy side of something, coming right up.'

Before she got started on the dinner, Maddie first poured herself a glass of white wine and stood watching her family enjoying playing cards together.

As she started preparing the food, her thoughts shifted to thinking about Clayton Tyler and their recent interaction. Having looked at every photo, video and file within the DUI folder several times over, she'd sent him a message asking him to call her, knowing that he would do so on a secure line or at least where he couldn't be overheard. He

223

had called her straight away from a phone near where he worked. 'I need you to pass my sincere—*really* sincere—gratitude to Eva Hyatt,' Maddie had said.

Clayton had laughed. 'Let me think. No. I'm sure I don't know what or who you're talking about.'

'Well, if it ever comes to you, tell her that it means so much to me and that I will use the information wisely. And it will never trace back to her.'

'She'll be relieved to hear it,' he'd replied. 'What do you plan on doing with the information that I don't know what you're talking about?'

'As soon as lockdown's over, I plan to take a little trip down to DC and Maryland,' she'd replied.

'Any chance of you meeting up with that friend in Philly at the same time? Maybe Eva Hyatt could meet you there and maybe get a bite to eat?'

Maddie had smiled. At the end of working on the case that had brought Wayne Wolsey to justice, Clayton had told her to look him up if ever she were in the area, and she'd told him about her friend in Philadelphia. 'Sure, why not? Eva can take me out for a Philly cheesesteak and whatever beer it is that you have over there.'

'AleSmith Speedway Stout,' he'd answered. 'I'd like that… I mean, she'd like that.'

'Me too,' Maddie had found herself agreeing. Maybe it was because she was in the safe bubble of lockdown impossibility that she'd so willingly agreed, but also perhaps she was finally accepting that Michael wasn't going to be coming back. Besides, one dinner with one guy at some point in the future wasn't going to hurt and didn't even need to be a *date*. In fact, the more that she thought about it, the weirder the situation seemed. She was planning on going out to dinner with a cop who was helping her to find her absent husband. Too weird. No, it would have to be just as friends. But surely the same thoughts had occurred to him? Maddie hated herself for it, but she couldn't help but question Clayton's motivation. Was he helping her out so much because he was a genuinely nice guy and wanted to assist her, or because he had designs on her and felt that his chances would be better if Michael were more definitively out of the picture? As usual, when it came to Michael, her thoughts spiraled and wound right back to where they started.

The food was ready, but Go Fish was still in full swing. It was such a rare glimpse of simplicity and happiness in the house that she had delayed dishing it up and regretted having to interrupt them finally to serve their food.

'Who's winning?' Maddie asked, setting the last plate down on the table.

'Grandma is,' Nikki revealed, unable to hide the surprise from her voice.

Her mom winked and tapped her temple. 'I'm not done yet, my girl.'

'Well done,' Maddie said, hoping as it came out that she didn't sound patronizing. Her thoughts were still lingering on Clayton Tyler, and she was suddenly taken with the idea that now might be the right time to tell them all about the information that he'd supplied. 'So, I can't say where it came from, exactly,' Maddie began, 'but I've got the full folder of documents from Emmanuel Gribbin's DUI arrest.'

'Who?' her mom asked.

'Emmanuel Gribbin: the guy whose fingerprint was found on Michael's truck,' Maddie answered.

'Wow,' Trenton said. 'And what does it contain, exactly?'

'I'll show you after dinner, but basically it contains a report of the investigation, an intake questionnaire about where he drank, what he drank, meals eaten, how much sleep he'd had, how he paid for drinks, friends who were with him and that kind of thing. There's a video of his pre-arrest and a video of his arrest, photos of his car, Miranda form, mug shot, blood test results, rap sheet… The list goes on.'

'That's incredible,' Nikki said.

'So…now what are we going to do with the information?' Trenton asked, setting down his fork.

Maddie knew that this was big news for him. 'I've got a few things that I can chase down now: looking into his associates from the night of the arrest, for example. But my main objective is to take a road trip to DC—and his hometown in Maryland—and see what I can dig up.'

'You can't go down to DC and Maryland!' her mom blurted out.

'Not now, Mom,' Maddie replied. 'But at some point, I will.'

'But what's that going to achieve?' her mom asked.

It was a good question. Maddie had no idea of what it might achieve, but she had to do it.

'Well, it's more than Defective Scorpion is doing,' Trenton said. 'I really want to see the video. Do you see his face?'

Maddie nodded. 'Very clearly. Very drunk.'

Maddie regretted that the revelation had killed the positive mood, and the meal progressed in near silence. She could tell that Trenton was simultaneously no longer hungry but also trying to eat as fast as he could so that he could get to see the computer.

When they'd all finished eating, Maddie cleared the table. 'Do you want to come down to see it, Mom?'

Her mom frowned and turned away, mumbling to herself. 'What? See a drunk man getting himself arrested? Let me see. No, I don't think so.'

With the kids trooping behind her, Maddie headed down to her computer in the basement. She leaned over the desk, pulled up the file and then stood back.

Trenton jumped into the chair and took over.

'Click the arrest video,' Nikki said, resting her arms on the back of the chair.

'Not yet,' Trenton said. 'We need to be methodical.' He turned to face Maddie. 'Could I have some scrap paper and a pen, please?'

'Sure,' she said, placing the items beside him. She watched as he went through the folder systematically, impressed by his meticulousness. He took notes which Maddie considered highly relevant as he went. Nikki watched intently, saying nothing.

When he'd finished, he re-read his notes, then opened up Google Maps, typing in Emmanuel Gribbin's home address. 'Look at that,' he said pointing at the screen. 'He gave his occupation as a pilot, and look; College Park airport is less than two miles from his home address.'

'So?' Nikki said.

Maddie immediately recalled the journal that Trenton had compiled during his time down at Green River and knew where he was going with this.

Trenton turned to face them both. 'Dutch John Airport is close to where Dad parked his truck. Emmanuel Gribbin's fingerprint was found on the trunk catch. He was a pilot who lived near an airfield. It makes perfect sense.'

'What makes sense?' Nikki asked. 'You're saying that this Emmanuel guy did what? Overpowered Dad, bundled him into his truck, drove him to Dutch John Airport and then flew him to College Park Airport?'

'Pretty much, yes,' Trenton confirmed.

Nikki began to cry. 'But why?'

Trenton shrugged.

'Mom?' Nikki said through her tears, staring at Maddie.

Maddie put her arm around Nikki, saying nothing. She couldn't fault Trenton's logic. It made more sense than anything else that family, friends or the police had come up with so far.

Chapter Twenty-Six

Saturday, April 18, 2020, South Jordan, Utah

Maddie hadn't slept well and had, yet again, found herself in the basement at some ungodly hour of Saturday morning. Her nocturnal brain had thought it helpful to choose now to supplant Trenton's ideas with something out of an action movie involving guns, car chases and, ultimately, Michael being shot. She had got up, used the treadmill for a half hour, taken a shower and then headed down to the basement with a very large coffee.

The DUI folder was still open on-screen, and Trenton's journal and scribblings from last night were on the desk beside the keyboard.

Maddie double-checked that Trenton had transcribed the names of Emmanuel Gribbin's drinking buddies correctly. He had: *Jonas Morse and Steve De Angelis.* The three of them sounded like they should be in a rock band together.

Logging in on the Spokeo background-check website, Maddie typed in Steve De Angelis's name.

57 people named Steve De Angelis found in New York, New Jersey and 19 other states.

In the top-left of the screen was a map of the United States, with red drop-pins where the name was located. In a long central column was a brief summary of each individual.

Maddie clicked the red drop-pin for the District of Columbia, thereby bringing the search results down to just one. Beside his name was a black box with *SEE RESULTS* in white lettering, which Maddie clicked.

Steven De Angelis
Age: 54
Current Address: 1700 K St NW, Washington, DC

Maddie printed the whole page to show Trenton when he woke,

then she slowly analyzed the profile. It was devoid of information: no social media; no phone numbers; no family; and no wealth information. But there was something highly significant that she had not anticipated: his email address was given as *s.deangelis@thelarkingroup.com*

Maddie flopped against the back of her chair, stunned. Emmanuel Gribbin hanging out with a man clearly employed by The Larkin Investment and Finance Group was huge and could not be written off as coincidental.

She quickly edited her search for Jonas Morse. His background profile was fuller, giving the details of his family and some past addresses. Maddie moved down the page, studying every detail. His work history gave various security jobs dating back to the 1980s. His position at the time of the DUI in 2014 stopped her in her tracks.

Head of Security, The Larkin Investment and Finance Group
Washington, DC
2008-2018

'What the…?' Maddie breathed. Both men drinking with Emmanuel Gribbin were employees of Andrew Larkin.

Now what?

Maddie drank her coffee and considered her options. She intended to dig further into Jonas Morse and Steve De Angelis, but something told her not to contact these men directly.

If Trenton's theory was correct, then would any record have been kept at Dutch John Airport of the planes that had taken off on March 8, 2015? Maddie knew next to nothing about flying or private planes or what airport documents might exist, but she had a college friend, Kirk Wennerstrom, who was a pilot and flew his own light aircraft. She opened up her emails and sent him a message.

Hi Kirk
Hope you're doing well. I have a slightly strange question that I'm hoping you might be able to answer. Would there have been any record of aircraft departing Dutch John Airport in Utah in 2015 and would these records have been kept? I'm hoping to find evidence of an airplane that took off from there at some point on March 8.

Thank you.
Maddie

She sent the email and thought for a moment. One thing had become abundantly clear, Michael had not banged his head and ended up living somewhere with amnesia. Nor had he been attacked by wild animals or drowned in the Green River. Someone—probably Emmanuel Gribbin—had done something bad to him.

'Hmm,' Hudson muttered to himself. Even though his house was presently reassuringly empty and there was no work-related necessity for him to be here, he found himself sitting outside of the Family History Library working on his laptop. It was colder today, with heavy clouds sitting over the city, but, thankfully, there was no sign of snow.

With his two clusters closed, Hudson was now working on reverse-genealogy, where all known descendants of the confirmed common ancestors to the genetic network were traced, searching for the overlap between another cluster. Technically, he was jumping the gun. Maddie liked to assign the team to specific areas to make sure that they weren't wasting time duplicating research efforts, but he knew that Becky and Kenyatta had yet to close down their second clusters and Maddie would likely be busy with her family.

He'd just found something that might be happenstance or might well be a significant discovery. One of the killer's confirmed ancestral couples, Vladislav and Kristina Hohnstein, had had a daughter, Taisiya, who had married a man named Peter Rawson. That surname had seemed familiar.

Hudson entered the Twin Falls killer's kit details into the FTDNA website and accessed his Y-DNA matches. Sure enough, one of the fifteen men with whom the killer shared patrilineal DNA was called Clive Rowson. There was a vowel difference between the two names, which could denote the same family but with a spelling variant, or it could indicate that they were in fact two entirely distinct families.

Hudson clicked the Time Predictor tool, which estimated the common ancestor to Clive Rowson and the killer as around twenty generations back. Exploring Clive's link to the killer was something

230

that was neither feasible nor worth doing, but researching Taisiya Hohnstein and Peter Rawson's descendants was.

As he clicked on Taisiya's profile within the speculative tree, Hudson realized that if the Rawson link was *not* simply a coincidence, then that would pull the killer's Russian heritage over to his paternal side.

Taisiya Hohnstein had settled in Weld County, Colorado where she'd married Peter Rawson. Hudson found them easily on several censuses, discovering that the couple had had six children. Since his theories were concerned with the paternal side of the killer's family, it was with some dismay that Hudson found that all six of their children had been boys. If those six Rawson boys also had sons, then the potential lines of descent to the killer would be numerous.

Starting with the eldest Rawson son, John, Hudson began to work his way through all the genealogical resources at his disposal, gradually building up a picture of John's life.

He had just discovered that John Rawson had had four sons of his own, when Reggie abruptly appeared in front of him. He was masked, wearing his usual orange jacket with a matching beanie hat pulled down over his bleached hair.

'Hey,' Hudson said with a smile, genuinely pleased to see him.

'It's a Saturday, man,' Reggie said, taking his normal seat a few yards away. He removed his mask. 'I would have got you some coffee if I'd thought you'd be here.'

'Honestly,' Hudson explained, 'I don't need to be here, but I quite like it. You know, just getting out of the house.'

'Things not going well with your wife?' Reggie asked. When Hudson flinched, he added, 'Wait. Sorry. That's personal. Ignore me.'

'Actually, it's fine to ask,' Hudson decided as he heard himself say it. 'She's moved out and won't answer my calls.'

'Oh, sorry to hear that,' Reggie said.

'Yeah... It's a very complicated situation,' Hudson admitted.

'Do you want to talk about it?' Reggie asked. 'I'm only here to escape from my parents, so if you want to chat about it, that's fine. And...if you want to work, that's fine, too.'

Nobody outside of him and Abigail knew the whole story, yet there was something about Reggie—perhaps the very fact that he was a total stranger—that allowed Hudson to open up. He placed his laptop down beside him and took a long breath in. He decided to start at the beginning. 'So, I'm trans.'

'I want to begin by saying that I'm sorry,' Kenyatta said.

'Okay,' Tabitha said, drawing the word out. 'Apologize to me? What for?'

Kenyatta looked at the camera on her laptop. 'For being such a snappy little so-and-so in our therapy session, last Saturday.'

Tabitha curled her lip as though she could barely remember what Kenyatta might be referring to. 'You don't need to apologize.'

'No. I do,' Kenyatta insisted. 'It's not me to be like that; to be so defensive.'

'We can all have moments where we're not being the person we'd like to be; the best version of ourselves. Why is it, do you think, that you felt defensive?'

Kenyatta laughed. 'And there we go, straight in. I guess because you were asking me about Jim, and I didn't want anyone shining a light on that part of my life.'

'Why? Your marriage is dissolved; you're entitled to move on and have new people enter your life. And that might well be people on a level that ends up going beyond friendship,' Tabitha said.

Kenyatta gazed at the keyboard. 'I know. When Otis left, I filled my life with work and just continued. The thought of dating anyone just didn't enter my head. I also didn't feel particularly good about myself, you know, physically.'

'Okay. So, what's happened in the last seven days to make you think, feel or see things differently?' Tabitha asked.

Kenyatta gave a wry smile. 'Your questions about him got right under my skin, and I guess I was forced to confront them. I almost bailed on seeing him Thursday at the SLC Homeless Kitchen but changed my mind and went anyway.'

'And how did that go? I presume you had more of an open mind than before when you saw him?'

Kenyatta laughed. 'Truth be told, I felt like some dumb fourteen-year-old. But do you know what happened?'

'Go on.'

'He basically said we could pretend that we were on a date while we were at the Homeless Kitchen. You know, since we can't very well go on an actual proper date.'

Tabitha smiled. 'I see. That's very sweet. So, you both acknowledged this shift. And did your date go well?'

'Yeah, I guess it did. We've fixed another for the same time and same place next week. Who knows what might happen in the future, though? I mean, right now it's exactly like high-school dating but what happens when this pandemic is over, and he invites me out to a meal for real; or worse, if he wants to go back to his place? I mean, what on earth, then?'

Tabitha smiled. 'Do you think it is helpful to think about that already? Take it one step at a time. Use this unusual time that we're living through to just see what happens without over-thinking it.'

Kenyatta nodded, knowing that what her therapist was telling her made sense. Still, it terrified the life out of her. 'I'll certainly try my best,' she promised. 'But... I finally got a text from Troy—the first since the family dog died—and he asked me to stop my work with the homeless so that Otis would let them see me.'

'That must have been a difficult message to receive.'

'It was,' Kenyatta admitted. 'But the court case is on Friday, so I'll wait and see what the judge has to say.'

'How are you feeling about the court case?'

'More than anything, nervous that it will get postponed because of the pandemic. All criminal jury trials and all civil jury trials have been suspended for a time. At the moment, district courts are continuing with what they call *mission critical functions* via videoconferencing, which, as long as nothing changes between times, does include enforcement of custody and parent-time orders.'

'So, let's assume that the case is heard as scheduled. What are your thoughts about the potential outcomes?'

Kenyatta had considered every eventuality that her lawyer had told her was possible. She spoke at length to the therapist, running through each scenario and how it might make her feel or react. The session came to an end with Kenyatta feeling upbeat, prepared and confident about her personal life.

When it was over, she made herself a grilled cheese sandwich, grabbed a can of Coke from the refrigerator and returned to her laptop. As much as she wanted to continue her work on the *Boys Under the Bridge* case, she felt under pressure to close down cluster seven, despite its pronounced difficulty.

Already this morning, Kenyatta had spent a few hours working on Henry Getman and his wife, Anna Kaufmann, determined to expand on their significant link to Russia. But she'd managed to get nowhere fast. Her friend and Russian genealogy expert, Marina Brizhatova, had come up with a few further suggestions, but none had yielded any results. The bottom line was that the records, which she needed, hadn't existed since World War II.

Kenyatta returned to the other five names within the cluster. The problem was that they all matched the Twin Falls killer at less than thirty centimorgans. The link could be a long way back and, if it were via Russia, then the chances of finding it were marginal to zero. But she had to try. She wanted something positive, a forward step in the case before the briefing on Monday.

None of the other five names within cluster seven had added a family tree or included any surnames that appeared in their tree, so she picked a man to research, named Otger Bryce, owing to his having the more unusual name.

'Twenty-seven centimorgans,' she bemoaned to herself as she logged in at FTDNA. Once she'd accessed the killer's autosomal matches, she viewed Otger Bryce's profile. Nothing but a Hotmail email address.

'Here we go,' she said, creating a speculative tree for Otger and then running his email address through all the background search websites to which the company had access.

It was going to be one long day.

Another email had dropped into the Venator inbox, asking for a progress update on the Sexual Assault Kit Initiative case that Becky had been working on. She'd also been reminded that April was Sexual

234

Assault Awareness Month and that it would be good all-round if some of the SAKI cases under review could be closed in that time.

Even though she was feeling the pressure to close her genetic network in the Twin Falls case, Becky had spent the day so far trying to identify the serial rapist who had preyed on young women and girls in Houston, Texas in the 1980s. The man was a monster and because some of his victims were children at the time of the assault, there was no way that, once he was caught, he could do as many suspects had done and plead that the encounter had been consensual.

Becky sipped a decaf coffee that she'd just made herself and was back at her computer working on the rapist's family tree. When this case had been considered for investigative genetic genealogy, it had been given a high-priority status because the rapist's closest relation on GEDmatch, a man named Craig Millar, had come in with a hefty 494 centimorgans of DNA. Becky had quickly managed to identify Craig's grandparents as the most recent common ancestors to him and the Houston rapist. She'd then managed to triangulate several more matches to create four confirmed ancestral couples for the Houston rapist.

Now she was doing reverse-genealogy on Craig Millar's grandparents, Charles and Betsy Millar, working to identify all known descendants and hoping to find an overlap with some of the names from the other three genetic networks that she had created.

Fortunately, Charles and Betsy Millar only had three children. Notwithstanding the outlying possibility of endogamy, the number of centimorgans ruled out Craig's father and all of his other offspring as being possible suspects, leaving just two siblings for Becky to research.

Becky chose Judy Millar, the eldest child of Charles and Betsy, to work on first. She knew that she'd been born in 1899 in Dallas, Texas and was present in that city for the 1900, 1910 and 1920 censuses.

Opening up the page for the 1930 Census, Becky entered Judy's details and hit search. The results appeared unworkable with 33,088 hits, but as she scrolled down the page, Becky found that only the top six were an exact match for Judy Millar. But none of their places of birth gave the right state. Still, Becky checked out each one in turn. None appeared correct, possibly because she had married by that point and was no longer recorded under her maiden name.

Returning to Judy's profile within the speculative tree, Becky clicked on the hints that were deemed to pertain to her. The first—as always—were public family trees that Becky rarely found to be accurate, but which might just give a clue or a source that could be corroborated.

In the first tree that Becky clicked on, she gasped. This tree had Judy Millar marrying one Norman Sheldon, a name which had cropped up in one of the other clusters. Luck continued to be on her side because the person who had compiled the tree had also included a copy of Judy and Norman's marriage certificate which confirmed that this was indeed the correct person.

Becky felt that she was on to something as she saved the information to her tree and then took a look at Norman Sheldon's family.

Within minutes, Becky had attached Norman Sheldon to one of the genetic networks that she had previously identified. Judy Millar and Norman Sheldon were very likely to be the Houston rapist's grandparents.

Becky quickly drank her coffee down, anxious to get on. Unless Judy and Norman had had a whole bunch of kids and grandkids, this case could very soon be solved.

After a short while of searching, she'd found that Judy and Norman had had just two children, both girls. One appeared to have remained her whole life in Dallas. She had married and had one son and two daughters. The other had moved to Houston and had had one son.

Becky was now down to just two male candidates: one in Dallas and one in Houston. Given the locations of the assaults, she prioritized with the latter man, Phillip Hollingsworth.

Running his name through BeenVerified, Becky found an address history that ran back into the 1980s. She cross-referenced the locations of the six assaults and applied the circle hypothesis. Phillip Hollingsworth lived directly inside of it.

She took a screenshot of the map, digitally annotated it, then printed it out, knowing that it would be a key piece of evidence when law enforcement came to build a case against him.

Returning to the BeenVerified results for Phillip Hollingsworth, Becky felt sick when she looked down at his employment history. *Kindergarten teacher. Youth Pastor. Boy Scouts of America leader.* He had worked in various churches, schools, and youth organizations throughout the 1980s and 1990s. Becky was certain that if Phillip Hollingsworth was indeed the perpetrator, then more victims would surely come forward after his eventual arrest.

She drew a breath and had to remind herself that Phillip Hollingsworth was not necessarily guilty of committing these crimes. Apart from knowing that his first cousin, James Reynolds, appeared to have lived in Dallas, Becky had done very little research into him so far. At this point, either man could still potentially be the perpetrator. Law enforcement would use her findings as a lead; only they could finally determine his guilt by processing his DNA through CODIS.

Leaving nothing left to chance, she continued her investigation into both men's lives.

Two hours later, Becky zipped up a folder of evidence and emailed it over to Maddie who would scrutinize her work, challenge her with questions, check her sources and pick it apart, looking for holes or oversights. If Maddie was then happy, she would send her work to the detective responsible for the case at Houston Police Department.

Becky exhaled as her computer made the whizzing sound which meant that the email had gone. The main Word document that she'd just sent contained a sourced summary of her findings, including DNA analysis and in-depth genealogical research and records. Her conclusion pointed to one man overwhelmingly: Phillip Hollingsworth whose photograph was in front of her on the computer screen right now. She'd found it in an online church archive, and it was a picture of him with his arms around two girls whom Becky estimated to have been around ten years of age. The image was captioned *Summer Camp, 1988.* Exactly the timeframe when the Houston rapist was committing his assaults.

The work had exhausted her, and she was about to close her computer down for the day and suggest to Ross that they get some takeout, when she remembered her virtual date with Jerome in less than an hour. Truth be told, she wasn't really in the mood. She sat back, removed her glasses and rubbed her tired eyes. She had no idea how tonight was going to go. All Jerome had told her was to be ready by seven o'clock.

'Okay, let's do this,' she muttered, putting her glasses back on and leaving the guest bedroom. She found Ross with his AirPods in, watching a webinar on Y-DNA.

He grinned as she entered. 'I come from the Horn of Africa, twenty-two thousand years ago.'

'Congratulations,' Becky said. 'I'm going to shower and get ready for my virtual date.'

'Have fun.'

Becky took herself off to her bedroom, showered and then spent an age deciding what she should wear. After the heavy day that she'd just had, she simply wanted to put on something comfy and collapse on the sofa, but she felt from the way that Jerome was talking about the evening that he was going to be making an effort. She chose a simple black dress and applied a little make-up. She stood back and looked at herself in the full-length mirror, suddenly finding it very weird that she'd gone to all this trouble to sit alone in her bedroom.

Just as Becky looked at the clock and saw that it was almost seven, the door buzzer sounded. She went out into the hall and pushed the button to talk. 'Hello?'

'Hi. Food delivery for Becky Larkin?'

Becky smiled. 'I'll be right down.' She hurried down to the main entrance, finding an UberEats driver with a discernible wide grin on his masked face, a bag of food in one hand and a bunch of red roses in the other. 'Just so you know straight off, these aren't from me,' he clarified.

Becky laughed and took the flowers and food, thanked the driver and returned to the apartment.

Ross raised his eyebrows and smiled when he saw what she was carrying. 'Someone likes you!' he sang.

Becky opened the food package, finding that Jerome had really gone to town. The order was from Fleming's Prime Steakhouse & Wine Bar, probably the most expensive takeout that he could find during the pandemic.

'What he get?' Ross inquired, reaching to open the bag to see.

Becky slapped his hand and pulled several items out. 'Crab cakes to start, prime tomahawk steak—'

'What?' he interrupted. 'They're like almost a hundred bucks! Did he put anything for me in there?'

Becky laughed. 'Nope. And I've got North Atlantic lobster and mashed potatoes, with roasted asparagus as a side and New York cheesecake for dessert.'

'Oh my God, what a feast.'

'And a bottle of white to boot,' Becky added, picking up a plate and some cutlery and heading off to her bedroom. 'Goodbye.'

'Enjoy!' he called after her. 'I'd be happy with any leftovers, by the way. And that's the food or the man.'

Becky laughed as she closed her bedroom door and put the food down on her dressing table. She looked at it all, impressed. She went to text him and saw that he was already video-calling her. 'Hi,' she answered. 'I can't believe all this amazing food. Really. Thank you so much.'

Jerome grinned. 'You're very welcome. I hope you like it. I've got the exact same, so get yourself organized and put me somewhere I can see and talk to you, and then we'll get on with this date.'

'It's really sweet,' she said, noticing that he was wearing a shirt and tie. She stood her cell phone up beside her, angling it as best she could, and began to decant the food onto a plate.

'So, how was your day?' he asked.

'Good, thank you,' she said, before giving him a brief summary of the SAKI case that she hoped she'd closed. 'How was yours?'

Jerome laughed. 'By comparison to yours, dull and boring, I'd say. Not even worth talking about to be honest. Which reminds me, those files that you wanted me to look at. Well, they were also very dull and boring. Was there something in particular that you wanted me to look for in there?'

'Just if there was anything out of the ordinary among the numbers. Anything like tax evasion, or money laundering, or anything illegal or suspicious-looking,' she said.

Jerome shook his head. 'Not at all. Just your usual, very uninteresting accounts. The Larkin Investment and Finance Group are basically funding major reconstruction works in Haiti; that's the bottom line. What makes you think there's something amiss in the accounts?'

Becky thought for a moment. Although she trusted Jerome, she hadn't known him for all that long and didn't want to divulge the real reason for her inquiry. 'I don't... It's some people who were working on this financial package got into trouble a few years back, that's all,' she said, totally underplaying the seriousness of the situation. 'I just wondered if there was something untoward in there that might have offered a clue.'

'Not that I could see, no,' he said. 'Are you ready to eat?'

'Yep, you bet,' she confirmed, eager to get started with the delicious-looking food in front of her.

'Bon appétit,' he said.

'Thank you so much,' Becky said, beginning to eat. In the quietness of their eating, she considered the finance project that Michael Barnhart, Artemon Bruce and Jay Craig had been working on. If this had not been the reason for their suspicious deaths or disappearance, then what could have been?

Chapter Twenty-Seven

Sunday, April 19, 2020, South Jordan, Utah

Maddie was just finishing analyzing the SAKI file that Becky had sent over last night. She had scrutinized every aspect of the file, starting with the DNA and the clusters that Becky had created, through the reverse-genealogy phase and on to her final conclusions. As she always expected to be the case, Maddie had found Becky's work to be airtight and fully supported the findings and conclusion. Copying Becky in on the email and acknowledging it to have been her work, Maddie sent the file over to the Houston Police Department. She guessed that they would take their own time digesting the information and would no doubt undertake a trash DNA sample which they would then run through CODIS to receive confirmation that Phillip Hollingsworth was the perpetrator for whom they'd been searching for the past forty years.

At the top of her inbox was a reply from her aviator friend, Kirk Wennerstrom.

Maddie,
How nice to hear from you. I'm good thank you and hope you're all well.
In answer to your question about Dutch John Airport, I'm afraid it has no services. No fuel, no attendant, no control tower, no airport beacon, I'm not sure even the runway is lighted. It doesn't even appear to have a bathroom, much less an FBO (fixed-base-operator) that would offer a room with a sofa and a vending machine. Some tiny airports have a 'guest log', (like small/old hotels) where pilots can write down the date, aircraft registration number, where they're coming and going, and a little note. But I highly doubt that here. It would be perfectly legal (and safe, and likely common) to take off or land at that airport with a private plane without even so much as talking on the radio.
Sorry this wasn't more helpful. Give me a call if you have any further questions.
Sincerely,
Kirk

Maddie sighed. If Trenton's theory were correct, there would be nothing to corroborate it at Dutch John Airport. Even if they had a guest log, which Kirk had thought unlikely, it was absurd to think that Emmanuel Gribbin would have signed it and stated the reason for his visit.

She sighed. Another avenue closed. Maybe Trenton's theory was a little outlandish, anyway. She pushed her chair out and went upstairs to tell him, having promised that she'd keep the kids totally in the loop. He was in the living room, watching TV. Her usual instinct would have been to tell him to get up and do something constructive with his weekend, but where was he supposed to go?

'So, I've just heard back from Kirk,' Maddie said.

Trenton sat up and paused the TV. 'And?'

'You can read the email in full, but, basically, he said that Dutch John doesn't have a bathroom, much less anything that would keep records of flights heading in and out.'

Trenton blew air from his cheeks. 'That's crap,' he said. 'Did he talk about landing at College Park?'

'I didn't ask. We don't actually know that he *did* land there,' Maddie replied.

'But with other Larkin Group employees with him in Washington and him living close by, doesn't it stand to reason that's where he would have landed?'

'I guess so,' Maddie agreed.

'Please, Mom,' Trenton begged. 'Ask him if there would be any record of Gribbin landing at College Park.'

'Okay,' she said, taking her cell phone out of her jeans pocket and dialing him. She'd make the call right in front of Trenton so that he could see it not playing out and that she had tried. 'Hi, Kirk, how are you?'

'Good thanks, Maddie. You?'

'Yeah, not bad. Thank you for your email. I'm sorry, but I'm afraid I do have a follow-up question for you, if that's okay?'

'Sure, go ahead.'

'So, if the pilot took off from Dutch John Airport and flew to College Park in Maryland, would there be any record of that flight landing?' she asked, looking at Trenton and bracing herself for his

242

negative answer.

'Absolutely, there would be.'

'Oh,' Maddie said, taken aback. 'Can I put you on speaker so my son can hear what we're talking about?'

'Of course,' Kirk replied.

Maddie hit the speaker button as Trenton moved closer to the phone. 'Go ahead.'

'College Park, by dint of its proximity to Washington D.C., has *a lot* of security measures in place. Since 2003, D.C. has been surrounded by a 30-nautical-mile radius Air Defense Identification Zone—ADIZ for short—plus there's a tighter, 10-nautical-mile radius ring around D.C. called the Flight Restricted Zone—FRZ for short—controlling that airspace. Some pilots call it the Circle of Doom.'

'Okay,' Maddie said, scanning the room urgently for a pen and paper. 'What does this all mean, exactly?' She found a pen but couldn't find any paper. Then she remembered her mom's crossword book and pulled it out from down the back of the sofa, the act receiving a baffled look from Trenton.

'ADIZ means that no aircraft is allowed within the ring without being in positive control of ATC and squawking a discrete transponder code. Any airplane that does not would promptly be escorted out by armed helicopters or jets, forced to land and met by armed officials on the ground. FRZ means that no airplane is allowed in or out without the pilots' having been security vetted via a background check, fingerprinted, that kind of thing. Any flight in or out of the FRZ must file a special flight plan and be in constant communication with Air Traffic Control. As a private pilot, I went through the process of getting permission to fly to College Park and I had to fill out paperwork for a background check, have a verification interview with the FAA, get fingerprinted by the TSA, and undergo a security procedures test. In the end, a pilot is issued a special, private security code. Whenever they wish to fly into or out of College Park, they have to call a phone number for Potomac Approach before taking off, file the flight plan, and disclose their unique code. If the code and name of the pilot don't match what's on file, the flight plan would be denied for sure.'

243

'And do you know if the special flight plans would still exist from March 2015?' Maddie asked, scribbling notes around the side edges of one of her mom's abandoned crosswords.

'Yes,' he answered.

'Really? And is this something I'd be able to access?'

'Yes. Go to flightaware.com and select custom reports. They have twenty-four years' worth of data on there.'

'Well, gosh, that's amazing,' Maddie said, underlining the web address. 'Thank you so much again.'

'You're welcome. You just go on and give me a call, or drop me an email, if you have any other questions.'

'I will. Thanks, Kirk,' she said. 'Goodbye.'

Trenton was already out the door, carrying the crossword book with him. She pocketed her cell phone and followed him downstairs to the basement.

'I'll do it,' Maddie said, seeing that he was about to slide into her chair.

She sat down, opened a fresh web-browser tab and accessed the flightaware website. She selected *Rapid Reports & Data Subscriptions*, then scrolled down to *Airport History* which promised *A full flight operation history for any airport* once she had entered the airport code.

'I don't suppose you know the—' Maddie began.

'33U,' Trenton said.

'Thank you,' she said, wondering where he'd procured such precise information and once again being impressed by his investigative skills. Maddie entered the airport code and hit search. It was a paid service— ninety-seven dollars for one month's access—which promised to include FAA-registered owner name and address for aircraft. She went through the registration process, paid the subscription and clicked to have the report sent to her email address.

'Come on. Open it,' Trenton said, probably thinking he'd be doing this twice as fast if she had only let him. 'Come on, already.'

'I am, I am,' she retorted, opening her emails and clicking the report. A very long Excel document opened with several columns, arranged in date order. She scrolled down the page until she got to 2015, then slowed up until she reached March.

'There,' Trenton said, pointing at March 8.

Maddie scrolled a little further and stopped. Just one flight was recorded as having left Dutch John Airport.

Ident: N409PT
Type: PC-12
Origin: 33U
Origin Name: Dutch John
Origin City: Dutch John, UT
Destination: KCGS
Destination Name: College Park
Destination City: College Park, MD
Departure Time: 3/8/15 16:03
Arrival Time: 3/8/15 23:19
FAA registered owner: The Larkin Investment and Finance Group
FAA registered address: S Main St, Salt Lake City, UT 84101

Maddie and Trenton looked from the computer to each other and back again, not needing to say anything about the results.

His theory was checking out to be correct.

Hudson had slept terribly. He was lying in bed with a coffee, looping round his social media, watching inane videos and seeing his friends' depictions of their lockdown lives. He felt simultaneously relieved and anxious about everything that he had confided to Reggie, yesterday. It was not something that Hudson was in the habit of disclosing to relative strangers. Several bad past experiences, including with his own parents, had taught him to be strictly guarded about his past. Besides which, it was a personal matter, and he felt that he didn't owe anybody an explanation about his life. But something had compelled him to be honest with Reggie about his current problems with Abigail, the adoption and the Wanda Chabala case. Reggie had listened quietly and carefully, making no comment or judgment on what Hudson was telling him. When he had finished, Reggie said, 'Wow, you've sure had a really rough time of it lately.' They'd carried on talking for a long time and, when Hudson had gotten up to leave, Reggie had stood, too. 'If it

245

weren't for the pandemic, I'd give you a really big hug, man.' Hudson had felt his eyes moistening as he'd said goodbye. He'd walked home with a strange inner peace that he had not felt in a very long time.

He finished his coffee and hit refresh on the KARE11.com webpage that he checked every day for Minneapolis news. And there it was, the story that he had feared but that he knew would be coming. Two side-by-side photographs, one of Francesca Chabala and the other of Warren Mercaldo, sat above a shocking headline.

FRANCESCA CHABALA'S STEP-FATHER ARRESTED FOR HER MURDER
(KARE) - Police arrested a suspect in connection with the 2005 murder of Francesca Chabala.
Minneapolis Police Department arrested Francesca's stepfather, Warren Mercaldo, 48, of Frindley in connection with the victim's death. He was booked at the Anoka County Jail for rape and murder in the first degree, but he has not been formally charged. Anyone with information related to the case is urged to contact the Minneapolis Police Department at 612-673-3000

Hudson wondered what Wanda or law enforcement had discovered in the past seven days that had made Warren the prime suspect over his brother. Was it trash DNA or some other piece of evidence? He briefly considered contacting Wanda to ask but thought better of it. Although he wanted to know the outcome of the case, he knew that he needed to keep his distance from now on.

He could not imagine what Wanda must be going through, having unsuspectingly lived with her daughter's killer all these years. He also wondered how soon Brandon Blake, the man falsely imprisoned for the crime, might be released. If past miscarriages of justice were anything to go by, the state would not be in a great hurry to release him. Especially in this case, where prosecutors believed Brandon was not the only person present at the rape and murder. Without an outright confession of guilt and sole responsibility from Warren Mercaldo, Brandon's defense team would probably have their work cut out in proving his innocence. Hopefully, in time the complete truth would come out and Wanda Chabala and Brandon Blake could move forward with their lives.

Although the news story had not talked about DNA or investigative genetic genealogy specifically, it was out there now, and Hudson felt obliged to copy a link to the story and send it to Maddie.

He'd had enough of looking at his cell phone. It was time to get up and get on with the day ahead. Before he did, though, he typed out a quick message to Abigail.

Hope you're okay.

Since she'd left the house without a word, he'd heard nothing from her, and his messages had gone deafeningly unanswered. He'd reached out to her sister who had confirmed that Abigail was staying with their parents and wanted some space.

Heading into the kitchen to make breakfast, Hudson looked out of the window to see thick gray cloud covering the Wasatch Mountains. The possibility of snow, plus the heavy unburdening of yesterday, made Hudson decide to stay home today. He would fix himself a nice breakfast, stay in his PJs all day and work on the reverse-genealogy for the six sons of Taisiya Hohnstein and Peter Rawson.

Kenyatta looked at her cell phone disbelievingly. She'd just received a text from her son, Jon, that she couldn't quite comprehend. She read it again.

Mom, I think Troy might have killed Dougie. I don't have any proof but there are just a few things that he's said that make me wonder. I haven't told Dad or anyone else.

The very idea of her own son, Troy, killing the family dog was just completely absurd. He loved animals. She was certain that Jon had to be mistaken or had misread something Troy had said. She thought for a moment longer and then tapped out a reply.

Troy wouldn't do that. I think you're reading something into whatever it was that he said. He loved Dougie as much as the rest of us but is probably just not able to express that. He's probably being dismissive or flippant, so he doesn't have to show you that he's upset.

Kenyatta sent the message and then tried to put it out of her mind and concentrate on some work, but there, too, she was in quite a quandary. Yesterday's research into other members of cluster seven had not gone well. She'd spent several hours working on Otger Bryce's family tree, trying to work it back to make a link to the cluster lead Ray Marshall's family. She believed that the connection would be on the Russian side of Ray's family on either his maternal grandfather Henry Getman's side or his maternal grandmother Anna Kaufmann's side, but so far, she'd found no ties to these names or to Russia.

She returned to the cluster and the other three names which appeared alongside Ray Marshall and Otger Bryce as matching the Twin Falls killer. These people hadn't included any tree or ancestral names, and the quantities of shared DNA fell below twenty centimorgans for all of them.

Kenyatta didn't know what to do for the best outcome. She could easily spend the day researching one of these three names and not get anywhere. Or, since it was a Sunday and technically not a workday at all, she could continue with the *Boys Under the Bridge* case.

After more thinking and heavy sighing, she opted for the latter.

Thus far, she'd put her energies into mining as much information from the DNA as she could. Now it was time to do genealogy and to trace Arthit and Preeda Tang's descendants. Somewhere on that tree were two little boys who had wound up in Turkey Creek, Penrose, Colorado, with bullet holes in the backs of their skulls. Kenyatta opened the speculative tree that she had created for Angela Spooner and her cousin, Kanda Phasuk, working her way up through the generations to Arthit Tang.

Her first port of call was the Research Wiki page at FamilySearch, which led her to a link for Phetchaburi province in central Thailand where the Tang family lived. The page that loaded was woefully empty. The only genealogical records that it linked to was a simple list of cemeteries within the province. At Ancestry, she typed *Thailand* in the search catalogue, finding a link to two unrelated datasets. A search in the *Collection Catalog* at MyHeritage gave *0 collections found for Thailand*. A search at FindMyPast within all record sets found nothing either.

This wasn't going to be easy, she realized, wondering why there was nothing out there. She ran a general Google search for genealogy in Thailand and, after a little research, she found the answer. Vital records for the country were not kept until 1909 and it didn't become a legal requirement to register births, marriages and deaths until 1917, and, even then, record-keeping was sparse until the 1970s. The issue of the language difference, coupled with a completely different script and unrelated alphabet, meant that very few—if any—Thai vital records had been translated into English.

Kenyatta stared despondently at Arthit Tang's name, wondering what her next step ought to be. Between Angela Spooner and Kanda Phasuk's family, who had emigrated out of Thailand, she had few avenues still left to explore. She just had to hope and pray that the two boys were at least second-generation Americans, and that some documentation would exist for them in the United States.

With a disappointed sigh, Kenyatta returned to Kanda Phasuk in the speculative tree. She shared a slightly higher number of centimorgans with the boys than with Angela Spooner, so Kenyatta started her research with her, fleshing out her great-grandparents and their kids who had been the first in the family to settle in the U.S.

'Kob Sook Tang,' Kenyatta said to herself, clicking *Search on Ancestry* to see what wonders the mysterious algorithms could come up with.

As she waded through the list, her cell phone pinged with a text message. It was from Jim.

Hey Kenyatta. Barb's not feeling well and she can't come down to the kitchen this afternoon. Do you fancy filling in for her?

Kenyatta smiled and replied, *Is this you asking me on another date??*
It sure is! he sent back.
I'll be there then, she replied.

Moments later, Jim sent her a love-heart emoji. There really was a first time for everything, it seemed.

Becky was eating dinner with Ross. 'This is really good,' she commented, enjoying the last of the pesto tortellini salad that he'd made for them.

'Thanks,' he replied. 'You know, it's not *quite* on the Fleming's-Prime-Steakhouse-&-Wine-Bar level, but I did my best.'

'No, that it is not,' she agreed with a grin.

'Haha. So, you haven't really said much about the date. You didn't come out of your room, so...'

'We ate, we watched *50 First Dates*, then—'

'Okay, several questions,' he interjected. 'First, *how* did you watch it? You were literally in two different parts of the city.'

Becky jabbed her last piece of pasta and scraped it around the remnants of the sauce. 'We got the movie up on Netflix and then pressed play at the same time.'

Ross grimaced. 'That's so corny.'

'Romantic is the word you're striving for, there.'

'Okay, sure. Second question: *why* did you watch it? Could he not come up with something more recent? That movie is like decades old.'

'About fifteen years old, actually,' she corrected. 'It's sweet; he'd really thought about it. The movie is about a girl who suffers from short-term memory loss, so she can't remember the day before and her boyfriend has to keep reintroducing himself to her every day afresh.'

Ross set down his cutlery and stared at her. 'And? How precisely are we thinking that that's well thought out, or in any way sweet?'

'He said it was like our situation with the pandemic.'

'Because you also have short-term memory loss and can't seem to remember who he is every day?'

Becky laughed. 'Shut up. It made sense when he explained to me why he'd chosen it.'

'And did he say anything about the Haiti files? Or did you forget to ask him because of your awful daily recurring memory loss?'

Becky rolled her eyes. 'It was the *first* thing we talked about. But there wasn't much to say. He found nothing at all out of the ordinary there. Just boring statistics and standard contract stuff. Literally *nothing* suspicious.'

'Oh. So, what does this mean, then?'

'I don't know… I've got to figure out what else might link the three men, if it wasn't the project itself. Maybe it's nothing to do with my father's company after all,' she said hopefully.

Ross's eyes widened. 'Yeah, about that… Not looking likely, Becks. Didn't Mrs. Restroom say something about her husband being different after a trip to Haiti?'

'Uh-huh,' Becky confirmed. '*WC* said that when Jay got back from the trip in January 2015, he was withdrawn and refused to talk about what he'd seen out there.'

'Maybe they got to see some part of the business that they shouldn't have,' Ross suggested. 'But which was unconnected to the project itself?'

'It could literally be *anything*,' she said with a shrug. 'With the only three people who worked on the project now dead or missing, I don't know who else to ask.'

'Go back to Lois Strange, maybe?' Ross suggested.

Becky shook her head. 'I really think she's told me everything she knows. There's no reason for her to keep anything else from me at this point. I don't want to keep hassling her, as though I think she's holding back on something. We're trying to re-build. I'm wondering if it's time to hand what I know over to Maddie and let go of the reins.'

'Maybe,' Ross said, finishing his dinner.

'I'll sit on it for a bit and see if I can't come up with something else,' Becky said, clearing the table. 'I only really want to talk with Maddie about it when I've got something to say. At the moment, everything I have is purely circumstantial.'

'I'm sure the two of you will figure it out,' Ross said, moving into the kitchen. 'What are your plans now?'

'I'm going to work on my cluster for a bit. After spending time on the SAKI case yesterday, I need to have something to show at the briefing tomorrow. What about you?'

Ross pointed at the TV and gestured as though her question were ridiculous.

'I hopefully won't be too long, and then I'll join you,' she said, heading into the guest bedroom and sitting at her desk. She took a moment to remind herself of where she had left off on Friday with trying to close down cluster two. Although she'd only established the identities of four of her cluster lead Heather Newton's great-great-great-grandparents, Becky was taking a gamble that because of their links to Idaho, these were the areas worth prioritizing. She opened up the quick and dirty tree that she'd started for another person within cluster two, Janelle Prendergast, hoping to find a link to Idaho or the surnames Govier, Lonsdale, Hesp or Williams.

Other than her email address, the only information that Janelle Prendergast had included was one entry below *Ancestral Surnames.*

Brown (Chatham County North Carolina)

Becky copied her email address over to BeenVerified to run a background check.

No Results found

'Interesting,' Becky commented. No results at all often pointed to the person's not being in the U.S. and thus out of the reach of the background check. Another possibility was that the email address had been set up for the specific use of registering her DNA and for nothing else. Becky turned to Google and ran an open search for her name. As expected, there were hundreds of thousands of results, the topmost being populated by Instagram, Facebook and YouTube profiles. She added *Chatham County* to the search. Becky scrolled down the results list, pausing at a link to the Geni.com website. She clicked through to a genealogy profile.

Stephen Prendergast
Gender: Male
Birth: February 10, 1916
Immediate Family: Son of Elijah Prendergast and Mercy Longley
Added by: Janelle Prendergast on September 30, 2013

Becky clicked on Janelle Prendergast's name, which in turn opened up a new profile.

The information was sparse. Becky noted down that this Janelle Prendergast had married someone with the surname of Neal and had had two children, although she still didn't know for certain if this was the correct person, or not. Beside Janelle's name were two options: *Send Message* and *View Tree*. Becky clicked to view the tree. An extensive pedigree starting with Janelle Prendergast through to the majority of her great-great-grandparents opened up, displaying names and dates for each individual.

Becky scanned down the list of surnames. Although none of the names that she was searching for appeared, she did find someone by the name of David Brown and, remembering what Janelle Prendergast had added to her FTDNA page, clicked on his name.

David Brown
Birth: 1814 in Chatham County, North Carolina
Death: 1881 in Chatham County, North Carolina

The addition of Chatham County gave Becky the confidence that this Janelle Prendergast was the same person who shared DNA with both Heather Newton from cluster two and the Twin Falls serial killer. She just needed to work out how.

Becky returned to the base of the tree and systematically worked her way up each line. She found that, although both of Janelle's parents had died in England, her paternal grandfather had been born in North Carolina. So far, no sign of any links to Idaho or the four family names that she'd identified in Heather Newton's tree.

As she was nearing the end of the paternal-line search, she spotted that Janelle's great-great-grandmother, Sophie Evans, had been born and died in Boise, Idaho. Becky clicked the arrow beside Sophie Evans's name, which opened up a further generation.

'Bingo,' Becky said, seeing that Sophie's mother's name had been Ann Williams. Ann's profile revealed her to have been the daughter of Benjamin Williams and Ann Hesp who were the great-great-great-grandparents of Heather Newton.

Becky had just closed down cluster two and successfully identified another set of the Twin Falls serial killer's direct ancestors.

Chapter Twenty-Eight

Sunday, April 19, 2020, Sawtooth Mountains, Idaho

He was sitting on a camping chair in the camouflaged hunting shelter that was barely big enough for two people to stand up in. Not that he ever brought anyone else up here. This was *his* place, not somewhere to be shared. In spite of the falling snow and the temperature outside being five below, he wasn't a bit cold. He was dressed head to foot in clothing that he'd fashioned from the skins and furs of the mountain lions, elk and wolves that he had hunted. On his face he wore a pronghorn stag skull mask which he had crafted and always wore when he hunted. Rising from each side of the skull's temple were black horns that rose ten inches upward and then curved inward to a spiked end. Circular eyeholes, bored into the front of the skull, served both to give him excellent forward vision and to produce heightened terror in that which he hunted.

It was getting dark now and he switched on his night-vision headgear, focusing it on the barrel thirty feet away up the mountain. This was the hide that he used in the afternoons and evenings, downhill from the drafting winds. The barrel was a damaged pony keg, a blue 25-gallon drum chained to a hemlock tree. There was a square hole in the top side that two weeks ago he'd filled with bread, grain, dog food and restaurant grease. The combined mixture was slowly seeping its way out of a hole in the bottom of the barrel; it was an unmissable feast for the black bear.

Without making a single sound, he slowly surveyed the mountainside around the barrel. The snow was continuing to fall, sticking with a thick layer on the evergreen hemlock, cedar and Engelmann spruce trees that dominated this area on the mountain. In his peripheral vision, he saw movement and shifted his sight over to the left and raised his Trapper.

It was an elk. A fine-looking bull. He tightened the focus on the night-vision gear. The elk was maybe 380 pounds with a six-tine rack that would look great hanging from his cabin walls.

The animal lowered his handsome head in order to inspect the smelly grease oozing from the bottom of the barrel.

He placed his finger more firmly on the trigger of the Trapper, watching the elk and wondering whether or not to take the shot.

He could easily take it down, but he wanted to wait for the top prize; just like he was doing with Debra Towers.

The beast took a quick and suddenly wary look over his shoulder before turning and trotting away.

He adjusted the angle of the night-vision aid toward where the elk had looked moments before. He grinned as his eyes settled on a 400-pound black bear.

The bear ambled over toward the barrel and began to scoop up the fatty food in his front paws, shoving it into his mouth.

The man watched for a few moments, then aimed the Trapper directly at the bear's head and pulled the trigger.

The shot rang out, sending the animal falling backward into a drift of snow. It lifted one paw in pathetic protest, then stopped moving.

He readied the gun to fire again and waited for any further movements. But the bear was dead.

Perfect shot.

The man got out of his camping chair, opened the hide door and trudged toward the black bear that was now just a dark mound, incongruous with the foot-thick snow that surrounded it.

He placed an expectant hand on the warm fur and an immediate sense of elation enveloped him, bringing with it a feeling of calm and relief from somewhere deep within him.

The man was sitting in the dark on a tree stump, illuminated by the fire that he'd made. The dead bear was slumped where he'd fallen just a few feet away.

He took a swig of the liquid bear fat from his mug and sighed with pleasure at how tasty the drink was. Fresh, warm bear fat was better than any beer, or any other drink in the world for that matter.

He sighed with a deep contentment spreading through him. There were few times in life that felt as good as this.

From the bag beside him—the sack of gold, as he knew it—he

took a handful of fatty meat from one of the bear's hind legs and tossed it onto the pan over the fire.

Only one thing was better than this, but he had to be patient, something he wasn't very good at. For now, while he waited, he had the next best thing. He licked his fingers, wiped the oily residue onto his pants, then took his tablet from his rucksack. Opening up an internet browser, he logged in at *Utopia100*. Yesterday, he'd completed Laredo, Texas and was now about to begin St Petersburg, Florida. *Welcome Rodger. Which weapon today?*

'Why, I think I'll go with my old lucky charm, here,' he said, nudging his gun with his foot. He selected the computer version of the 6.5-in barreled Marlin 1895 Trapper that he was marveling at beside him.

Go!

He entered the city of St Petersburg. Just in front of him five young women were talking outside of a shop. He smiled as he put a bullet into each of their heads.

Roasties 5 / 129,100

The chunks of bear meat sizzled and spat as the man shook the pan. 'Nearly there,' he muttered, his voice emerging as a squeak. But he didn't care how he sounded way out here; the nearest neighbor was a clear fourteen miles away.

He entered a small virtual grocery store, walked around it and took out all the women shopping in there.

Roasties 21 / 129,100

The food was ready. He paused the game, put the tablet down, took the pan off the fire and stuck a fork into one of the pieces of meat, letting it cool in front of his face in the freezing night air. It looked perfect.

He held the meat to his lips, inhaling the satisfying odor of cooked bear. It was a smell like no other. Then, he tore a piece off with his front teeth and began to enjoy the exquisite flavor in his mouth.

He washed the chunk down with more liquid fat, then took another piece of meat from the pan. As he began to chew, his cell phone sounded an alert. He took it out of his pants pocket. It was a Facebook notification: *Debra Towers has updated her status.*

The man clicked the notification and was taken to Debra Towers'
Facebook page.

*Thanks for all your messages about Gareth's mom. She's doing okay. She's
isolating at the family home. Gareth's gone up to see if he can help his dad out.*

The Chad had gone.
Debra was alone.
The man stood up, took an apologetic glance toward the bear, then
pulled on his pronghorn mask and picked up his Trapper.
It was time to go hunting again.

Chapter Twenty-Nine

Sunday, April 19, 2020, Twin Falls, Idaho

Detective Maria González was wading through the list of three thousand one hundred and seventeen names that the analysts had pulled out of the state hunting-license database. The file contained all the data extracted plus additional information that Maria had requested, including each man's current address. Any that fell within the circle, previously identified by the Venator team as the probable area of his residence, were highlighted yellow. Maria looked at those eighteen names but none of them was familiar to this investigation. The analysts were working on background and criminal checks for each of the men.

Maria scrolled up to the top of the list and exhaled. Then she noticed that one of the geeky analysts, Reuben Wright, was standing awkwardly in front of her desk, clutching some papers in his hand. He swept his hair over and muttered something.

'Pardon?' Maria said.

'Sorry to disturb you, Detective,' he said. 'I think I've found something.'

He had her full attention. 'What have you got?'

He laid the papers on her desk. 'I think our guy might be an incel,' Reuben started.

'A *what*? A unicell?'

Reuben smiled awkwardly and then cleared his throat. 'An incel. It's short for involuntarily celibate. It's basically a group of guys who consider themselves physically ugly and who can't get dates. They direct their anger at women who they think are to blame.' He placed a print-out of an article from *The New Yorker* on her desk. 'This kind of explains it.'

Maria picked it up and quickly scanned down the text, catching phrases like *notions of white supremacy* and *diabolically misogynistic*. She wanted to know more from him before she took the time to read the entire article. 'What makes you think this guy is an...*incel*?'

'Apart from it entirely fitting with his M.O., there's the black pill.'

'What black pill?' Maria asked.

'Each of the victims had capsules in their stomachs that contained the Amobarbital and Secobarbital. I checked with the Ada County Forensic Pathologist, and he confirmed that the capsules were black.'

'Right…' Maria said, trying hard not to get impatient about where this conversation *wasn't* going very fast.

Reuben laid another print-out on top of the previous article. He drew her attention to a highlighted section.

The incel community, believed to number tens of thousands within the U.S. alone, follow a deeply sexist ideology that they call the Blackpill, the principal belief of which is that all women are coarse, shallow and will only choose the most attractive men based on unalterable physical traits. Incels are not out for sex, they want total (white) male supremacy and extol their beliefs in dark web forums, where encouragement for rape and murder is commonplace.

'It's certainly an interesting theory,' Maria said, meeting Reuben's stare. 'You're saying that the killer has turned saddo forum rants into reality?'

'Uh-huh,' Reuben confirmed. 'I'm not aware of anyone who has actually used a black pill to represent their anger before, but he isn't the first incel to revenge-kill women.'

'Have you got anything else that would link him to this…cult, or whatever it is?'

'That's it so far.'

'Hey, Maria!' her detective colleague, Mike Davis, called over from his desk, cutting across whatever Reuben had been about to say.

'Yeah?'

Mike rotated his cell phone ninety degrees toward his shoulder. 'We might have a problem on our hands. The Patrol Unit has just arrived at an address in Adams Street after a request for a welfare check on the owner. It's a young, single woman.'

'Name?' Maria asked, visibly sagging at the news that they had all feared would be coming sooner or later.

'Debra Towers,' he answered.

Maria wrote her name down on the pad in front of her, then turned back to Reuben. 'Have you looked into these dark web forums?' she asked.

'I've had a trawl through some of the postings on Reddit and Braincels to try and find a link to Twin Falls or any mention of the victims, but nothing yet.'

'Okay, this could be interesting. Keep digging,' Maria instructed, watching as Mike returned the cell phone to just below his mouth. 'Yeah, go ahead.' He turned it again and relayed to Maria, 'No response at the address. They're going in.'

Maria jumped up and headed over to the large wall-map of Twin Falls. She located Adams Street. 'Shit,' she muttered. The road fell in the circle between Wendell Street and Harmon Park Avenue, again, where the Venator team had predicted that the killer probably resided.

'We'll be right there,' she heard Mike say into his cell phone. 'Maria! They're in. We gotta go. It looks like he's struck again.'

Chapter Thirty

Monday, April 20, 2020, South Jordan, Utah

Maddie arrived down in her basement, carrying what would likely be the first of several cups of coffee. She woke her computer and pulled up her emails. From the thirty-three unread, which had arrived overnight, she searched for and found one in particular. After discovering yesterday that an airplane belonging to the Larkin Finance and Investment Group had flown from Dutch John Airport in Utah to College Park in Maryland, she had taken a screenshot and sent it over to her aviator friend, Kirk, asking if he could add anything to the information included in the report.

Maddie
The airplane is a Pilatus PC-12 turboprop that is commonly used for executive / VIP transport and would be the natural choice for a company-owned aircraft. The airplane could make the journey from Dutch John to College Park in a non-stop five-hour flight. The arrival time of 23:19 is interesting as the offices would all be closed, local staff at home, and little likelihood of a local pilot or the 'weekend warriors' still being present. There would be security cameras running but local pilots do have gate access, so they can drive their cars up to the plane (I just called the Fixed-Base Operator for you to confirm that). The FAA database doesn't give you any more information about the airplane or its ownership than you already know. That's probably all you're going to get out of the records from 2015. Maybe the Larkin Investment and Finance Group keep their own records? Hope this helps.
Sincerely,
Kirk

Yes, it had helped. But it had unfortunately given more credence to Trenton's theory that Michael had been on that airplane, probably against his will. And, if he *had* been on that plane, where had Emmanuel Gribbin taken him upon landing? To the Washington D.C. Larkin Investment and Finance Group offices? To what end? If they were intent on killing him, then why go to the bother of dragging him halfway across the country, first?

Maddie needed to see the security video for the night that the Pilatus airplane had landed at College Park. She opened her cell phone and typed out a message.

Hey. Hypothetically, if someone needed to see footage from security cameras at College Park Airport, MD from 2015 how would they go about it?

She had just clicked to send the message to Clayton Tyler when the cell phone began to ring in her hand. It was Ross, which usually meant that it was a Venator-related question that needed an immediate answer.

'Hi, Ross,' she said.

'Hi, Maddie. I've just had a call from Detective González. She sounded tense and wants an urgent Zoom meeting at ten o'clock with the whole team.'

'Oh, okay. Did she say what it was regarding?'

'No, just to impress upon you that it was ultra urgent.'

'Okay. Thanks, Ross. Can you get a link out to the team and include Detective González on it, please? Also send a text message to alert everyone to the meeting, please?'

'Sure,' he confirmed. 'See you in an hour.'

'Okay, bye.' Maddie put her cell phone down, wondering about the meeting. It sounded ominous. She pulled up the local news for Twin Falls with some trepidation, expecting to see that another body had been discovered, but there was nothing, which came as a relief.

Maddie waded through the rest of her unread emails, made herself some fresh coffee and got ready for the Zoom meeting.

At two minutes to ten, she admitted everyone to the meeting. 'Good morning,' she greeted.

There was a short exchange of greetings and pleasantries with everyone speaking at the same time, then Maddie said, 'Detective González, did you have something that you wanted to know or to share about the investigation?' Whatever it was, judging by Detective González's tired and grave face, this was not going to be good news.

She nodded. 'We haven't released this information to the public as yet, but—and this has to remain confidential—he's got another victim.'

Maddie gasped, echoing similar reactions emanating from the rest of the Venator team assembled.

'The killer has taken a twenty-six-year-old woman from her home in Twin Falls,' Detective González relayed solemnly.

'Are you sure? Is it definitely him?' Maddie asked.

'Yes, it's definitely him,' she replied. 'And if he repeats the same pattern as the other four victims, we've got just a few days before she winds up dead. I understand the way you work and that you might not have any definite names until your work is done, but is there *anything* else you can give us?'

'We've successfully identified ten of the killer's great-great-great-grandparents—'

'Apologies…that's twelve,' Becky corrected.

'Twelve of the killer's great-great-great-grandparents,' Maddie continued, 'and we're about to start the reverse-genealogy phase of linking these twelve families together, kind of like an inverse pyramid. Hopefully at the bottom of that pyramid is one man's name.'

'Any idea how long that might take?' the Detective asked.

'We could find the links in a few hours, or…it may take longer. One problem we have is the influence of the Russian side of his family; the records just don't exist that we need.'

Detective González exhaled and the meeting fell silent.

'Can I ask where she was taken from?' Becky eventually asked.

'Adams Street,' Detective González replied. 'It's within the circle that you already identified to help us home in on him.' After another short silence, she added, 'Please could you contact me any time of the day or night, the second you've got even an *idea* of a remotely possible name. A few hours—hell, even a few minutes—could make all the difference, here.'

'I will,' Maddie confirmed.

'Thank you,' Detective González replied. 'I'll let you get on. Bye.'

Maddie said goodbye, waited for the detective to leave the meeting, then said, 'While we're all here, let's do a quick briefing. Becky, it sounds as though you've closed your genetic network. Is that right? Or had I miscalculated the number of common ancestors we've identified?'

'Benjamin Williams and Ann Hesp are the common ancestral couple for cluster two,' she confirmed, bringing up their family tree for everyone to see.

'Well done,' Maddie said.

'I was right to have followed on the trail of Heather Newton's Idaho family,' Becky said, 'as this was where I found the connection. Benjamin and Ann came from Boise, Idaho, just a stone's throw away from Twin Falls. I've yet to undertake any kind of reverse-genealogy, so, for now, you all need to keep a look out for Williamses in Idaho.'

'That's great. Good job,' Maddie praised. 'Kenyatta, do you have anything to share with the team? No is a perfectly acceptable answer, since I told you all not to work the weekend.'

Kenyatta smiled. 'I've no need to share my screen because I've got literally nothing to share, but *not* through lack of trying. I spent literally *hours*'—she dramatically dragged out the word—'on Saturday, working on trying to link someone else—a guy called Otger Bryce—to my cluster lead. No connections to him or to Russia came up. I don't know what the problem is, here, but it's going nowhere fast.'

'I think, given what we've just found out from the police, it's probably time to call it on cluster seven,' Maddie said. Kenyatta was her deputy in all but name and she knew that if Kenyatta couldn't break the cluster, then it probably couldn't be broken, at least not with the limited amount of time that they had left to work it. 'Hudson, do you have anything to report on from your weekend?'

'So, I *might* be onto something with the Russian side of the killer's family. *Might*. The common ancestral couple for cluster four, Vladislav and Kristina Hohnstein,' he began, pulling up the speculative tree that he'd created, 'had a daughter called Taisiya.' He clicked on her profile. 'She married a man, named Peter Rawson.'

'Isn't that name in the Y-matches?' Becky asked.

'Sort of,' he replied. 'The killer matched someone called Clive Rowson, R-O-W-S-O-N. Not the exact same spelling and the common ancestors are back twenty-something generations ago. But I've got this hunch that it's *not* a coincidence.'

Kenyatta leaned in closer to her camera and said, 'If you're correct, then that means the Russian side would be paternal, right?'

'Right,' he confirmed. 'So, yesterday, I spent a few hours doing reverse-genealogy for the six sons of Peter Rawson and Taisiya Hohnstein. Nothing more to report as yet on that front.'

'I think you're probably onto something,' Maddie agreed. 'It does seem too much of a coincidence for the two names to appear like that. Well, we've definitely tipped over into the reverse-genealogy phase, which is a fantastic achievement. Well done, everyone. Ross, could you bring up the full list of common ancestors that we've identified, please?'

'Sure,' he said, tapping his keyboard and then displaying the Word document that he had populated with every name, location and piece of relevant information that the team had produced. At the top, in red type, signifying factual information, was a summary of the case so far, including victim details. Below that, were the key findings from the team, headed with the names of the common ancestral couples that had been identified.

'Take a good look at those names and locations, people,' Maddie said. 'Somehow, somewhere, they intersect and combine with one another, culminating in the target name of the Twin Falls serial killer.'

The team fell silent as they purposefully read through the list of surnames: *Randazzo. Longo. Pernicano. Messina. Welch. Manefield. Murton. Davis. Hohnstein. Williams. Hesp.*

'So,' Maddie eventually said, looking at the names on her screen. 'Let's assign the common ancestors. Becky, since they're fresh in your mind, do you want to take Benjamin Williams and Ann Hesp? Kenyatta, do you want to pick back up with Vincenza Pernicano and Rosa Messina? Hudson, are you happy to carry on with Vladislav and Kristina Hohnstein? And I'll work on John Murton and Minnie Davis. Everyone good with that?'

The team sounded their agreement.

'Great. Given the urgency of this case, if anyone makes any startling discoveries, please notify the team immediately and keep Ross updated with your findings. I'm not sure yet, whether we'll have a briefing tomorrow morning or tomorrow afternoon. We'll see how we do. Any questions?'

'Nope,' Hudson replied.

'I don't think so,' Kenyatta answered.

'I'm all good,' Becky said.

'Great. Good luck, then, everybody,' Maddie said. 'More than any other case before, I think we need it.'

Maddie said goodbye and ended the meeting. She sighed, rubbed her eyes and sat quietly for a moment, hoping that she'd not bitten off way more than she or her team could chew with this case. If this latest victim should die, she knew that the whole team would be deeply affected by it. She had to remind herself that investigative genetic genealogy was simply another tool for law enforcement who were themselves running their own parallel investigations as they usually would. All they could do was their very best to support that.

Maddie spun her chair around and stood up at the whiteboard where she began to add the names of the killer's latest common ancestors. Ordinarily, they would each have been written on an orange slip of paper, giving the team a clear, visual, top line of ancestors from which they would work downward, searching for how the people had become connected, until they reached the killer. But this would have to do.

Returning to her computer, Maddie opened the speculative tree that she had created for John Murton and his wife, Minnie Davis. Before she got engrossed in the work, she took her empty cup upstairs to make some fresh coffee.

'Hey,' Maddie said, seeing her mom gazing out of the kitchen window. 'You okay?'

Her mom turned and tried to smile, but Maddie could see that she'd been crying about something.

'What's the matter?' she asked, placing a hand on her mom's shoulder.

Her mom shook her head. 'It's nothing. Really.'

'Mom,' Maddie said. 'Tell me.'

Her mom took a long breath, staring at the floor. 'I just went into the bathroom, and I couldn't remember how to wash my hands. I looked at the faucet, the soap and the towel, and I just couldn't remember what to do first or how...'

'Oh, Mom,' Maddie said, squeezing her gently.

'I mean, it did come to me eventually, obviously, but…'

Maddie didn't know what to say to reassure her. These kinds of things would be happening more and more often, she knew. 'As soon as this pandemic is over, we'll go to the support group down in Draper.'

Her mother shot her a critical look. 'And that'll help me remember how to wash my hands, I suppose?'

'No, Mom. But, you know, it might just help you cope with these changes,' Maddie said.

'Hmm,' her mom muttered. 'I'm going for a nap.'

'Please come talk to me if you need to,' Maddie called after her, but her mom kept on walking. It broke Maddie's heart to watch her shuffle away, a slowly shrinking version of the strong, intelligent, resilient woman that she had always been.

As she poured the coffee, Maddie wondered what the future might look like for their family. Her mom would need an increasing amount of care and support, and Maddie's already-thin hopes that Michael could one day return were quickly disintegrating.

As much as the future frightened her and needed carefully planning, she reminded herself that a young woman was right now being held captive somewhere by a serial killer. Knowing the barbaric and gruesome details of his other victims' injuries, it was downright obvious that this woman was being held in unimaginable terror.

They had to catch him before it was too late. As bizarre and incongruous as it was, the best way that she could help this latest victim was to return to the basement and get on with the reverse-genealogy phase of the work.

On the computer screen in front of her was one set of the killer's confirmed direct ancestors, John Murton and his wife, Minnie Davis, whom Maddie had traced back to a small village called Slaugham in Sussex, England. How on earth this couple came to be the direct ancestors of a serial killer from Twin Falls, Idaho, who also had a strong Russian and Italian heritage, was anybody's guess. She hoped that the killer's having such distinct elements in his family tree might do them a favor.

Having already tracked John and Minnie's son, Alfred's line all the way down to Joey Seymour, Maddie focused on their other two children, William and Harriet, about whom she knew nothing at all except for their birth dates and locations.

According to the 1881 and 1891 England censuses, Harriet Murton had been born in the village of Slaugham around 1880. At some point after 1891, Harriet had left the family home and couldn't be located on the 1901 Census, which Maddie presumed was either because she had married or died.

In the *England & Wales, Civil Registration Marriage Index, 1837-1915* record set, Maddie ran a search for a marriage for Harriet Murton. The fourth result looked promising. The union had taken place in 1899 in the registration district of Cuckfield, which, according to ukbmd.org.uk, was in Sussex and encompassed the village of Slaugham.

Maddie returned to the marriage entry and clicked *View Record.* The link was merely an index providing little in the way of genealogical information. What she did learn, however, was that Harriet's spouse had been recorded as Thomas Walker.

Switching back to the 1901 Census, Maddie edited her search for Harriet Walker, born around 1880 in Slaugham. The top result appeared to be correct. She clicked to view the scanned copy of the original record, finding Harriet living with her husband, Thomas Walker, in the village of Slaugham. Living in the adjacent house were her parents, John and Minnie Murton.

Now that Maddie knew that she had found the correct Harriet, she looked her up on the 1911 England and Wales Census, finding that she and Thomas had had five children.

Once Maddie had added the children to the speculative tree, she paused and drank her coffee, wondering what to do next. Ordinarily, she would have fleshed out the lives of each one of those five children, identifying their spouses, children and grandchildren, until she had reached a sufficient depth to have established any overlap by that point with the other clusters. But this case was different. She could literally spend *hours* working on Harriet Murton's descendants when it might not be her line that contained the killer at all, but rather her brother, William's. At some point in time, *someone* from this family tree must have emigrated to the U.S., since the team had discovered no other links to the U.K. Maddie was sure that searching for this someone was the key.

Going for a low-hanging-fruit strategy, Maddie reviewed the hints that were offered against each of Harriet Murton's five children. Among the variety of records suggested for each sibling, none of them had any obvious connection to the U.S. Of course, that didn't mean that emigration hadn't occurred in the generations below theirs, but it was enough to convince Maddie to turn her attention first to Harriet Murton's brother, William, before pursuing her children.

William had been born in 1878. Like his sister, he had been present in the family home in Slaugham in 1881 and 1891 but had also left by the time of the 1901 Census to which Maddie now returned.

Using his approximate birth year and location, Maddie ran a search for him. The first result showed him living in London with his wife, Agnes, and an eight-month-old son, George. Although Maddie was confident that she had found the correct William, she needed to be absolutely certain and so ran a search for his marriage, finding that it had occurred in 1898 in the district of Paddington. Just like the record for his sister, Harriet, it was only an index. Although she was sure that Paddington was somewhere around London, she confirmed it on the UKBMD website. Then, she opened up the *London, England, Church of England Marriages and Banns, 1754-1936* record set and searched for the marriage. She was in luck. A scanned copy of the original record loaded on her screen, providing her with confirmation of William Murton's father's name and occupation. This was indeed the correct family.

Maddie saved the marriage certificate to the speculative tree, then looked for William and his wife, Agnes, on the 1911 Census. They were still living in London with their six children.

As she saved each new child to the tree along with the census record, Maddie began to wonder if she was embarking on a wild-goose chase with this family. Then the hints beside each of the children's names began to populate and Maddie could see that, by the time of the 1920 U.S. Census, the whole family had been recorded living in Billings, Yellowstone, Montana.

She was relieved to have made the right call. Now she had to research each of the six Murton children's lives in the U.S.

'Here you go, Mom,' Nikki said, placing a plate of food down on the desk beside her. 'Since you're not reading your texts...'

'Oh, thank you so much,' Maddie said, taking her eyes off the screen and blinking for what felt like the first time in several hours. 'You sent me a message?' She picked up her cell phone to see that she had left it on silent mode. 'Oops.' She had unread text messages from Nikki, Trenton, Clayton and a thread on the Venator group.

She would deal with them in a moment, she thought, choosing now rather to give Nikki her full attention. 'Thanks for cooking. How's your brother and grandma?'

'Good, I think. They've both had dinner. Trenton's on a video game and Grandma is washing the dishes,' Nikki relayed.

'Washing the dishes?'

'Uh-huh,' Nikki said. 'I didn't have the heart to tell her that we have a dishwasher.' Nikki looked at her computer. 'How are you doing? Any closer to finding this guy?'

'Yes...and no,' she answered. She'd made good progress on the first four of William and Agnes Murton's children and thought she had made a breakthrough when she'd discovered one son living in Pocatello, Idaho, just 114 miles away from Twin Falls. But, just a few moments ago, Maddie had found that he had died apparently single and childless. The disconcerting thought that he could also potentially have fathered a child that had gone undocumented was clouding her mind. If that were the case, then no record would exist that showed an overlap with the other clusters and they would just be chasing shadows.

'Are you going to stop or take a break at any point?' Nikki asked.

'I'll take a break to eat now,' Maddie replied. 'Thank you.'

'You're welcome. I'm going to use the treadmill, take a shower and then watch a movie before bed,' Nikki said, moving toward the door. 'Don't work too hard.'

'I won't,' Maddie answered, but that ship had sailed; she had already worked too hard. She tucked gratefully into the dinner of chicken, French fries and salad as she picked up her cell phone. She read Nikki's messages first.

How are you doing down there? Trenton and Grandma are asking what's for dinner.
I'll cook.

Maddie smiled, sent her daughter a love heart emoji and then read Trenton's messages.

Are you still alive down there?
Hello???
Okay, so I presume you're dead so I'm just going to spend the whole night playing video games

She sent him an eye-roll emoji back and said, *I'm turning the internet off at 10pm.* Next in the list was a thread on the Venator group, started by Kenyatta.

PURPLE SLIP!!! Vincenza Pernicano and Rosa Messina's son, Carlo married Silvestra Randazzo and Marie Longo's daughter Onofria in Sicily.

The rest of the team had quickly jumped in to congratulate her on finding the first pair of the killer's great-great-grandparents. Maddie hastily typed out a message.

Well done! Sorry for taking so long to respond. Cell on silent. Good work! No major breakthroughs from me as yet…

Last was a message from Clayton Tyler in response to her message inquiring about access to security camera footage in College Park Airport.

Ok. Did a bit of research on this. All video at airports is controlled by regulation from TSA and Homeland Security. You could try requesting a certain camera or two if you know the location and state you think something was stolen. Give the date and approximate time. For fuller access the geeks in my office who do this all the time just said a lot easier would be to hack it. Take an expert 5 minutes.

The message was followed up by another.

To answer your next question, yes, I do happen to…if you'd like.

It took Maddie a moment to work out to what the second message was referring and then she realized what her next question would have been: *Do you know someone who could hack into the security cameras at College Park Airport for me?*

Wow. Had it really come to this? Maddie wondered, finding herself typing out a reply that read:

Yes, please. A Pilatus PC-12 turboprop landed at College Park at 23:19 on March 8, 2015. Any footage of the plane, pilot, anyone going to or from the plane would be amazing. Thank you.

Maddie took a breath, not sure how life had gotten her to this point. She finished the dinner, constantly checking her cell phone, as if the security footage might just magically arrive. It hadn't and Maddie pushed the plate to one side, sent a thank you message to Nikki for the dinner and then resumed her work.

'Bessie Jane,' she muttered, pulling up the profile for the final child to William and Agnes Murton. She had been born in Paddington, England in 1909 and had emigrated with the rest of her family to Billings, Yellowstone, Montana in 1913. She was recorded with the family on the 1920 and 1930 U.S. censuses. After that, Maddie had lost track of her. She clicked to view the fifteen hints associated with Bessie Jane. She stopped about half-way down the page at a link to FindAGrave and clicked through.

Bessie Jane Pernicano
Birth: 4 Nov 1909, England
Death: 3 Apr 1984 (aged 74), Pocatello, Bannock County, Idaho, USA
Burial: Mountain View Cemetery, Idaho, USA

Maddie excitedly enlarged the photo of the memorial, finding that Bessie Jane's husband had been called Stefano Pernicano. She picked up her cell phone and typed out a quick message on the Venator group chat.

Did Carlo and Onofria Pernicano have a son named Stefano?? (please say yes…)

273

While she waited for a response, Maddie checked more of the records that Ancestry suggested might pertain to Bessie Jane.

Yes! Came Kenyatta's response, to which Maddie replied:

Then I think I've just earned myself a BLUE slip of paper thanks to Stefano Pernicano and Bessie Jane Murton!

The link looked solid, but Maddie needed to shore up her research with further corroborative documentation to be absolutely certain. Accuracy and sourcing were critical at this stage of their investigation. But right now, it appeared as though she'd just identified two of the Twin Falls serial killer's great-grandparents.

Chapter Thirty-One

Monday, April 20, 2020, Sawtooth Mountains, Idaho

Life in his cabin in the Sawtooth Mountains was amazing right now. He was lying back on the beat-up couch with his legs crossed at the ankles, his feet just a few inches from the burning fire. A dozen crushed beer cans were lying discarded on the floor beside him. Resting on his thighs was an empty bowl with only the greasy residue left over from the chunks of bear meat that he'd just eaten. Only two things were wrong. One was the weather. A damned truckload of snow had fallen in the past few hours, slowly riding up the windowpanes in front of him. The second problem was the women. He had just twenty-two roasties left to find before he would complete St Petersburg, Florida. But he'd been trudging the streets, looking for hours now, and all he saw were white men everywhere. He liked a challenge, but this was getting stupid. Plus, the game creator, Death2Girls, had released a special upgrade that he'd promised players would love. The only clue he'd given them was to try *not* killing the women, which made absolutely no sense to him at all.

He got up and shuffled drunkenly into the back room where the orange glow from the fire barely reached.

'Where do you whores all like to hang out?' he mumbled.

Silence.

He laughed as he remembered that, as well as blindfolding Debra, he'd gagged her to stop the incessant, penetrating screaming. She was sitting on the floor with her back to the wall, hands tied behind her back and feet tied off at the ankles. He loosened the tie at the base of her neck and repeated the question.

'I…don't…know wh-what…you mean,' she stammered.

'Oh, you know exactly what I mean,' he said, his voice jumping an octave. It was the first time that she'd heard it happen. He saw her look in his direction. She didn't show it, but she was sure to be laughing at him on the inside. Mocking him. 'What's funny?' he demanded, his voice remaining normal.

'Nothing,' she replied softly. 'You're the internet guy, aren't you?

The one who came to my house. Steven…? You seemed like a real nice guy.'

'I *am* a real nice guy,' he squeaked. 'A supreme gentleman.'

'Then, let me go,' she sobbed.

'Oh, I will,' he responded. 'We just need the damned snow to let up. It's no fun hunting in this weather, I can sure as hell tell ya.'

Just like the others, she began to wail, too, and he re-tightened her gag. There was literally no danger of anyone hearing the noise; he just couldn't concentrate on playing *Utopia100* with all the racket she was creating.

Beauty salons, hairdressers and nail parlors: that's where they'd go, he thought, feeding off an anger intensifying inside of him.

He finished the last dregs of beer, crushed the can, belched and then hit the *Navigate* button, which brought up a searchable map. He typed in *Nail parlor* and two downtown city buildings became highlighted in red. He tapped the closest and an arrow appeared in the sky, directing him on.

It was a few blocks until he finally reached *Natalie's Nails*. Inside, he found three women having their nails painted by another three women. He aimed his Trapper at the head of the first woman, but then remembered what Death2Girls had said. Instead, he aimed at the first woman's arm and pulled the trigger. The bullet split open her bicep as it always would have done. But this time, she looked at him, screaming, shouting and swearing about how much pain she was in.

He laughed. Nice touch.

She still just stood there, screaming, while all the other women carried on obliviously with their nails.

They didn't even bat an eyelid when he'd blown the woman's head clean off, right in front of them.

Chapter Thirty-Two

Tuesday, April 21, 2020, Liberty Wells, Salt Lake City, Utah

Hudson was exhausted. He had been working late last night and then had set his alarm for 6 a.m. this morning. He nursed a cup of coffee between his hands as he read the email that had just come in from Wanda Chabala.

Hudson, I just want to thank you for the work that you did on behalf of my daughter. I can appreciate that the findings put you in a very awkward position and I totally understand why you felt you had to back away from the case. I'm not sure if you've seen the news or not, but Warren was arrested on Sunday for Francesca's rape and murder. My heart has been broken again but at least now justice will be done for my daughter and also for Brandon Blake. Unless you wish it to be otherwise, your name remains unconnected to the case. After a tip-off, a surreptitious DNA test was obtained which confirmed that my worst nightmare was in fact real. The two people that I loved most in the world are gone from my life forever. But the truth is now out. Thank you again, Wanda

The email hit Hudson hard from multiple angles simultaneously. He felt desperately sorry for Wanda and the cards that life had dealt her; putting her in the position of watching her husband being tried for the rape and murder of her daughter. He also felt relief that his name and the work that he'd undertaken had been kept out of the case. It also made him think about Abigail. She'd not made any contact with him, even when he'd forwarded the email that had come back from Utah Adoption Specialists agreeing that taking a pause during the pandemic was a wise, healthy and well-considered decision that wouldn't negatively prejudice their application going forward. Hudson was sure, though, that there was simply no way that he could feel any less like adopting a child than he did right now. Maybe that would change if his ailing relationship with Abigail could be salvaged.

He forwarded Wanda's email to Maddie, without adding any comments. His resignation still hung in the air but, right now, he didn't have the emotional energy to think about that.

Minimizing his emails, Hudson pulled up the speculative tree that he had been working on. He'd given hours last night to continuing his research into the six sons of Peter and Taisiya Rawson, who had all emigrated to the U.S. as young men. The 1880 Census showed the brothers living in Denver, Arapahoe, Colorado, working as carpenters, farmers and laborers. Despite their nearest neighbors having an eclectic range of birthplaces ranging from Switzerland, Norway, Bohemia, France, Ireland and several U.S. states, four of the brothers had married other Russian immigrants. One of the brothers had died unmarried and the final brother had married a woman who came from Missouri.

Given the killer's genetic heritage, Hudson's gut instinct was pointing him toward the four brothers who had married other Russian immigrants. He had fleshed out biographies for three of the brothers, adding detailed and sourced documentation to the tree and bringing their lines down a further two generations. So far, there was no sign of any of the surnames that the team had identified.

He clicked to view a record in *U.S., Passport Applications, 1795-1925* on Ancestry for one of the fourth brother's sons, Paul Rawson. The typed document from 1902 confirmed his date and place of birth, as well as his father's name and place of birth. A third of the way down the page was the *Disposition of passport*, which interested Hudson:

I am about to go abroad temporarily and intend to return to the United States within six months with the purpose of residing and performing the duties of a citizen therein; and that I desire a passport for use in visiting the countries hereinafter named for the following purpose: Russia for a pleasure trip.

Although the record served to provide confirmative evidence of Paul Rawson's name, date of birth and his relationship with his father, it was the final five words of the statement that stirred Hudson's intrigue. He'd already found Paul Rawson on the 1910 Census, living in West Sheridan, Arapahoe County, Colorado, with his wife, Eva, and their four children, Harvey, Joseph, Lewis and Lena. Significantly, Eva had given her place of birth as Russia and her immigration year to the U.S. as 1902, the same year that Paul Rawson had travelled to Russia

278

on his pleasure trip.

According to the 1910 Census, Paul and Eva had married in 1903. So, using the Research Wiki at FamilySearch, Hudson navigated his way through to vital records for Arapahoe County, Colorado, which took him to a search page at FindMyPast. Entering the details for Paul Rawson and an approximate marriage date of 1903, Hudson hit search. Of the 264 results suggested, number one looked right. He clicked to view a scan of the original record.

State of Colorado Division of Vital Statistics
MARRIAGE RECORD REPORT

County: Arapahoe
Husband's Name: Paul Rawson
Age: 22
Wife's Name: Eva Semenov
Age: 19
Place of Marriage: Littleton, Colo.
Date: Apr. 8, 1903

The record was brief and didn't provide any evidence that the pair had met during Paul Rawson's trip to Russia. Not that it mattered.

Hudson followed both Paul and Eva through the censuses and vital records until their deaths, then began to build a fuller picture of their children, three more of whom had been added to the tree.

He started working on their eldest child, Harvey Rawson, who had been born in 1905. Hudson found Harvey living with his parents until his marriage in 1928. They were still residing in Arapahoe County at the time of the 1930 Census but, by 1940, with his wife, Amelia, two sons and one daughter, he had moved. Their new address made Hudson sit up with ignited interest: Cassia County, Idaho.

He ran a Google search for the county. It was adjacent to Twin Falls.

Even though none of the surnames that the team had found had yet shown up, he felt like he had to be on to something.

Hudson waited to be admitted into the afternoon's briefing. Since the news had come in yesterday from the Twin Falls detectives, he'd worked so much harder than usual. He knew that the rest of the team would have been doing precisely the same thing. But what if it were not enough? The killer had taken the latest victim two days ago. Her time was running out. He had made good progress today but still didn't know if the families that he was working on actually connected directly to the killer.

The screen changed in front of him, and his image was bounced into the briefing, along with the rest of the team.

'Everyone okay?' Maddie asked, inclining her head and voicing what Hudson himself immediately noticed. 'My, you're all looking tired, out there.'

After a brief silence, Kenyatta spoke. 'Look… I know you said that we shouldn't work ourselves to the bone on this case, but I'm guessing that I speak for the rest of the team when I say that we just can't *not* give it our all. I confess to pulling a late one last night and then getting up with the birds first thing this morning to carry it on.'

'Me too,' Hudson agreed.

'Me three. Same,' Becky chipped in.

Maddie exhaled. 'Yeah, busted. Same for me. Okay… But all of us being this tired isn't good for us *or* for the case, if we make mistakes or overlook something important because we're not firing on all thrusters. So, after this briefing, I want you all to take at least a couple of hours off. Okay?'

The team agreed, although whether they would stick to it, or not, was a separate matter. Hudson thought that he might take the whole evening off, get some rest and get up very early to resume his work in the morning.

'One second,' Maddie said, standing and disappearing from camera. Moments later, she slid a whiteboard into view upon which she'd written the names of the Twin Falls killer's twelve known great-great-great-grandparents. She pointed to the names below those and said, 'Since yesterday's briefing, Kenyatta found that Carlo Pernicano married Onofria Randazzo, providing a link between clusters six and three. Well done, Kenyatta.'

'Why, thank you,' Kenyatta said, taking a bow, chest up.

Maddie continued, 'Then, with a little luck on my side, I managed to link their son, Stefano Pernicano, to Bessie Jane Murton from my cluster five...'

Kenyatta and Becky clapped at this information.

'Thanks,' she said. 'I have done what I hate doing, which is sending out information before we're done with a case. But on this occasion, I thought I would break my own rules and I sent Detective González some of the names that we've confirmed are linked to the killer to see if they showed up in any of their searches or databases, or whatever else it is they're working on. I got a reply back about a half hour ago to say that—so far—the names had *not* appeared in connection with this case, unfortunately. So, we keep going... Kenyatta and I have been productive today. We've been working on the descendants of Stefano and Bessie Jane. Rather typically, they had twelve kids.'

'Uh-huh,' Kenyatta said with a short, incredulous laugh.

'But, despite this, we found that—sorry—*Kenyatta* found that one of these twelve kids, Rosa Pernicano, married a guy named Ronald *Williams*,' Maddie continued, standing up and writing Rosa's name below those of Stefano and Bessie Jane.

'Oh!' Becky exclaimed. 'I don't think I have a Ronald on my Williams tree yet. When was he born?'

'Nineteen thirty-two,' Kenyatta answered. 'This could just be a coincidence as we've yet to work back on Ronald's tree. All we know so far are the names of his parents. Maddie, do you want to show the tree?'

'Sure,' Maddie said, getting up the profile for Ronald Williams. She circled her cursor around the names of his parents, Elijah and Lydia Williams. 'Here they are.' She clicked on Elijah Williams. 'Born 1900 in Boise, Idaho.'

'That's *exactly* where the Williams line in cluster two comes from,' Becky confirmed. 'I'm sure he must be from the same family as I'm working on. We just need to find that elusive link.'

'What is interesting,' Kenyatta said, 'is that Ronald and Rosa Williams's four kids were all born in Twin Falls.'

'Oh, my goodness,' Becky said.

'That's amazing work,' Hudson praised. 'That's a green slip.

Getting closer.'

'And that's where we're at,' Maddie finished, slumping back in her chair, feigning complete exhaustion.

'Shall I go next?' Becky asked.

'Sure, go ahead,' Maddie encouraged.

Becky brought up her screen which showed the children of the couple, Benjamin Williams and Ann Hesp. 'As you can see, they were a big family who liked to evade the census, move around a lot and have generally been slippery to trace. I've got three of their kids, right down to the 1990s and another down to the 1950s, but still have one boy and a girl to go. Now that I know about this Elijah Williams character, I'll concentrate on the son. That's all from me.'

'Good work, Becky,' Maddie said. 'Hudson, how have you got on?'

'Not bad,' he replied, sharing his screen for the Rawson family. He talked through what he'd been working on all day, concluding with the discovery that Harvey and Amelia Rawson had raised their children in Cassia County, Idaho… Right next to Twin Falls.

'Brilliant work,' Maddie said. 'Becky, are you happy trying to work out if Elijah Williams connects to your tree?'

'Of course,' she answered.

'Hudson, are you happy to continue with the Rawsons?'

'Yep,' he replied.

'Since Williams is the third most common surname in the U.S., Kenyatta, you and I can take two each of Ronald and Rosa's kids. That okay?'

'Suits me fine,' she confirmed.

'Hey, that's cheating,' Becky mocked. 'I had to do the whole Williams tree by myself, you two slackers.'

Maddie laughed. 'You're younger than us.'

A laugh and a nod from Kenyatta was followed by a short silence. Hudson presumed they were all feeling eager to end the meeting and continue their research.

Maddie leaned forward, placing her elbows on the table. 'I really feel that we're on the verge of getting somewhere, here, you know. Thank you all for working so hard on this case. We're doing everything that we can and so is law enforcement up in Twin Falls but remember that we're up against a total psychopath, here. Whatever he does next is absolutely *not* within the bounds of our control. You've all of you got to hold tight to that perspective, okay?'

They verbalized their agreement and said goodbye to one another, and, with that, the meeting ended.

Hudson looked out of the window across the street at the school, thinking on Maddie's parting words. He figured that she was preparing them for the worst. Had she heard something? Hudson wondered, running a Google search for the local news in Twin Falls. News of the woman's abduction had broken and was now public. Under a grim headline, which shouted *FEARS FOR SERIAL KILLER VICTIM NUMBER FIVE*, was the photograph of a good-looking woman in her mid-twenties. The caption below the photograph read, *Fears are rising for Debra Towers, believed to be the latest victim of the Twin Falls serial killer.*

Hudson felt nauseous as he read the article. Debra had spoken to her boyfriend on Sunday morning but, when she had failed to answer his repeated calls, a friend had gone to the house, finding no sign of Debra. A welfare check by city police had found clear evidence of an abduction that matched the kidnapping style of the killer of the other four victims. The article went on to say that Police were checking nearby security video and Ring doorbell footage, as well as conducting house-to-house inquiries. But the tone of the article was generally pessimistic with obvious references to the typically short gap in time between the abduction and discovery of the other victims' bodies. The story left Hudson feeling that the authorities were not optimistic about finding Debra alive.

He shared a link to the article on the Venator text group then considered what to do next. Any notion that he had entertained of his possibly taking the rest of the evening off evaporated. He got up, took a microwave dinner from the freezer and, shortly afterward, returned with it to his computer.

He had resolved that he was not going to stop tonight, until he'd traced every one of Harvey and Amelia Rawson's descendants.

Chapter Thirty-Three

Wednesday, April 22, 2020, Salt Lake City, Utah

'Becks!' she heard again.

She groaned as she fumbled on her nightstand to switch off her cell phone alarm. She found it, turned it off, curled herself back into the fetal position and closed her eyes.

'Thank you!' Ross called from his bedroom.

After the late night that she'd just had, she desperately wanted to go back to sleep and return to the dream that had been rudely interrupted by Ross's inconsiderate shouting. In her reverie, she had been skiing with Jerome at Park City, and it had felt absolute bliss: perfect snow conditions, blue skies and warm sunshine. Best of all, the weight of her investigations into the Haiti project and the Twin Falls serial killer, not to mention her strained relationship with her parents, had not existed. But they slammed back into focus, filling her head and heart with dread and anxiety. After a lengthy conversation with Ross, yesterday, Becky had decided to present everything that she knew about Michael's connection to the Haiti project to Maddie later today after the briefing.

As she dozed, her mind wandered over to the case. The stark image of Debra Towers from the news story that Hudson had shared last night formed before her: smiling at the camera in a relaxed, informal pose. Becky thought back to the anger-retaliatory category that the killer fell into and wondered if Debra Towers' undoubted beauty had been the reason that he had chosen her. What had happened in the killer's life to make him wreak such brutal revenge on these poor innocent women?

She rolled over and opened her eyes. There was no way that she would be going back to sleep now. Swinging her legs out of the bed, she twisted her hair up into a ponytail, put on her glasses and headed out to the kitchen.

Ross was sitting in his pajamas at the breakfast bar already, drinking coffee. He growled doglike at her as she entered the room.

'What?' she said.

'Why, pray tell, am I awake at six o'clock in the morning?' he asked, running his hand through his just-out-of-bed hair.

She draped her arm over his shoulder. 'Sorry. I don't know why. I... I was in such a deep sleep.'

'So was I,' he replied.

Becky yawned. 'Let me make you some breakfast. What's your top request?'

'French toast from Eva's,' he replied. 'And a ton more coffee.'

'How about I make you eggs on toast instead?' Becky suggested.

Ross stretched. 'Sure. That might compensate a tiny bit for the lack of sleep.'

Becky playfully slapped him on the back before going over to the refrigerator to get a half-dozen eggs.

'So, you were considerably late to bed last night. I saw your light still on in the early hours,' he mumbled.

Becky nodded. 'Yeah, I was determined to find the connection between the Elijah Williams that Kenyatta and Maddie found and the Williams family that I'd been working on.'

'And?'

'And I found it, of course,' she revealed with a satisfied grin. 'Even though it was highly likely that the two families were linked, I wanted to make sure that I had enough documentary evidence and sourced data to support it. I got everything together around two in the morning, then finally went to bed, utterly spent.'

'So, why are you—why are *we*—up again so early?' Ross complained.

'To carry on. This latest victim, Debra Towers, has only a few hours left to live in all likelihood. She may even be dead already, and I'm standing here, fixing breakfast.'

'Fair enough.'

'In fact,' Becky said, leaving the kitchen, 'I need to message Maddie to ask her what she'd like me to work on next.' She entered her bedroom, took her cell phone from her nightstand and sent a message on the Venator text group as she crossed back to the kitchen.

Hey everyone - I found the connection between Elijah Williams and the Williams family I was working on. Elijah married Lydia Welch, who was the granddaughter of Clifton Welch and Julia Manefield from my cluster one! Maddie, can we Zoom whenever you're ready so you can tell me what you'd like me to work on next?

Becky set her phone aside and finished making their breakfast. She sat down to eat with Ross. 'So, I'm thinking of venturing out into the big wide world, later,' she said.

'Oh, really?'

'Uh-huh. This place is starting to feel a little *too* small now. I think I'll go for a long run up toward the Arcadia Trailhead,' she revealed.

'What? Are you mad?' he asked. 'It's practically vertical and you've not done much exercise for a couple of weeks. And you're tired…'

'I'll take it easy,' she said with a dismissive wave of her hand. The road up to the trailhead was very steep but it gave amazing views out over the city and should be quiet with all that was going on right now. She knew she wouldn't be able to think straight until she had released some of her pent-up stress.

Just as Becky was finishing her breakfast, Maddie sent a reply.

Great job, Becky! I'm at my desk. I've sent a Zoom link. Join me when you're ready.

Becky quickly ate her breakfast while moving toward the sink, placed her dirty plate next to a few other items. 'See you in a bit,' she said to Ross as she headed into the guest room and woke her computer. Maddie's link sat at the top of her inbox. She clicked to join it, then realized too late that she hadn't yet looked in the mirror this morning.

'Jesus,' she muttered upon seeing herself pop up.

'What's up?' Maddie asked, suddenly appearing on-screen.

'Just the state of me. Sorry. I guess I should have gotten ready first,' Becky replied with a coy laugh.

'Hey, look at me,' Maddie said, also laughing. 'Most mornings, I just head straight down to the basement and get right to work, maybe showering and getting dressed, if I'm lucky, at some point during the day.'

'Glad it's not just me, then.'

'I think it's probably the majority of the country, actually,' Maddie said. 'So, anyhow… Great job on connecting Elijah Williams.'

'Thanks. It didn't take too long to connect the dots together, but I wanted to get a lot of evidence saved to the tree.'

'That's great. Kenyatta and I are currently working on the four kids of Ronald and Rosa Williams, so do you want to help Hudson with what he's working on?'

'Sure,' Becky answered.

'Give him a call and see where he's at and take it from there. Okay?' Maddie suggested, sounding as though she were about to end the call already.

'Before you go…' Becky began, 'I've been doing some separate digging—you know—into Michael's disappearance.'

'Oh, okay,' Maddie said, clearly taken aback. 'I thought you got worried about the damaging repercussions with your parents?'

'I was. I am. But I still went ahead and did it anyhow. I just couldn't sit back and think that my dad's company had something to do with it. I guess I was looking to exonerate him, maybe?'

'And did you?' she asked.

'Not really, no. Listen, I don't have all the answers and what I have found out has just raised more questions, basically. I'm at a point, now that, other than taking a trip to Haiti, I'm at a dead end.'

'Haiti?' Maddie interjected. 'Has the trip that Michael took right before he disappeared got something to do with it?'

'I think so…but I don't know how,' Becky said. 'Let me tell you everything that I know…' And, so, Becky spent time laying out exactly what she'd discovered, answering Maddie's various questions as she went.

'Gosh,' Maddie exclaimed when Becky had finished. 'I had no idea that Artemon and Jay were dead. This is incredible.'

'Yeah, I wonder if the fact that they both were… that they both died out of state happened for a reason?'

'So that the three of them would less likely be linked?' Maddie intuited.

'Uh-huh,' Becky said, fully aware that the implications of what she was saying were that Michael was also dead.

'But what, do you think, can possibly have happened in Haiti to cause all this to follow?' Maddie asked.

Becky shrugged. 'I don't know. Did you notice a difference when Michael got home from his trip with Artemon and Jay? In his general demeanor, I mean.'

Maddie took a long breath in, clearly casting her mind back. 'Yes, actually. He was normally very keen to share what went on during his trips abroad; wanting to show photos, bringing gifts home and generally talking about the places he'd been. But Haiti was different. He didn't bring anything back for the kids, didn't want to talk about it at all. I just put it down to the fact that the trip must have been hard. You know, seeing all that devastation everywhere after the earthquake. It wasn't exactly a vacation.'

'That's exactly what Jay Craig's widow said.'

'God…' Maddie muttered, holding her head in her hands.

'Sorry. I know it's a lot to take in.'

'Yeah,' Maddie agreed. 'I've been doing my own investigations, too, actually.'

'Oh?'

Maddie took in another long breath. It seemed to Becky that, whatever was coming next, she might not like to hear it. 'Do you remember that, after I had Michael's truck swept again by CSI, the only fingerprint they found belonged to a guy called Emmanuel Gribbin?'

'Uh-huh.'

'So, not long after Michael received that telephone call from the Larkin building downtown, a flight left Dutch John Airport which is right next to where Michael was last seen. It flew to College Park in Maryland, practically in D.C. The plane was owned by your dad's company, and it looks as though Emmanuel Gribbin was flying it.'

Becky gasped and instantly felt queasy. 'What?'

'I know…'

'Jeez. But why? Do you have any idea what happened next?'

'Not at the moment but I'm working on it.'

Becky couldn't help it and suddenly burst into tears. 'I'm so sorry, Maddie.'

'Hey, please don't apologize. Whatever went on has literally nothing to do with you,' Maddie tried to reassure her.

'But it's my *dad's* company,' Becky sobbed. 'It has plenty to do with me. His company and money pay for my apartment and my allowance. Oh my God… What could have happened, Maddie?'

'I really don't know.'

Becky dabbed her eyes on her pajama sleeve and sniffed back another wave of tears. 'As soon as I can, I'm going out to Haiti.'

'Becky, you really don't have to do that,' Maddie said. 'What do you think you're going to find out there, anyway?'

'I don't know,' she answered quietly. 'But you need answers and so do Artemon Bruce's and Jay Craig's families.'

A heavy silence lingered on the call. Becky guessed that Maddie was also trying—and failing—to build a picture from their shared information. But it made no sense and felt as though they were trying to piece together two completely different jigsaw puzzles.

'Are you okay?' Maddie asked softly.

Becky nodded. 'I think so. I just need to get back into work mode and let my brain think on it a little. What about you? Are you okay?'

Maddie took a while to answer. 'I'm confused more than anything, to be honest. I just don't understand…'

'Between the two of us, we'll find the answers,' Becky said, her determined strength returning to her voice. 'But for the moment, let's focus on catching this sick monster in Twin Falls.'

Maddie nodded her agreement. 'Yes, let's do that.'

'Okay, I'll see you at the briefing.'

'Thank you, Becky…for all you've done for me. I appreciate it. I know that it can't have been easy for you.'

'It's the least I could do after all you've been through,' Becky replied.

Maddie thanked her again, said goodbye and ended the meeting, leaving Becky staring at her computer screen in deep contemplation. Whatever had happened in Haiti with those three men, her father was implicated. She'd meant what she had said to Maddie: when it was possible to do so, she was going to Haiti in search of answers. The files that WC had sent over detailed the precise locations that the three men had visited during their trip. Despite its being a long shot, she had to follow up. With that resolution in mind, Becky turned her focus back to working on the Twin Falls case, starting by sending Hudson a Zoom link to discuss assisting him with his research.

She sent Hudson a text message to say that Maddie had asked them to work together and moments later he appeared in the meeting.

'Hey, Hudson,' Becky greeted. 'How are you doing?' Just like her, he too looked ashen and drained.

'Great, thanks,' he answered, his words sounding mechanical. 'Well done for finding the Williams link.'

'Thanks,' she said, noting that he hadn't asked how she was doing or commented on her own disheveled appearance. Something beyond the demands of this case was up with Hudson, she was sure of it.

'Give me a moment. I'll just share my screen, so you can see where I am,' he said, jumping right in to work mode.

'Sure, great,' she replied, trying to sound as cheerful and normal as she could as he mirrored his screen. After Ross's previous observations, she immediately checked out the tabs open in his web browser. There were so many that it was impossible to see anything except the icon belonging to each address, most of which she recognized as being genealogy related.

From the open family tree, Hudson pulled up the profile for Harvey Rawson. 'As I mentioned in the briefing yesterday, this guy and his wife, Amelia, had three sons that they raised in Cassia County, Idaho, right next to Twin Falls. The three kids were born in the 1930s, so I think we probably need to go down another generation or two before we can make the link across to Ronald and Rosa Pernicano's kids who were born in the 1950s and 1960s. I started by concentrating on his eldest son, Pierce, and his descendants.'

Hudson displayed Pierce Rawson's family tree. He had five children, two of whom were male. 'These guys are the correct generation to have married into the Williams family, but, as you can see, there's no evidence of that happening.'

'NPE?' Becky asked, wondering if they could be searching for a paper trail that simply did not exist because a non-paternity event would mean that a liaison between a Rawson and a Pernicano would have occurred outside of a documented relationship.

'It's possible, yes,' Hudson answered. 'Plus, we still don't know for sure how the Rawson family connects to the killer. More than ever, we seem to have taken a whole lot of educated guesses that we hope we can substantiate at the end.'

'Okay, so what are you working on right now and what do you want me to do?'

'I'm now working on Harvey and Amelia Rawson's middle son, Ryan. Do you want to take the youngest, Lee Rawson?'

'Sure,' she said. 'I'll get right on it. Is everything you know about him on this tree?'

'Yeah…which isn't much right now. Good luck.'

'Thanks. You, too. We'll talk if we find anything, otherwise I'll see you again at the briefing later.'

'Bye,' he said, leaving the meeting.

Even though Becky knew something had to be up with him, he clearly didn't want to talk about it and she had enough on her own plate without trying to second-guess what his problem might be.

Starting with Peter Rawson, Becky worked her way down the tree to the three sons of Harvey and Amelia. She clicked on their youngest, Lee, finding that the only information contained in his profile had come from the 1940 Census which showed him as a four-year-old boy living in the family home in the city of Burley, Cassia County, Idaho.

Becky ran a map search for Burley, finding that it was just 38 miles from Twin Falls. This family had to be closely related to the killer.

There were three Ancestry hints for Lee Rawson's name. The first was a grayscale photograph taken from the *U.S., School Yearbooks, 1900-1999* collection. It was an individual portrait picture from the 1952 Burley High School yearbook, giving Lee's age as sixteen years.

The second hint was taken from the *U.S., Obituary Collection, 1930-Current* which Becky clicked to view.

Name: Lee Rawson
Gender: male
Mother: Amelia Rawson

Although no further information was provided, Amelia Rawson's name was highlighted in blue, so Becky clicked it and was taken to a page with further information.

Name: Amelia Rawson
Gender: Female
Death Age: 85
Residence Place: Twin Falls, ID
Death Date: 19 Mar 2007

Becky's eyes settled on the place of residence, *Twin Falls*, then she hurriedly clicked to view the source information which provided a URL to Legacy.com. Becky copied and pasted it into a new browser tab.

Amelia's name, in large white letters, dominated the left half of the screen, while on the right half was her obituary.

Rawson - Amelia (Zalewski). Having just celebrated her 85th birthday, Amelia passed away quietly, March 19 after a short illness. Amelia was raised in Burley, ID, where she met her future husband, Harvey Rawson. After the birth of their three children, Amelia became active in church life and involved with the local cub scouts. For many years, Amelia ran a successful drapery business, which opened a second branch in Twin Falls in 1972, employing many family members including her children and grandchildren by two of her sons who lived in the city. Amelia was predeceased by her son, Lee Rawson and granddaughter, Maeve. She is survived by her husband, Harvey; sons, Pierce Rawson and wife Julie, Ryan Rawson and partner Lori; by her grandchildren, Todd Rawson, Jennifer (Rawson) Turner, Miles Rawson, Ben Rawson and Jim Rawson. Amelia had nine great-grandchildren. In keeping with her wishes, cremation has taken place. Donations to the Disabled American Veterans.

'God,' Becky said, studying the obituary carefully. She was fairly confident that this document contained the name of the Twin Falls serial killer.

It was time to work out who that was.

Becky was about to save the obituary and flag it to the rest of the team when a message came through from Maddie.

Zoom meeting in five minutes. We've got something.

Chapter Thirty-Four

Wednesday, April 22, 2020, South Jordan, Utah

'Thanks for joining at such short notice, everyone,' Maddie said when the whole team assembled on-screen in front of her. 'As I said in the message, we've made a significant breakthrough.'

At that moment, Kenyatta cleared her throat.

Maddie smiled. '*Kenyatta* made a significant breakthrough.'

'*Very* significant,' Kenyatta corrected.

'Okay, *very* significant,' Maddie conceded. 'Bring up the tree and show everyone.'

'Ta-da!' Kenyatta said, sharing the speculative tree for Ronald Williams and Rosa Pernicano. She circled their four children who had all been born in Twin Falls in the 1950s and 1960s. 'As you know, Maddie and I have been working on these four kids. This one right here'—she ran her cursor over Loretta Williams—'has been the most difficult to track down. I don't believe she ever married but she seems to have had several children with several different men, and also went by various names and configurations of Loretta. Birth records for post 1929 are only available at the County Courthouse; so, they're out. But I did manage to find Loretta's mom's will and probate records, and it mentioned all of Loretta's kids by name.' Kenyatta clicked Loretta Williams' profile and circled her mouse around the names of her five male partners. 'Notice anyone familiar?'

'Ryan Rawson!' Hudson read jubilantly.

'I've literally just saved Amelia's obit to the tree, and it mentioned Ryan's partner, Lori,' Becky exclaimed.

'That's one of her aliases, yeah,' Kenyatta confirmed. 'It seems that Ryan and Loretta had four boys.'

'And these four boys are now our main suspects,' Maddie added solemnly. 'Miles, Benjamin, Jim and Todd Rawson, all born in the 1970s in Twin Falls. I suggest we take one son each: I'll take Miles; Kenyatta, Benjamin; Becky, you take Jim; and Hudson, Todd. Anything at all that rules them out or in get it to the team quickly. Okay?'

When everyone had given their agreement, Maddie ended the

meeting and called Detective González.

'Hi, Maddie,' she answered almost immediately. 'Any news for me?'

'Yes, actually.'

'Go ahead. We need anything we can get right now.'

'I just need to caveat what I'm about to tell you and say that we haven't yet finished. There may be other names, these names may not be relevant. There's al—'

'Yeah, yeah. I get it, Maddie,' Detective González interrupted. 'Please…'

Maddie slowly inhaled, then revealed the team's discovery, 'Four brothers born in Twin Falls in the 1970s: Miles, Benjamin, Jim and Todd Rawson.'

'This is amazing, Maddie,' Detective González gushed. 'Any one of them more or less likely from the DNA?'

'We can't distinguish between full brothers' DNA, I'm afraid. I'll email over everything we have but, so far, we've not researched these men fully. Each member of my team will be working on the brothers for the rest of the day, and I'll get back to you if I've got anything that eliminates or incriminates any of them.'

'Thank you so much, Maddie. Thanks to your team, too. Maybe we can still save Debra Towers' life.'

'God, I really hope so.'

Chapter Thirty-Five

Wednesday, April 22, 2020, Twin Falls, Idaho

Detective Maria González dropped her cell phone down onto her desk and waited impatiently for the email to arrive from Maddie. 'Come on, come on…' she mumbled to herself breathlessly again and again.

Then it came.

Detective González,
These are the people whom we've identified as <u>*potential*</u> *suspects, as I said during our…*

Maria skipped down to the all-important names.

Miles Rawson born 1974
Benjamin Rawson born 1975
Jim Rawson born 1977
Todd Rawson born 1979

She took a photo of the screen, leapt up and dashed over to the large bulletin boards at the front of the Criminal Investigation Division office. In large red letters, she carefully copied the four names to the center of one of the boards, then turned to face the forty-plus detectives, officers, analysts and support staff who were working this case with her. As she took in a long breath, she caught the eye of Captain Pritchard. She nodded him over, then clapped her hands several times. 'Guys, I need everyone's full attention.'

Captain Pritchard sidled up next to her, staring at the latest addition to the bulletin board. 'Where'd this come from?' he whispered.

'Venator,' she replied, then spoke to the room. 'These four names'—she turned and pointed to the board—'have just come in from the investigative genetic genealogy team. They are at *great* pains to tell me that they've not finished their research, but these four brothers are our main suspects and, right now, they're our best lead. Janice, I want current addresses for all four men, plus any other properties the family owns. Marcus, get your team on criminal background. Reuben and Janet, get your team cross-referring the names against anything and everything we've done so far; check it all again. Dean, get a team together to pull every record we have for them—I want vital records, DMV, cell phone data, partners' and parents' details, employment records—everything you can get on these guys. The rest of you, keep going with what you were doing but be mindful of these names. Go, go, go!'

Captain Pritchard leaned in closer to her and lowered his voice. 'What's the plan?'

She knew that she was against a wall. Despite Debra Towers possibly only having hours left to live, Maria's choices were severely limited. There was no way that a judge would sign a warrant based solely on four possible addresses and part of the contract with Venator stipulated that investigative genetic genealogy be kept out of the warrant. Exigent circumstances, which would allow them to enter a property forcefully without a warrant, would only be possible if they had seen or heard Debra Towers inside and could demonstrate that her life was in extreme danger. 'Get surveillance on each property, try and collect some surreptitious DNA,' she said finally. 'I'll get warrants written for each property, ready to go as soon as we have further information.'

Pritchard nodded his agreement. 'Just don't mess this up. Make sure they don't find out we're onto them.'

'Agreed,' she said.

'I've got the addresses,' Janice yelled, rushing over with a piece of paper.

'Thank you,' Maria said, snatching it from her. 'Get it onto the bulletin boards, to Reuben and Janet, and Mike.' She turned toward Mike Davis's desk. 'Mike, can you head up and co-ordinate four surveillance teams at each brother's home address. We also need to obtain trash DNA...*without* being seen.'

'On it,' he said, rising from his desk.

With the piece of paper in hand, Maria moved over to the large wall-map of Twin Falls. Pritchard followed her over, watching as she stuck four pins to denote the addresses of the Rawson siblings. Two of them fell within the circle hypothesis where Venator had suggested the killer could reside. A third address was within a mile of the circle perimeter. The fourth address was to the north of the city. It was good, but not good enough to focus them in on a single name.

'Have you got anything else?' Pritchard asked quietly. 'Anything on this *incel* thing?'

'Tech is working on the IP addresses of some usernames on these dark websites. Friendly-sounding people using names like Death2Girls and AllWomenDie.'

Pritchard shook his head and looked at the floor, then asked, 'Have you got teams in place near the churches?'

'Uh-huh,' she confirmed. Small observation teams were stationed strategically close to every church in the city, preparing for the moment that now seemed inevitable when the killer would dump the body of his fifth victim, Debra Towers.

Chapter Thirty-Six

Wednesday, April 22, 2020, Sawtooth Mountains, Idaho

He quietly entered the dark back room of his cabin, carrying a pan of elk meat. The pronghorn-skull mask covered his face, and he wore his goat fur over the back of his shoulders. Debra was lying motionless on the bed, her hands clasped together above her head and tied to the iron frame. Thick rope bound her ankles to the outer edges of the bottom of the bed, keeping her legs splayed apart.

He watched her for quite some time as the familiar burn of anger began to rise inside of him yet again.

He clenched his fists around the pan handle and gritted his teeth to push back against his feelings.

His white knuckles were quivering as he stared at her, unblinking.

The shaking got so bad that the pan fell from his grasp, banging nosily and landing upside down on the wooden floor.

She woke, looked over at him and screamed.

He bent down, picked the pieces of meat up from the floor, placed them back into the pan and slowly walked toward her.

She wriggled violently and continued to scream for help. 'Let me go, you piece of shit!' she yelled. 'The police will be out looking for me, right now. You'd better let me go.'

He stood silently waiting until her screams subsided and evolved slowly into long and yelping sobs.

'Please,' she pleaded. 'I swear I won't tell anyone anything. Just put the blindfold back on me and drop me somewhere…in the middle of the forest. I don't care…'

These were the moments that he liked the best, when they begged and showed him deserved deference. Women who wouldn't normally give him a second glance, much less go on a date with him, were suddenly subservient. Now he was Alpha. But that showed just how shallow they really were; willing to trade *anything* for their freedom. The disgust that he felt for her curdled with the bile of hatred and loathing that pumped through his heart.

'Please,' she muttered quietly. 'I really honestly thought—when you

299

came to my house—that you seemed like a good guy and… I didn't… I don't care about that thing that happens…with your voice.'

The rage crescendoed through his body and he threw the pan of meat at her face with a roar of fury. She screamed as it hit her on the side of the head, showering her face with hot oil and fat. She writhed in pain as blood trickled determinedly down from a cut above her left eye.

He wanted to shout at her but held back through fear that what might come out of his mouth would result in still more mockery, as it had done his whole life since puberty had dealt its cruel hand.

'Help! Somebody, help me! I'm being held captive in here! Please help me! Help me!' Debra shouted.

He stormed from the room, slamming the door behind him. Every cell of his body was throbbing. He had to unburden himself…tonight. The only way was to administer her punishment and set himself free. He looked out of the window at the darkening mountainside. The snow had stopped. Perfect.

He needed to calm himself down. The way that he was feeling, right now, the hunt would be over before it had even begun. He'd get some rest, prepare his equipment, then it would be time to release her and for the hunting to begin.

Chapter Thirty-Seven

Thursday, April 23, 2020, Salt Lake City, Utah

Kenyatta yawned and looked at the clock: 12:03 a.m. It was way past her usual bedtime. She had just sent an email to cancel her therapy session in the morning in spite of its being short notice. She figured that she would either still be working, or, if they'd managed to narrow down the pool of suspects even further, she would be tucked up in her bed fast asleep. Either way, the therapy session to help her to prepare for the court case was not going to happen. Even though Maddie had warned the team when they took on this case that she didn't want them to burn out, they had all agreed to work through the night and continue until they had done all they could.

She was working on Benjamin, the second eldest of the Rawson brothers, who'd been born in Twin Falls in 1975. Right now, thanks to his Facebook profile, she was looking right at his face. He looked like an idiot, but he didn't look like a killer. But then they rarely did, until they were wearing orange jumpsuits and staring coldly out of their law enforcement mugshots. His Facebook profile picture showed him with his eyes crossed, tongue out, facing the camera, both hands sticking up the middle finger. A young girl of eight or nine had her arm around his shoulder and was pulling the same face and also sticking up her middle fingers. Kenyatta found herself wondering what on earth would possess someone to take such a photograph, never mind post it on social media for all the world to see. 'Classy.'

Kenyatta double-checked the predicted phenotype for the killer: very pale skin, brown hair and blue eyes.

Benjamin had light skin, brown hair and blue eyes.

Could it be him? she wondered, saving the photo to the speculative tree.

Once she had saved the picture, she scrolled back further through his timeline, finding evidence of what official records for the state of Idaho could not provide: that he'd married in 2018, something that he'd obligingly confirmed under *Life Events*.

Kenyatta looked at his recent posts which, by comparison to

301

previous years, seemed to be few and far between, making her question why. The most recent post had been dated February 26 of this year.

Opening the general document file from the shared Venator drive, Kenyatta looked at the timeline for the case.

'Oh,' she said to herself, reading that February 26 had been the day that the third victim, Jasmine Jaconski's body had been found.

She looked again at the post that he'd made that day. It simply said, *Yeah!!!* above a meme that read *The Bill of Rights. If I had to choose between freedom of speech and my gun, I'd choose my gun. (and then I'd say whatever I wanted because I have a gun).*

Kenyatta took a screenshot of the post and added it to Benjamin Rawson's family tree gallery. It might mean nothing at all or simply be his idea of a joke, but the fact that he'd posted it the day that Jasmine's body had been discovered could not be ignored.

Having trawled through his Facebook profile, Kenyatta switched her focus to trying to find out more about Benjamin's recent past. On the BeenVerified background check website, she ran a search for his name and the location of Twin Falls. There was only one matching profile which she now clicked to view.

According to the site's records, Benjamin and his wife, Katie, had lived at their current address for two years. Again, Kenyatta returned to the main case file and opened up the map that Becky had saved that showed a translucent circle superimposed over a map of Twin Falls in which the killer might possibly reside.

It took a moment for her to find Benjamin Rawson's current address of Tyler Street. It was right bang in the middle of the circle.

'Okay,' she muttered, reaching for her cell phone and typing out a message on the Venator text group.

According to BeenVerified, Benjamin Rawson lives on Tyler Street - right in the center of the circle. And look at his photo compared to the predicted phenotype…

She sent the message with Benjamin's picture, then thought for a moment. In the context of his address, Benjamin's most recent Facebook post was highly relevant. She took a photo of the meme and sent that to the group, too.

Kenyatta looked at Benjamin, seriously wondering if she was looking into the face of an active serial killer and shuddered with both fear and disgust.

Becky had her laptop resting on her thighs. She was sitting in the living area of her apartment, working on the profile of the third Rawson sibling, Jim, who had been born in 1977. Background check websites had provided her with Jim's long work history with P&R Trucking in Twin Falls, a handful of drug-related convictions, an address in the north of the city—just outside of the circle hypothesis—and a link to his Twitter account. It appeared so far that Jim had never married or had kids. She had yet to see a photo of him to know if he, like his brother, Benjamin, matched the predicted phenotype.

'Can you get the dates of the attacks, please,' she said to Ross who was working on his own laptop beside her.

It took him just a few seconds to get the document. 'Here,' he said, angling his screen in her direction.

'Thanks,' she replied, returning to her own laptop and starting to scroll back through Jim's highly numerous tweets. 'Jeez, despite only having twenty-three followers, this guy is tweeting like a celebrity, five times a day.' She paused when she got to last Saturday, the date of Debra Towers' abduction. 'Just baseball and poker retweets,' she commented. 'What's the date before that?'

'April second, when Molly Hutchison was killed,' Ross relayed.

'April second,' Becky parroted, rolling back through Jim's tweets. The first on that day was a retweet of a video showing a toddler wearing a diaper standing in front of a TV screen, copying every movement of some fitness guru.

'I mean, that is *very* cute,' Ross said.

'I guess,' she half-agreed.

The next tweet that day made Becky meet Ross's disbelieving gaze.

It's a proven fact that how you run in poker is in direct correlation to how good of a person you were in your past life.
Another interesting fact, I used to be a murderer of young orphan children.

'Jesus,' Ross muttered. 'Would he be so brazen?'

Becky considered the profile that she'd produced about the type of killer that he was at the start of their investigation. 'Yes, he definitely would be so brazen.'

'Do you think it's him, then?' he asked.

'I'm not sure yet,' she replied, taking a screenshot of the troubling tweet and saving it to his tree profile.

The next tweet that day was a view out of his truck cab window. Beyond the snow-covered foreground was a frozen lake and behind that was a run of single-story homes in the distance. The caption above the picture read, *mary alice lake all frozen up*.

'Look,' Ross said, pointing to the bottom right corner of the picture. It was the sideview mirror of his truck. Becky noticed what Ross had seen and enlarged the photo. She zoomed in further to see a clear reflection of Jim Rawson's face. He was bald with a dark beard, pale skin and blue eyes.

'Isn't that what Hudson said he'd look like? Ross asked her.

'Uh-huh,' she answered, taking a screenshot and saving it before sending it to the rest of the team, along with the tweet from the day that Molly Hutchison had been killed.

Hudson looked at the time. Two thirty-four in the morning. He'd just sat back down at his computer with yet another coffee. He'd lost count of how many he'd guzzled in order just to stay awake and be able to focus on this case. He was trying to find anything that he could about the youngest of the Rawson brothers, Todd, who had been born in Twin Falls in 1979. But there was hardly anything out there. After Kenyatta had sent a photo of Benjamin, and Becky had sent a photo of Jim, Hudson had wanted to see one of Todd, but, despite in-depth searching, he hadn't found a single social media profile for him. Open Google searches also produced nothing that could concretely be attributed to him. The email address registered to Todd, puahate1979, also yielded no linked accounts or additional information. The only thing of substance that the background check sites had provided him with was Todd's address. He lived at Borah Avenue West—just a few streets away from his brother, Benjamin—right in the circle where

Becky had predicted that the killer would live.

He yawned and then drank some coffee as he thought about what to do next. Of paramount importance was knowing what Todd's movements had been in the past four months since the attacks had started. But without any kind of social media, that was going to be very difficult. From the messages coming in from the rest of the team, it appeared that rather than eliminate some of the brothers, they were actually uncovering potentially substantiating evidence against each one of them.

The thought then entered his mind that perhaps more than one sibling might be responsible. How likely was it that multiple siblings grew up to be serial killers? Not very, he reasoned, but still unable to discount the idea fully.

He drank more coffee and returned to the scant information at BeenVerified. Other than some convictions for drug possession and a traffic infraction a few years back, there were only his occupations listed.

Walmart shop assistant 1995-1995
Ken's Guns & Ammo 1998-1998
Red's Trading Post 2002-2002
Wildlife Technician, Idaho Department of Fish and Game 2003-2004

The combined list of jobs bothered Hudson. Clearly Todd Rawson was an outdoorsy kind of guy with experience of guns and hunting. And, unless there were other places of employment that hadn't been registered, which was entirely possible, then it appeared that Todd Rawson couldn't hold down a job.

Hudson drank coffee and stared at the screen, feeling very uneasy about this man.

He'd had no luck so far in finding an up-to-date picture of Todd but could maybe track down something from his school days, he thought, as he opened up classmates.com and logged in using the Venator credentials. Navigating through the state, city and then to Twin Falls High School, Hudson selected the year of 1995. From the sidebar menu, he clicked *Who's in this book?* and an alphabetized list of students loaded in front of him. He scrolled down to the letter R and saw Todd Rawson's name with a hyperlink to a page on which he featured. Hudson clicked the link and was taken to a double-page scan of the yearbook titled *Boots, Chaps, and Cowboy hats*. The pages featured the members of the Rodeo Club and at its center was a black and white image of someone on horseback, driving cattle. Above it was a smaller image of the six club members. Hudson read the identifying caption and then zoomed in to the image. Todd Rawson was standing at the back of the photo, wearing a Stetson and a checked shirt. Unlike his fellow classmates, Todd was not smiling. Hudson zoomed in closer. Although the image was black and white, he could easily see that Todd had much pastier skin than his teammates and brighter eyes. The hair that was showing from under his cowboy hat was dark.

He took a screenshot of the photo and saved it alongside Todd's employment history to his profile. As Hudson finished his coffee, the feeling of unease grew inside of him. This guy lived in exactly the right area, was experienced with guns, animals and outdoor life, and seemed unable to hold down a job.

He shared his disquiet with the rest of the team.

It was after 3:30 in the morning and the house was silent. Maddie was reviewing the evidence that was being sent through to her. Rather than eliminate any of the Rawson siblings, the findings built strong suspect profiles for each of them. She had just received Hudson's message with a photo of Todd's work history and, out of all of the team's findings so far, this left Maddie feeling the most perturbed.

Even though she knew that Detective González would be working under significant pressure right now and would not appreciate having her time wasted, Maddie couldn't help but pick up her cell phone to call her.

'Maddie. Hi. Have you discovered something else for me?' Detective González asked right away.

Maddie suddenly felt stupid for calling. 'Uh, no. No, not really. Not yet. All four brothers seem to have a checkered past—'

'Yeah, that's what we're finding from our side, too,' she concurred. 'So…?'

306

'One of the brothers, Todd, worked as a wildlife technician for the Idaho Department of Fish and Game between 2003 and 2004, and… I was just connecting the dots to hunting and the removal of the victims' molars…'

'Between 2003 and 2004 did you say?' the detective checked.

'That's right.'

'I'm out of the office right now, but I'll get on it. Thank you. Anything else?'

'That's it for the moment, but we're—'

The call was terminated.

Maddie held on to her phone and sighed, hoping that she hadn't just sent the detective or one of her team off on a wild-goose chase, just when time and resources were at their most critical.

She turned her attention back to the eldest of the Rawson brothers, Miles. Born in 1974, he'd married three times, had two children and had a host of assault convictions behind him. Although he lived outside of the circle that Becky had thought he might inhabit, just like his brothers, his appearance matched the phenotype exactly.

Before Hudson had sent his message, Maddie had been mid-way through a backward trawl of Miles Rawson's latest wife's Instagram posts, which were mainly dominated by photos of their kids. She was already back in late-December 2019 and decided that, when she reached the start of that month, she would change tack to another line of inquiry. She moved past photos from New Year's Eve and Christmas Day, through snowy pictures in their backyard, until she reached early December. A series of photographs threw Maddie off, as they showed Miles, his wife and kids seated around a room in t-shirts and shorts, opening Christmas presents. She checked the date of the post. December 13. Why were they opening presents two weeks early? And why were they dressed like that? Maddie wondered. The accompanying text answered her question. *Early Christmas vacation to moms.* The location was given as Key West, Florida. Unless the photo was fake or the location incorrect, then it ruled Miles out as a potential suspect since Lorena Baly's body had been discovered that very day.

Maddie continued to look through the Instagram posts, seeing several pictures of beaches and landmarks from Key West completely spanning the period of Lorena Baly's abduction. She was as sure as she could be that the photographs were genuine, which meant that Miles Rawson was ruled out.

She picked up her cell phone to share the news with the rest of the team and then with Detective González just as a message came in from Becky.

Jim Rawson looks to be out of the running.

Becky had also sent some screenshots from Jim's Twitter account that showed him in Nevada on the day that Carla Eagleton had been abducted and in Utah on the day that Jasmine Jaconski's body had been discovered.

'And then there were two…' Maddie said to herself, then re-dialed the detective.

Benjamin or Todd Rawson had to be the Twin Falls serial killer.

Chapter Thirty-Eight

Thursday, April 23, 2020, Sawtooth Mountains, Idaho

The agony inside of him was almost unbearable. He was sitting beside the dying fire in his cabin, trying to concentrate on *Utopia100*. He'd reached Lubbock, Texas by now but he just could not settle. He swigged back another beer, but it did nothing to ease his torment. Only one thing would. And it was high time. He picked up his skull mask and carefully put it on his head, then pulled on his full hunting furs.

He was ready. The Trapper was cleaned and good to go, as was the Idaho Hunter SRE fixed-blade knife, currently sheathed on his right thigh.

He took a candle from the box on the table, placed it into a holder and then held it to the fire. Once lit, he walked over to the door to the back room.

He pushed it open with deliberate slowness, knowing that the drawn-out, aching creak would strike more fear into her.

And it did.

She looked terrified, just as he wanted her to.

'Please,' she cried. That was her favorite word, it seemed. *Please do this. Please don't do that. Please, please, please…*

She also looked emaciated. She had been skinny beforehand but, after refusing to eat anything he'd offered her, she was now looking pathetic. It was just plain laughable that she'd turned down his food because she was some kind of a *vegetarian*. Just when he had thought that he couldn't have hated her any more strongly, she had gone and told him that.

Without speaking, he placed the candle down onto the floor and proceeded to slowly unsheathe the hunter knife.

Debra gasped and began to cry.

He walked toward her at what he hoped was a sufficiently menacing, slow pace.

'What are you doing?' she cried. 'Please don't hurt me.'

She flinched as he raised the knife.

He held it aloft for several seconds, before bringing it down hard and fast onto the rope that bound her ankles.

She cried out in terror and gathered her knees to herself as he leaned over, slashing the rope around her left wrist. Her tears turned into wailing. 'Oh, God. Please don't hurt me…please…'

He cut the rope to her right wrist and stepped well back. When he'd reached this point with Jasmine, she'd launched herself at him, kicking him hard in the groin and then fleeing through the open door. If he hadn't been in such agony, he might have found it amusing that she had done exactly what he'd wanted her to do.

Debra, though, now clamped her arms around her knees and pushed herself up to the top of the bed, retreating and cowering away from him.

He raised the Trapper to eye level and aimed it at her.

'No! No! Please, don't,' Debra screamed.

He pushed the large loop lever forward and then backward, loading the rifle.

'Oh, God,' she wailed desperately.

Holding the Trapper in position, he extinguished the candle flame between his thumb and forefinger, plunging the room into near-complete darkness.

'You can go,' he said, his voice featuring a pathetic squeak. He was sure that she went to laugh at him, and he roared, 'Go!' This time, his voice boomed much lower, echoing around the walls of the cabin.

'What?' she asked.

'Get out. You can go!' he yelled.

Debra ran from the room, barefoot and crying loudly, out the door and onto the dark snowy mountain.

Beneath his mask, he smiled. He left the room, picked up a pack of beers, his night-vision goggles and the Trapper.

Now…may the game begin.

Chapter Thirty-Nine

Thursday, April 23, 2020, Twin Falls, Idaho

Maria parked her black Dodge Charger behind the surveillance van on Tyler Street. Unable to sit and wait back at the station, she was doing the rounds of the surveillance teams. They had decided that it would be best to keep all brothers under watch for the time being. The road was pitch-black and silent as she stepped out of her car. She took a brief look around her at the bare trees that lined the sidewalk and the small, single-story homes that were set back behind thin strips of grass.

She knocked gently on the back of the van and its door was immediately opened by Mike Davis.

'Come on in,' he said, stepping back to allow her to enter.

Maria climbed into the back, acknowledged one of her colleagues, Jessica, who was looking through the viewfinder of a camera with a long telescopic lens pointed out at Benjamin Rawson's property through the blacked-out windows. The interiors of the vans had been modified for the specific task of surveillance, with high-backed seats on sliding casters that could easily be moved and repositioned along the lengths of the side and rear windows. Below the windows was a ledge that held the mounted tripod and, in the center of the van was a narrow table on which was an assortment of tech, candy wrappers, empty party-size chip bags and half-drunk bottles of Coke.

'Anything?' Maria asked.

'Two minutes ago, a light went on in the bathroom,' Mike informed her. 'Possible female, but not confirmed.'

'Okay,' Maria said with an impatient sigh. Since the surveillance team had assembled close to Benjamin's home yesterday, there had been no confirmed sighting of him, just movement inside the property.

'Any developments in the investigation that prioritizes one of the brothers over the rest?' Mike asked.

'The genealogy team think that Benjamin over there, or his brother, Todd, are the most likely. But they've all got criminal records, so I'm not ruling any of them out as yet.'

'So, we keep watching,' Mike replied.

'Yeah, keep monitoring closely,' she said. 'I'll be in touch as soon as we know more.' She pushed open the rear door and stepped down onto the street.

She walked quickly back to her car, got inside, started the engine and sped through the empty streets over to Borah Avenue West. Her breathing was fast but shallow, as though she'd just got in from a long run and adrenalin was rushing around her body. It made her feel sick to imagine what was probably happening right now; she was sure that Debra Towers' dead body was going to show up at some point tonight. If they couldn't save her life, then Maria at least wanted to catch him in the act of disposing of her body.

She drew up behind the second surveillance van, got out of her Dodge and, once again, took in the surroundings. She knew from her days on patrol that this neck of the woods was poorer with several dilapidated and rundown buildings. She tapped lightly on the back window of the van, which moments later was opened by her colleague, Derek Cousins. 'Good morning, Maria,' he said, sounding way too jolly for the hour and the task.

'Anything?' she asked, stepping inside and getting straight down to business.

'Nothing whatsoever. Not a peep,' he replied.

Maria sighed. 'Literally no movement at the house since you arrived yesterday?'

'Nothing at all,' he clarified.

Maria rubbed her tired eyes and moved over toward Danny Munroe who was staring through the camera viewfinder out of the window at Todd Rawson's apparently deserted property. Was Todd not there because he was out on the mountains someplace chasing after Debra Towers? Or was he a hermit or away somewhere?

'Can I take a look?' Maria asked Danny.

'Sure,' he said, sliding out of the way.

Maria peered through the viewfinder. A night-vision aid bathed Todd Rawson's property in a dull shade of green. The single-story house was covered in dirty and broken off-white shiplap. Two of the windows had been boarded up and part of the roof was covered by a tarp weighed down with blocks. 'Nice place,' she commented.

312

'Oh, yeah. Your real, five-star palace, right there,' Danny agreed with a chuckle.

'So, really, nobody going in or out of the house?' she asked Danny, taking her eyes away from the camera.

'Zero movement,' he confirmed. 'No lights have gone on. Nothing.'

Maria returned her eye to the viewfinder and said, 'Oh, shit.'

'What?' Derek asked, instantly alert.

'Old lady, ten o'clock,' Maria said.

Derek and Danny both leaned closer to the windows.

'Looks like we've been rumbled,' Danny muttered.

'Swap,' Maria directed, getting out of the seat and allowing Danny to return to the surveillance.

Just as she had expected, seconds later there came a sharp, insistent knocking on the back doors.

'Tortoise,' Derek whispered, giving the word for everyone to keep perfectly still and ignore the distractions going on outside the shell of the van.

None of them moved.

'I know you're in there. I've seen you,' the old lady yelled, banging hard again. 'What are you doing here? I'm going straight home to call the police.'

'She's going to wake the whole neighborhood,' Maria said, deciding that it was better to open the rear door and confront her.

The old lady, wearing a face mask, cream nightdress and purple slippers, took a step backward. 'What do you want, here?' she demanded.

Maria got out of the van and closed the door behind her. She flashed her badge. 'I'm Detective Maria González and we're here because we're worried the serial killer might be active someplace nearby, tonight.'

The old lady gasped. 'Do you think I'm in danger?'

'No, ma'am. He's targeting women in their twenties; I think you're safe. Perhaps you could tell me who lives around you, though?' Maria said, gesturing vaguely toward Todd Rawson's house.

'Well, there is a young lady—Rose McCullen, she's called—and she lives across the street from me,' she said, pointing. 'She must be in her twenties.'

'Okay, thank you. And what about in that house, there?' Maria pointed at Todd's house. 'It looks empty. Is that right?'

'Oh, no. That's my neighbor, Todd's place. It's in a little need of work, but it's not empty.'

'And does he live by himself?' Maria questioned.

'Yes,' the old lady answered, lowering her voice. 'Very much a loner. Poor boy, he had a terrible upbringing. His father was hardly ever home and—' she lowered her voice again to a whisper '—he used to bring home a string of young women, all the while his alcoholic wife was strung out on the couch.'

'Right,' Maria said.

'You needn't worry yourselves about Todd's place. You won't see any young women over there. Keeps himself to himself… When he's there, that is.'

'When he's there? Where else does he go when he's *not* there?'

'He's got a cabin up in the woods.'

'Do you know where, exactly?' Maria asked.

'Oh, someplace up in the Sawtooth Mountains.'

Chapter Forty

Maria's blood ran cold. 'Is he there now…at the cabin?'

'I imagine so. His Jeep's gone. He wouldn't be anywhere else at this time of the night, to my mind.'

'Do you happen to know exactly where this cabin is?'

She shook her head. 'Just somewhere remote where he can hunt.'

'Thank you very much, Mrs…?'

'Mrs. Staniforth.'

Maria clumsily took out her cell phone, thinking fast. She called the station, asking for Reuben Wright.

Mrs. Staniforth was staring at her.

'You can go to bed now, thank you, Mrs. Staniforth.'

'Are you sure I'm safe?'

'Lock your doors and windows, and you'll be fine,' she said hastily.

'Detective González?' Reuben asked uncertainly.

'Reuben, I need you to get the Fish and Game Regional Office hunting license database up,' she ordered, watching as the old lady shuffled off back toward her home.

'Now?' he asked.

'Now,' she commanded, wishing that Mrs. Staniforth would hurry the hell up and get inside so that she could get back to the station. While she waited, she knocked on the back of the surveillance van door and said to Derek Cousins, 'I'm calling it. Todd Rawson is now our main suspect. Can you direct the other teams to stand down and get back to the station? I don't think he's here, but I want you to stay and watch the house, just in case…'

'I'm in,' Reuben told her on the phone.

'I need you to look up Todd Rawson for the dates 2003 or 2004,' she said, carefully enunciating his name and the years as she ran back to her car. She fired up the engine, put her cell on speakerphone and then drove fast toward the station.

Twenty seconds later, Reuben said, 'I've got him!'

'Is there an address for a place in the Sawtooth Mountains?'

315

'Uh-huh,' he confirmed.

'Get that address to Pritchard and tell him to get a SWAT team there, right now. And I mean, right now.'

'Got it,' he said, ending the call.

'Damn it,' she yelled, slamming her fist into the steering wheel. Maddie had given her that information and those dates several hours ago, but she'd been too preoccupied with checking on the surveillance teams to follow it up.

As she pulled into the parking lot next to the police station, she knew that she'd never be able to forgive herself, if those lost hours had cost Debra Towers her life.

Chapter Forty-One

Thursday, April 23, 2020, Sawtooth Mountains, Idaho

She was good; he had to give her that. The other four had been next to useless at trying to escape. This one was actually making a real effort, rendering the hunt all the more of a challenge for him.

He was standing in a camouflaged shelter that he'd built on a vantage point halfway down the mountain. It was perched on a rocky outcrop and gave a wide view over the snow-covered Douglas firs and Engelmann pines down to the valley below.

He pushed back his pronghorn mask, took a long swig of beer and then put on his night-vision goggles. Slowly and methodically, he surveyed the mountain from left to right, searching for any signs of movement. So far, nothing. After this many minutes of escape, all four of the other women had been hunted down. They had chosen the obvious, well-trodden path that zig-zagged down the mountain past his series of hides. Carla Eagleton had screamed the entire way down, totally not understanding the point of the hunt. Putting a bullet in her leg and felling her like a tree had only made her screams more persistent.

But Debra Towers had not taken the easy, obvious route down and, right now, he had no idea where she was. He swept back to the left through the goggles and saw a slight movement behind a clump of bushes fifty yards down the mountain, almost directly below him. He smiled, although he was also slightly disappointed that his hopes of a challenging hunt seemed likely about to be dashed. If he'd not been so desperate to relieve the burning desire to enact his punishment, he might have chosen to extend the game.

He raised his Trapper to eye-level, pushed the large loop lever forward and then snapped it backward to load before aiming the front sight at the bushes and waiting for her to move again. Then, he'd pump one of the copper hollow-points—the type designed for soft-skinned animals—into her leg.

There was movement to the right of the bushes, and he swiveled his aim accordingly. She moved out from behind the bush but, at that moment, he saw that it hadn't been her at all: it was an elk.

'Damn you, Debra Towers,' he squeaked, lowering his rifle.

She was really putting him to work. He finished the can of beer, tossed it to the ground and then left the shelter, making his way back toward his cabin. When he got there, he pushed open the door, wondering if perhaps she'd thought herself smarter than him and hidden somewhere closer by. Maybe she thought she'd find herself a phone or another gun. There weren't any, but there *were* knives and other implements that could certainly do him some damage.

The cabin was virtually pitch-black. He lowered the pronghorn mask, raised the Trapper and cautiously entered.

'I know you're in here,' he called, stalking the shadows and edging his way around the dark room. He side-stepped behind the beaten-up couch, but she wasn't there. The only place she could be was in the back room where she'd been tied up previously.

He pushed back his mask, put on the night-vision goggles and allowed his eyes to adjust to the muted green light. Then, he crept toward the door to the back room, trying to figure out where she could have been hiding.

He took a step closer and crouched down. He could see that the bed was empty and that she wasn't under it. The only place that she could be, now, was just inside the door.

He leapt into the room, hoping to make a lion-like roar, but the sound that came out was more like a pitiable new-born kitten. He swung around and checked the room. She wasn't there.

He cursed her for the lost time. How long had she been gone, now? Twenty minutes? Twenty-five minutes? It was irrelevant, really. She could be running in any direction for more than an hour before she could hit on another property. He'd find her long before that.

He rushed back into the main living room of the cabin and took the flashlight from a shelf above the fireplace. Outside of the front door, he swung the light beam until he saw the prints of her bare feet.

She seemed to have taken a dangerous, steep route down the mountain. He'd be really disappointed if she'd fallen and hurt herself or, worse still, had gotten herself killed. How ironic that would be.

Using the flashlight, he continued to follow her footprints through the forest. She was either very smart or very dumb in choosing a zig-zagged path down the mountain. Probably the latter, he thought. It would certainly make it harder for him to get a clean shot, but that was what hunting was all about.

He stopped when the path opened out onto a clearing in the trees, and the beam from his flashlight fell on a partial footprint. She'd deliberately changed direction and gone over the south-facing, rocky ground where swathes of the snow had melted.

If she kept going in this new trajectory, she would end up in Sawtooth City. Not that it mattered, the name was a misnomer. It was a ghost town, abandoned after the old mining days.

As he raised his night-vision goggles to scope out the area and try to ascertain which way she had gone, he heard an unusual noise and cocked his head to listen.

It sounded like a helicopter, somewhere over the mountain behind him. He turned to look but couldn't see anything. They did come over occasionally, ferrying rich people to prime hunting ground, but not usually at this time of the night. The sound of the chopper blades seemed to be holding steady and unmoving, making him wonder what it could be doing in this neck of the woods. The thought briefly entered his mind that perhaps they might be here for him. But there was no way that they could have known who he was, never mind how they might have tracked him here. No way.

He ignored the noise and switched on the night-vision goggles, returning to the task of carefully scanning the vista.

About a hundred yards below, he spotted movement. He focused in and instantly saw that it was her, weaving through the pine trees. There was no chance of him getting an accurate shot from here. He needed to get closer.

Switching off the goggles, he replaced them with his pronghorn mask and began descending dexterously in Debra's direction. She was slowing down and, at that pace, he would see her dead in under ten minutes. Then he'd revive her and kill her again.

Let the hunt resume.

Chapter Forty-Two

Thursday, April 23, 2020, South Jordan, Utah

'Hi,' Maddie said, welcoming the team to a briefing. 'How are you all holding up without any sleep?'

'I'm literally existing on caffeine alone,' Hudson replied.

'Me too,' Maddie agreed.

'I'm not entirely sure *I am* still awake anymore,' Kenyatta quipped.

Becky yawned, laughed and then apologized.

'Listen, guys,' Maddie began, 'you've all worked so incredibly hard these past days, especially last night and into this morning. I couldn't have asked any more or for a better team. Thank you so much for everything you've done.'

'Have you heard anything back from the police yet?' Becky asked.

Maddie shook her head. 'Not since I confirmed the two most likely suspect names.'

'I don't think I'll be able to sleep until I know what happened to that poor Debra Towers,' Kenyatta said.

'Me neither,' Becky concurred.

'I'm sure it won't be long,' Maddie said, holding back from almost adding 'either way'. 'We just have one final task to do before we can rest and that's to double-check our work to make sure that there are no oversights and that the DNA findings corroborate our belief that these two guys have been correctly identified.' She pointed to the whiteboard behind her, on which the names BENJAMIN RAWSON and TODD RAWSON were written in red marker pen below the heading of SUSPECTS. 'Kenyatta and Hudson, I'd like you two to cross-check each other's work. Becky, you and I will do the same. Let me know on the group text as soon as you're done, and we'll have a quick final meeting and then get some well-earned rest.'

'Hallelujah,' Kenyatta sung.

'Bye for now and well done again,' Maddie said, ending the briefing.

She sat back in her chair with a long sigh. What a night. She yawned and looked at the clock: 5:48 a.m. In another half hour or so, it would be sunrise on a new day.

'Let's get this done,' she said to herself, opening up the speculative tree that Becky had created for the lead of genetic network cluster one, Latasha McNaughton, who matched the killer with 87 centimorgans of DNA. Becky had identified Latasha's great-great-great-grandparents, Clifton Welch and Julia Manefield as the common ancestors to her and the killer, making them fourth cousins once removed to each other.

Opening the Shared cM Project Tool from the DNAPainter website, Maddie inputted the figure of 87 centimorgans. Of the many ways in which Latasha and the killer could be related, fourth cousin once removed was a possibility, albeit an outlier.

Next, she opened the file for cluster two and repeated the task, finding Becky's research to be accurate, just as she had expected it to be.

Once she was satisfied that the DNA matches worked out correctly, she moved on to verify the speculative trees that Becky had created, ensuring that the Genealogical Proof Standard could be applied to her conclusions.

Finally, she verified all the documents that Becky had attached to Jim Rawson's profile page, agreeing that evidence from social media meant that he was unlikely to be the main suspect.

Maddie was the first to put on the Venator text group that she was all done.

She slumped back in her seat, trying to recall a time when she'd felt quite so thoroughly exhausted. In just a few moments, her eyes began to grow heavy, and sleep tried to lure her in. She couldn't; not yet. She stood up, rolled her neck around, stretched and then thought that she would check her emails to keep herself busy while she waited for the rest of the team to finish their cross-checking process.

Scrolling her way down through the unread mails, she paused. There was another email from Eva Hyatt. With an attachment.

Chapter Forty-Three

Thursday, April 23, 2020, Sawtooth Mountains, Idaho

Considering she was barefoot and could see almost nothing of the dangerous terrain that she was clambering through, Debra Towers was making solid progress down the mountain. So far, she'd played the hunting game much better than the other four, for sure. If he hadn't despised her and everything that she stood for so much, he might have had an inkling of respect for her.

In spite of her efforts to escape, he was gaining on her fast, driven forward by the adrenalin-fueled anger inside of him that he was just moments away from unleashing.

He knew this terrain like the back of his hand and was able to cut corners in anticipation of the direction in which she was headed.

She was about forty yards away now, still weaving in and out of the dense pine trees. Keeping one eye on her and one on the changing ground beneath him, he moved closer and closer to her.

He glanced up at her, watching as she tripped and fell. Debra cried out in pain as she rolled down a short bank and crashed sideways into a tree stump.

Then, she noticed him and screamed the loudest that he'd heard any of them scream. She seemed pinned to the spot as he continued trudging toward her.

She was now twenty feet away.

'Run, then, bitch,' he shouted, his voice emitting the deep masculine boom that he hoped it would.

'No,' she replied.

Her refusal surprised him, but it didn't really matter.

He shrugged, raised the Trapper, closed his left eye and aimed the sight at her right leg. 'Maybe this will change your mind,' he said, his voice oscillating mid-sentence.

He hitched the load lever back and forth, aimed and began to squeeze the trigger, when she deftly dived out of the way.

This was more like it!

She began to run, deliberately choosing a thick Douglas fir to shield behind.

This was his kind of hunt. He hurried forward, side-stepped, took a quick and clumsy aim and then fired.

It missed by a cat's whisker.

He laughed, running after her, reloading the rifle as he went.

She made a fatal error and dithered when a bush blocked her way.

Without taking aim, he fired off a shot and the resultant bullet smashed into her right thigh, knocking her straight to the ground with an agonized scream.

He lowered the Trapper and took a long inward breath. He just stood, taking great pleasure in her pain. He slowly edged forward, knowing that his slow gait and masked face would only add to Debra's terror.

She was lying prone, clutching her bleeding leg, her screams intensifying with every menacing step that he took toward her.

His hands began to shake from the anticipation of watching her face as he would strangle her to death for the first time of many. He was hoping that with such fighting spirit, he might be able to revive and kill Debra Towers at least three times over.

He stood over her, taking great pleasure in the terror on her face.

Over the top of her screams a shot suddenly fired and, in the briefest of moments, he glanced down, baffled and wondering how the Trapper had gone off without his having reloaded. With the instant realization that it wasn't his gun at all, came the excruciating pain in his chest, quickly followed by the sound of another shot.

He met Debra Towers's gaze as the Trapper fell from his hand and his legs buckled under him.

Chapter Forty-Four

Thursday, April 23, 2020, South Jordan, Utah

'So, you're all happy with each other's work? No oversight, confirmation bias or DNA matches that just don't match?' Maddie asked the team.

'I'm happy,' Kenyatta said, 'in an exhausted kind of gotta-sleep sort of way.'

'Happy,' Hudson confirmed.

'Yep, you did well,' Becky said to Maddie with a grin.

'Okay, I'll get a message off to Detective González, reaffirming that we're of the belief that Benjamin or Todd Rawson are the main suspects as we initially thought.' Maddie smiled. 'Yes, you're all free to sleep. And I don't want anyone working now until midday Monday, got that?'

'I'm good with that,' Becky agreed.

'Well,' Kenyatta began, 'I might just—'

Maddie's cell phone began to ring. 'Sorry,' she told the team. 'Detective González calling. Hang on there a second.' She muted herself, then answered her cell. 'Hi.'

'Hey, Maddie,' Detective González said. 'I've got some news for you.'

Maddie instantly stood and walked away from the camera, sensing from the detective's voice that it was going to be bad. 'Go on.'

'We've got Debra Towers…alive,' she told her.

Maddie gasped and couldn't help but cry. 'Oh, God. Is she okay?'

'She's got a non-life-threatening injury to her leg and hypothermia…but she's alive and should make a full recovery.'

Maddie couldn't stop the tears from flowing. 'Sorry… I'm just so happy that you were able to save her.'

'No. You saved her,' Maria corrected. 'You and your team. You did it, Maddie.'

Through her tears, Maddie mumbled, 'Are you able to tell me what happened?'

'He'd taken her off to his cabin in the Sawtooth Mountains. He'd released her and was hunting her down when the SWAT team got there. He was seconds away from killing her, Maddie. Literally seconds…'

'Is he—'

'He's dead, Maddie.'

Maddie was unable to speak. As much as she would have liked him to have faced trial and the rest of his life in jail, this had to be seen as the next best thing. Maddie took a few long breaths. 'Which brother?' she sobbed.

'Todd Rawson,' she answered. 'The brother you suspected because of his employment at the Idaho Department of Fish and Game.'

Maddie was silently processing everything, filtering it through her exhausted mind.

'Do you know why he targeted those women in particular?' Maddie asked.

'We're still trying to piece things together, but from what we can gather from initial digital forensics, he was an incel—involuntarily celibate. The women that he targeted he chose because they represented a type that he perceived hated him. In his estimation, they were young, beautiful and had a choice of any man that they wanted, yet would never ever choose him.'

'Wow,' Maddie muttered.

'Yeah. He had the typical unstable background that we see in these types of cases: alcoholic mother, semi-absent father who apparently brought a slew of young women back to the house, in front of his wife, drug abuse in the home... You get the picture. Where Todd differed from his brothers, though, was that he suffered from bad acne as a teenager that left him scarred and feeling ugly, and he also suffered from something called muscle tension dysphonia. Basically, it meant that his voice would involuntarily come out mid-sentence in a much higher pitch…like a girl's. You can imagine the bullying that would have gone on.'

'The red flags were flying,' Maddie commented, wondering how on earth he hadn't come to the attention of authorities sooner and whether early intervention might have prevented this tragic outcome.

'I dread to think how many more bodies would have ended up on the pathologist's slab if you hadn't worked your DNA magic. Please can you pass my very, very deep gratitude to your team?' Maria asked. 'We couldn't have done it without you; and that's a fact.'

'I will,' Maddie said. 'Thank you.'

'Take care,' Maria said. 'Goodbye.'

'Bye,' Maddie said, lowering her cell phone and wiping her eyes, before sitting back in her seat and turning to stare at the camera. She could see that the rest of the team were reading bad news in her face. She unmuted herself. 'She's alive... Debra Towers is alive. Apparently, they got there just in time.'

There was a collective audible reaction from the team, full of emotions.

'Who was it?' Kenyatta asked.

'Todd,' Maddie confirmed. 'Todd Rawson. He's dead.'

Chapter Forty-Five

Friday, April 24, 2020, Salt Lake City, Utah

Becky Larkin was running hard and fast. This was the first run that she'd completed since before lockdown and it felt amazing. The sky was clear and, for the first time in as long as she could remember, because of the lack of vehicles out on the road, the air quality was just perfect.

Right before she reached the turning circle that terminated the road and the Arcadia Trailhead began up the mountain, Becky stopped to gain her breath and to take in the panoramic vista. In the far distance were the snow-capped Northern Oquirrh Mountains and in the bowl between there and where she now stood was her beloved Salt Lake City. Somewhere in that sprawling mass of houses, streets and businesses was the dormant Venator office. She longed to get back there, back to normality and back to solving cold cases in the usual way.

This morning's news headlines were dominated by Debra Towers' dramatic rescue and Todd Rawson's death. According to various media outlets, Debra was recovering from surgery in the hospital. All the quotes and soundbites coming out of the Twin Falls Police Department office contained praise for the Venator team and that, without them, Debra Towers—and possibly more women besides— would be dead. Becky had watched as Captain Pritchard had stepped forward in front of the cameras and had been asked his opinions on using investigative genetic genealogy to solve live cases. He'd blushed red and mumbled, 'I will admit that I was initially a little skeptical about how useful this new method would prove to be, but now the team would always have my full support in any future cases. They have mine and my department's sincere gratitude.'

Becky breathed in the wonderfully clean mountain air as she continued to stare at the city. Also down there someplace were her parents. She wondered how they were doing, coping with the pandemic and wondering what effect the lockdown would have on her father's business. Not that she really worried about it. Big businesses like his would always survive. He would always survive, no matter what mud were thrown at him. But she was going to find out what he or his company had done to Michael Barnhart, Artemon Bruce and Jay Craig. Whatever it took.

She took one last long breath in and then began her run back down the mountain.

She returned to her Sugar House Apartment in record time, sweating, exhausted and satisfied.

'How's it going?' she asked Ross, who was frowning at his laptop and typing fast.

'Don't ask,' he replied without looking up. 'But, since you have, I'm fielding about a million billion emails from news outlets wanting to speak with Maddie and about another million billion emails from a variety of people wanting our services. I guess when Maddie gave everyone the weekend off, she forgot about little ol' me.'

Becky smiled. 'Shall I make us some breakfast?'

'That would be great, thank you. You might need to spoon-feed me, though.'

'I can do that,' she said, filling up a large glass with water and drinking it all down in one go.

Ross looked over at her. 'Oh, and you had a message from Maddie: Phillip Hollingsworth was arrested last night for the 1980s Houston rapes.'

'Oh, thank God,' Becky said. 'That's two monsters out of the picture in two days. Not bad going, I'd say.'

Hudson Édouard walked slowly to the FHL, arriving with two take-out coffees. As he expected, Reggie was sitting on the wall outside. 'Hey,' he said.

'Hey, man. Good to see you,' Reggie replied. 'You got coffee but no laptop bag?'

Hudson shrugged as he handed Reggie his drink. 'I'm taking the weekend off but wanted a walk.'

'Well, it's good to see you,' Reggie said, setting his laptop down on the wall. He raised the drink. 'Thanks for this. If you don't mind me saying so, you look shattered, man.'

Hudson smiled. 'I am. Very. We worked through the night and into yesterday morning.'

Reggie's eyes widened. 'Oh, yeah. The Twin Falls dude. Congratulations, that's amazing that you guys saved that girl.'

'I think technically the SWAT team that shot him saved Debra, but I'm happy to take some of the credit.'

'So you should.'

'Now I just need to get some sleep and recover,' Hudson said.

'Why aren't you in bed now?'

'Good question. I can't sleep. Abigail called and said she wasn't coming back.'

'Oh. I'm sorry, man,' Reggie replied. 'That must've been hard to hear.'

Hudson took in a long breath. 'Yeah…and no. I guess I could see it coming a mile off.'

'So, what's happening now?'

'She's going to stay at her parents' place until the pandemic is over, and then come over and get her stuff. She wants to sell the house, but I'd like to keep it. I don't know. She's entitled to half the money I got for the Wanda Chabala case but said she doesn't want any of it. So, I could buy her out, I guess. Oh, and good news: Maddie has said that I can keep my job.'

'That's amazing. You deserve to keep it. You just caught a serial killer, man.'

Hudson grinned. 'Well, actually—'

'Yeah, yeah… The SWAT team,' Reggie finished his sentence.

'I was going to say that I was working on Todd Rawson right at the end and had this gut feeling that *he* was our guy.'

'There you go. I can see why you wanted a break from home. It's been quite a few days for you, all round.'

'Yeah, I could really use a vacation right now, but this place'—he glanced up at the library behind him—'will just have to do…for now.'

'Could you go back home, once this is all over? For a break, I mean?'

Hudson grimaced. 'My mom wouldn't want to see me and, even if she did, she'd be dead-naming me the whole time. No, my family is right here in Salt Lake.' He drank his coffee and then asked, 'What about you? How's things going at your place?'

Reggie threw one arm into the air. 'Let's just say if this damned pandemic isn't over within the next few weeks, the cops are going to be at *my* house because of a murder. And they won't need investigative genetic genealogy to find the culprit; I'll hold my hands up and gladly admit to the crime.'

Hudson laughed.

'You can laugh, man, but you live alone,' he said with a smile.

'Well, you're welcome to the guest room at my place,' Hudson said.

'Are you serious?' Reggie asked.

Hudson thought for a moment. Was he serious? He'd barely known the guy a few days. But right now, he could use the company. 'Let's see how the next few weeks go—pandemic-wise—and then, yeah, maybe you could move in.'

'You're a good guy, Hudson. You know that?' Reggie commented.

Kenyatta Nelson ran up to Jim in floods of tears. He was standing behind a table in Pioneer Park, handing out bowls of soup to a long line of the homeless.

'Whatever's the matter, Kenyatta?' Jim asked her, steadying himself and pulling her into an embrace.

'You two shouldn't be doing that,' Lonnie commented from the line. 'You do know, it's not called social distancing for fun.'

'I won,' Kenyatta sobbed. 'I won.'

'The court case? Kenyatta, that's fantastic!' Jim cried, lifting her off the ground. 'I'm so happy for you.'

Kenyatta squealed until he put her down. She dabbed her eyes with a handkerchief. 'The judge said there was no case here, that I have to see them every other weekend and half the week. She said categorically that if Otis prevents me from seeing them, he'd go to jail.'

'That is just the best news,' Jim said.

'When you two have finished with your theatrics,' Lonnie said, 'I'd like some of this chicken soup, and preferably today. So long as it doesn't have chilies in it like last time, that is. Who wants chilies in a soup, for God's sake?'

330

Kenyatta grinned and began to ladle some soup into a bowl. 'One bowl of chicken soup coming right up, Lonnie.'

He walked up to the front of the table, lifted his face mask and, despite his being largely toothless, took a bite of a bread roll. Ignoring crumbs falling back out of his mouth, he took on a conspiratorial air. 'I see you got your Twin Falls serial killer, huh, Kenny?'

'Yeah, we got him. And just in the nick of time,' Kenyatta answered.

Lonnie huffed. 'You know the FBI estimates there are between twenty-five and fifty *active* serial killers out there right now in the United States? I read it.'

'That's a very big number,' Kenyatta answered.

'Uh-huh. You guys had better get back to work. Don't know what you're doing standing round here, wasting time flirting with *him* all day,' he said, taking the bowl of soup and shuffling away.

Kenyatta laughed.

'I'm not even kidding,' he said without turning around. 'Twenty-five to fifty active serial killers.'

Kenyatta looked at Jim and smiled. She could see from the sparkle in his eyes that beneath his mask he was smiling too. He reached out and took her hand in his.

Kenyatta returned home the happiest that she'd felt in a very long time. Now that she was here, in this headspace, she was better able to tell that she had actually been unhappy for a very long time. But now life was going in the right direction, and she'd even started dating.

She took a health juice from the refrigerator and opened the speculative tree for Angela Spooner. Even though Maddie had warned the team not to work this weekend, Kenyatta wanted to carry on fleshing out the family. It was a big tree and would take a long time, but at least some progress had been made.

She was just about to start, when there came a knock at the door.

Kenyatta frowned, set the laptop down on the couch and headed over to see who it could be. She was grateful that she was still wearing the decent clothes that she'd put on to go down to the SLC Homeless Kitchen earlier in the day.

She pulled open the door to see her three sons smiling back up at her and Otis's miserable face way back on the sidewalk.

'Thank you,' she said to him.

He nodded and walked to his car.

'Oh, thank you, God, for bringing these boys home,' she beamed, pulling them all into a hug. She never wanted to let them go again.

Maddie woke with a start. Her head was throbbing, and her neck ached from the way she'd been slumped, asleep at her desk. It was her cell phone ringing that had woken her, she realized, groping around in her pocket for it. It was probably a journalist ignoring her requests to have interviews arranged via Venator, not her private cell phone. 'Oh,' she mumbled. It was Jenna. Thankfully, given the disheveled state in which she currently felt she must look, it wasn't a video call.

'Hi, honey, how are you?' Maddie asked, trying to feign wakefulness, and barely managed to stifle a yawn.

'I'm okay,' she replied.

Maddie could tell from her tone that she was still annoyed, but she also knew Jenna well enough to know that she wouldn't be calling if she hadn't moved some way toward forgiving her.

'Congratulations on the case,' Jenna said. 'Thank God the police got there in time.'

'Yeah, it was a close one,' Maddie said, happy to be talking again, even though it did feel slightly stilted. 'I'm glad we got our guy, though.' Just before she'd fallen asleep, she'd received off-the-record word from Detective González that Todd Rawson's DNA had been put into the FBI CODIS database and was a one-hundred-percent match for the Twin Falls serial killer.

After a pause, Jenna exhaled loudly. 'Look, I don't want to fall out with you, Mom. It hurt that you kept something so monumentally huge from me and I can't pretend that it didn't, but I want us to move on from it.'

'Thank you, Jenna,' Maddie said. 'I mean, thank you for your understanding and compassion. I know that I let you down and I really am sorry.'

'I know,' Jenna said. Then, after a brief silence, she added, 'I've

332

decided, I don't want to know his name right now. Maybe one day that might change. Rick thinks I'm crazy for not wanting to find him, but… I don't know. Maybe it's all the uncertainty over Michael who was my father in every way except biologically.'

'I totally get it, Jenna,' Maddie agreed.

'So, what are your plans for today?' Jenna asked, sounding suddenly much more like her old, usual self and clearly wanting to change the subject.

'Sleep and a bath would be unbelievably welcome right now.'

'But?'

'But I've got a whole raft of media interviews scheduled,' she answered. Although she didn't particularly enjoy being interviewed, it was good publicity for Venator and was good promotion for investigative genetic genealogy, generally. 'Plus, I've found something out…about Michael. I'll share it with you later.'

'Sounds intriguing,' Jenna said.

'Well, don't get too excited. As usual, there are more questions than answers. My brain's not working at the moment.'

'Well, I'll let you go and get some rest, and we'll talk later about whatever it is you've found out. Give me a call when you're ready.'

'I will,' Maddie promised. 'Thank you, Jenna.'

'Bye, Mom.'

'Bye.'

Maddie stood up from her desk, ran her hands through her hair and then headed upstairs. Trenton was sitting on the couch in the living room, apparently studying. She was half-tempted not to disturb this miracle but wanted to get something out of the way.

'Trenton, could you get your sister and come down to the basement, please?'

He put his book down and asked, 'Are you going to kill us?'

'Uh-huh,' she said, yawning.

'Okay, then,' he said, leaving the living room and yelling Nikki's name at the top of his lungs in the hallway.

Maddie rolled her eyes.

'What's with all the shouting?' her mom asked, appearing with a fierce look on her face.

'I've just got something to show the kids,' Maddie whispered. 'It's about Michael.'

'Oh?' her mom said. 'You didn't say anything to me. Did you think I'd blurt it out or run around the streets telling everyone?'

'No, you don't need to get so defensive. I've been so busy with the end of the case—and now all the interviews—that I just haven't had the time to do anything else. I haven't even showered in three days, you know?'

Her mom turned her nose up. 'Well, that's not something to be proud of.'

'I'm not proud of it,' she replied as Trenton and Nikki arrived. 'I've got something I'd like to show you on my computer.'

Maddie led the whole family down to the basement. She wriggled her mouse to wake her computer. On the screen was a paused video.

'What's this?' Nikki asked, staring at the screen.

'It's security footage from College Park Airport,' Maddie said.

'What?' Trenton said. 'How did you get *that*?'

'A friend… She's called Eva,' Maddie answered.

'You haven't got a friend, called Eva,' her mom declared.

Maddie ignored the comment and placed her hand over the mouse. But she couldn't quite click to start the video. Theories about the flight from Dutch John to College Park were all that Trenton talked about, so she knew she had to show them the footage. But what it showed was hard to see.

'It's okay, Mom,' Trenton said, placing his hand on her back. 'Nikki and I are prepared for the worst.'

'Worst of what?' her mom asked.

Maddie clicked to play the video and stood back to watch it once again.

The grainy and low-resolution video footage began, showing a black Chevrolet Suburban with dark, tinted windows pulling alongside a small aircraft with the identifier *N409PT* legible on the fuselage.

'Is that the airplane that left Dutch John?' Nikki asked, squinting at the screen.

'Yeah, it is,' Trenton confirmed.

The foursome watched as the driver's door of the Chevrolet

opened and a stocky man jumped out, popped the liftgate of the truck and ran over to the door of the plane, getting there just as it opened.

Trenton and Nikki leaned in closer, just as Maddie had done when the footage had reached this point. They watched as the pilot dragged a heavy-looking dark and solid bundle to the plane door. The Chevrolet driver took one end of the bundle, gradually drawing it out to its full length. The pilot jumped to the ground, taking the other end, and the two men loaded the object into the back of the waiting truck. The men appeared to exchange words as the trunk was pushed down, and then the Chevrolet driver got in the driver's side and drove the vehicle out of shot. The forty-seven-second video ended.

'Was that him?' Nikki asked, welling up. 'In that bundle?'

'I don't know,' Maddie answered truthfully.

'I think it was Dad,' Trenton said solemnly, again placing one hand on Maddie's back and gripping Nikki's hand with the other.

'Where *is* Michael?' her mom asked. 'I haven't seen him for a very long time. Is he coming home?'

'I don't think so, Mom,' Maddie replied.

Acknowledgments

I must confess to having been a little nervous when *The Chester Creek Murders* was published. Although I had done my homework, countless hours of research, reached out to experts and undertaken a great deal of analysis of my own and others' DNA results, I was concerned that the book wouldn't stand up to the scrutiny of the experts and people who work in this field. Fortunately, and much to my relief, the book was received very positively by readers, genealogists and those working in investigative genetic genealogy. To all of you who read, reviewed or recommended the book, I would like to offer my sincere gratitude.

For more than any other fiction that I have written, *The Sawtooth Slayer* required the significant assistance of many knowledgeable people, all of whom have so willingly shared their particular areas of expertise with me. I'm very grateful to all of you for helping me to make this fiction as factual and true to life as possible. Your help really has made the book much richer. Any oversights, exaggerations or mistakes are all mine.

My first thanks go to those who assisted with my numerous police procedure questions and so willingly volunteered their knowledge: Chief of Police at Green River Police Department, Tom Jarvie; Detective Thomas Fedele; Detective Brian Savelli; and Captain Jim Collins.

For answering several emails regarding the narcotics mentioned in the story and providing expert information in reply, I would like to thank Brianna Smyth.

For gently guiding me away from using California law as a basis for Wayne Wolsey's trial in Pennsylvania and providing the correct legal terminology, I'd like to thank *The Legal Genealogist*, Judy Russell.

I'd like to thank Barbara Rae-Venter for answering further questions regarding the field of investigative genetic genealogy.

I'm very grateful to Angie Bush for giving me information about Salt Lake City during the lockdown, the city's homeless and for the top tip of using the FHL Wi-Fi from outside the building, something that you may have noticed Hudson finding particularly useful.

To Pat Richley-Erickson, my sincere thanks for spending a good deal of time chatting on Zoom with me, discussing lockdown in Salt Lake City, including schooling, internet and takeouts among other things.

Several people kindly responded to my pleas on social media for specific enquiries, so my thanks go to: Noreen Baker and Bob Adams for supplying information about Delaware prisoner outfits; to Laura Davenport for 'recommending' good places to dump bodies in Twin Falls; to Terry Ager for visiting the First Baptist Church used in chapter one and for identifying the tree species outside; to Diane Gould Hall for information regarding the releasing of bodies after autopsies and for putting me in touch with Captain Jim Collins.

To Lee Ann Schlager, I would like to extend my thanks for her knowledge of Volga German genealogy.

I would like to thank Megan Smolenyak for supplying information about *Unclaimed Persons*, an online group of volunteer researchers who assist coroners and medical examiners in identifying unknown deceased individuals. For more information, please visit unclaimed-persons.org.

I am very grateful to those people who not only supplied me with expert information, but who also willingly appeared as themselves in the story: Gene Turley, the Twin Falls Coroner; Scott Fisher, host of *Extreme Genes*; Stephen Caraccia for his Italian translations; Kirk Wennerstrom for sharing his expertise as a pilot and for information on the airports mentioned in the story; and Marina Brizhatova for her time taken to research Russian genealogical records, specifically for Voronezh.

As usual, I need to offer great thanks to my sixth cousin, Patrick Dengate, for another fantastic book cover, and to his son, Andrew Dengate, for modeling for it.

A big thank you must go to my wonderful early readers: Mags Gaulden, Cheryl Hudson Passey, Helen Smith, Connie Edwards, Dr Karen Cummings, John Lisle, Natalie Levinson, Lorna Cowan, Elizabeth Swanay O'Neal and Laura Wilkinson Hedgecock. The seriousness with which you undertake this role is truly appreciated. Your comments, feedback, corrections and suggestions make the book much stronger.

As always, I am eternally grateful to those groups, bloggers, writers and individuals who have kindly championed me and my writing over the years. In particular, Peter Calver at *LostCousins*; *The Genealogy Guys* (Drew Smith & George Morgan); *DearMyrtle* (Pat Richley-Erickson); Scott Fisher at *Extreme Genes*; Bobbi King and Dick Eastman; Sunny Morton; Lisa Louise Cooke at *Genealogy Gems Podcast*; Amy Lay and Penny Bonawitz at *Genealogy Happy Hour*; Andrew Chapman; Diahan Southard; Karen Clare and Helen Tovey at *Family History* magazine; Sarah Williams at *Who Do You Think You Are?* magazine; Randy Seaver; Jill Ball; Shauna Hicks; Cheryl Hudson Passey and the *GenFriends* team; Linda Stufflebean; Sharn White; Elizabeth Swanay O'Neal; Wendy Mathias; James Plyant; Denise Levenick and all of the family history societies around the world, too numerous to name individually, which have run reviews of the books.

My final thanks go to my husband, Robert Bristow, for his constant encouragement and support with the writing and production of this book.

Further Information

Website & Newsletter: www.nathandylangoodwin.com
Twitter: @NathanDGoodwin
Facebook: www.facebook.com/NathanDylanGoodwin
Instagram: www.instagram.com/NathanDylanGoodwin
Pinterest: www.pinterest.com/NathanDylanGoodwin
LinkedIn: www.linkedin.com/in/NathanDylanGoodwin

The Chester Creek Murders
(Venator Cold Case #1)

When Detective Clayton Tyler is tasked with reviewing the formidable archives of unsolved homicides in his police department's vaults, he settles on one particular cold case from the 1980s: The Chester Creek Murders. Three young women were brutally murdered—their bodies dumped in Chester Creek, Delaware County—by a serial killer who has confounded a slew of detectives and evaded capture for over thirty-eight years. With no new leads or information at his disposal, the detective contacts Venator for help, a company that uses cutting-edge investigative genetic genealogy to profile perpetrators solely from DNA evidence. Taking on the case, Madison Scott-Barnhart and her small team at Venator must use their forensic genealogical expertise to attempt finally to bring the serial killer to justice. Madison, meanwhile, has to weigh professional and personal issues carefully, including the looming five-year anniversary of her husband's disappearance.

'Both educational and entertaining, this fast-paced glimpse into an entirely new technology is a must-read for anyone interested in genealogy, law enforcement, or mystery'
Blaine Bettinger

'Nathan Dylan Goodwin continues to deliver captivating genealogical mysteries that draw us into the latest cutting-edge investigative methods. *The Chester Creek Murders* will have you rooting for a new cast of characters as they solve this intriguing cold case using genetic genealogy'
Lisa Louise Cooke, Genealogy Gems YouTube Channel

'This is a novel for all family history fans. The plot unfolds with twists and turns, keeping us guessing to the end. I thoroughly look forward to the next book…'
Family Tree magazine

'Nathan Dylan Goodwin is the creator and master of the genealogical thriller genre. *The Chester Creek Murders* is his latest offering, taking us on a can't-put-the-book down hunt for a 1980s era American killer. Informative and captivating, the reader will learn how cold cases are now solved using genetic genealogy'
Scott Fisher, host, Extreme Genes

'At the end of the book there were several open storylines, so now I can't wait for the next instalment in the series! Thoroughly recommended for anyone who enjoys genealogical mysteries and/or crime stories – no detailed knowledge of DNA is required'
LostCousins

'The book is full of juicy details for family historians, as well as a pacey read with lots of surprises, twists and turns that will appeal to fans of crime fiction. The research is thorough, the clues well laid and the story delivered with style, while the characters' back stories are gently revealed. Highly readable and believable, *The Chester Creek Murders* heralds a new series that should be as enjoyable as Goodwin's books about forensic genealogist Morton Farrier'
Who Do You Think You Are? magazine

'Nathan Dylan Goodwin's latest novel is a gripping crime story that explores how DNA is used to solve historical and current cases. He introduces a set of completely new characters, all of whom caught my attention. Most importantly, the story is a genuine page-turner, alternating between the events of 1983 and 2020 in riveting fashion. Highly recommended'
Jonny Perl, DNA Painter

'It's a great read for those who want to understand the mechanics of how forensic/genetic genealogy is used to solve cold cases, and the characters all feel like people we know. If you haven't yet, I recommend snagging a copy'
Megan Smolenyak

'This was a great story from start to finish due to the attention to detail given to everything from the description of the bar at Beerhive to the research process used by Madison and her team'
Angie Bush

Have you tried *The Forensic Genealogist* series,
featuring Morton Farrier?
Start the series with the short story, *The Asylum*,
available to download for FREE from
www.nathandylangoodwin.com

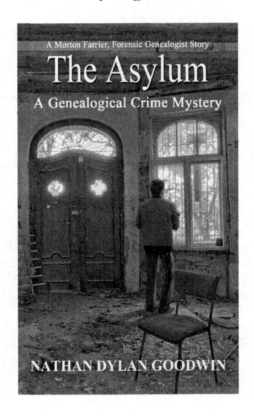

The job presented to forensic genealogist, Morton Farrier, ought to have been simple and easy. But the surprise discovery of an additional marriage to his client's father leads Morton on an enquiry, revolving around a mysterious death in the county asylum. Requiring his various investigative genealogical skills, Morton must work to unravel this complex eighty-year-old secret and finally reveal the truth to his client.

This is the first story in the Morton Farrier genealogical crime mystery series.